ROSE AMONG
THORNES

Terrie Todd

HERITAGE BEACON
FICTION

Heritage Beacon Fiction is an imprint of LPCBooks
a division of Iron Stream Media
100 Missionary Ridge, Birmingham, AL 35242
ShopLPC.com

Cover design by Hannah Linder Designs

Library of Congress Control Number: 2021937484

All Scripture quotations, unless otherwise indicated, are taken from the Holy Bible, King James Version.

Chapter Six contains an excerpt from Prime Minister Winston Churchill's 1941 Christmas Eve speech delivered via radio from Washington, D.C., while visiting President Roosevelt at the White House. The Epilogue includes portions of the apology to Japanese Canadians delivered by Prime Minister Brian Mulroney from the House of Commons in Ottawa, Canada, on September 22, 1988.

ISBN-13: 978-1-64526-304-3
Ebook ISBN: 978-1-64526-305-0

PRAISE FOR *ROSE AMONG THORNES*

An emotion-packed story of pain and forgiveness, friends and enemies, love and war that will leave you thinking about the characters and their journeys long after the final page.

~**Anne Mateer**
Author of *Playing by Heart*

Terrie Todd's novel, *Rose Among Thornes*, is a powerful story of man's struggle to forgive and to make restitution; to stop hate and to find love; and to let go of fear long enough to grab hold of God. Though Terrie's story is about two families on different sides of the interment of Canadians of Japanese during World War II, we've seen much the same inhuman treatment of those of different cultures and beliefs throughout the history of mankind. Filled with a cast of well-developed characters, this accurately researched novel with its heart-wrenching scenes reminds us to stay vigilant. Thankfully, the ending brings readers an abundance of hope and healing.

~**Clarice G. James**
Author of *The Least of These,* her fifth women's contemporary novel

Thoughtful and timely. In *Rose Among Thornes*, Terrie Todd shows the difficult conditions faced by Japanese-Canadians in World War II—a topic rarely explored in novels—as well as the horrific treatment of prisoners of war. Both Rose and Rusty have reasons to hate, reasons never to forgive. Through their struggles, we see the cost of not forgiving and the blessings of forgiveness. A beautiful story that makes you feel—and think. Highly recommended!

~**Sarah Sundin**
Bestselling and award-winning author of *When Twilight Breaks* and the Sunrise at Normandy series

Dedicated with admiration to
the Japanese Canadian community in Manitoba

ACKNOWLEDGMENTS

I'd like to thank my friend Terry Tully and his mom, Osono, for providing the inspiration behind Rose's story. See my Author's Notes at the end for more on this and for the many books referenced during the creation of this one.

Thanks to George Otsuji for the interview, Kelly and Cheryl Ronald for the loan of their book on sugar beet farming, Anita Janzen-Gemmell for leading me to her Great-Uncle Isaac Friesen's journey from Winnipeg to Sham Shui Po prison, and to Peter Ralph for his assistance in creating Bert's hot rod. Thanks to author Sarah Sundin for guidance on how the Japanese ships were named. I'm grateful for author Rachel Hauck, who helped me kick-start Rose's journey, and for the encouragement of everyone at the 2019 Deep Thinkers Retreat. Thank you to my critique partner, Clarice James, whose books I love and who patiently lets me rant. I'm incredibly blessed to still have access to the memories of my mother, Norma Oswald Klassen, when trying to imagine farm life in the 1940s. I'd also like to acknowledge pianist Linda McKechnie who blended Beethoven's Fifth Symphony with "How Great Thou Art" on her CD, *Worship in the Key of Life*.

This book wouldn't be in your hands without my editor, Denise Weimer, and the creative team at Iron Stream Media. Thanks for believing in this project. And to my readers, without whom writing stories would be completely pointless.

My deepest gratitude, as always, is due my redeemer, Jesus Christ, master storyteller and main character in the greatest story ever told. Thank you, Lord, for pushing me to tackle this challenging story and for finally convincing me it really was mine to tell.

CHAPTER ONE

Vancouver, Canada - October 1941

She had expected it to be an ordinary Saturday afternoon at the movies. But suddenly, Rose Onishi knew beyond any doubt that she was staring directly at her future. She stood on tiptoe, mesmerized, gazing into the storefront window, her friend Freda tugging on her arm.

"C'mon, Rosie." Freda was the only one allowed to call her *Rosie*. "We'll miss the start of the movie!"

Rose wouldn't budge. "This is it, Freda. This is the one." The black satin dress was the most elegant creation Rose had ever seen. Its hem hung gracefully around the mannequin's ankles, while a generous strip of shimmering silk draped over one shoulder and fell halfway down the back. Simplicity at its most beautiful. "It's perfect."

"For your recital?" Freda finally stopped smacking her gum long enough to take a good look, her reflection in the store window emphasizing the contrast between the two girls. Freda's five feet, nine inches were topped with a mop of wild blonde curls, while her own long, ink-black hair refused to curl no matter how frequently she begged God. Together at every opportunity, the pair had become known as Mutt and Jeff.

"It's not just *any* recital." Rose glanced at Freda long enough to scowl, then turned back to the exquisite dress. "It's everything! It determines whether I get the scholarship or not. Which determines whether I *go* or not. Everything has to be perfect, including what I wear."

She imagined herself in the dress, the satin sliding over her arms and swirling around her body like a refreshing dip at Vancouver's

Kitsilano Beach on a hot July day. She saw herself stepping to the stage and taking her seat on the piano bench, the spotlight catching the glimmer of the fabric and whispering "winner" into the judges' ears before she even began to play.

Freda resumed her gum-chewing. "Your mom can make it for you."

Rose nodded. It was the only way. Not in a million years would her parents ever buy the ready-made dress even if they had the money. And never in a million years would they ever have the money.

"She can." Rose sighed. "But she won't."

"Of course she will. Why wouldn't she?" Freda leaned down to re-roll a bobby sock. "She's the best seamstress anywhere."

"I know. But she'll say it's not practical. Or I'm too young. Or it's a waste of fabric she could use for a customer's dress, or it's too much trouble for something I'll only wear once, or ... who knows? She just won't."

"She wants you to get into the University of British Columbia, doesn't she?"

"Yes. She says she does. I mean, I've explained it a thousand times." Mama seemed to think Rose had gone as far as she needed to go when she passed her Grade Ten Royal Conservatory exam, but her father understood. "I get the scholarship, I get into the music program, I become a concert pianist, I travel the world—"

"You mean *we*. *We* travel the world." Freda wagged her thumb back and forth between them.

"Right. *We*."

Freda was skilled on the violin, but every time Rose had accompanied her on the piano for one of Freda's recitals, the judges and music teachers ended up flocking around Rose after the performance. Freda's mother finally grew indignant enough to find her a different accompanist, but Freda merely shrugged and said a girl could still dream. She remained Rose's biggest fan.

"Maybe your dad will buy you the dress."

Rose raised her eyebrows at her friend. "Dad? Can you see my dad doing something without Mama's say-so? You can't be serious." The two girls had been in and out of each other's homes since Grade One. Freda knew better than anyone what Rose's parents were like.

"Well, okay. Maybe not." Freda tugged on Rose's arm again. "But where's the harm in showing your mom the dress? Maybe she'll surprise you. Now come on! *It Started with Eve*—we've been dying to see this. We'll miss the beginning."

"No, we won't. We'll only miss the newsreels. Who wants to see all those bombs and guns?" Rose shuddered as she followed her friend, the October breeze causing her to pull her red cardigan close around her.

"Besides, does it really matter what you wear?" Freda reached up and pulled a heart-shaped leaf from a low-hanging Katsura branch and took a deep whiff before twirling it between her fingers, releasing its burnt sugar scent. "Why should they care how you look if you can knock their socks off with your playing? And you already know you will. You knock *every*one's socks off."

Rose grinned. "It *all* matters. I want them to see me as a concert pianist from the minute they lay eyes on me. I need that dress."

"Maybe you can earn the money yourself." Freda shrugged, ever the optimist.

Rose laughed. "Did you see the price tag? I'd need to teach piano lessons around the clock for six months. I've only got five, and I need to spend every spare minute practicing. I shouldn't even be going to this movie. You're a bad influence."

"Yes, I am!" Freda tossed her head back in a devious laugh. Then she craned her neck to see who was entering the Roxy Theater up ahead. "Hey, I think Ted and Tony are going in. C'mon, maybe we can sit with them." Freda had been in love with Ted Rogers for at least six weeks—a new record, even if it was unrequited. "You can sit with Tony."

There was no point protesting. If Rose was honest with herself, she'd love to sit beside Tony Sutherland.

When they reached the Roxy, four uniformed soldiers leaned against its outside wall. "Hello, ladies," one of them said, tossing his cigarette to the ground. "You live around here?"

Rose ignored them and reached for the door handle, but Freda stopped to chat. "Sure do! Where are you boys from?"

The same fellow who had initiated the conversation answered for all. "Rivers and me are from Alberta. Private Thompson here comes from Manitoba, and Atkins is all the way from Halifax, Nova Scotia." He dragged out 'Nova Scotia' like a radio announcer selling some grand opportunity.

"Wow." Freda grinned at the one called Atkins. "Coast to coast, eh?"

"Something like that, yeah. I think I might like *your* coast better."

Freda laughed way too loudly, and Rose pinched her elbow to make her stop.

The boy from Manitoba opened the door to the theater's lobby, and the fragrance of popcorn wafted out. He smiled at Rose. "Going in?"

Rose focused on her shoes.

Freda answered. "You bet. You fellas here to see the picture too?"

Rose wanted to strangle Freda. She grabbed another pinch of her elbow skin and twisted it, pulling her friend aside.

"What?" Freda practically hissed.

Rose whispered between clenched teeth. "Why else would they be here, you ninny? We are *not* sitting by them. Not unless you never want to see another movie with me as long as you live. Which might not be all that long if they sit with us."

Freda sighed and rolled her eyes. "Who's gonna know? Tim's not tagging along behind us, is he?" She glanced over her shoulder for Rose's nine-year-old brother, but Tim had decided he'd rather play ball than sit through a musical.

Rose glared at Freda. "Old Mr. Kiosaki runs the projector on Saturdays, and he's got eyes like a hawk. If we sit with those soldiers, you know Dad will hear about it within the first thirty minutes and drag me out of here by my ear. Worse yet, Mama. Chattering in Japanese all the way. I'd rather die."

Freda opened the door to the lobby and looked around. "Doesn't make any difference now, anyway."

Rose followed Freda's gaze. The four soldiers had purchased their tickets and were going inside the theater.

"Good." Rose sighed.

"Spoilsport." Freda marched to the ticket counter. "Two, please."

The girls handed over their quarters for admission, then used their dimes for a bag of popcorn and a drink to share. At the door into the theater, a pimpled usher took their tickets and pointed a chin at Rose. "She's supposed to sit in the balcony."

Freda pressed her face toward him, leaving about a half inch between his nose and hers. "We'll sit where we want."

The usher backed off as he always did, and Rose tried not to blush. As she always did.

The girls stood still until their eyes adjusted to the dim lighting. They spotted Tony and Ted in the back row with a bunch of other kids, and Freda tossed her head as though she hadn't noticed them at all. As they made their way down the aisle, the newsreel was still playing. Rose wanted to plug her ears to the explosions and close her eyes to the images of fighter planes and bombs dropping somewhere over the Atlantic. She shuddered. Her big brother James had been trying to enlist for two years and been turned away every time. Though Mama and Dad sympathized with his growing frustration, Rose suspected they secretly felt relieved the Canadian military adopted an unwritten "No Orientals" policy. The very idea of James in one of those bombers, or firing from a foxhole somewhere, or peering through a periscope, made Rose's heart pound. Dad's stories from the Great War should have been enough to frighten James too. But who could figure out boys?

Rose relaxed when she spotted the four soldiers seated down in front beside the giggling Porter twins. Freda led the way to seats near the middle of the theater.

Before she sat, Freda looked up at the projection booth. "You were right." She stuck her tongue out. "It's Mr. Kiosaki."

Rose prayed the man didn't catch her friend's rude gesture as she grabbed Freda's arm and pulled her into the seat beside her.

Freda pointed to the red velvet curtains on either side of the silver screen. "See that shade of red? That's the color dress I want for prom."

Suddenly, she bounced on her seat. "Hey, I've got it! Tell your mom if she makes the black satin dress, you can wear it for the recital *and* for the prom."

Rose let out a snort. "You bozo. Who's going to ask *me* to the prom?"

"Tony Sutherland."

Rose could feel the heat rising in her face. "Never."

Freda sucked up too much Coca-Cola through her straw and let out an unladylike burp. "You know he likes you."

"I don't know any such thing."

Rose did indeed hope Tony liked her. She liked him, too, and who wouldn't? He had the dreamiest blue eyes and cutest grin. But what was the point? "Tony asking me to the prom would be like Art Nakamara asking *you*. You know *that's* not going to happen."

Freda gave Rose a blank stare. "Why would I *want* that to happen?"

"You don't. That's not my point. Tony Sutherland is not going to ask a Japanese girl to the prom."

"You're not Japanese. You're Canadian."

"I know, but … you know what I mean. He's never asking me."

Freda grinned and leaned in. "That's not what he told Joe." Freda's brother Joe was a year older and in Grade Twelve, like Tony.

Rose turned wide eyes to her friend. What had Tony told Joe?

"Last week, when you played 'O Canada' for assembly?" Freda pulled her gum from her mouth and stuck it to the bottom of her seat. "Tony wasn't singing or looking at the flag. He was staring at the piano player. And as you walked back to your seat, he watched you, all googly-eyed, the whole time. I bet he's watching you right now." Freda craned her neck toward the back of the theater.

Rose punched her arm. "Don't you dare!"

"I'm telling you, Rosie, he's planning to ask you."

"Don't say things you know aren't true." Rose nibbled a piece of popcorn. Freda might be a dear friend, but she really had no clue what life was like for Rose. When your last name is Smith, no one ever calls you a *dirty Jap*. "Besides, who's got time for boys? I shouldn't even be here with *you*."

"So you said. Fourteen times already. As if one minute away from your piano will cost you the whole scholarship and you'll be stuck here on Powell Street teaching piano lessons for the rest of your life."

"That's exactly what will happen if I don't win this thing." Rose could imagine it all too easily. Her piano teacher, Mr. Bernardi, always told her she possessed a rare gift that needed to be shared with the world. How could she share it with the world if it all ended in March with the loss of this fierce competition? "Maybe I should go home. Chopin's 'Nocturne in E-flat Major' is not going to memorize itself."

Freda let out a huff. "Would you stop it? You need a break from your piano once in a while. Those skinny fingers of yours will wear themselves to the bone. Speaking of fingers, I've already got nail polish the color of those curtains. You can borrow it for your recital."

Someone behind the girls shushed them, and they turned their attention to the screen. Rose tried to relax into her seat. The credits were fading and the opening music resolving. Deanna Durbin starred in this picture. Rose and Freda admired Deanna the most because she was Canadian-born like them and had the most amazing vocal range. Deanna's picture even graced Rose's bedroom wall. She settled in and let Hollywood carry her away, far from the concerns of recitals, proms, and fancy dresses.

When the movie ended and they reached the lobby, Freda turned to Rose. "See? Now aren't you glad you came? I was right, wasn't I?"

Rose laughed. "I hate to admit it, but you were. I needed that. Thanks."

Freda turned her attention to something—or someone—behind Rose. "Don't look now, but—"

She was interrupted by a masculine voice. "Hi, Rose. Can I talk to you a minute?"

Rose turned around to see who had spoken and nearly stepped on a boy's foot. Right in front of her, grinning his adorable grin, stood Tony Sutherland.

"Can I walk you home?" Tony smiled down at Rose, a twinkle in his blue eyes.

Rose's palms immediately grew sweaty. She began to shake her head, her eyes searching for Freda. But her friend had already anticipated what was happening.

"She'd love that." Freda waved and started to leave the theater. "I have an errand to run for my mother before I head home, anyway, so this is perfect. 'Bye, Rosie."

And just like that, Freda was gone. How dare she? Rose looked up at Tony again and tried to smile.

"Okay, then." Tony held the door open for Rose, and she walked through. They headed down the sidewalk together. "So … you and Freda have been friends for a long time."

Was that what this was about? Did Tony secretly like Freda and want to pump Rose for information? Well, that she could deliver easily.

"Yes. We met as preschoolers at the Anglican Church." Their congregation was well represented by white and Japanese, with a few others thrown into the mix. Rose thought it normal. Even at school, her class was about a quarter Japanese. "When Freda and I ended up in the same Grade One class, we became inseparable and have stayed that way for these past ten years."

While the adults complained of all the challenges during the Great Depression, the girls had enjoyed their childhood. Rose had her piano and Freda her violin. They played together when they could.

"We went to Girl Guides at the church every Thursday night, and now to youth group."

Tony shoved his hands in his pockets. He wasn't saying anything, so Rose kept talking about her friendship with Freda.

"Our birthdays fall only a day apart—June fourteenth and fifteenth. The year we turned nine, we hatched a scheme for me to sleep at Freda's house the night of my birthday, the morning of hers. The next year, we did the same at our place and have continued the tradition ever since."

Rose had once overheard her mother's friend, Mrs. Oohashi, criticizing her mother for allowing the sleepovers, but the Onishis trusted the Smiths. Rose knew their home as well as she knew her own, and Freda knew theirs. They'd survived their awkward pre-adolescent years and helped each other earn top marks at school. Their shared love of classical music set them apart from their peers and got them through many a potential teenage spat.

"Now you're both sixteen?"

"Yes."

"Me too."

"Freda and I share everything. Well, except clothing." She was rambling, but she couldn't seem to stop. "Oh, we've tried a few times. It always ends in a fit of hysterical laughter."

"I can imagine." Tony chuckled.

"I'll try wearing one of Freda's skirts only to trip over it when I walk. One time, on an unplanned overnight stay, I gave Freda a spare *nemaki* to wear."

"What's a nemaki?"

"Like a housecoat. Nightwear."

"Okay." Tony nodded. "I'm guessing it didn't fit?"

Rose laughed. "It stretched tightly across her shoulders and barely reached her knees. She ended up in one of my big brother's."

"Boys wear them too?"

"Oh sure. Boys and men. James was about fourteen at the time. He turned beet-red when Mama offered Freda his nemaki. Probably embarrassed a ten-year-old girl could fit something of his." They had reached Rose's apartment building. "Well, this is where I live."

Tony raised his eyebrows, then peered up at the three-story brick building. "That was a short walk. And all we talked about was Freda."

"Isn't that who you wanted to know about?"

"Well … sure … I guess." Tony suddenly seemed fascinated by his feet. "But maybe next time we can talk about you."

Next time? Rose could feel heat in her face. Why was it so much easier to talk about Freda or music or anything but herself? Why hadn't she asked Tony anything about himself? "Okay, well … I better go on up. I'm practicing for an important piano recital."

Tony said goodbye, and Rose dashed up the stairs to the Onishis' living room window overlooking the sidewalk. But Tony had already rounded the corner and was out of sight.

CHAPTER TWO

Winnipeg, Manitoba - October 1941

P rivate Russell Winston Thorne shivered in his sleep. It was the same
dream he'd had a thousand times.

He's fifteen again. His brother Jack lies dead in a back alley in a
faraway city, but somehow Rusty can see Jack's body. Jack opens his
stone-cold eyes and levels them straight on his little brother. The words
Jack speaks usually startle Rusty into consciousness. This time, the
dream is interrupted before Jack can say them.

"Wake up, pal. Movie's over." His buddy Bert Johnson was punching
him in the shoulder. "How can you sleep through Deanna Durbin?"

Rusty opened his eyes to the credits rolling on the silver screen. "I
guess I'm that tired. Furlough's exhausting." Rusty dragged himself to
his feet. The two friends made their way up the aisle of the Colonial
Theater and out into the bright Winnipeg sunshine.

"You hungry?" Bert pointed to a burger joint across the street.

Rusty shook his head. "Naw. Told Mum I'd be home for supper.
I think she's a little miffed because I took time away from the family
when I'm only home for a couple of days."

"Nieces and nephews getting on your nerves?"

"It's not the kids. It's their mothers." Rusty's two older sisters,
Shirley and Claire, almost hadn't recognized him when the whole
family had met him at the train.

"Claire's first words to me were, 'You're a man! A real, grown man!'"
He mimicked his sister's voice by making his own high-pitched. "And
then Shirley pokes me in the ribs and goes, 'Where's your baby fat,

Rusty? It's all gone!' They haven't stopped picking on me since."

Bert laughed. "The tan from our stint in Jamaica probably doesn't hurt either."

"That's another thing they won't let go." Rusty wiggled his fingers on both sides of his face in his impersonation of Claire. "'You look like The Golden Boy!'"

"Aw, that's just their way of telling you they're proud." Bert led the way down the sidewalk. "And you gotta admit, you've changed a lot."

"Yeah, well ... not fast enough to hang onto Susie." Rusty had received Susie Pierce's *Dear John* letter mere weeks into basic training. A young doctor had moved to Spruceville, and Susie had decided her prospects were better with him.

"You can do much better than Susie Pierce." Bert kicked a small stone down the concrete. "I always thought so."

Rusty shrugged. "She was in church on Sunday with her new fella."

"I noticed. I also saw you march right over, bold as brass, and shake the man's hand."

"Figured I might as well take the bull by the horns and make the first move. I welcomed him to the community and told him Spruceville needed a good doc."

"That was big of you. What did Susie say?"

Rusty laughed. "Pulled me aside and said, 'If I'd known how handsome you were going to turn out, I might have waited.'"

Bert's eyes widened. "She didn't."

"She did."

"Like I said, you're better off without her."

Pals since childhood, Rusty and Bert had signed up the minute Canada declared war on Germany in September of '39. Rusty was only eighteen at the time, but his parents didn't try to discourage him. Dad had fought in the Great War. Both his parents, although born in Canada, held to the British tradition that if your country needed you, you volunteered.

"I don't know about better off, but it's safe to say Susie no longer wants to be Mrs. Russell Winston Thorne." Rusty's mother always claimed to be a third cousin of Winston Churchill, and that's how Rusty got his middle name. Of course, Churchill was a mere secretary of state when Rusty was born, but his mother had followed the ups and downs of the man's career and cheered whenever Churchill took a step up the parliamentary ladder.

They reached Bert's car, a 1930 Ford. Since the age of thirteen, Bert had used all his charm, every penny he could save, and every spare minute to acquire the car, then remove the four-cylinder motor and replace it with a flathead V8. It was his pride and joy.

"Wanna drive?" Bert dangled his car key beside his cheek. "Since you already enjoyed a nap. I wouldn't mind taking one on the way home."

"This old rattle trap?" Bert must be awfully tired if he was making the offer, but Rusty couldn't resist the chance to ruffle his buddy's feathers.

"Scared you can't handle her?"

"If I must." Rusty caught the keys and drove the hour back to Spruceville. As they passed the church he'd grown up in, his lips twisted into a wry grin. His family had sat proudly together in their regular pew on Sunday, eager to show off their soldier. Rusty couldn't help wondering if his presence in uniform was supposed to compensate for the shame his parents had endured when Jack left. Those months of not knowing Jack's whereabouts had taken a horrible toll on his family. While this community was filled with kind people, they had enough of the other kind too. He could still recall the comments Susie's mother, Justina Pierce, made to his own mother at Jack's funeral years before: "Your boy proved the Bible true. Jack reaped what he sowed, and his awful death can be a good lesson to all our young people."

So comforting. The best lesson had come from Mum's response. She didn't say a word but maintained her strength, her dignity, and her faith that God would exact justice without her assistance. Rusty had drawn on her example through basic training and his first military assignment whenever he felt unfairly treated.

As they approached the Thorne family farm, Rusty's heart warmed at the familiar sight of the big red barn. The old two-story house might be in need of some new paint, but the apple tree out front was alive with fall colors. It was the only home Rusty had ever known. He climbed out of his friend's hot rod, and Bert carried on down the road to his own place.

Four nieces and nephews immediately skipped around his feet. When five-year-old Benjamin begged Rusty to swing him around, Rusty obliged—which only prompted the three younger ones to chime in. "Uncle Rusty! Swing me next, Uncle Rusty!"

Not to be left out, Lady, his German shepherd, nearly plowed Rusty over. He knelt to give her a good rubdown. "Hey, girl. *You* won't be findin' yourself another fella, will ya?"

The kids trailing him around the outside of the house, Rusty found his father washing up on the rear porch.

"Good picture?" Dad grabbed the towel and rubbed his tanned face.

"It was all right." Rusty poured fresh water into the basin and plunged his hands in. "You haven't filled me in on how the harvest went for you, Dad."

Dad worked the towel over his arms and elbows. "Well, every able-bodied man, woman, and child pitched in. Lost a few beets, but that's to be expected. Our usual hired hands are all off fighting. As it should be."

"Been tough?" Rusty caught the towel Dad tossed him.

"Yeah. Our bunkhouses stayed empty all summer. No strong young fellas around anymore."

Guilt rose to the surface, but staying home to work the farm would only induce greater guilt because Rusty wouldn't be serving his country. Besides, if the rumors of a coming conscription were true, he'd eventually have no choice, anyway.

"Maybe by next harvest, the war will be over." Rusty wished he could believe his own words. "You know I'll come back and help you make a go of things. And there'll be plenty of fellas looking for work then."

"Yeah, maybe." Dad pulled the screen door open and waved the kids through. "We pray for a swift end to it every day."

Rusty hung up his towel and followed the ruckus into the warm kitchen. Mum had supper on the table, and Rusty inhaled deeply. The aroma of roast ham, mashed potatoes, and corn sure beat the chow line back at camp. Mum had even made a chocolate cake.

"Been saving sugar rations for something special." Mum's light brown curls stuck to her forehead as she carried the cake to the sideboard. "Your brief visit home before shipping out again is about as special as they come."

Rusty smiled. "Thanks, Mum."

The big old kitchen table had seen better days but was now set with Mum's finest china for the adults and her chipped everyday set for the kids. Rusty's sisters, Claire and Shirley, settled the children before their husbands joined them from the living room. Once everyone was seated, Dad reached out to hold hands with Mum on his right and Rusty on his left. When everyone's hands were thus clasped, he cleared his throat.

"Lord, thank you that we can all be together like this and celebrate Rusty's presence here with us for one more night before he ships out again. Thank you for this bounty we're about to enjoy from your hand. Amen."

A round of *amens* followed and was immediately accompanied by the clinking of dishes and silverware. Conversation focused on the food, the harvest, and the weather as though no one wanted to acknowledge the war or Rusty's imminent return to it. He closed his eyes for a moment to savor the laughter of the children, the aromas of his mother's food, and the warmth of his family's love.

Only one figure was missing from the idyllic family scene. Though no one mentioned Jack, his shadow hovered over every conversation, every snippet of story, every trill of laughter, and every tear.

Nobody around the table mentioned Susie Pierce either.

After their meal together, the family convinced Rusty to take a seat at the piano, where he accompanied his sisters while they sang

"After the War is Over" in sweet harmony. Mother pulled down her hymnbook and turned to "Great is Thy Faithfulness." Rusty played and his family sang along. He knew the words by heart from childhood, but had he ever truly tested God's faithfulness? Would the next leg of his journey provide that test?

Wednesday morning, Rusty's parents accompanied him to the train station, where he met his unit for their next adventure. Shirley and Claire arrived together, for once, with no kids. His family kept their goodbyes brief and unemotional, but his parents' tense faces and moist eyes testified to their fear of losing their only remaining son. The melancholy honking of Canada geese overhead darkened his mood as his parents left the platform. *At least, if I die in the war, I'll be remembered as the good and honorable son.*

He tried to rest as the wheels made their hypnotic chug on the tracks below. He had never minded the gentle rocking motion but allowed it to lull him into near-slumber even as he picked up pieces of conversations in progress all around him.

The train had started in Valcartier, Quebec, and had already picked up reinforcements in Montreal, Ottawa, and other stops before reaching Winnipeg. By now, it was common knowledge they'd be joining C-Force from Eastern Canada, but naturally, the troops of the First Battalion of the Winnipeg Grenadiers had not been told where they were headed. It would be considered a breach of security. But rumor mills could be pretty accurate, and the boys weren't born yesterday.

"At first, I figured we were heading to Jamaica to replace your company," one of the soldiers with an east coast accent told Rusty as the endless, monotonous prairie rolled past. "But when we kept chugging farther and farther west across Canada, those hopes were dashed."

By the time they reached Alberta, the prevailing notion was Singapore. Wherever they ended up, it seemed clear that they would travel via Vancouver. They'd stopped in Melville, Saskatoon, and Edmonton, adding more men with each stop.

"Hey, Rusty!" Bert moved into the empty seat beside him and poked Rusty in the ribs with a bony elbow. "Open your eyes, pal. You're missing the scenery. Never saw anything like this back home."

Rusty sat up a little straighter and gasped at the view out his window. The sun was rising, and they were in the Rockies. Already, words began to form in his head for his next letter home. But how exactly could one describe the majestic, breathtaking beauty? He'd never imagined such stunning color—the glorious hues of blue and purple mixed with gray, the snowy white peaks, the lush green of the pines around the bottom of each range. Bible verses about mountains that he'd memorized as a kid began to bubble up from wherever they were archived, and the words of old hymns surfaced, telling of the wonders of God's creation. Surely, those hymn writers were viewing the Canadian Rockies when they wrote things like "I sing the mighty power of God, that made the mountains rise ..."

Now the tune was stuck in Rusty's head. Mother would be proud.

The train stopped in Jasper, and the men were allowed outside for some exercise in the cool October air. While most of the others lit cigarettes, Rusty and Bert admired the colorful Haida totem pole towering over the small town. The gorgeous mountain view and bright morning sunshine filled Rusty's heart with hope and a renewed conviction that Canada and everything about her was worth fighting for.

More men joined them, and the train continued on through the incredible Rockies. When the mountain range fell behind them and they chugged through the interior of British Columbia, he relaxed against his seat and closed his eyes again.

Bert wouldn't let him sleep. "This would go a lot faster if we were flying."

The initial dream for both had been the air force, like their hero, Wop May. The Canadian flying ace of the First World War had been born near their own home in Manitoba and had survived pursuit by the famous Red Baron. But Rusty had failed the eye exam for pilots and joined the army instead.

As if to make a point, he pushed his glasses higher on his nose.

"Hey, don't blame *me*, pal. I didn't force you to follow me. You could be flyin' around up there right now."

Bert hadn't yet admitted he'd changed his mind about the air force out of loyalty to Rusty. "I still think they could have taken us as a team. I could be the eyes and the brain. You could be the brawn."

Rusty gave him a punch to the upper arm. He never could understand why God had made him take after Mother's side of the family—stocky, baby-faced, and only five-foot-eight. If his brother, Jack, was going to throw it all away, why did God make Jack the tall, dark, and handsome one? If Rusty had resembled Jack, would the air force have overlooked his glasses? It's not as though his eyes were that bad. And he *was* strong.

Jack had always found the breaks, thanks to his charm and good looks. Captain of every sports team, star of every school stage production, Jack had never lacked for dates or awards. Would Jack be in the air force now, flying bombers for his country, if he hadn't grown so bored with life on the farm? If he hadn't resented Mum and Dad's rules or rejected their faith?

Rusty would never forget his father's words after Jack's funeral. "You're our only son now, Russell." Dad only called him Russell when he was terribly serious or angry. And he almost never got angry at Rusty. Rusty was the good one. Never gave his parents an ounce of trouble. Determined to be the most devoted Christian, ideal son, and best soldier he could be. They deserved nothing less, especially now.

You're our only son now, Russell. Thank God we have you. We know you'll do us proud.

The words had carried Rusty to the valedictorian's platform at high school graduation, then through the backbreaking work of another sugar beet harvest, then through basic training, and most recently through his company's stint in Jamaica. Surely, they would continue to carry him through whatever lay ahead.

Wherever we're going, Lord, he prayed, *help me make my parents proud. Help me do it right.*

CHAPTER THREE

Rusty's train arrived in Vancouver at 0800 on October 27. By that afternoon, the men found themselves on board the New Zealand liner the *HMT Awatea*. Rusty and Bert found a small plaque explaining the name was a Māori term meaning "bright pathway." Rusty sure hoped it would be true for them. The officer in charge waited until Vancouver's harbor was a speck on the horizon before assembling his troops on deck.

"Gentlemen, we are going to Hong Kong. Prime Minister King has promised Prime Minister Churchill two battalions from Canada to help the British defend their colony on the southeast coast of China against a possible attack from Japan. We should disembark in mid-November, and you'll receive your orders upon arrival."

After they were dismissed to their barracks, Bert voiced his usual optimism with a slap to Rusty's shoulder. "Can you believe our luck? Just think, Russ. We could be sloggin' around in the muck fighting Germans, and instead, we get to visit all these exotic, warm places. God is smiling on us, man."

Rusty only grinned. If Churchill figured he needed reinforcements in Hong Kong, there must be a valid reason.

The air grew warmer. The *Awatea* made a stop in Pearl Harbor, and that night Rusty began a letter home. After describing the Rocky Mountains the best he could, he wrote:

Never thought I'd see Hawaii. It's certainly beautiful from the ship! We weren't allowed to go ashore, though the men were itching to. Hawaiian ladies in grass skirts and flowers around their necks and in their hair danced for us, waving from the shore.

Rusty didn't tell about the Canadian dollar bills that floated from the ship to the waiting women or that he kept his own hands and money firmly in his pockets.

As we pulled away from Pearl Harbor, I stayed on deck a long time. Mother, you think our prairie sunsets are something? I wish I could capture for you the most amazing one I've ever seen, over the Pacific. For a moment, I thought the harbor had been set ablaze, so brilliant were the reds, corals, and golds. I remembered us singing "A Sunset Nearer" at Jack's service, and the tune sort of lodged itself in my head for the rest of the evening.

I'm not allowed to say where we're headed, but by the time you get this, I'll be there. I'm sure glad I don't get seasick. Bert's not doing as well, but he combats it admirably. He says to give his family his love and he'll write when we have solid ground under our feet again. Love, Rusty.

Vancouver

By November, Tony and Rose were, in Freda's words, "an item." They sometimes ate lunch together at school and had seen *Dumbo* together at the Roxie.

"We're not *an item*," Rose argued when Freda dropped by after school one afternoon. She closed the door to her bedroom. "We're just friends."

"Sure, sure." Freda would not be swayed. "You think I didn't see you practice-writing Rose Sutherland in your notebook?"

"Shh!" Rose clapped her hand over Freda's mouth. Rose's mother was at her sewing machine just outside the door. "My parents would throw a fit if they thought anything serious was going on."

"You really like him, though, right?" Freda lowered her voice to a whisper as she lay back on Rose's bed.

Rose shrugged. "Most of the time."

"What kind of answer is that?" Freda flopped over onto her stomach and swung her feet back and forth in the air. "Did he ask you to prom yet?"

"He mentioned it. But it's still months away. A lot could change."

"Like what?"

"Oh, I don't know. He's cute and all, but … he's not keen on piano like I am."

"Are you kidding? What boy is? If you hold out for that, you'll be waiting a long time, my friend." Freda had still not managed to draw the attention of Ted Rogers, but she confidently imparted advice about Rose's love life. "Forever, probably."

Rose sat at her dresser and picked up a hairbrush. "That's not true. Just because we don't know any boys like that doesn't mean they don't exist."

"Boys like what? Sophisticated? Like us, ya mean?" Freda blew a huge bubble with her gum and let it pop around her lips.

Rose laughed. "Yeah. Like us."

Freda peeled the pink mess away from her lips with her tongue and pulled it back into her mouth. "Hey, did you ever ask your parents about the dress?"

Rose pulled the brush through her hair. "I did. Mama and I walked past the window on our way to deliver some sewing, and I pointed it out to her."

"What did she say?"

"Nothing. As I expected."

"So … what will you wear for the recital?"

"My Sunday dress, I guess." Rose sighed. "It'll be fine."

"Aww. Don't give up so easily."

"My parents have far more pressing matters to worry about."

Every evening, George and Sono Onishi glued themselves to the radio to hear what was going on with the war. The Japanese were threatening the Allies left, right, and center. James was still being rejected for military service at every attempt. Although none of it affected Rose personally, her parents worried about the ramifications for all Japanese Canadians.

After nineteen days at sea, the *Awatea* arrived in Hong Kong harbor on November 16 and sailed to Holt's Wharf at Kowloon. Rusty and the other men cheered as they disembarked.

"Gotta love this tropical heat when you know winter is settling in with a vengeance back home." Bert raised his face to the sun and wiped his forehead with his arm. The men stood gawking at the beautiful women while throngs of smiling island inhabitants waved to them. Rusty tried to imagine how he'd describe the exotic scents, intense colors, and intoxicating air in his next letter home.

On the wharf, a uniformed official greeted them in a crisp British accent. "Welcome to our island, men. I'm Sir Mark Aitchison Young, governor of Hong Kong. On behalf of Prime Minister Churchill, your presence here is appreciated."

Rusty had never seen such a congestion of people in his life. He turned toward Bert. "What do you suppose these folks would think of the wide prairie skies of Manitoba?"

"Or the long stretches of road without a single farmhouse or human being in sight?" Bert shook his head.

The men marched in formation down Nathan Road, about four miles to their barracks at Sham Shui Po, next to the dockyard. The place had been built in 1927 for and by the British and came with a well-appointed courtyard and manicured lawns. Chinese boys scurried around, eager to shine shoes, cook, or help the men with their gear. After finding their assigned bunks and unloading, a tour of the grounds led Rusty and Bert to another breathtaking view. Steep cliffs overlooked the harbor.

"I feel like the emperor myself." Bert stood tall, sticking out his chest as they surveyed the brightly colored sails ferrying goods back and forth.

The next three weeks did indeed feel like a holiday. Their major reminded the men that they were obliged to behave themselves. Canada was counting on them to represent their country and their regiment respectfully. With that, he let them follow the road leading into Kowloon. They spent their time visiting the cafes, riding rickshaws, playing baseball with a Portuguese team, and scouring local shops. They could exchange each of their Canadian dollars for six Hong Kong dollars, and they saw plenty to buy. Rusty picked out lengths of fine, colorful silk for his mother and sisters and mailed it all home along with his letter—which had stretched to four pages. The men and their families back home had been advised to write short letters more often. That way, if one letter didn't make it through, maybe the next one would.

Regardless, a strange urging told Rusty he should send all four pages at once.

CHAPTER FOUR

The first weekend of December started out like any other. Rose spent Saturday at her piano. Her little brother, Tim, spent it at his friend Henry McGregor's house. When he got home, he wouldn't stop talking about how they'd played Lone Ranger, listened to the radio, drank milk, and ate shortbread cookies.

On December 7, *Ojiisan*—Grandpa Onishi—joined them for Sunday supper, like always. After their meal of rice, fish, and *misoshiru*, the adults gathered around the radio. This time, the news was too horrifying to imagine. The Japanese had dropped a bomb on the United States! When Rose first heard it, she imagined Washington, DC, or maybe New York City. Then the announcer explained it was Hawaii that had been attacked—a place called Pearl Harbor. Rose had never heard of Pearl Harbor, and Hawaii seemed a lot more foreign and far away than the U.S. mainland. Still, the news was devastating. The adults stared at each other, expressions somber and fearful.

Ojiisan suddenly looked small and frail to Rose, as though every one of his seventy years had been lived with great effort. Had he foreseen any of this decades ago when he bravely embarked with some of the first Japanese to sail to Canada seeking a better life? When he worked day and night until he could afford his own fishing boat? When he arranged for his "picture bride" to join him, or when they deliberately gave their children English names they themselves could not properly pronounce?

To this day, Ojiisan spoke little English—he pronounced it "Ingerishu"—but he understood everything. Enough to grasp perfectly that he had never been truly welcome, only tolerated, in Canada. Enough to understand that the two nations he loved were at war with one another. Rose wanted to cry for him. Did he wish he'd never left Japan?

Rusty was finishing his breakfast of eggs and coffee in the mess hall on December 8. It was Monday morning, but he was thinking about how it was still Sunday the seventh back home. His parents would have attended church that morning and were probably sitting down to supper now. Or perhaps they gathered around the radio for the latest news before heading out to milk the cows.

His imagining was disturbed when an alarm went off. Bert came running in, his eyes filled with panic. "Rusty! Let's go!"

Rusty shoved his chair back with a metallic screech. "What's going on?"

"The Japs are coming! They bombed Pearl Harbor four hours ago!"

Rusty's heart began to race. Pearl Harbor? Rusty recalled the idyllic sunset and couldn't imagine the beautiful islands under attack. Surely now, the United States would enter the war.

Bert dashed for the door, yelling over his shoulder. "They've hit Guam too. And they're coming here—maybe fifty thousand of them! Hurry!"

Rusty followed his friend back to the barracks, where men were getting into their gear and everybody was shouting. He tried to remember what they'd been taught in basic training, but it was rapidly flying out the window in the cacophony surrounding him. They'd been told the ship loaded with trucks and other equipment intended for Hong Kong had been rerouted to the Philippines by mistake. How could they defend anything with so little artillery and the lousy ratio of men?

Eventually, the Winnipeg Grenadiers were assigned to defend the west side of Kowloon under Commander Maltby. With no trucks, the men set out on foot. Their orders were to shoot to kill if they saw any Japanese troops landing. Rusty's throat felt so dry, his "yes sir" was barely audible.

Help me, God. Rusty prayed as he marched, keeping his gaze on the sky. It would be his first real combat, and with only fourteen thousand troops against fifty thousand Japanese, chances were, he was marching to his death. *I can't die, God. Mum and Dad have already lost a son. Please. I'll take a bullet if I must. Just help me live.*

The men were split into groups of three to set up rustic camps where they could take cover in some bushes while keeping an eye on the sky and water. Rusty and Bert were still together. Their third partner, Private Brooks, was no more experienced than they.

From the confusing map they'd been issued, Rusty concluded they were in the middle of the island, where the elevation was highest. Steep slopes made their every move treacherous and required their full concentration. By the next morning, planes flew overhead almost constantly. Explosions in the distance told them something was happening, but all they could do was obey orders to stay put and shoot any Japanese that appeared. None did, for days. Or was it weeks? It became impossible to keep track.

Rusty tried to get some sleep when it was his turn, sharing cans of bully beef when they grew too hungry to wait any longer. Every few days, a runner would arrive with fresh supplies—water and rations. His news was never good. Japanese ground forces were moving in from the north and fanning out to the east and west, advancing up the valleys leading to high ground. Their government was demanding surrender. Hong Kong kept refusing, even though two British relief ships had been sunk and the Chinese were in no position to give aid. Hundreds, if not thousands, of their men were already dead.

"We're sitting ducks." Bert's usual optimism was swiftly disintegrating.

Rusty thumped him on the back. "We need to keep our wits about us, pal." He didn't share the snippet of Winston Churchill's words to parliament he'd read in the Sunday paper: "If Japan goes to war, there is not the slightest chance of holding Hong Kong."

Rose nearly cried for her little brother, but she put on a brave face. On December 8, Tim returned home from school with his glasses broken. When Mama demanded to know what happened, he told the story through tears. He had run across the playground to join his friends in a soccer game only to be greeted with the words "Dirty Yellow Jap" from his best pal Henry, whose home he'd played in forty-eight hours before. Poor Tim had no idea what he'd done. The school he loved was no longer a safe place. Overnight, the Onishis had become the enemy in their own town.

Almost immediately, Ojiisan's fishing boat was seized along with thousands of others and tied up in New Westminster. When his fishing license was suspended, Ojiisan came to live with Rose and her family. Tim moved into Rose's room so that Ojiisan could bunk in with James.

Suddenly, curfews were imposed. No Japanese were to be outside their homes after sundown. Rose stopped attending youth group because she couldn't get home before dark. In solidarity, Freda valiantly offered to skip the meetings and spend those evenings at the Onishi home instead, but Freda's parents forbade it. Not that they were opposed to the girls' friendship. Rose appreciated Freda's loyalty and understood that Mr. and Mrs. Smith were merely looking out for their daughter's best interests.

The days dragged on, one running into the other without relief. One night, Rusty was awakened by a sharp blast. He drew his rifle, expecting to fire it in combat for the first time. But it was only Brooks, firing into the bushes in response to a snapping twig. A brown rabbit hopped out unharmed and raced across the open space to find cover elsewhere.

Too keyed up to go back to sleep, Rusty took over the rest of that watch. As the sun rose, black specks appeared in the sky off to the south. He had not heard or seen any planes. Were his eyes playing tricks on him? Maybe they were only birds. He cleaned his glasses on his shirt and replaced them. More black specks appeared. Finally, the thrumming of a plane overhead—where was it? Before Rusty could warn Bert and Brooks, a commotion behind him made him jerk his rifle to his shoulder and turn around. Enemy soldiers, about a hundred yards away, were running in his direction.

He didn't think. He just fired as he'd been taught. He had no idea whether he was killing men, and he didn't really want to know. The sky blackened with enemy aircraft roaring overhead, and heavy gunfire split the air. Rusty took cover in a clump of trees and fired into the surrounding woods. Where were Bert and Brooks? Were they already down? What about other troops who had camped nearby?

When his ammunition ran out, he began to run. Suddenly, a blow to the back of his head sent him sprawling. As the ground came up to meet his face, Rusty's sharpest impression was of his sister Claire and her two little girls. As his world dimmed, he saw them dressed in colorful silk, holding hands in a circle. He could almost hear them singing, "Ring around the rosy …"

Then everything went black.

CHAPTER FIVE

When Rusty opened his eyes again, he stared into the face of a Japanese child dressed in a soldier's uniform. Or so it seemed. The pain in the back of his head made it difficult to focus. The young soldier held a rifle with a bayonet aimed at Rusty's midsection.

Without moving his head, Rusty tried to survey his surroundings. His own rifle was nowhere to be seen. Where were Bert and Brooks? Men groaned behind him, but in front of him were only more Japanese, dozens of them. Most were covered in blood, but judging by their freedom of movement, the blood was not their own. Somehow, all Rusty could think about was how young they all looked. Was he being taken captive by children?

A heavily accented voice sounded through a megaphone. "The war is over. I give you safe passage to surrender."

Rusty had read about Japanese military ideals, how surrender was the ultimate humiliation. To be taken prisoner made you loathsome scum, deserving of every horror they could dream up. He'd learned the word "Bushido," the teaching that death or suicide was valued over surrender or capture. The code was loyalty and honor until death. Now he and the other men were being offered the choice to give in, which would earn their captors' contempt as cowards, or to resist in any way they could, which would mean swift and certain death.

Choose life.

The words from some long-forgotten Scripture surfaced in Rusty's muddled mind, and his vision began to clear. He spotted Bert about fifteen feet away. Despite a bloody shoulder, he was rising to his feet. Rusty did the same, as his guard motioned with the tip of his bayonet.

"Hands behind heads!" The voice came over the megaphone again.

Rusty clasped his fingers together behind his aching head and felt the lump there. Nothing seemed to be bleeding, so he must have been hit with the butt of a rifle or some other blunt instrument.

Divested of weapons and hands raised, the men moved along, prodded by gunpoint. When they reached a clearing, Rusty counted thirteen Canadians and estimated at least seventy-five Japanese. A rugged rock wall towered above them, and the enemy soldiers order them to line up against it.

Were they going to be shot? Probably not. From all he'd heard, shooting would be too merciful and a waste of bullets. Rusty tried not to imagine a slow death from a bayonet. His mouth went as dry as if he'd been sucking on rusted nails.

His head began to spin, and he closed his eyes and attempted to pray away the vertigo. When he opened them, the Canadians were being tied together at the wrists with barbed wire. The brusque and stoic efficiency of the Japanese, even in the face of the prisoners crying out, made it clear this was not the first time they had completed such a task. When Rusty's turn came, he held his wrists out but refused to watch. Instead, he made eye contact with Bert, who nodded slightly and held his gaze. By focusing on Bert's face and taking slow, deep breaths, he managed to stop the shaking that threatened to control his body.

Once they were finished, the soldier ordered the men to start marching. It took every bit of concentration Rusty could muster to stay in rhythm with his fellow prisoners, to keep the barbs from cutting into his wrists. By the time they reached a road, most of the men's hands were covered in blood, including his own.

Thirst soon trumped fear and pain as they shuffled along. Rusty couldn't remember the last time he'd had anything to eat or drink, and he'd slept maybe four hours in the last week. Although, who knew? The nights had all run together, and he had no idea what day it was. He thought back to the days leading up to enlisting, how he'd been certain he was doing what God wanted him to do. Could this possibly be part of that plan?

Why hadn't he spent those first three weeks in Hong Kong memorizing landmarks, connecting with the locals, even learning a little of the Chinese language? Or maybe Japanese. Researching the ways of the Japanese army so when they attacked, he'd have been more prepared. For a guy who'd always tried to do things with excellence, he'd sure messed up. *Lord, what kind of soldier gets captured on his first real mission? I need to keep my wits about me better than this if I'm going to survive whatever's ahead. Help me stay alert, to be aware of my surroundings.*

Whenever one of the prisoners spoke a word, the guards would scream for silence. Rusty decided to risk it, anyway. If the other men were as fear-filled as he, they needed words of hope.

"Heads up, fellas. Stay strong." His words were just loud enough for the soldier in front of him to hear.

Then that man repeated the mantra. "Stay strong."

Maybe it would get passed up the line. As they kept moving, he tried to take in his surroundings. Chinese people lined the road. Some scuffled along, keeping their heads down and minding their own business. Others stopped to watch, sorrow on their faces. In all his years growing up back home in Manitoba, he'd never seen either a Chinese or a Japanese person except in pictures. He'd never met a black-skinned man or woman until he went to Jamaica. Although he'd attended school with kids from the Indian reserve and some of their parents worked for his dad at harvest time, he hadn't gotten to know any of them well. His church was filled with white faces like his own. Now God was broadening his horizons, literally and figuratively, and opening his eyes to the differences and similarities of people. He thought about those lovely, brown-skinned women on the shore at Pearl Harbor. How many of them had perished in the attack?

A young boy stood watching from the side of the road, and Rusty made eye contact with him. So innocent. What would happen to him? Would he get to grow up? And if he did, would he be filled with hatred and revenge?

What about you?

The words were clear, and Rusty was learning to recognize the voice—not his own thoughts, but the Lord speaking to him. It was a good question. If he managed to survive whatever lay ahead, he'd be no good to anyone if he allowed his experiences to make him bitter.

As a kid, he'd studied the paintings in the big family Bible his mother kept on a corner table in the living room. The most fascinating picture was of Jesus, bowed low by the weight of the cross on his shoulders, his head adorned with a crown of thorns, and blood trickling down his face. That image came to Rusty now as he staggered along with the barbed wire cutting into his hands. He found it strangely comforting.

Landmarks became familiar, and Rusty realized they were once again on Nathan Road. Were they being taken back to Sham Shui Po? What a relief that would be. He allowed himself to imagine a cool drink of water, a meal, a shower, and a cot. Medical attention for his hands.

Then a sight startled him back to the horrors of his new reality. Along the edge of the road lay a line of soldiers, still tied together with barbed wire like Rusty's group, all in Canadian uniforms. All dead, slashed with bayonets. Rusty tried to find a familiar face, but it was too hard to tell. The angle at which they lay and the grimaces upon most of the faces made it impossible to recognize anyone. They told a tale Rusty did not wish to witness. He tried to count them as they walked by, but when he reached nine, he cried out.

"He's still alive!"

The tenth man had let out a groan.

"Quiet, Thorne," the private behind Rusty whispered.

But Rusty was too horrified. "One of them's not dead yet! You gotta do something! You can't just leave him—"

"Silence!" The butt end of the guard's rifle came down hard on Rusty's left shoulder, pushing him to the ground. The whole line of men went down with him.

Rusty realized his mistake. *Oh God, help us.* Had he just dealt the death blow to this whole group of men?

The guard who appeared to be in command marched back and forth, shouting in Japanese. Somewhere along the way, the one with the megaphone who spoke at least some English must have gone a different direction. Rusty had no clue what the man yelled, but he was clearly angry enough to kill. Someone behind him let out a whimper.

"Silence!" Then, "Up!"

With great difficulty, the men struggled back onto their feet. They were ordered to continue their march. Rusty didn't dare turn to see if the dying soldier still showed signs of life. He heard nothing and prayed it was over for the poor man. How long until the dead soldiers' families learned of their fate?

Another quarter mile and Sham Shui Po came into view. But it bore little resemblance to the place Rusty had spent his first three weeks in Hong Kong. The impressive structures were in ruins, windows shot out on every building, walls pockmarked with bullet scars. Rubble covered the once-beautiful grounds. Everything of value was gone—probably looted—and replaced with the shattered and broken. Had the Japanese taken over the facility for use as a prisoner of war camp? All of Hong Kong must be under Japanese control.

Churchill's plan had failed.

With darkness falling, the men collapsed in one corner inside the fence. The ground beneath them felt rock-hard, but at least they were horizontal. No food or water was offered. The barbed wire remained, and the men lay as still as possible to avoid injuring one another. Rusty prayed for them all to survive the night. He closed his eyes and remembered the breathtaking sunset at Pearl Harbor. The words of an old hymn came to mind again, beckoning him to bolster the courage of the men around him.

Lord, give me strength.

With his mouth too dry to swallow, Rusty somehow started to sing. It began as little more than a croak, but as he continued, his voice grew stronger and the melody clearer.

A sunset nearer daybreak, when suns will set no more;
This evening we are nearer than we have ever been before
A sunset nearer every night, a sunset nearer glory bright.

Gradually, the moaning sounds faded as the exhausted men fell into fitful sleep.

CHAPTER SIX

Rusty and Bert were able to stay together as the weeks passed at Sham Shui Po, and it was the one thing for which they could truly feel grateful. At one point, civilians from the other side of the fence cranked up the volume on a radio broadcast so that the men could hear a snippet of Churchill's Christmas speech—recorded in Washington, where he was spending the holiday with President Roosevelt.

"Let the children have their night of fun and laughter. Let the gifts of Father Christmas delight their play. Let us grown-ups share to the full in their unstinted pleasures before we turn again to the stern task and the formidable years that lie before us, resolved that, by our sacrifice and daring, these same children shall not be robbed of their inheritance or denied their right to live in a free and decent world."

The Japanese guards began yelling. The recorded voice abruptly stopped. The radio was confiscated. And the word that jumped out at Rusty was "years." Surely, the prime minister could have chosen a better word. Weeks. Months, even. But *years*? If Churchill believed the war was going to continue for years, what hope was there for Rusty and the other prisoners? The men could not last here for years. On rations of one moldy rice ball and a three-inch square of dry bread each day, they rapidly lost weight. The unsanitary conditions kept many of them sick. The first time they'd been escorted out of the confines of the camp, hope soared for a moment. But they soon learned they were being tasked with collecting dead bodies, piling them up, dousing them with fuel, and setting them on fire.

Now the hellish job was behind them, but the images were seared into his memory for life. The stench of death and decay, the blast of heat charring his own skin, the awful hissing and popping sounds all came back when he closed his eyes at night. He thought back to bonfires with his youth group and wondered if he would ever be able to enjoy a bonfire again. He tried to pray, asking God for a few brief hours of peace, only to have it all come back in dreams. It was always a relief to wake up—until he remembered where he was.

Every few days, a new captive or two arrived. Sometimes these soldiers had been wounded beyond belief and left in ditches to die— but they'd survived. Though their captors meant it as a lesson to do as you're told, the prisoners used it to encourage each other. If these men could survive, they could too.

Christmas and New Year's Day came and went. It was 1942, and Rusty tried not to think about what his family must be feeling. Did they have any idea he'd been captured?

Somewhere near the end of January, orders came to be ready to load onto trucks at eight in the morning. The rumor mill among the prisoners ground out a bit of everything. Some said they were setting sail for Japan, others that they were being lined up and killed on the edge of a cliff so their bodies could drop in the water below where the sea could deal with them. No one dared hope the war was over and they would be freed, but at least something new was happening.

The men climbed into the back of a cargo truck lined with canvas and rode in pitch blackness. Four guards joined them, making sure no one spoke. The motion put Rusty to sleep, and when he awakened to the shouts of guards and bright sunlight streaming in the back of the truck through open canvas flaps, he had no idea how long they'd been driving.

Soon enough, he learned they were at North Point, another prisoner of war camp. He was still on the island of Hong Kong.

Conditions here were no better. Every morning and evening, the men lined up in a central parade square and were counted. Sometimes this went on for hours, in all kinds of weather. Searing heat, pouring rain—it didn't seem to matter. Once a day, they lined up for a cup of watery rice stew. Days were spent trying to avoid angry guards while being as resourceful and creative as possible to meet their own basic needs. Until now, Rusty had never wasted a thought on the way clothes wear out when worn day and night for weeks on end. With no means of washing or mending, the men pooled whatever resources they could. Needles and thread became a hot commodity. Cigarettes were the currency. One of the men joked that if anybody had any paper cash, they may as well use it for toilet paper since the latter was far more useful.

For the most part, the Japanese guards allowed the men to fend for themselves. When a couple of fellows scrounged an abandoned truck tire and managed to turn it into crude sandals, Rusty was certain he caught a brief glimpse of admiration on the face of one of the guards. Though frequent beatings took place for no apparent reason, actions of resourcefulness were rarely punished.

The men talked about escape all the time, but it was mostly just something to talk about—something to give them hope. One night shortly after Rusty fell asleep, the alarm went off, and everybody staggered out to the parade grounds to line up and be counted. They'd been forced to learn their numbers in Japanese. Over and over, Rusty found himself repeating, "Ichi … Ni … San … Shi … Go …"

Hours later, when the sun started rising, they still stood there, being counted over and over, with much yelling from the guards. Five or six rifle shots rang out from somewhere beyond the fence, and the men were finally allowed to return to their barracks—some so weak from hunger and standing they required support on both sides.

The next day, they learned four prisoners had managed to escape—but not for long. Their bodies lay on display in the parade grounds until the prisoners were given permission to bury them. As challenging as it might be to escape the camp, the greater challenge lay beyond its fences. How do tall, half-starved white men in ragged uniforms stay hidden in Hong Kong, find enough food to survive, or reach safety with no idea in which direction or how far away that safety might be?

Following that event, their guards initiated a new rule. The men were placed into groups of ten. If anyone from a group attempted escape, the other nine would be executed immediately.

Even before this, Rusty had entertained no grandiose ideas of escaping. Only of surviving and helping as many others survive as he could. He couldn't help all the men, but perhaps he could encourage the nine others in his group. Besides himself and Bert, the group was made up of two other Canadians, three Americans, and three Brits.

Rusty made it his goal to initiate an individual conversation with each one. He'd ask where the soldier was from, what he did before the war, what his family was like, what his parents did for work. He asked about the man's schooling and faith. Some had none, or if they ever did have faith, they'd given up on it now. Mostly, he'd try to get each man talking about what he hoped to do after the war, to help him envision a brighter future. He took mental note of each man's dream and prayed for wisdom to offer hope in meaningful ways. Speaking words to bolster his comrades' spirits and provide a listening ear gave him a worthwhile project, a purpose to live for each day.

Gradually, the men stopped talking about possible escape. The hottest topic of conversation became food. They would spend hours describing in detail the dishes their mothers or wives made for them back home. It became a bit of a competition to see who could elicit the deepest groans from the others. When Rusty's turn came, he talked about the meals his mother and sisters would bring to the sugar beet field during harvest time. Hot corn on the cob, freshly picked from the garden and rolled in homemade butter that would run down your chin. Fresh red tomatoes and cucumbers in August, sliced thick and salted. Mounds of fried chicken or slices of ham. Homemade bread and chokecherry jelly. Mashed potatoes and chocolate cake.

Was all the talk of food helpful … or harmful? If it gave them something to live for—something to imagine on the other side of the war—it was worth every painful pang.

Meanwhile, many of them battled dysentery from the unsanitary conditions and lack of clean drinking water. It was hard to watch these once-athletic and virile men turn into weakened skeletons and to realize he must look the same. One item in high demand was any kind of cord they could find to hold their trousers up as their bodies became more wasted.

One of the Japanese guards stood apart. Rusty didn't know what his real name was, but the men had nicknamed him Scrappy after the cartoon character, presumably because of his round head and short stature. Despite his name, Scrappy didn't yell like the others. He seemed curious about the westerners and showed an interest in learning *Ingerishu*. English. When he was certain he wouldn't be caught, Scrappy was even known to show kindness to the prisoners. One day, he came in with a small supply of blank newsprint and the promise to do his best to mail letters for the men if they could improvise envelopes.

Rusty and some of the others had pencil stubs in their kits, which they gladly passed around. The men took great pains to use tiny lettering so they could say as much as possible on a small scrap of paper. They tried to phrase their letters to minimize their families' worry but also pass censoring.

Envelopes proved more challenging. By saving a grain or two of cooked rice, however, the men figured out how to fold paper into an envelope and glue it closed with the starchy rice. The sacrifice of even a single grain felt almost unbearable, especially knowing the letter might never reach home. Rusty prayed his would find its way to his parents and at least assure them he was still alive.

As he prepared to write, pencil stub in hand, he pictured his mother in her kitchen, punching down a massive pillow of risen dough until her liberally greased hands were buried to her elbows. He saw her turning it over in her gigantic, speckled enamelware bowl, then carefully covering it with a clean tea towel. She'd wipe her hands on her apron, smooth out a stray strand of hair with the back of her wrist, and turn to her next task—perhaps peeling potatoes for supper or sweeping the floor while she waited to form the dough into loaves for baking. She'd hear a motor running and peer out the window. Their neighbor, Mr. McCarthy, would rattle into the yard in his old Chevy truck and step out almost before it stopped. He'd wave an envelope in his hand and call out in excitement.

"Frank! Anna! You've got a letter from Rusty!"

Dad would come running from the barn and Mum from the house. They'd thank Mr. McCarthy for bringing their mail from town, promise to share with the congregation on Sunday whatever news the treasured envelope held, and hurry inside the house. They'd sit together at the kitchen table, Mum's hands shaking as she opened Rusty's homemade envelope—careful not to tear any precious bit. She'd unfold the paper, both sides filled with words, and tilt it toward the window for best lighting. She'd read it aloud.

What did Frank and Anna Thorne most need for their hearts to be at peace? What if this letter contained the last words they ever received from their one remaining son? Maybe Rusty shouldn't be thinking that way, but he had to consider it. Odds were not in his favor. If he were to provide his family with any comfort, he would need to do it in half-truths and not reveal the dire conditions under which he and his fellow prisoners survived each day.

Help me write the words they need to read, Lord.

He touched the pencil to paper and began.

Dear Mum and Dad,

You may have heard by now that Bert and I were involved in the battle in Hong Kong. Maybe you know we were captured. We are both all right. Your stories from the last war are serving a purpose now, Dad. You always said it was the war that made you a man and sealed your faith. Like you, I hope to come through this a stronger man and a more devoted Christian than I was before. Mum, you'll be glad to know I still have my Bible. One of the fellows offered me good money for it, but he wanted only to tear out the pages to use for rolling cigarettes. I told him to use his cash instead. I'm trying to remember the things you've taught me over the years, to not focus on my circumstances but to find ways to do good. I try to encourage the other men and to see our captors through the eyes of Christ. They are made in his image too.

As Rusty read over what he'd written, he could hear two Japanese guards on the other side of his barracks wall, talking and laughing. He had no idea what they said to each other, but the sound of their language alone was enough to make something sour rise inside him, even as he wrote words of compassion. *You're a hypocrite, Thorne. Jesus said to love your enemies, and you've got nothing but contempt for yours.*

He shook the thought away. It wouldn't do him or his parents any good to reveal his growing hatred. Besides, he had to be careful what he wrote to make sure his letter would pass the inspection of whoever censored these things. What else could he tell Mum and Dad?

I caught a bit of Churchill's Christmas Eve speech, but that's the last time I heard a radio. It's hard to know what's going on in the world. Did you and the girls receive the silk I sent? Tell them I look forward to seeing them wearing it, so they better get busy sewing if they haven't already. And tell those kids not to grow too much. I want to be able to recognize all my nieces and nephews when I get home! I hope it will be in time for harvest, Dad, but if not—please hire more help.

There's a fella here from Nova Scotia. Told me all about lobster fishing, and I explained sugar beet farming to him. We've got this little bet going about which job is harder, and we plan to visit each other to see who's right. So maybe by next year, we'll have some extra help—if you can call that help. He won't know what he's doing with a sugar beet knife, and I won't know what I'm doing on the boat!

Mum, I miss your home cooking. Most of the guys seem to think their mothers are the best cooks, but I don't bother arguing with them. I know you are.

Rusty was rapidly running out of space.

Give my love to all. If Bert's folks don't get his letter, let them know he's okay. Hope to see you soon. Love, Rusty.

The voices outside the barracks had become louder, and some sort of scuffle seemed to be underway. Rusty tucked his letter inside his Bible and went to investigate. The lobster fisherman he'd mentioned in his letter, Eli, lay sprawled on the ground, face down in the mud, hands behind his head. Two Japanese guards, rifles in hand, kicked him repeatedly in the ribs. With each blow, Eli tried to curl his body into a protective position, but the guards only found fresh places to kick. There was little use trying to come to Eli's defense because it would only get them both shot. He'd seen it. Nor was there any point wondering what Eli had done to warrant the guards' wrath because it was probably nothing. But could he distract them somehow?

He didn't need to. A ruckus began outside the fence. Daily, poor Chinese beggars would approach the fence with hopes of selling a piece of fruit or a pair of sandals to a prisoner. Usually, they knew enough to wait until the guards were out of sight. But today, a skinny little boy had come. What he was offering, Rusty couldn't tell. Quickly, an older Chinese woman came running to pull him away from the fence.

She was too late. A shot rang out, and the little boy slumped to the ground. The woman let out a wail, and Rusty feared she would be shot next. But the guards didn't want to waste another bullet—or deal with the dead. The woman gathered the child in her arms and carried him away, weeping uncontrollably. On the ground lay a small, dirty blanket, soaked in the boy's blood. The blanket must have been what he'd hoped to sell.

With the two guards who'd been kicking Eli gone to investigate, Rusty moved in. Eli was unresponsive, but his chest still rose and fell. He was bleeding from his head and knees, his body so covered in bruises and dirt it was impossible to tell where the worst wounds were. Rusty, weak himself, tried to pick Eli up by getting a grip under his arms. Another prisoner came over to help. He took Eli's feet, and together they managed to carry him to the barracks.

That night, Rusty lay awake watching to see if Eli would pull through. The men had taken to lying huddled together for warmth on the cold concrete floor where they could avoid the bedbugs and lice infesting their bunks.

Not that the men slept much. Nearly all of them suffered from burning feet, which became markedly worse at night. Some of the fellows called it "electric feet," and others even nicknamed it "happy feet" because it made them stamp their feet or keep moving in whatever manner they could to relieve the pain. To Rusty, it felt like sharp, shooting electric pain relentlessly running through his feet. Soaking them in cold water brought momentary relief, but that, too, was almost useless. By the time he lay down again to sleep, the pain was back. One of the other prisoners had been a medical student at Dalhousie and took meticulous notes about the burning feet syndrome. He kept the notes hidden away, determined to take them home and use his findings for good. He held to a theory that the pain was caused by the men's lack of nutrition and ongoing infections in their bodies. Rusty didn't care what caused it. He only wanted it to stop long enough to allow him to escape into sleep.

He envied Eli, lying unconscious. The med student had ministered to Eli's wounds as best he could, but he knew there must be internal injuries he could do nothing about. With no reserves of good nutrition upon which to draw, his body couldn't fight back. By morning, Eli was dead. He would not be visiting Manitoba to learn about farming sugar beets, and Rusty would never catch lobsters from Eli's boat.

Rusty's letter remained unchanged.

CHAPTER SEVEN

Determined to give Eli a decent burial before the guards threw his body to the stray neighborhood dogs, the men agreed to dig a grave behind their barracks. With only one shovel, it would take fifteen weakened men working in ten-minute shifts most of the day to get the hole deep enough in the hard-packed ground.

"Thorne." One of the fellows grabbed his attention as soon as they carried Eli's body out of the barracks. "You should say a few words. You're the closest we got to a preacher."

Rusty didn't respond but took his turn digging. His thoughts tortured him, and his soul felt as empty as his belly. All the things he'd believed, all the Scripture verses he'd memorized, seemed to mock him in this place of torture and death. Either God did not see him and the other men, or he didn't care, or he was not as powerful as Rusty had believed. There didn't seem to be any other explanation unless they were all being punished for something. But he'd confessed every sin he could remember ever committing, and some of them twice. When he and Bert took a few minutes away from the others, Rusty confided in his friend.

"How can I say anything, Bert? God has turned his back on us." They sank to the ground and leaned against the barracks wall.

Bert sighed. He didn't try to argue. "Well, I don't advise you to say that."

"It's all I got."

Bert shrugged one bony shoulder. "You could recite the twenty-third Psalm. Pray the Lord's Prayer."

"It would be meaningless." Rusty swallowed. "I don't know if I believe any of it anymore. God hasn't even provided our daily bread when we ask. How can we trust him for more? I'd feel like a hypocrite."

"It's not really about you, though, is it?"

Bert's challenge made Rusty mad, but he didn't defend himself.

"I mean, sometimes just saying the right words, even if you don't feel them in the moment, can give someone else a little hope and comfort—something to cling to."

Rusty sighed. "Yeah. I guess so. Maybe you should do it."

They watched while the men lay Eli's beaten and wasted body gently in the grave and began covering it.

"We could ask the men to say things about Eli," Bert suggested. "I didn't really get to know him very well. Any idea what he did to rile the guards?"

"No. Could have been anything—or nothing at all. I know he started a letter to his family, though. He was working on it before he went outside, before the ruckus started. But he tucked it away with his kit before he went out."

"Want me to go find it?" Bert struggled to his feet. "Least we could do is try to mail it home for him."

Rusty nodded, and Bert went around the corner to search through Eli's meager belongings. Rusty pulled his Bible from his shirt pocket and opened it to the twenty-third Psalm. But instead of the familiar words, his eyes fell on the twenty-second, and he began to read.

Be not far from me; for trouble is near; for there is none to help. Many bulls have compassed me: strong bulls of Bashan have beset me round. They gaped upon me with their mouths, as a ravening and a roaring lion. I am poured out like water, and all my bones are out of joint: my heart is like wax; it is melted in the midst of my bowels. My strength is dried up like a potsherd; and my tongue cleaveth to my jaws; and thou hast brought me into the dust of death. For dogs have compassed me: the assembly of the wicked have inclosed me: they pierced my hands and my feet. I may tell all my bones: they look and stare upon me.

Rusty closed his eyes and the book. The words were King David's, he knew that much. Written centuries before Jesus came along, yet it described the suffering of Christ in detail. And Rusty could relate all too well, right down to the protruding bones on his body.

"God," he mumbled under his breath. "If you even hear me ... if you want me to say anything comforting or encouraging to these men, you're going to have to give it to me. I've got nuthin.'"

How could an empty vessel pour out anything good? Was there even a drop left in him? Rusty decided when the time came, he would open his Bible at random and read whatever his eyes fell upon. If it was completely inappropriate, so be it. Probably nobody was listening, anyway. And if they did listen and the words made no sense, then God could just look stupid. Rusty didn't really care.

He opened his eyes and watched while the last shovels full of dirt were patted down over Eli's grave. Bert came around the corner carrying one of the slips of paper Scrappy had provided for letter-writing. "Found it." Bert held it out to Rusty. "And I think you should read it."

Rusty didn't take it right away, although his curiosity had been piqued. "Doesn't seem right to read it."

"Well, maybe not. But I did. And I think you should too."

Rusty took the letter and began to read the tiny script.

Dear Mom and Dad, I want you to know I'm all right.

Rusty could almost hear Eli's Nova Scotian accent as he read the words his friend had written.

Life is hard here, but I try to focus on the thought of the war ending and coming home, and it helps me get through each day. My friend Rusty helps too. He wants to come fishing with us after the war, and he invited me to his farm in Manitoba. He talks to me about God and faith and helps me see a higher purpose in us being here. Some days, I think I'd give up if it weren't for Rusty. And I know that even if I don't make it, I'll be going to a better place to be with the Lord. You can be sure about that. I've made my peace.

46

The letter went on to give greetings to Eli's siblings and extended family, but Rusty's eyes had filled with tears. He handed the letter back to Bert and rose to his feet.

"You made a difference in his life, pal." Bert put a hand on Rusty's shoulder. "You need to hang onto that."

Rusty made his way slowly back to the crude gravesite where the men waited. Most of them appeared too weary to stand, so he needed to keep this short.

He made eye contact with each man around the circle. Their hollow eyes told it all. This was far from the first death they'd witnessed, and they all knew it would not be the last. Most of them probably wondered when their turn would come. Who would bury the last of them? Would even one survive to tell of the atrocities in this place? Without looking, Rusty stuck his thumb into his Bible, opened it, and let his gaze fall to the middle of the page. He began to read aloud.

"And fear not them which kill the body, but are not able to kill the soul: but rather fear him which is able to destroy both soul and body in hell. Are not two sparrows sold for a farthing? and one of them shall not fall on the ground without your Father. But the very hairs of your head are all numbered. Fear ye not therefore, ye are of more value than many sparrows."

Rusty stopped reading when Bert nudged him. His friend put a finger to his lips and nodded his chin toward something off to the side. A sparrow had landed a few feet away. The men were all gawking at the little bird, though it wasn't an unusual sight. Sparrows were everywhere and viewed by the locals as pesky as rats or mosquitoes. Some of the men had unsuccessfully tried catching them for food.

But this one was different. Fearlessly, it hopped forward between two of the men as though oblivious to the humans and made its way to the fresh mound of earth covering Eli's body. There it stayed while the men stared. No one moved.

In a voice just above a whisper, Bert repeated the last words Rusty had read from his Bible. "Fear ye not therefore, ye are of more value than many sparrows."

Still, the bird stayed. And the men stared. What each one was thinking, Rusty could only guess. He only knew what was going on in his own heart. If God could send a bird at that exact moment, there had to be something more going on than what could be seen. He was not abandoned. He would choose to believe it, even if it killed him.

Finally, the sparrow spread its wings and, in a glorious display of freedom, flapped its way higher and higher, then soared beyond the confines of the barbed wire until it became a tiny speck. And then it was gone.

CHAPTER EIGHT

By February 2, the War Measures Act required all Japanese Canadians to register themselves and their property. There would be no more owning land or growing crops. Businesses were being taken away.

But Rose clung to her own dream. She'd prayed for it from the time she first learned what a concert pianist was. Her first piano teacher, Miss Richer, had visited her parents when Rose was ten and told them she'd taken Rose as far as she could. She encouraged them to find a more advanced teacher and gave them a referral.

Mama had seemed resistant at first. She was the one who suggested Rose start giving piano lessons to kids in the neighborhood and earn money for her own lessons. Rose had sensed the plan was a yardstick of sorts—to measure how serious she was. Determined to pass Mama's test, she made posters offering piano lessons and hung them everywhere she could. Trouble was, theirs was the only piano in the neighborhood. A few parents came to their door, offering to pay for lessons if their children could practice at the Onishis' house. Mama said yes to the three who lived the nearest. The income from those three would not be anywhere near enough to pay for Rose's lessons with Mr. Bernardi, but any more and their piano would be tied up with children plunking out "Mary Had a Little Lamb," not leaving Rose enough time for her own practice.

Her parents had discussed it behind closed doors. Ojiisan was in on it too. Somehow, the three of them raised the additional money, and Rose had begun to study under Mr. Bernardi. He pushed her harder than she'd ever been pushed, and sometimes, she hated him for it. But mostly, she loved him for it—especially when she could see herself improving and when she took top scores at competitions. When the time came, he not only wrote a letter of recommendation to go along with Rose's application to the University of British Columbia, but he secured a music scholarship that would allow her parents to afford the remaining amount. One last hurdle to jump—her March recital—and she'd be all set.

If only Japan hadn't dropped those stupid, horrible bombs on Pearl Harbor.

When Rose returned to Mr. Bernardi's for her first lesson after the attack, a bomb was dropped on her heart as well.

"This will have to be our last lesson, Rose." He refused to meet her gaze. "I wish you well, but I can't continue to teach you."

Rose expected a repeat of Miss Richer's speech and argued with him. "But Mr. Bernardi, you still have so much to teach me. I–I feel like we've only begun. I need you to help me prepare for uni—"

He stopped her. "It's not that, Rose. It's the war. If I continue to teach you—or any other Japanese students—I run the risk of losing the others. I'm sorry. Let's hope for a swift end to the war, and then all will be right again, yes?"

Rose had been too stunned to speak and returned home in a daze. It made no sense. She told her parents what Mr. Bernardi had said.

"The coward," Mama mumbled.

Dad's eyes revealed his sadness. "It's all right. *Shikata ga nai.* It cannot be helped. You will make as much progress on your own."

Rose knew that wasn't true, but she practiced harder and kept teaching. Dad began a search for a new teacher who would take her, and things had just begun to sound promising when the newspaper reported that the government planned to move all Japanese Canadians east. They were to be relocated somewhere outside the hundred-mile area along the west coast—supposedly for their own safety.

"Do you hate being Japanese?" Tim asked Rose.

"I'm a Canadian," Rose told him. "And so are you. Never forget it."

A week later, James was sent to a road camp in the interior of British Columbia, helping to clear the forest for a new highway. Though they showed little emotion, Rose sensed her parents felt heartbroken to have their firstborn so far away. In the one letter they received from him, James wrote:

The conditions here are dreadful, but this will be my patriotic contribution to the war effort. Once a road is built, the army won't need to depend solely on trains to haul supplies across Canada. As things stand now, one well-placed explosion could set everything back by months if anyone wanted to sabotage the Allies.

Rose suspected James was telling himself what he needed to hear. Somehow, he needed to justify the humiliation of being carted off like a prisoner simply because his last name was Onishi.

If Freda squeezed Rose's hand any tighter, Rose feared her career as a pianist would be over. Or at least, seriously hampered. She wiggled her fingers to loosen her best friend's grip and tried to focus on not clenching her teeth as the pair of them stood watching the disaster unfolding before their eyes. How could this be happening?

But the notices were everywhere. The B.C. Security Commission had displayed posters and dispatched letters. Every person of Japanese descent, whether Canadian-born or not, had been given forty-eight hours' notice to vacate their homes before being sent to "clearing sites." When Rose had asked her parents where they would go, Dad admitted he didn't know.

"It's all right to cry, you know," Freda half whispered.

"Actually, it's not."

Rose motioned toward Mama, stoic as always though Rose knew it must pain her deeply to see all her most cherished belongings loaded onto a truck. At least, her sewing machine wasn't going into storage. The government poster recommended bringing sewing machines and enough clothing and food for an undetermined length of time—an impossible task when limited to a hundred and fifty pounds per person.

Next to Mama stood Ojiisan, his shoulders slumped and his eyes sad. Rose turned away.

Freda had tried the night before to talk Rose out of watching. "Stay at my place for the morning, Rose. Why torture yourself?"

"My parents might need me," Rose had told her, desperately hoping Freda would come over to support her.

She didn't need to ask. Mama and Rose hadn't even cleared breakfast away when a knock sounded on the door. Rose ran to answer it, and there stood her tall, blonde friend. They said nothing as Rose let Freda in. With one smile, she conveyed her gratitude.

Home was about to take on a much different meaning, and she would no longer have Freda. Last week, as she and Mama had sorted their things, determining what they could sell or give away or store, Rose had presented Freda with her most treasured possession next to the piano. It had been a gift from Ojiisan when Rose completed her Grade Ten Royal Conservatory exam—a miniature grand piano with a little music box inside that played Brahms' "Lullaby."

Freda had accepted the gift reluctantly. "Just for safekeeping, until you're home again," she promised. Then she gave Rose a postcard, addressed to herself and complete with a one-cent stamp. She made Rose promise to send it as soon as she was settled.

Now the two friends stood, holding hands and witnessing their lives take an uninvited twist.

"Rosie, look." Freda nudged her and tilted her head.

Tony Sutherland stood at the end of the block. He raised a hand in farewell, and Rose raised hers.

"You think he'll come over?" Freda squeezed her hand again.

"No. We said goodbye after school yesterday. Which is already more than he's allowed. Apparently, I can't be trusted." Tony's parents had forbidden him to see her since the announcement that all people of Japanese descent were to leave the city. Even so, Tony had sent her a note indicating his desire to accompany her to the prom.

Rose swallowed a lump in her throat as Tony turned and walked away, then gave her attention to the men loading the truck.

The worst moment had arrived. The upright grand piano that had been played more than it had stood silent, the piano that had helped Rose win acceptance for next year into the music program at UBC, was being loaded onto a truck to be hauled away. Rose could barely breathe.

Dad had rounded up friends and neighbors to load everything, but they weren't professional movers. What did they know about the delicacies of a fine instrument? They considered only the weight of it. Dad shouted his instructions in Japanese, guiding his corner while ten others surrounded Rose's most beloved possession. She had no memory of when the piano came into their apartment. As long as she could remember, it had stood in the living room, the center of their home and of Rose's heart. Now her heart was being torn away.

"You don't need to watch, Rose."

Freda meant well. But she didn't understand. When your last name is Smith, the government doesn't force you from your home or destroy your dreams.

"I need to see it safely loaded."

Even as she said it, Rose knew she would not have the opportunity to view the unloading or the place where it would be stored. Freda had tried to convince her parents to take the piano, "just for safekeeping until the Onishis return home." Her parents were willing, but when the girls' fathers took some measurements, they realized the piano would not fit through the living room door of the Smiths' already cramped home. Was that relief she'd seen on Mrs. Smith's face?

Rose's mother stepped over and placed one hand on Rose's arm. "It better this way, *Rozu.*" Mama always used her pet name when she hoped to comfort Rose. "This way, our things all stay together in one place until we return. *Shikata ga nai.* It cannot be helped."

Shikata ga nai was her parents' answer for everything, and Rose was sick of it. Even Dad, who'd been born in Canada and should know better, used it. At eighteen, Dad had served in the Canadian Army during the final months of the Great War. He never talked about it, but he'd returned to Canada convinced he would be recognized as a full

Canadian citizen, with voting rights and all.

But it was not to be. The *Issei*, or first-generation like Ojiisan and Mama, understood they would never be considered true Canadians, no matter how loyal they were. They taught their children, the *Nisei*, to keep their eyes down. "That way, they may not see you. That way, you offend less."

The message to disappear had worked its way deep into their hearts. Even Minister of National Defence Ian MacKenzie had publicly proclaimed it. "The intention of the government is that every single Japanese man, woman, and child should be removed from Vancouver as speedily as possible."

Vancouver was the only home Rose had ever known. She'd never even visited Japan, nor had Dad. Ojiisan had never returned to his homeland, and Mama had few memories of her early years there. When Rose read the words "Go home, Japs" painted on the side of Kokawas' grocery store, her first thought was, *Go home? But I* am *home!*

Freda shifted her attention from the piano movers to Rose. "I still don't understand why they insist you're Japanese. You don't even speak Japanese."

The irony almost brought a grin to Rose's lips. Freda had been the one to chide her for not working harder to learn her family's language. Dad and Mama had sent all three of their children to the Japanese Hall after regular school two days a week. They were supposed to be learning Japanese, but Rose resented the extra hours away from her piano. James had taken to it and would likely be considered fluent by Canadian standards. Tim and Rose had not.

"If *my* family knew another language," Freda always crowed, "I would want to learn it."

"I understand it well enough." Rose had always preferred to focus on things that made her fit in, not stand out. She didn't mind her flat nose and dark, almond-shaped eyes. But her parents' and grandparents' traditions meant little. Oh, she stayed respectful on the outside. As long as they never left Powell Street, they were one of many Japanese Canadian families. But in the white stores, or when Dad and Mama came to her school for parent-teacher events, they could be embarrassing.

"There. It's safely loaded." Freda's soft voice brought Rose back to the moment. Though her eyes had remained on the piano, her thoughts had wandered, probably as some kind of coping device. Two of the men threw an old blanket over her piano and tied it securely into place with a thick cord. How long before she would see it—or any piano—again?

Everything was loaded, and the men began to disperse. Dad's friend Harvey Nakahara walked over to him and thumped him once on his back. "*Kodomo no tame gaman shi masho,*" he said. "For the sake of the children, let us endure." The same group of men were heading to Harvey's house next.

Freda turned back to Rose once more. "How are ya holdin' up?"

"I feel as though my piano is encased in a coffin, ready for burial." Tears welled up, and Rose blinked them away.

"It will be fine." Freda's statement sounded feeble. Was she talking about the piano or about how their next step was to say goodbye? Rose turned to embrace her quickly. When she pulled away, Freda tucked something into Rose's palm and folded her fingers over it. "Don't look until I'm gone."

Rose squeezed her eyes shut, but the tears escaped, anyway. "But I have nothing for you."

Freda pressed her lips tightly together, then turned and walked away.

CHAPTER NINE

Rose clutched whatever Freda had placed in her hand while her friend began the eight-block walk back to her apartment building. She made up her mind not to peek at it until bedtime.

"Time to go, Rose." Dad placed a hand on her shoulder and firmly turned her toward the pile of belongings they would carry to their new lodgings. Rose pushed Freda's gift deep into her pocket and followed her father. She and Tim each grabbed two suitcases while Mama slung a knapsack on her shoulders and lifted a deep basket in each hand. Dad took another knapsack and the sewing machine. Ojiisan carried a duffel bag and a cardboard crate full of rice, tied with string.

At the bus stop, other families already waited. When the bus pulled up, the driver took one look at them and sneered. "Load your stuff at the back, then come around to the front and get in one at a time. Show me your papers."

Seats had been removed from the back of the bus to make room for their belongings. Once settled inside, people began exchanging stories.

"How kind of our government to protect us from the hysteria of neighbors we've known for years," someone muttered.

As the bus moved down the street, Rose glanced back at the windows of the apartment she called home. Something fluttered in her parents' bedroom window, and Rose's first thought was to tell Mama they'd left a window open. Before she could open her mouth to speak, however, her jaw dropped. Was her imagination playing tricks? Swaying so gently in the window hung a long, shimmering drape of black fabric uncannily similar to her beautiful concert dress. She stared until the bus turned the corner and the dress disappeared from sight.

Rose turned around and focused on the scenes going past as they rode down the city streets, each block becoming less familiar as she left behind the only neighborhood she'd ever known.

They pulled onto the Pacific National Exhibition grounds at Hastings Park.

She pressed her nose against the window. "We were here once for the fair, remember?"

Tim shook his head. "No."

"You were too little, I guess." Rose squinted, trying to grasp onto comforting memories. "James bought us popcorn and cotton candy and let us ride on the carousel." What had been set up for them at this formerly happy site?

Nothing could have prepared her.

It took everyone a couple of hours to unload and register at the administration building—most of that was spent standing in line.

"How old is the boy?" The woman at the desk peered over her glasses.

"Ten." Mama kept a hand on Tim's head.

"Ten is the cut-off age." The woman thumped a paper with the rubber stamp in her hand. "He'll stay with you. Men, you go that way." She pointed to another building in the opposite direction from where Rose, Tim, and Mama were to go. When Mama reached for Tim's hand, he let her hold it only a moment before pulling away.

The building to which they were directed had been one of the livestock barns, and the smell would have given that detail away even if Rose were blind. The pungent odor of animal feces and urine assaulted her nose immediately. Once her eyes adjusted to the dim lighting inside, Rose could not believe it. Endless rows of bunk beds, as far as the eye could see. Several had sheets or blankets hung around them for some semblance of privacy. Rose closed her eyes and prayed for a corner bunk.

They were not that fortunate. A monitor guided them to their assigned bunks, surrounded on all sides by bunks and more bunks. On each unoccupied bed waited a large bag filled with straw and two army blankets. When they reached the set to which Rose had been assigned, an elderly woman lay on the bottom bunk. Mama struck up a conversation with her in Japanese, but they spoke too quickly for Rose to understand.

"What did she say, Mama?"

"She's been here a week. She is all alone in the world, except for a grandson who was sent to the road camps, like James."

Rose tried to imagine what possible threat this poor old woman could possibly present to the security of Canada's west coast. In the previous week's newspaper, a fellow named Ken Stuart—some high-ranking muckety-muck in the Canadian army—had been quoted as saying of Japanese Canadians, "From the army point of view, I cannot see that they constitute the slightest menace to national security." Yet here they were. And here the old woman was. Strangely enough, she smiled widely at Rose when Mama introduced her and Tim as her children. She murmured something Rose didn't understand, and Mama translated again.

"She says she feels blessed to have a warm, dry place to sleep and such a lovely young lady for a bunkmate." Mama gave Rose a look that conveyed that she had a lot to learn from this old woman.

Would her dear old Ojiisan fare as well?

They made up their beds, and Mama managed to find one extra sheet to hang between them and the strangers on one side. The remainder of the day was spent becoming oriented to their surroundings, including an enormous impoundment area filled with cars and trucks.

"See all those vehicles, Tim?" Rose pointed. "They all belong to Japanese Canadians. I wonder when they'll get them back." The Onishis had never owned a car.

"You suppose our radio and camera are here somewhere too?" Tim wondered aloud. Both had been confiscated a month earlier "for safekeeping."

"I don't think so." Rose shook her head. "I don't know where they are."

Rose had never seen so many Japanese in one place at the same time.

One big building was set up as a mess hall with long tables and benches. When a bell rang, they joined the supper line—keeping their eyes out for Dad and Ojiisan. The old woman stayed with them, happy to connect with somebody. Her name was Sachi, and her sunny smile made it easier for Rose to tolerate her slow walk. Rose helped her up the ramp leading into the mess hall. It had narrow boards nailed across it, designed to keep hooves from slipping on a wet surface—further evidence that they were eating and living in buildings intended for animals.

Eventually, they reached the front of the line, where they picked up metal pie plates. The serving line was staffed by Japanese women, each wearing a blue ribbon tied around her left upper arm. As they went down the line, they were each given a baloney sandwich, an apple, and a tin cup filled with milk. That was supper. They managed to find space for the four of them, and Mama insisted they bow their heads to give thanks before they ate.

Rose muttered a prayer of her own. "God, make me grateful." Then she tore her sandwich in two and gave half to Tim. He might be little, but he possessed the appetite of a teenager, and this meager fare would not last him until bedtime.

They never did spot Dad or Ojiisan in the crowd.

Next, they searched for the toilets. Ten shower stalls were provided for what had to be fifteen hundred women or more. No curtains, no privacy. A woman was doing her best to wash out diapers in cold water, and Rose found something new for which to be thankful. At least, her family didn't have a baby. Toilets were nothing but troughs made for animal waste with water constantly running through them. Even with lime sprinkled around the troughs, the smell was unbearable.

"Well, at least, we don't have to remember to flush," Tim joked.

They wandered the grounds some more. By dark, they had still not seen Dad or Ojiisan. They finally gave up and returned to the livestock-building-turned-dormitory and found their beds in the sea of bunks. Rose struck up a conversation with another girl around her age.

"We've been here three days." The girl rolled her eyes. "My sister and I left the grounds and went to a restaurant for a decent meal. All you need is a pass from the administration building—and some money for the restaurant, of course."

Rose didn't know whether her parents had any money, but even if they did, she doubted they'd let her go to a restaurant.

A young mother with an infant occupied the bunk closest to Rose's head. Her baby would not stop howling, and the mother was crying too. Mama approached her, spoke gently, and reached out to take the baby. While Mama bounced back and forth, trying in vain to hush the child, Rose overheard the young woman's story.

"I came here on a boat from Sea Island. My husband had already been taken to one of the road camps. I have not heard from him, and I don't know where he is. Now he has no idea where I am!" She wiped a tear from her cheek. "I got so seasick and so distraught on the way. Now I have no milk for my baby. I've dried up."

"When is the last time he had anything?" Mama offered the baby her finger to suck on, but he only howled more.

"Yesterday."

Mama's caring expression changed to indignation. She managed to flag down one of the dorm monitors and explained the child's plight. The monitor promised to return with some canned milk for the baby and hurried off. Mama stayed with the mother until the monitor returned as promised. It took another half hour for the baby to settle down.

Mama gave Tim and Rose each an orange from her basket, and she shared one with Sachi. They climbed into their bunks fully clothed. It was still late February and far too cold to undress, not to mention the lack of privacy. Rose sat in the middle of her bunk, surveying the massive shed. The smell had not become any less unpleasant. Tim sneezed and coughed from the dust. Rose pulled her blanket tightly around herself and shivered. When her tummy rumbled, she hummed to drown it out. This place was far too noisy for sleeping. Between the constant crying of babies and children and the even more heartbreaking sobbing of old and confused women, Rose closed her eyes and tried to imagine herself at home. She envisioned a keyboard in front of her and ran her hands over it, going through her scales first, then Brahms' "Lullaby"—willing the melody in her head to somehow break through to reality and lull people to sleep.

It didn't work.

Finally, she reached into her pocket for Freda's gift and opened her eyes. As she'd suspected, it was a necklace. But not just any necklace. It was a beautiful gold treble clef. Inside the loop of the clef nestled a small gemstone—a purplish-blue alexandrite. Her birthstone, and Freda's. Rose had seen this necklace many times. It had been a gift to Freda from her parents on her sixteenth birthday. Rose had watched Freda open it and her mother place it around Freda's neck. Her friend had worn it every day, maybe all night as well.

How did I not notice it missing from her neck this morning?

That morning now seemed like weeks away.

For the first time that day, Rose let the tears flow unchecked. She gazed at the beautiful necklace and allowed the ache to rise inside. *Oh, Freda. You should not have given this to me.* Did Freda's parents know? She undid the clasp and fastened it at the back of her neck. Maybe tomorrow she'd be able to write a letter, tell Freda where she was, and thank her for such a thoughtful gift. Tell her she'd return it next time they were together. Perhaps that was Freda's intent. Perhaps she figured Rose needed to hang onto something "for safekeeping" as well.

Suddenly, the lights went out in the building. The noises did not stop, but Rose lay down and rested her head on the straw mattress, trying in vain to form a pillow.

"Goodnight, Rozu," Mama crooned from the bunk next to hers. "Goodnight, Timothy."

"Goodnight, Mama," Tim and Rose answered in unison.

Rose curled up on her side as tightly as she could and clutched Freda's treble clef in one hand, trying not to wonder what tomorrow would bring. This had been the longest day of her life so far. She lay awake, certain that in the morning, they'd discover it had all been a huge, dreadful mistake.

CHAPTER TEN

Somehow, Rose must have eventually slept, because the next sound she heard was childish laughter. She wanted to keep her eyes closed and imagine herself at home, in her own bed—the laughter coming from neighborhood kids on the street outside her window. Slowly, she opened her eyes and leaned over the edge of the bunk. Three little boys chased each other down the rows between beds, giggling and happy just to be with friends. Someone shouted for them to be quiet, which was ridiculous in a building filled with constant talking and crying. Rose doubted it could have been any noisier when filled with agitated cattle.

Another voice cried out, "Let them be. It beats the crying."

A pair of young mothers chased the kids down, and the game ended. A thrumming sound was added to the mix, and it took Rose a minute to realize it was rain hitting the metal roof. She groaned. Would they have to stay inside this dismal, stinking shed all day? She remembered the old woman on the bunk below and imagined what her response might be.

The rain is not dripping on my head, and for that, I can be grateful.

Mama had thought to bring an umbrella. She, Tim, and Rose huddled under it as they made their way to the bathrooms first and then to the mess hall. Something actually smelled good, and Rose's stomach growled as they got nearer. Inside, servers dished out some kind of porridge with milk. A glob of it hit Rose's tin plate with a *glich*. Was it oatmeal? It certainly wasn't rice, and it smelled better than it tasted.

Rose turned to Mama. "Why don't they give us rice?"

"Shh, Rozu. *Shikata ga nai.*"

Rose rolled her eyes, but there was no point arguing with Mama. Her parents had always said difficulties make us stronger and should be embraced for the character they would build.

The next server handed Rose a small bowl of stewed prunes and a tin cup of what appeared to be diluted canned milk. She found a seat on the end of a bench, and Tim squeezed in beside her. This time, she didn't share. She felt hungry enough to get the food down, but she would need to be far hungrier still to feel truly grateful for it. Tim ate his without complaint.

"Did you get any sleep in all that racket?" she asked him.

"What racket?"

Rose shook her head. "You could sleep through anything."

"Just think, Rose." Tim leaned toward her and tilted his head. "We always wanted to go to camp."

Rose was still chuckling at her brother's optimism when she heard her name. "Rose! Sono!"

Dad and Ojiisan had spotted them in the crowd and were making their way over. Rose hadn't been this happy to see them since the time Ojiisan lost his helper and Dad had joined him on his fishing boat for a whole week.

Dad was practically dancing. "Are you done eating? Come! Come outside where we can hear each other. I have news. There's been a mix-up."

I knew it! Just as she'd hoped, the morning had brought good news. It had all been a horrible mistake, and they would return home. She'd be back in her own bed that night and in her classroom the next day. She gathered their plates and cups and dropped them in a big metal tub filled with soapy water. Then she followed her family outside. The rain had let up, but everything was muddy, and it was still cold. Rose didn't care. They were leaving this horrible place.

Dad pulled a piece of paper out of his jacket pocket. "The administration made an error."

Rose waited to hear when they could return home. She and Freda would laugh about their tearful goodbye, only to be reunited the next day. She could almost hear her friend saying, "Well, don't I feel silly?"

"What kind of error?" Mama sounded doubtful.

"This place is not for us because we live in Vancouver. It's for those coming in from other places. We were sent the same letter as they received, but in error."

"But what about all the others on the bus yesterday?" Rose frowned. "Aren't they from Vancouver too?"

"Yes. It seems about eight families from here all got the same letter. They're sorting it out now. We need to leave to make room for others coming in from Tofino and other areas."

Rose wanted to jump for joy or throw her arms around her father's neck, but public outbursts of any kind were not their way.

Mama looked skeptical. "Where will we go next?"

"Go back to your building. Gather your belongings and meet us at the administration building. We'll do the same." Dad was already hustling toward the building where he and Ojiisan had spent the night.

When they arrived at the administration building, Rose recognized some of the other people from the bus. Everyone talked at once, but from what Rose could gather, they were to be loaded onto another bus. Her optimism dimmed when a Royal Canadian Mounted Police officer held up his hand for silence and began to speak.

"Load your things in the back of the bus and find a seat. Once everyone is seated and quiet, I will explain what's happening."

It seemed to take half the day, but eventually, they were all inside the bus, seated if not quiet. The uniformed officer stood at the front and held up one hand, waiting for silence.

"Raise your hand if you do *not* live in Vancouver."

No one raised their hand.

"This bus will take you to the train station, where you'll catch the next available train to one of the internment camps in the interior."

Rose's heart sank. A ruckus arose that reminded her of a referee's bad call at a ball game. The officer rolled his eyes heavenward and held up a hand again. People kept shouting questions.

"Which camp?"

"Where?"

"How can I get word to my son?"

Rose placed her hands on the back of Dad and Mama's seat in front of her. Using its surface as a pretend piano, she ran her fingers through some scales until the din finally settled. The officer held up a sheet of paper.

"I do not know which camp you will end up at, and even if I did, I could not say for security reasons."

"Hogwash," a male voice behind Rose muttered.

"It seems a few people received a letter intended only for those outside Vancouver," the officer continued. "The Vancouver people will be going directly to the interior by train. Now I'm going to read out this list of names as one final check. If you do not hear your name called, please get off the bus and return to the administration building with your belongings."

He then began to read a dozen or so family names, including "Onishi, family of five." Rose leaned back against her seat. At least, they didn't have to stay here. Nothing could be worse.

"See?" Tim whispered, leaning into Rose so closely she could smell the porridge still on his breath. "Now we'll get to go to a *real* camp!"

Rose pushed him away but couldn't help smiling at his goofy grin. What did a ten-year-old know about anything? He was simply excited to be having an adventure. Her mother stared straight ahead, poker-faced. Dad leaned across the aisle to Ojiisan and spoke softly in Japanese.

They waited another twenty minutes before the bus began to roll. Rose took a last look back as they pulled off the grounds and onto the street, remembering the sunny day she'd once spent here with James. She would choose that memory over this one if ever her mind wandered back to Hastings Park.

The bus grew eerily quiet, and Rose closed her eyes again. The bus smelled of wet wool and diesel fuel. She pressed a mitten to her nose, hoping for the scent of soap or perfume. But her clothing had absorbed the odors of the livestock barn. It seemed the stench of horse urine permeated everything quite effectively.

At the train station, the Onishi family gathered their belongings around them and found seats together on a long wooden bench. Tim and Rose had taken a train trip once before with Mama when they were about eight and two. Mama had taken them to visit her cousin, whose name Rose could not recall. Where they went, she never really knew. She only remembered that it had taken half a day, and they'd enjoyed a lovely meal served on pretty dishes in a special dining car.

The day dragged on, and their tummies rumbled again. No lovely meal, then. But Mama surprised them by pulling *onigiri*—rice balls— from her basket. Rose felt torn between gratitude for the provision and annoyance that Mama had withheld them until now.

The station was full of anxious people, all of them Japanese, half of them children, and most dressed in their Sunday best. A police officer stood on a box with a rifle in his hands, surveying his domain.

Trains came and went, but they were not told to board any of them. A mailbox stood in one corner, and Rose pulled Freda's postcard from her coat pocket. Should she send it? She knew she wasn't "settled" yet, but what if the place they were going had no post office? This might be her last chance. Besides, she already had so much to tell. She borrowed a pencil from Dad and filled the card with words.

Dear Freda, You won't believe it! We were sent to Hastings Park by mistake—that was an adventure it will take me all day to tell next time I see you. Trust me when I say it's not something I feel eager to relive. We're waiting to board a train for one of the camps now. I heard someone mention "Slocan" and someone else "Tashme." I will write as soon as I can. I miss you. Love, Rose.

Rose wanted to erase what she'd written and start over. Say something more meaningful. But at last, it seemed something was happening. People were being organized into groups of forty and told to put everything they didn't need with them into the baggage car—

one suitcase per person. Rose and Mama went to work sorting stuff out while Dad and Ojiisan carried most of their belongings to the baggage car for loading.

Rose ran to the mailbox and dropped her postcard through the slot. The instant it left her hand, she regretted it. *I forgot to thank Freda for the necklace! How could I be so stupid?* She peered into the slot, hoping beyond reason the postcard might have somehow stuck to the edge where she could grab it, but it was gone.

"Rose, come!" Dad called.

With a sigh and one last, longing glimpse at the mailbox that had swallowed her postcard, Rose promised herself she'd write another at the earliest possible moment. Then she turned and joined her family in the lineup.

Eventually, they boarded a train car and found two bench seats facing each other. Mama, Tim, and Rose squeezed into one side, facing Dad and Ojiisan on the other. The car smelled of coal oil and orange peelings.

"At least, we are together." Dad relaxed against the back of his seat.

Mama gave a small shake of her head but said nothing. Rose knew her mother was thinking about James. They were not all together.

Tim took it all in, entranced with the conductor and other train workers. Everything seemed to be covered with a fine layer of soot from the coal engines. Mama attempted to wipe things down with a handkerchief, only to shake her head as it came away black. She hadn't made a dent.

The sun was going down by the time the train began to move. Mama pulled yet more rice balls from her basket for each of them. They shared some oranges, then took turns using the lavatory at the back of the train car. It needed cleaning, but Rose tried hard to feel grateful for it. At least, it was an improvement over Hastings Park.

As the world around them grew darker, they left the city behind, and Rose could no longer see anything out the window. Their car grew quiet as tired people—even the children—fell asleep. Although Rose was still too cold and too hungry, she found the rocking of the train a far more pleasant way to fall asleep than her experience of the previous night.

Rose folded her fingers around Freda's necklace and tried not to imagine what tomorrow held in store.

CHAPTER ELEVEN

When Rose woke up on the train, the sun was rising, and steep mountain peaks surrounded them on all sides. Oh, how she wished the family still had their camera! The Rockies had always been a backdrop, not something you could reach out and touch. If only she knew how to sketch.

Rose kept staring out the window at the amazing view as the train chugged on. It labored so heavily going uphill, she wondered if they'd make it. Tim started singing, "She'll Be Comin' 'Round the Mountain," so Rose picked out the tune on an invisible piano in front of her. Dad laughed when Rose muttered a "no" and started over.

"How can you tell if you've made a mistake?" Dad squinted at Rose's hands as though trying to see her imaginary keyboard.

Rose shrugged. "I don't know. I hear it in my head. I've got it right now." She picked her way through "Go, Tell It on the Mountain" and "I've Been Workin' on the Railroad" before the game got old. It wasn't the same when others couldn't hear it. When she stopped, she caught a glimpse of her father's haunted expression, brows drawn down as he gazed out his window. It seemed they all wondered where they were going and when they would arrive, but nobody talked about it.

Someone produced a deck of cards, and they played rounds of gin and Go, Fish to help pass the time. The train car was cold, so they all kept their mittens and gloves on, which made playing cards a rather humorous challenge. Mama's food supply ran low. A lady at the back of the car complained loudly in Japanese, and Rose picked up enough to know she thought they were being treated like pigs. Then the woman began to cry. The look Mama gave Rose said it all: *We will not stoop to such undignified behavior, no matter what.*

Rose closed her eyes and tried to pray. Though Ojiisan still considered himself a Buddhist, Mama's family were Christians, and the family had attended church for as long as Rose could remember. Dad once told her that Mama would have refused to marry him if he hadn't agreed their children would be raised as Christians, and he had no problem with that. He came to church with them, too, but out of respect for his father, Dad kept his prayers to himself and taught his children to do the same. But in her Sunday school class and at youth group, Rose had learned to pray out loud. If only she could do so now. Maybe there'd be a better chance of God hearing her. *God, all I want is to graduate and start university as planned. Then to go on to be a concert pianist.*

At nightfall, the train stopped. The passengers were told to unload with all their belongings, including the heavy box of rice Dad guarded as though their lives depended on it. Hours passed as everyone reorganized themselves, many asking where they were going but receiving no answers. Rose couldn't remember ever longing for a warm bed so much in her life.

After loading into the backs of big military trucks, the Onishis found themselves squeezed in like sardines. "Not that we can see much, but I don't think we're even on a real road," Rose told Tim. "It feels like a trail."

Whenever the moon came out from behind the clouds, it revealed the surrounding mountains. The smell of pine trees filled the air. She and Tim clung to each other for warmth. They were so tired, they managed to doze off between the bumps, dips, and jostling of the truck. Rose ached for Ojiisan, sitting silent and stoic on top of the rice box.

Finally, after about a three-hour ride, they arrived at their destination and were told they were at Tashme Camp. Rose could make out two big barns silhouetted against the night sky as they climbed down from the truck. Smaller buildings stood in rows. A policeman with a loudspeaker ordered them to line up in families and assigned each family to a house. A Japanese woman led them to theirs.

As they walked, Rose's energy lifted. "Finally, Tim. A real house with our own rooms. I can't wait to crawl into an actual bed!"

But she could not have been more wrong. The house was nothing more than a shack, and it was already filled with people—strangers with whom they were expected to share the space.

"This is the Kokura family." The volunteer introduced them with a wave of her hand.

A mom, a dad, a boy about her own age named Kenji, and a girl about twelve named Tamika offered solemn nods in greeting. The shack was made of rough boards and lined with tar paper. Rose had seen more sophisticated construction in a neighborhood kid's treehouse. The room contained a roughly hewn table, benches, and a stove for both heating and cooking and was strung with clotheslines from which hung damp shirts, trousers, and sheets. The smell reminded Rose of wet burlap.

Just as she was trying to figure out where everyone would sleep, a little girl who appeared about six came running inside, breathlessly shouting.

"Bears! I saw three bears up a tree! Just outside the outhouse!"

"Tsuyuko." Her father tried to settle her down. "It was merely shadows."

But the slight nod he gave Dad told Rose it was entirely possible his daughter had indeed seen bears. Petrified to visit the outhouse alone, Rose agreed quickly when Dad suggested the whole family go together and wait for each other before returning to the relative safety of the shack.

As both families huddled around the stove to warm up, Mrs. Kokura scowled at all of them, making her displeasure clear, as though the place was hers and they had no business intruding.

"The men here spend our days cutting trees for firewood," Mr. Kokura explained. "But the properly dried wood has already been burned, and the green wood doesn't burn right."

They soon learned that off the main room were two "bedrooms," one of them previously occupied by Mr. and Mrs. Kokura. Now their whole family crowded into the other, leaving one for the Onishis to share.

The room held a double bed for her parents and a cot for Ojiisan. Tim and Rose made pallets for themselves on the floor with the blankets they'd been issued—two each. Once everyone lay down, not a square foot of floor space remained. They heard every sound from the other family's side, and even baby cries coming from other shacks around them.

As they snuggled together for warmth, Tim said, "At least there are no mosquitoes!"

Sunlight filtered through the cracks in the wall boards and the tar paper, accompanied by the steady thumps of an ax on wood. Tim slept soundly beside her, but the adults were missing from their beds. Rose quickly pulled on her clothes and folded her blankets. Why had Mama let her sleep in?

Mama and Mrs. Kokura were cooking rice on the woodstove, Mrs. Kokura complaining loudly in Japanese about Mama's method. With no windows and no electricity, the room seemed darker than the night before when an oil lamp burned. Rose wrapped her warm coat around herself to step outside and was nearly blinded by the brilliant sunshine reflected on white snow.

Once her eyes adjusted, the scene stopped her in mid-stride. She stood amid the most gorgeous wilderness she could have ever imagined—mountains, trees, and water all lay within her field of vision. Strains of Greig's "In the Hall of the Mountain King" played in the back of her brain and made her smile. If only she could stay focused on the natural scenery and pretend she was on some lovely vacation, avoiding the sight of her nearer surroundings where the stark reality hit her—rows and rows of little shacks like the one she'd just exited.

The contrast between the beauty of God's creation and the sadness of man's struck Rose like a punch to the gut. How many people lived here, and for how long? When would they be allowed to leave? She needed to finish high school this year in order to start her classes at UBC in the fall. Was there even a school for her and Tim to attend? How would she ever keep up with her piano? She normally played for two to four hours every day, and she'd already missed several days.

"You just going to stand there?"

Rose turned toward the voice. Kenji Kokura was splitting firewood about twenty feet away. Rose couldn't tell if he was teasing or being mean.

"It's … my first time out of the city." What she meant was, she'd had no idea how beautiful the rest of the country was.

He stared at her a moment. "Outhouse is that way." With a nod in the general direction of the crude facility, he returned to his work. He must be wondering whether she had a brain in her head.

She used the outhouse, thinking of Freda back home in her warm house with indoor plumbing. Wait until she heard about this! One of their old Sunday school lessons came to mind when the teacher had admonished, "Gratitude leads to freedom." Freda and Rose had thought themselves ever so mature for understanding the meaning. It wasn't difficult. Until now. Rose was not free to leave this place, not free to go home, to take a hot bath, to eat as much as she wanted—no matter how grateful she might be. It would take a lot of effort to free her heart if she allowed herself to feel like a prisoner in this place.

When she came out, Kenji was carrying wood to the shack. He walked with a pronounced limp.

"Want some help?" She stepped toward him.

"Sure."

Rose picked up the last few pieces and walked with him. Filled with questions, she really wanted to start a conversation with this boy, but shyness and awkwardness rose to the surface as her face grew warm. Maybe she'd have better luck with the older daughter. Where was Tamika, anyway?

She worked up her courage. "How long have you been here?"

"Three weeks. I got pulled out of UBC along with the other Japanese students."

"UBC?" Rose couldn't believe it. "That's where I'm going in the fall!" Now she really had questions. What program was he in? What were the profs like? Did they pile on the assignments?

"Don't count on it." Kenji's voice held a bitter tone. "I was set to graduate this spring. Won't be happening now. Who knows when they will ever let us back in?"

"Graduate?" The shock on her face must have been obvious. Was he older than he looked, or advanced for his age? He didn't volunteer an answer.

"I'm going to be a teacher. At least, I was going to be one. That's why I got sent here, instead of to the road camps." He laid his wood down along the outside wall of the shack. "I'm supposed to be teaching the little kids."

He opened the door and nodded for Rose to carry her load inside, where he began feeding it into the stove. Mama handed them both bowls of hot rice, and Rose held hers in both hands to warm up. Dad, Ojiisan, and Mr. Kokura sat on the bench while the rest ate breakfast standing. Kenji's sister Tamika remained silent and would hardly look at Rose or Tim. The little girl, Tsuyuko, talked enough for all of them. Between mouthfuls, she described again the bears from the night before. When she'd covered that topic, she turned to Tim.

"After breakfast, you can help me make a snowman. You know, just until you get to know some of the boys. You hear that baby crying? She's a brand new little baby girl, born just last week, in the house right over there, and I got to see her the very next day. She looks like a little doll. They didn't have any girls yet, only boys. So they were very happy to get a little girl baby, and I'm going to play with her when she gets big enough. You can play with the boys."

Rose was stunned that anyone would have to give birth in one of these shacks, but Tsuyuko was already changing the subject again. She told them she would be starting school soon.

"And I'll be the favorite one in the class because my big brother will be my teacher." She beamed with pride at Kenji.

"Enough now." Her mother scowled. "Eat your food."

Over the next few days, the family received answers to a few of their questions. No one knew how long they would be there, but people spoke in terms of months—even years. Not weeks. Rose closed her ears to it, refusing to believe. A chat on the way to the outhouse with Tamika, whose quiet voice could be quite informative when her little sister wasn't around, helped fill in some of the blanks.

"The real reason Kenji wasn't sent to the road camps like your brother is because of his bad leg," she told Rose in a near whisper. "He had polio when he was little."

"Oh." Rose wasn't sure Kenji would appreciate his sister sharing this information.

"He's a brain." Tamika entered the outhouse but kept talking through the closed door. "School came so easily for him, the teachers didn't know what to do with him. He finished Grade Twelve at fourteen."

"Wow." Rose could feel her eyes widen involuntarily.

"Then he studied on his own for a year while he helped Dad in our store, then he started university at fifteen. He zipped through that too." She stepped out, and Rose took her turn in the outhouse, listening while Tamika continued the explanation.

Now eighteen, Kenji had been charged with starting a school. The problem was, the camp provided no place to meet, no desks, no books, no anything. Only children, and lots of them. The kids were becoming increasingly restless and getting into trouble for lack of structure and activities. One boy had nearly drowned in a creek shortly before the Onishis' arrival, so the pressure was on to start a school. Rose didn't want to believe she would be in this place long enough for it to matter.

During the day, Dad and the other men were put to work cutting trees or building more shacks for newly relocated Japanese families. Mama did her best to keep the family's clothes clean and make meals from whatever she could afford to buy at the little store. She was also trying desperately to get word to James so he'd know where they were.

She wrote a one-page letter and addressed it to his last known location, praying he would still be there when it arrived. But when she handed the letter, along with her penny for a stamp, to the official in charge of mail, he opened it, then quickly handed it back and shook his head at them. "English only."

Mama brought her letter back to the shack, found another precious piece of paper, and asked Rose to sit down and write to James. Even though Mama's English was quite good, trying to write proper English sentences proved far too overwhelming. Rose unfolded Mama's letter and bit her lip. She dared not admit how little of it she understood.

Mama guessed. She told Rose what she'd said, and Rose started fresh in her own words. Mama warned her to not say anything negative or anything that might give authorities cause to black out lines or refuse to deliver the letter. And not to give James any reason to worry.

CHAPTER TWELVE

A month had passed, and the Onishi family were still in the camp. Rose tried to be as helpful as she could for Mama's sake, and as cheerful as she could for Tim's. He didn't seem to mind anything about their new lives. He quickly made friends, and they spent their days exploring the camp or organizing games. He had no idea why they were there, that they were viewed as a threat to their own country or that they might be spies. For Tim, it was delightful to be surrounded by other kids who looked like he did and never once called him a dirty yellow Jap.

The only thing Tim seemed to miss was food. Their meals consisted mostly of rice—which they loved—and oatmeal, which they didn't. At the little store, Mama could buy canned vegetables and fish. Occasionally, fresh pork or chicken became available, and Mama made it stretch by experimenting with soups and stews. Ojiisan made plans to plant a vegetable garden if they were still there in May. Rose prayed they would be home by then.

Most nights, she was tired enough to fall straight to sleep. But when she allowed herself to think about how much she missed Freda and her piano, she couldn't stop the tears. At least once a day, she ran through her scales at the kitchen table. She tried to do it when Mrs. Kokura was out of the house because the woman clearly thought Rose was crazy. She'd fire a contemptuous look in Rose's direction and order her away from the table if she needed the space. Tamika would patiently explain, in a mixture of Japanese and English, what Rose was doing and how she needed to practice. But her mother only shook her head and ranted in Japanese.

"She says you are wasting time and space. You should be doing something useful." Tamika's tone sounded apologetic.

When Mama witnessed these tirades, she took Mrs. Kokura's side and gave Rose some other task to do. Keeping the peace had always been more important to Mama than Rose's musical skills.

In late March, a shipment of school supplies arrived, and a former barn was set up as a classroom. Kenji recruited Rose to help him organize the teaching materials—readers for the earliest years, paper and pencils for all. Another girl Rose's age named Margaret agreed to help as well. The kids from age six through ten were to show up at nine o'clock and stay until noon. Word passed through the camp. On the first day, thirty-five children arrived in their Sunday best, with clean faces and combed hair. Their well-groomed appearance was a tribute to their mothers.

They didn't have desks or even child-size tables yet, so the kids sat on benches. At nine o'clock, Kenji asked Rose to lead in the singing of "O Canada." Nervously, Rose found the key of G in her head and began, breathing a sigh of relief when the older children joined in. When she reached the words "true north strong and free," a lump formed in her throat which was difficult to sing around. They were patriotic Canadians, but they were not free. The little kids didn't seem to notice and sang heartily, some of them learning it for the first time. They seemed happy to be in school. Tim didn't admit it, but Rose could tell he was glad for something more structured to fill his time.

The young teachers spent their first hour trying to assess what levels the kids were at and group them accordingly. Rose took the youngest bunch of nine children, most of whom had never been to school. Margaret worked with those who could already read through the basic Grade One reader, and Kenji took the older ones. Rose's hands trembled more over trying to teach these kids than they ever had for a piano recital, but once they started, the time passed quickly, and she enjoyed it.

With no curriculum to work from, she tried to remember back to Grade One. How had she learned to read? One letter at a time, she guessed. But what good is one letter if it has no meaning in and of itself? She had no memory of learning how, but she supposed it must be a bit like learning to speak or anything else. So she read their reader to them and told them they would soon be able to read it for themselves.

She taught them A, B, and C, and they practiced printing those. Rose even wrote a little song for the letters to the tune of the actual notes in the scale. That way, once they reached G, they'd be able to sing the whole scale, and she'd know which kids had an ear for music.

Her biggest challenge was trying to make Tsuyuko understand she wasn't free to talk incessantly. Every sentence Rose spoke was, apparently, a reason for Tsuyuko to launch into a story that held the attention of the other students far better than anything Rose could say. She began to wonder if she could somehow teach Tsuyuko everything first and let her teach the others. Ironically, the little girl seemed the last to catch on to each new idea.

When they broke for recess, Kenji took everyone outside for some fresh air and sunshine. With no playground equipment, they tried to remember games that required only their bodies. The smaller children liked "What Time is it, Mr. Wolf?" and "Red Light, Green Light." The bigger kids played "Red Rover" and "Prisoner's Base." Kenji suggested they find a different name for Prisoner's Base in light of their current circumstances, so they decided to simply call it "Freedom."

As they made their way back inside, Tamika pulled Tsuyuko aside and spoke to her in hushed tones but with a stern expression. After that, the little girl was quieter, although Rose could tell by her wiggling that she was itching to speak.

Kenji stayed behind to prepare for the next day, while the two sisters walked "home" with Tim and Rose at noon. Their mothers had hot rice waiting for them. While they ate, Tsuyuko filled them in on their school day. She surprised Rose by singing the ABC song, but it still wasn't enough to earn a smile from her mother.

Rose pitied the Kokura children. Their mother never seemed to stop scowling or complaining. Her moodiness wore Mama down too.

For the first while, Mama had replied with her usual *"shakata ga nai,"* but Mrs. Kokura responded with a loud and angry stream of Japanese words Rose did not know. After that, Mama kept her opinions to herself. She was always the first to volunteer to retrieve water from the communal tap, and Rose suspected it was an excuse to get away from Mrs. Kokura for a few minutes. She was likely to find other, friendlier women drawing water at the same time. The adults did not have many socializing opportunities, but they made the best of it and set an example for their children.

That first day of school turned out to be the best day ever in the camp, at least for the Onishis. When Dad returned to the shack, he carried a surprise for Rose and a surprise for Mama. Rose's surprise was a wood plank about five feet long. Somehow, Dad had scrounged the materials he needed to sand it down nice and smooth. He'd meticulously drawn a piano keyboard on it using a carpenter's pencil. The "white" keys were the original wood, but the "black" keys were painted with some brown paint. He laid it across the table, and Rose sat down to "play." With no sheet music, she had to do so from memory, but she could hear the music in her head almost as clearly as if it were a real piano.

Tsuyoko immediately wanted to learn too. She sat beside Rose, and Rose taught her to play the ABC song they'd learned at school, singing along. Mrs. Kokura soon began nattering and gave the little girl a chore to do.

Dad placed a hand on Rose's shoulder. "Maybe you should take the piano board outside."

Rose leaned it against the outside wall of the shack. When she came back in, Dad reached into his pocket and produced a letter from James. The family gathered around the table, and for once, Mrs. Kokura disappeared into their family's bedroom, taking her girls with her.

Mama opened the letter and handed it to Rose to read.

Hello everyone,

I received your letter, and I'm glad you're all safe and together. I am still at Yard Creek, which is a pretty little stream we've been able to pull some nice fish from. Our overall job here is to break bush for a new road, so there are guys who know how to run bulldozers and stuff. I guess because I'm a city kid, I got relegated to the camp kitchen, but I don't mind. We have to get up very early in the morning to get breakfast going, but after we've cleaned up, we get some free time to rest or read until we start supper. The food is plain but plentiful. I'm learning a few things about cooking, but I may never know how to cook for only four or six people! There were 104 of us to start, but some of the fellas opted to go to Ontario, and some of the married ones went to work on farms with their families. I think there are about 80 of us now—the younger ones like me are all Canadian-born, and the older ones are Japanese nationals. The two groups work well together, but in our leisure time, we are clearly two different groups, two different languages. I have become the go-between person, it seems. I'm the only one who can speak, understand, and write both languages fluently. When an argument breaks out, I can sometimes help settle people down—especially if it's only a misunderstanding because of language. I'm glad I can do that.

About once a week, I go with some of the other fellas to one of the Finnish farms near Cambie, where, for 25 cents, we can use their sauna. We're hoping to build our own bathhouse soon.

Our guards are vets from the Great War. (Did you know some are beginning to call it World War One? I guess that makes the current situation World War Two.) They walk around with their rifles, some in their old uniforms. Nobody wants to make trouble, though. Truth is, most of us younger guys would rather be joining up and serving shoulder-to-shoulder with other Canadians, but—

At this point, someone had blacked out two lines of James' letter. Rose held it up to the light, but she couldn't make it out. After the black lines, he ended with:

There's much more I could tell you, but paper is scarce, and it's time to

get back to the kitchen. Rose, I hope there is a piano at your camp. Tim, try to stay out of trouble. I'm glad you are all together.
    James

The relief on Mama's face was a joy to behold. She hummed as she went about preparing supper. Afterward, Dad helped Rose set her piano board across two stumps outside, and she practiced scales until it grew dark. People walking by their shack stopped to watch, a few nodding as though they could appreciate what Rose was trying to do. Most laughed and shook their heads. Rose didn't care.

That night as she fell asleep, Rose didn't need to ask God to make her thankful. She already was.

CHAPTER THIRTEEN

April arrived and with it, milder temperatures and more hours of sunshine—all of which contributed to an improved atmosphere in the camp. The little school was growing, both in numbers of students and in curriculum.

"How's it going so far, Rose?" Kenji asked one morning.

"Truthfully? I'm amazed my students are learning to read, in spite of my lack of training."

"Good."

Rose hesitated. "And … I guess I'm even more surprised by how satisfying I find it to hear them sounding out words from their readers."

Kenji smiled broadly and nodded. He made a schedule for which subjects would be covered and how much time should be allotted to each.

"My goal is that the children will be able to fit back into their regular grades when our internment ends," he explained.

Rose agreed. "We need to allow for an hour of music instruction each week as well."

"How can we, with no instruments?" Kenji raised one eyebrow. "And don't tell me your fake piano will do it."

"The brain and the heart are the only musical instruments one truly needs."

Kenji chuckled. "All right. One hour a week."

Rose wondered how on earth she could follow through on her bold statement. But she couldn't have been more pleased, under the circumstances. On Fridays, the day for music class, she lugged her piano plank to school. They had a chalkboard by this time, and she drew a music staff on it. Since the kids were learning their alphabet at the same time, it worked well to teach them the corresponding music notes. Of course, Rose had to use her voice to give them the right notes. They made as many words as they could using only the letters *a* through *g*, like *bag* and *cab* and *beg*. Then they found the notes on their piano scale and sang the letters of each word, creating tunes that made little sense musically but made the children laugh. Rose figured if she could help spark the love of music in them now, at least some of them would follow through with real lessons if the opportunity ever presented itself.

She'd written to Freda as soon as she could after their arrival at the camp, and a long letter finally came from her friend. Freda enclosed a photo of herself standing in front of their school, and envy flooded Rose's chest. Freda was still on track to graduate in June. Then she revealed a mystery Rose had not allowed herself to contemplate since leaving home.

Rosie, I don't know if your mom told you about the concert dress. She made it for you after all (I told you she would!), and it's even prettier than the one in the store. Your parents meant it to be a surprise and swore me to secrecy. But I saw it hanging in the window the day you left, and I couldn't bear the thought of someone else getting your dress. With some conniving (which I won't go into now), and some assistance (from someone who wishes to remain anonymous), I was able to retrieve your dress and am keeping it safe for you. Let me know if I should mail it. Otherwise, I will guard it with all my strength until you return.

Freda always did have a flair for the dramatic. Still, Rose's heart swelled with a rush of love for her parents and for her friend.

The letter included news of all the goings-on at school and church, all the things the two girls would have discussed before the war. Then it took a nasty turn.

Don't mention this to your parents, but I've heard rumors that the belongings placed in storage by the Japanese families have been auctioned off. I don't know if it's true—I hope not. They say the government has justified it because they need to pay for the internment somehow. I wanted to send you a clipping from the Sun, *but Dad said I shouldn't in case your mail is censored. Another article talked about the Japanese moving into the interior of B.C. and how the existence of the ultra-British valley, as we know it, is "seriously threatened."*

The editorial was titled, "We Must Not Unload Our Japs On The Okanagan," and you won't believe what it said, Rosie!

"The Sun *has repeatedly pointed out that during 50 years of Oriental immigration to this continent, British Columbia has consistently fought against the Japanese infiltration … and just as regularly, we have been over-ruled by Ottawa. Now, for excellent military reasons, the Japanese are being moved inland. Can anyone blame us if we hope that by May Day we shall have seen the last of them—and for all time? We shall have to admit that we are gladly using a necessity of the war to give us a solution, a permanent solution if possible, to an immigration that was thoroughly distasteful and objectionable."*

You know what's even worse? The slogan across the top of the Sun *calls itself "a newspaper devoted to progress and democracy, tolerance and freedom of human thought." I used the page as an example of irony for one of Mr. Rutledge's assignments. He was not impressed and gave me a C.*

I went to the theater with Evelyn Parker. It wasn't the same as going with you, though. We saw To Be or Not to Be. *Did you know Carole Lombard died in a plane crash in January? So sad. She was beautiful in the movie, but I couldn't enjoy it much after seeing the newsreel. Next time, I might deliberately arrive late so I don't have to watch. Oh, they try to make the war sound glorious, but it's too horrible for words. One of the younger students brought a game to school called "Yellow Peril," and the kids played it at recess. I really hoped Principal March would take it away, but he allowed it.*

I want to scream, Rosie. I miss you so much. School isn't the same without the Japanese students. Please, oh please, if they move you again, keep writing so we don't lose touch with each other. I couldn't bear it.

Your friend forever,
Freda

Rose wiped tears off her cheeks and then read Freda's letter again. And cried again. The hope of returning home was growing dimmer instead of brighter. What if they never went back?

After supper, Mama asked Rose why she was so quiet. "You seem sad, Rozu. You miss your friend." She pulled out a hairbrush and motioned for Rose to sit on the floor in front of her chair. Gently, she began to brush. "Is Freda all right?"

"Yes, she's fine." Rose didn't want to pass along the news about the Japanese property being auctioned off, especially if it might not even be true. "Mama, do you think we will ever get to go home?"

"I don't know, Rozu. We must take each day as it comes and do our best with it."

"But we need something to look forward to," Rose argued. "Something to work toward."

"You are doing a good thing teaching the little ones." Mama set aside the brush and began to braid Rose's hair into a single braid. "Do your best every day. Make a better future for them."

But who will make a better future for me? Rose could still envision herself on a concert stage, playing a grand piano for a sold-out crowd, an orchestra behind her. But with every passing day, that dream grew less realistic. Perhaps it had never been realistic in the first place.

"It's not fair, Mama."

"*Shakata ga nai,*" she murmured. "It cannot be helped."

Two days later, a late blizzard blew through the valley. Once again, temperatures plunged to well below freezing, and the families, so used to milder coastal weather, were not prepared. Dad and Mr. Kokura worked hard to keep their little shack warm, but it was futile. They all huddled together, wearing every item of clothing they owned and praying for the weather to change. Ironically, some war bond posters had been delivered to the camp, encouraging all patriotic Canadians to invest in victory bonds. The picture on it featured a map of Canada with a Nazi on the east coast and a Japanese soldier on the west. "They menace Canada on both coasts," it read in bold letters. Both soldiers scowled hatefully, their hands reaching toward the map with gnarled fingers and sharp claws. "Canada stands squarely in the path of conflict," the finer print read, among other fearsome warnings. Dad managed to secure about a dozen of these and showed great pleasure in throwing them into the stove and watching them burn.

Kenji canceled school for two days so they wouldn't need to heat the classroom, but no one fared much better in their shacks. Everybody bundled up tightly and slept as much as possible, hoping the time would pass quickly and spring would return to stay. On the second evening, Rose's family ventured to the outhouse as a unit, which they still often did after dark. When they returned, the shack felt surprisingly warm. At first, they thought it was simply because they'd been outside. They wondered why the Kokura family was not huddled around the stove. Then Kenji appeared in the doorway to his family's sleeping quarters. His face was pale.

"I'm so sorry, Rose. I did not get here in time to stop her."

Rose couldn't imagine what he meant until her father glanced toward the empty corner where Rose's piano plank had been propped. Then he made a swift dash for the stove. He opened it to reveal the remains of Rose's piano board, broken into pieces and burning far more efficiently than anything they'd burned all winter.

Dad closed the stove. Rose continued to stand there, staring in disbelief. The one item of joy she had in her life, her father's sacrificial expression of love—tossed into the fire to be burned. It wasn't right! Her lip trembled.

Dad placed a hand on Rose's shoulder. "We'll make another."

Rose knew he meant it, but she also knew there was not a plank like that to be found anywhere in the camp, especially not after this cold spell.

"It will be your sacrifice for the greater good of everyone, Rozu."

Rose didn't speak. If she had, she might have reminded her father a sacrifice is something you make of your own will. She'd had no say in the matter. Unable to enjoy the heat generated by her so-called sacrifice, she crawled into bed and waited for sleep to bring some measure of comfort. When it did, all she could see were the gnarled claws of those enemy soldiers and their threatening grimaces. Except in her dream, the soldiers' faces had turned into a remarkable likeness of Mrs. Kokura.

CHAPTER FOURTEEN

Rose felt sick to her stomach.

Dad and Mr. Kokura had returned to the shack from a meeting, excited with a new possibility of leaving the camp. The prospect of going home had made her feel like dancing. But that hope was quickly crushed. To hear Dad tell it, they'd been offered a golden opportunity. They could go to Manitoba to work on farms.

Mama pressed her lips into a fine line before she spoke. "What do we know about farming?"

"They will teach us." Dad's eyes glowed with optimism. "They are short of farmworkers. All the young men have gone to fight the war. It would be our patriotic service."

Manitoba seemed a million miles away—and in the wrong direction.

"How would we get there?" Rose hung up the dish towel she'd been using.

"They will give us train fare to Winnipeg—the whole family—for free!" Dad was clearly bent on this new adventure. "From there, we'll go with a farm family who needs help, and the farmer will provide a place for us to live. We wouldn't have to share space with the Kokuras or anyone else."

Mama's face brightened. "We'd have our own place?"

"I'm sure we would. And a nice farm family to work with."

How could Dad be so sure they'd be nice?

"What about James?" Tim looked up from the science book on his lap. "How will he know where we are?"

"We'll write to him, same as now. Better yet—maybe he can leave his camp and join us. They need strong young people, and they said this would be a way for us to stay together."

Now Mama was definitely on board. "We could have James with us?"

"Maybe."

Rose needed to think. The weather had warmed, and she stepped out into the late April sunshine and sat on the step. Kenji was just returning to the shack.

"Heard the news?" He plopped down beside her.

She nodded. "Is your family going?"

"I don't know yet." Kenji was an interesting mix. He still carried resentment about the way they'd been treated. But Rose had also seen a much softer side to him. He cared about his students and the work he'd been given to do here. "I don't want to leave my classroom—certainly not to work in the fields."

"I know. It feels like a giant step in the wrong direction to me."

Kenji's eyes held compassion. "I don't want you to go, Rose. You're the only friend I have here. And you're a good teacher too. The kids love you."

Rose could feel her face growing hot. She'd grown fond of Kenji in spite of his sharp edges. She couldn't tell if he was considering her in a romantic light or not, but something stirred inside her. "I don't know what I want." She shook her head. "I'd gladly leave if we were going home."

"I know."

"But given the choice of staying here where at least I know how things are, and going east where I don't know how anything will be ... I think I'd rather stay."

"In spite of my mother?" Kenji grinned.

Thankfully, Rose didn't need to answer. Dad came out and sat on the step between them.

"Rose, I know this idea doesn't appeal to you, but I haven't told you everything." Dad let out a big sigh and lifted his eyes to the surrounding mountain peaks, as though seeking help. "The government is giving me two options. Staying here is not one of them. Not for me."

"What do you mean?" Rose glanced at Kenji, then back at her father.

"I can either take my family to Manitoba where we can stay together, or I can leave you, Timothy, and Ojiisan here with your mother and go work in the road camps."

Rose remembered the news story Freda had shared, how the B.C. government wanted them as far east as possible.

"They're forcing your hand, Mr. Onishi," Kenji shook his head. "Did they give my father the same ultimatum?"

"Not yet. He is a few years older."

Rose couldn't bring herself to speak. For her father's sake, she needed to be brave and cooperative. Tim would see this as another grand adventure. Mama would hold onto the hope of a reunion with James. Poor old Ojiisan had already accepted that others would make all his decisions. Rose needed to see a positive side to it, but for the life of her, she couldn't.

"Anyway," Dad continued. "Now you know how it is. We have until the end of the week to get ready."

The choice had clearly been made. Dad stood and walked back into the house. Kenji remained silent beside her. She didn't want him to speak, but she didn't want him to leave either. They sat there until she was ready to go back inside as well.

As predicted, Tim was optimistic. While they settled into their beds on the floor that night, he tried to cheer Rose up.

"Manitoba gets a lot of sunshine, Rose. That'll be nice. And we'll be on a farm, so we'll have all the food we want."

Rose rolled onto her side, facing him. "How do you know so much about it?"

"There's a book in the schoolhouse about all the Canadian provinces. With pictures too. The government building in Winnipeg has a golden boy on top of it! Fourteen feet tall and so shiny on a sunny day, you can hardly stand to look at it. That's what I want to see."

Rose didn't share Tim's enthusiasm for any statue—golden or not.

They'd likely end up much too far from Winnipeg to see it, anyway. She rolled onto her back and closed her eyes.

"But I'm sorry you'll miss out on the piano," Tim added.

Rose's eyes popped open. "What do you mean? What piano?"

Tim grew silent.

Rose faced him again. "What piano, Tim?"

"Nuthin'. I don't know what I'm talking about. Good night." He rolled away from her.

Rose grabbed his shoulder and squeezed. "Tim! What did you mean? What piano?"

With a big sigh, her brother flipped over toward her. "I thought you knew."

"Knew what?"

"I guess it was supposed to be a surprise. I shouldn't say anything. Especially not now."

"Tim!" Rose sat up in aggravation. "You have to tell me now. Come on!"

"It was Kenji. He managed to work things out for a piano to be brought into the camp. Probably just an old clunker, anyway."

Rose was speechless. Kenji had done this? How?

Tim studied his sister's face in the dim evening light. "It's supposed to arrive next week. After we're gone. Good thing you won't have to hear it, Rose. It'll sound awful, for sure, probably worse than no piano at all."

By the end of that week, they had packed everything once again and waited with others who were heading east too. Apparently, more internees were coming to take their places. Rose had said farewell to the students who were staying behind and now watched them say goodbye to their friends. If nothing else, she was learning not to grow attached. Not to people, places, or things. After Tim told her about the piano, she hadn't even cried. The old Rose would have wept herself to sleep. Instead, she'd lain back down without a word and without tears.

But Kenji had done something wonderful for her and for the children, for everyone in the camp, really. Surely, someone else could play it, maybe someone yet to come. Someone who would use the piano to teach, to bring joy to the whole community. She would focus on that.

The Kokuras were staying behind, at least for now. As Rose waited to board the truck for their return trip to the nearest train station, Kenji approached. He ruffled the top of Tim's hair.

"So long, Tim. Keep working hard. You're an excellent student and a very smart boy. You will succeed at whatever you set out to do." Then he shook Tim's hand like a grown man's, and her little brother's face lit up with the praise.

Kenji turned to Rose. "I'm glad I met you, Rose."

Rose hadn't let on that she knew anything about the piano, but she couldn't leave without showing her gratitude.

"I heard what you did." Suddenly shy, she looked at the ground. "About the piano. I'm sorry I won't be here to play it."

"I'm sorry I won't get to hear you play."

"Thank you for doing that. I don't know if anyone has ever done such a nice thing for me before." As soon as she said it, her cheeks burned. What an audacious assumption to think Kenji had done it only for her! "I mean—thank you for doing this for the whole camp and for the kids—"

Kenji put a hand on Rose's arm. "It *was* for the whole camp, Rose. But mostly for you. I need to say thank you too."

Rose scrunched her eyebrows. "For what?"

"You made this place bearable. Helped me adopt a more positive attitude." He nodded toward Tim, who was already scrambling into the back of the truck. "You and that squirt."

"Pretty hard to stay negative with him around." Rose smiled. "Goodbye, Kenji. I'm glad I met you too."

"Write when you're settled?"

"Sure."

Tim yelled from the back of the truck. "Come on, sis! Let's go!"

Rose turned and climbed in. Dad and Mama were already on board, and Ojiisan sat up front. The space was packed with people, the adults seated on their belongings. The smaller children stood, wedged between their parents' knees for balance. The truck began to move, and Rose waved to Kenji and the others who had come to see them off. How long before another family moved in and had to endure Mrs. Kokura's grumpy ways? Surprisingly, she, too, had come out, although Rose suspected it was more out of curiosity than anything. As she watched Mrs. Kokura turn and shuffle back toward the shacks, Rose was suddenly filled with clear knowledge about two things—she had not forgiven Mrs. Kokura for burning her piano plank, and, for her own sake, she needed to.

"I forgive you," she whispered as the woman's form become smaller with distance. Sudden compassion flooded her for this person who had made their time here so unpleasant. Who knew what heartaches she carried? If Rose didn't learn to forgive, she might one day become just like her. Heaven forbid! *God bless you, Mrs. Kokura.*

Rose took a deep breath and let it out before turning away from the camp. The majesty of the mountains around them seemed more beautiful than ever, and she drank in the scenery. Despite whatever hardships might lie ahead, for right now, she felt lighter than she had in a long time.

CHAPTER FIFTEEN

Rose's heart grew heavier as the train carried them farther from the direction she wanted to be going. She was beginning to think they must be at the end of the world. At first, it had been interesting to be able to see for miles across the wide-open prairies of Saskatchewan and the flat-as-a-pancake countryside.

"Look! A coyote!" Tim had shouted more than once.

Then the novelty wore off, and they kept going and going forever, in the endless nothingness.

While moving around on the train to stretch her legs, Rose noticed a girl around her age in the car behind theirs. She smiled shyly and Rose smiled back. Later the same day, Rose stopped to say hello.

The girl patted the seat beside her for Rose to sit. "My name's Mary."

Mary explained that she and her family had been at one of the other camps and, like the Onishis, had decided to go to work on a farm rather than be split up.

"I'm the youngest." Mary pointed at the others in her family, who were all either asleep or engaged in a card game. "Those are my two older brothers. My dad says our family will be one of the first chosen because we are all strong adults—no little kids or old people. Farmers will take the families with strong workers first."

This worried Rose. Ojiisan appeared feebler than he really was. And Tim was obviously still a child—surely, he wouldn't be expected to work, would he? That left Mama, Dad, and Rose—a tiny girl compared to the people who probably farmed this land. What would become of them if none of the farmers wanted them? When Rose returned to her seat beside Tim, she said nothing about any of this to her family though it kept cropping up in her mind.

When they first crossed into Manitoba, a few more trees and some rolling hills appeared on the horizon. Then more flatness. The odd small town. Lots of farms. Fields, waiting to be planted. It was nearly May, and skiffs of snow still clung to the shady side of ditches in places.

She wrote to Freda, her penmanship leaving much to be desired due to the jostling of the train. By the time the letter reached her, Freda would probably have graduated. As much as Rose loved and missed her friend, jealousy reared its ugly head. By now, her seat in the music program at UBC had no doubt been given to another student. Why should Freda get to finish high school and go on to continue her music studies when Rose's life was being, quite literally, railroaded? It wasn't her fault her ancestors came from Japan. Freda's came to Canada from somewhere else too. England, probably. Freda had nothing to do with that. It was so unfair.

Rose remembered the old lady at Hastings Park. She'd lost everything but continued to smile and be grateful. Maybe the reason she could stay positive was because her life was mostly behind her. She wasn't watching all her future hopes and dreams die slow, painful deaths.

Rose closed her eyes and wrapped her hand around Freda's treble clef necklace. None of this was Freda's fault, either, and Rose knew her friend would change things for her in an instant if it were within her power. She could be thankful Freda had not allowed herself to be swallowed up by the prejudiced thinking that surrounded her. She had remained a loyal friend and given Rose no reason to believe that would change. But would they ever see each other again?

After two days with little sleep on a moving train, the Onishis sat up straighter when more buildings appeared, signaling that they'd soon be completing their journey. Mama, who had been extremely quiet the whole trip, began to perk up and take an interest in the sights around them. Winnipeg was different from Vancouver, but at least it could be called a city. When they finally stopped at Union Station and left the train for good, it seemed the ground still rocked beneath Rose's feet. The sun shone, and she chose to take that as a good sign. Maybe God was smiling on them. Maybe they'd find a good situation, a real home with kind people.

The station itself was far more impressive than Rose expected—another good sign. As they entered, loaded down with all their belongings, she didn't know which direction to face. Japanese people were pouring off the train and into the station, which was already populated with soldiers waiting to board. When someone over the loudspeaker announced the train for Vancouver, she wanted to cry. She imagined herself sneaking onto one of the cars loaded with soldiers. While they were heading overseas, she'd be returning home. Maybe she could stay with Freda's family. Surely, they'd keep her hidden until the war ended and everything went back to normal.

But even as she thought it, Rose knew she was being ridiculous. She turned her attention to Tim, who stood craning his neck to stare straight up at the high, domed ceiling with all its pretty etchings. Rose followed his gaze, but between the wooziness from leaving the moving train and the strange sensation of the rotunda, she lost her balance for a moment. Jerking one foot out to catch herself, Rose stepped on something. She quickly looked down to see someone else's foot being yanked out from under her own.

"Clumsy Jap." A young man in an army uniform scuttled away, a duffel bag slung over his shoulder.

In that moment, Rose realized how sheltered she'd been in the camp all these months. She'd barely seen another person who wasn't Japanese and had all but forgotten that dreadful scorn. Disoriented, dirty, hungry, and exhausted, she crumpled onto a bench.

Tim sidled up. "You all right?"

"I wish I could snap my fingers and this place would empty itself of all but my family and me." She wanted to let the dizziness pass. To survey this magnificent place. To step outside and sit on green grass and soak up some sunshine. To walk around the neighborhood and get her bearings. From Tim's descriptions of Winnipeg, she knew they were within walking distance of its famous Golden Boy atop the legislative building. Surely, there were restaurants in the area too. How great would it be to sit down to a full-course meal and eat their fill, after days of stale sandwiches and *onigiri*?

But none of that was to be. They were herded like sheep into a large room where a man rapped a gavel on a wooden table to quiet everyone.

"In the next room are about twenty-five farmers waiting to meet you," he announced. "Some have already chosen the families they want to sponsor from a list. If you're on that list, you will be taken back to their farms immediately."

What about the others? Rose didn't have to wonder long.

"Those not selected today will go to a retention center that's been set up called Immigration Hall."

Rose's stomach clenched at the mention of another center. Was she an immigrant now? Weren't they still in Canada?

The farmers filed in. Names were read out. Farmers stood. Families stood. As Mary had predicted, her family had been pre-selected. They were given only a few minutes to exchange names and addresses with their Japanese friends before leaving with their farmer. Away they went. Which farmer had chosen Rose's family? Would it be the tall, skinny fellow in the brown suit with the hat in his hands? Or maybe the chubby, bald one who hadn't bothered to change out of his overalls?

Rose counted the remaining farmers and the Japanese still waiting. Only three families were left—hers, a couple in their thirties named Albert and Marie with six children ranging from infant to thirteen, and a group consisting of two elderly grandparents, a woman around forty, and a teenage girl named Linda with braces on her legs like Rose had seen polio survivors wear.

And no more farmers.

CHAPTER SIXTEEN

Three days later, Rose and her family were still cramped into one small room at Immigration Hall. The washrooms, shared with everyone else, were down the hall. With the other two Japanese families on either side of the Onishis, they heard a lot of noise from the family with the young children. The other family was quiet. Rose overheard Linda, the girl with the braces on her legs, offer to help the young parents by watching their smallest child. Did Linda gravitate toward the children because they didn't seem to be bothered by the braces or the way she swung her legs out when she walked?

The rest of Immigration Hall housed soldiers, and they always seemed to be coming or going. Rose's father warned her and Tim to stay clear of them. On their third afternoon, a bunch of these fellows, carrying all their gear, marched toward the train station.

"Where do you suppose they're headed?" Tim lifted a hand to shield his eyes from the bright sunshine.

Rose had no idea. With no radio and no money for newspapers, her parents had picked up only bits of news here and there. "If they go east, Halifax. If they go west …Vancouver."

"And after that?

"Could be almost anywhere, I suppose. England, maybe."

"Japan?"

"Maybe."

Tim stayed quiet a long time. "They won't all make it back, will they?"

For a ten-year-old, her brother was far too astute. "I don't know, Tim. I guess if they're being sent into an actual battle somewhere, then no."

He thought awhile. Then, in typical Tim fashion, he smiled. "Well, at least they'll have an adventure. C'mon, let's have one of our own."

He headed off down the sidewalk, and the pair spent the next couple of hours exploring this part of the city. When they turned down Broadway Avenue, Tim recognized Manitoba's legislative building with The Golden Boy on top. He lifted his fingers to measure the statue. "I thought he would be bigger."

"I'm sure he would look much bigger if he were down here instead of way up there," Rose mumbled. All the people they encountered on the sidewalks were white, and all of them stared. Though Tim was oblivious, Rose grew increasingly uncomfortable. She tried to stay focused on the buildings and other sights, keeping track of how many blocks they'd walked in each direction so they could find their way back.

Then the voice of a small child piped up behind her. "Look, Mommy! Japs!"

Tim turned around, but Rose grabbed his elbow and hurried him along. "Never mind, Tim. We should head back. Mama will be wondering where we've gone."

Sure enough, when they returned to Immigration Hall, their parents scolded them. Mama's brow lowered. "Rozu, where were you? We have a farmer meeting."

Dad paced the floor. "We're supposed to gather downstairs to meet the new farmers."

Mama began inspecting them, smoothing Tim's hair and instructing Rose to change into her best dress. "Hurry. We won't get picked if they think we are slow."

Rose changed quickly, and they headed down to the meeting room. As Mama predicted, the other Japanese families were already present when the Onishis shuffled in. A middle-aged white man and woman waited nearby. The man held his hat in his hand, revealing a farmer tan around his crown. His wife wore a periwinkle dress, brown curls peeking out from under her summer hat. The other farmer stood alone, chubby and wearing gray overalls. Rose found herself hoping for the couple.

The man in charge asked them to line up against the wall with the other Japanese but told them, "Stay in your own family groups. These gentlemen are both from the same community, and we're hoping that between them, they can take you all."

Rose stood silently beside her family and couldn't help thinking about the stories she'd read about slaves being auctioned off. Nobody was literally buying the Japanese Canadians, but they may as well have been. The two men and one woman scrutinized them, no doubt to determine how useful they would be in their fields. Rose pressed herself against the wall, wishing it could absorb her. Mama gave her a minuscule chin lift as if to say, *stand up straight*. When the farmer with the wife walked past, Rose straightened to her full height, pulled her shoulders back, and tried to look strong.

The farmer with the wife pointed at them. "I'll take this family."

The man in charge stepped over. "Mr. Thorne, this is George Onishi and his father, wife, and two children." He waved a hand around.

Dad and Ojiisan pressed their hands together and bowed slightly.

"George." To Rose's surprise, the man called Mr. Thorne put out his hand to shake Dad's. "Frank Thorne. This is my wife, Anna."

The men shook hands. Mrs. Thorne smiled and nodded at Mama and then at Rose and Tim. Then she placed one hand on her husband's elbow and pulled him aside. Rose tried to listen, but the other family's baby began howling. It appeared the other farmer was taking Linda's family. Rose caught Linda's eye and smiled at her. Would the family with all the children be left behind?

They were instructed to gather their belongings and meet at the Thornes' truck outside. As Rose walked past, Mrs. Thorne pled with her husband. "We can't just leave them here! What will become of them?"

"What would we do with all those children, Anna? They can't work, but they need to be fed somehow."

The woman continued her appeal as Rose left the room, somewhat comforted. Regardless of how this turned out, Mrs. Thorne was a compassionate woman.

When they finally reached the parking area where Mr. and Mrs. Thorne waited by a truck, it became clear that Mr. Thorne had won the argument. The family with all the children was nowhere to be seen. Linda's family was getting into a car with the other farmer.

"There's room for one up front with us." Mr. Thorne helped the Onishis load their belongings into the back of the truck. Ojiisan climbed into the cab with Mr. and Mrs. Thorne, while Dad, Mama, Tim, and Rose climbed into the back and tried to get comfortable among their boxes and bags. Perhaps they should be getting used to it by now, but she found something so humiliating about climbing into the back of a farm truck in the middle of a city while passersby gawked.

Tim leaned toward Rose. "Aren't you glad it's a nice day?"

She almost laughed out loud. As usual, Tim was looking on the bright side. It could be raining. Or worse. Rose raised her face to the sun and let it warm her. Far better to focus on the blue sky than on people who would only judge and stare.

Mr. Thorne held out a package of Beech-nut chewing gum. "You kids speak English?"

Rose nodded, accepting with a quiet "thank you."

"We all do." Tim also took a piece of gum and unwrapped it. "Except Ojiisan."

"Ojiisan?"

"Grandfather." Dad held up a palm to the offered gum. "But he understands what you say."

"Very good. It's an hour's drive, so I hope you can get reasonably comfortable back here. Our farm is five miles from a little town called Spruceville. We'll stop halfway to make sure you're all right." He nodded toward the vehicle pulling away with Linda's family inside. "The other family will be just down the road from us, so you'll see them around once in a while. Are we all good here, then?"

Dad nodded, and Mr. Thorne tapped the side of his truck before crawling in behind the wheel. He started it up, and they began to roll down the street and on to their next adventure.

Mr. Thorne must have forgotten his promise to stop halfway, but it was just as well. With the city behind them, they were soon on a gravel road, great clouds of dust swirling around them at every slow-down. Rose's chewing gum became gritty between her teeth. Mama had possessed the foresight to bring a small jug of water, and they passed it around several times. Rose never knew water could feel so good going down one's throat.

When they passed a sign that proclaimed, *Spruceville, Population 555*, Rose thought what an easy number it was to remember. Mr. Thorne stopped in front of a white building. The sign on the front read, *Grocery Store and Post Office*. Completely unimaginative, it provided no clue as to who might run the combined business.

Mr. Thorne got out of the truck. "Just going to check for mail. Feel free to stretch your legs." He went inside. Mrs. Thorne and Mama must have decided they didn't need to stretch because neither moved. Tim and Rose stood and scanned their surroundings without getting out of the truck. Dad hopped down and opened the passenger side door to check on Ojiisan. Rose could hear them speaking softly in Japanese.

"Our new town, Rose." Tim pointed a grimy finger. "I see a school."

Sure enough, across the street and down a bit stood a red-brick, two-story building. A big sign on the front read, *Spruceville High School*, and the Union Jack flew proudly from a tall pole in front. It looked so much like their school back home, a lump formed in Rose's throat. Most of her classmates would be graduating without her in a few weeks. A bell rang, and teenagers began leaving the building.

Tim tried counting the students but gave up. "How can such a small town have enough students to fill the building?"

Rose shrugged. "Maybe they live on surrounding farms."

Mr. Thorne returned, a handful of mail in his arms and a big smile on his face. His wife leaned her head out the window. "Anything from Rusty?"

He waved a package high. "Looks like a whole parcel!" He passed it through to Mrs. Thorne, then turned to Rose's father, who had returned to his place in the back of the truck. "Our son Russell is in the army, serving overseas. This is the first word we've had since Pearl Harbor."

The information meant little to Rose, who took special note of the post office's location. Mama would be writing to James as soon as possible to give him their new address. Would Tim or Rose be sent to town to get the mail? Would they attend school here, or anywhere?

They carried on through the little town, and Rose admired its pretty houses with front porches. If the drought and depression had affected Spruceville, it had recovered well. Most of the yards appeared to have been recently dug up and planted with vegetables, as advertised by makeshift wooden shingles staked into the ground with words like *carrots* and *tomatoes* carefully inked across them. Most were already sprouting. Some sported signs proudly declaring themselves *Victory Garden*.

Rose peered through the rear window into the cab. Mrs. Thorne had opened the package from her son and was reading a letter aloud, although Rose couldn't hear what she said. Several lengths of beautiful, silky-looking fabric lay folded on her lap.

The five-mile drive took them past three farms and a one-room schoolhouse on one corner, from which children walked home in all four directions. All of them stopped to stare. While none of the children appeared more affluent than the Onishi family, every face was white.

CHAPTER SEVENTEEN

One mile west of the school, the truck pulled onto the Thorne farm. At the sight of its storybook appearance, Rose dared to imagine a hot bath and ridding herself of the grit and grime of the road. A two-and-a-half-story white house with black shutters stood proudly surrounded by green grass and a variety of trees—some evergreen, some in bud with pink or white blossoms. A dog, which Tim identified as a German shepherd, trotted over to greet the truck, then barked when it spotted strangers in the back. A huge red barn dwarfed a chicken coop next to it. Brown and white chickens pecked freely around the space between. When a rooster crowed, Rose nearly laughed out loud. Had she stepped onto the movie set for *Rebecca of Sunnybrook Farm*? She'd be sure to tell Freda all about it in her next letter.

Mr. Thorne drove past the house, past the barn, and stopped in front of two much smaller buildings. Were they some sort of granaries? Rose had no idea how sugar beets were stored, but as they'd crossed the prairies on the train, she'd learned most farmers had grown wheat until the price dropped, and things like oats and wheat were stored in granaries. They climbed down from the truck, and Rose and Mama brushed dust from their clothing and hair. Tim didn't seem bothered by it.

"Our summer workers stay here." Mr. Thorne gestured to the two shacks. "Of course, our regular summer workers are single fellas traveling through, so they don't mind the rustic bunkhouses. Not really designed for a family, but you can take your pick or use them both if you want. I'm sure your wife there can fix it up however she likes." He began lifting things down from the truck as he spoke. "They're not set up for winter, but we'll get them insulated for you before the snow flies if you're here that long."

Rose hoped they wouldn't be here that long but said nothing. The whole family remained silent.

"'Course, we're hoping and praying this foolish war ends any day now." Mr. Thorne cleared his throat. "Then our hired men will come home, and our son, of course … and … you'll be free to …"

The dog came sniffing around them, wagging her tail. Tim knelt to pet her, and they seemed immediately smitten with each other.

"That's Lady." Mr. Thorne scratched the dog behind her ears. "She keeps away skunks, badgers, and foxes. The barn cats take care of mice and rats, so … you're welcome to bring a cat into your cabin if you want."

Rose didn't want to think about what he was implying.

"Outhouse is around back. The pump is just over there by the house, and we have lots of water. Even through the dirty thirties, that well never ran dry." He nodded toward the house. "I was born in that house. Never lived anywhere else."

Mrs. Thorne had remained in the truck, leaning out the window with her arms folded over the edge. "I made a large pot of stew this morning. I'll bring some over in an hour or so for your supper."

"After that, you'll be on your own for meals," Mr. Thorne clarified. "But once the garden's producing, feel free to help yourself to as much as you want."

"I'm sorry the bunkhouses aren't nicer," Mrs. Thorne added. "I thought we'd be coming home with several single men, or I'd have done some cleaning."

"You can have tomorrow off to get yourselves situated. There's plenty of firewood—our son Russell piled that up when he was home last fall, so it's good and dry." Mr. Thorne climbed in behind the wheel again. "Planting starts on Wednesday."

He started the truck and parked it beside the barn. Lady ran after them and walked with them toward the house. The dog flopped onto the porch while Mr. and Mrs. Thorne went inside.

Mama poked her head inside one cabin, then the other. "They're both the same," she called. "But no point using both."

After visiting the outhouse, Rose stepped inside the nearest cabin, where Mama was already going through their things. Two sets of wooden bunks took up half the room, a small window between them. The other half consisted of a wood-burning cookstove, a rickety table with four chairs, and floor-to-ceiling shelves. Most were empty. Others held an assortment of dishes, pots, and other utensils. A larger window by the table overlooked the farmyard, but it was in such dire need of cleaning that little light got in. Large-head nails stuck out from every stud. On one of them hung a square metal washtub. On another, a bucket. Mama made a beeline for the bucket. She could barely reach it, but she pulled it down and inspected it carefully. "First, we clean this place. Then, we clean us," she announced. She handed the bucket to Rose with instructions to fetch water from the pump, then sent Tim hunting for a second bucket.

Behind each cabin, Rose discovered a bench with two washbasins, another bucket, and a cracked bar of soap. More nails had been pounded partway into the outside walls, probably to hang towels. An old shaving mirror hung crookedly from one nail, and Rose caught a glimpse of her dirt-smeared face. No wonder the school kids had stared. The term *dirty Jap* echoed in her mind, and she sneered at her reflection.

Rose and Tim pumped four pails of water and carried them back while the adults organized their belongings. Dad made a fire in the stove to heat water, and Mama put them all to work scrubbing things down. By the time Mrs. Thorne appeared with a pot of stew, the sun was setting. Four beds had been made up. Tim would sleep on the top bunk above their parents. Rose would be on the top bunk over Ojiisan.

The stew smelled heavenly, and there was plenty of it. Mrs. Thorne brought a whole loaf of bread to go with it, butter, jam, and a basket containing a dozen or more apples. Rose's mouth began to water, but Mama stood waiting for Mrs. Thorne to take the lead. Would she leave or stay?

"Looks as though you're settling in nicely." Mrs. Thorne set the stew on the stove and wiped her hands on her apron. "Is there anything you need? More blankets?"

No one answered. For a moment, Rose dared suppose the woman would invite them inside her house for hot baths, but she did not. "I'll leave you to your meal, then. I trust it will fill you up and that you all have a good rest tonight."

She turned to leave, and Mama surprised Rose by speaking up. "Mrs. Thorne?"

The lady turned. "Yes, Mrs. Onishi?"

"Your son is okay?"

Mrs. Thorne smiled and nodded. "Yes. He is fine. Thank you for asking." She hesitated. "Do you ... have other children?"

Mama simply nodded, then Dad spoke up. "Our oldest son, James, is on a road crew in B.C. We hope he can join us here. He would be a great asset to you."

Mrs. Thorne nodded again. "Then, for all our sakes, I hope he can too." She left them to their meal.

Rose couldn't remember the last time she'd been able to eat her fill. Her belly ached afterwards, it was stretched so tightly. Tim wanted to take a walk around the farm, but Rose declined with an enormous yawn. Mama began filling the washtub with warm water, and Dad hung a blanket across the room so they could take turns bathing.

Rose fell asleep on her bunk with no thoughts of home, school, Freda, or even her piano. This was her new life, and she would make the most of it. Their space might be cramped, but at least they didn't have to share it with another family. They might not have all the conveniences they'd enjoyed in Vancouver, but it seemed there'd be plenty to eat. For now, it would have to be enough.

In the coming days, Mr. Thorne gave the Onishis lessons in sugar beet farming. Rose thought it ironic when he told them the seed he used was grown in British Columbia. "The rows are spaced twenty-two inches apart, the seeds two inches apart. The first ones we plant will be sprouting by the time we plant the last ones—with good conditions, they could be up in four or five days."

He explained why the seedlings required as much care as baby humans. "Every weed must be eliminated. Even more importantly, the beets must be thinned out when they've sprouted four leaves. Each seed sends up several shoots. Someday, we hope they'll develop monogerm seed—one beet per plant. Until then, we have to pull out all the little roots except the strongest one, being careful not to damage or stunt it." He removed his cap to scratch his head, then replaced it. "You'll get the hang of it. Most of the fellas around here still use the shorter hoes, but I switched to long ones. Easier on the back. A good beet hoer can weed and thin an acre a day, but don't worry, I won't expect that from you. At least, not at first." He chuckled.

By June, Rose's gratitude had disappeared, and even Tim's optimism dwindled. All five of them worked from sunrise to sundown, six days a week. Although Mr. Thorne worked alongside and expected no more from them than he did of himself, he was clearly far more used to this work. He moved at four or five times the speed of any of them.

"If his former hired hands kept pace with Mr. Thorne," Dad said on their first lunch break, "they must have completed the work much faster. We must learn and grow proficient, so the Thornes won't be disappointed. They are paying us a dollar a day."

They did get faster. By the time planting was done, it was time to start weeding and thinning the fields that had been planted first. By July, the temperatures climbed to the eighties and nineties. The clear sky and treeless prairie fields offered no relief from the merciless sun. It beat on them as though they were the enemy. In a way, Rose supposed they were. The only comfort was knowing Mr. Thorne endured it too. He continued to outwork them all, and Rose marveled at how he managed it, especially when her own much younger back ached. Ojiisan worked alongside him valiantly, determined to prove he could keep up. Even Tim worked, using a hoe with a shortened handle.

"Our chief foe," Mr. Thorne explained, "are the webworms. Watch for small, white eggs on the undersides of the leaves. Once they hatch, they can destroy an entire crop in a couple of days, so it takes diligence."

He showed them how to pinch the eggs or pull off an entire leaf and destroy them.

What he didn't tell them was how the larvae stick to workers' clothes and crawl on hands and faces.

In typical Tim fashion, Rose's little brother made a game of it. "You get to make a wish for each little worm you find on yourself," he announced as he pulled several off his arm. "I'm running out of things to wish for."

The summer dragged on, and Rose's hands grew black with ground-in Manitoba soil. Her knuckles went from blistered to callused, and she wondered what her piano teachers would think if they could see her hands now. On rainy days, they washed clothes and cleaned their cabin. If the rain stopped, they hung their clothes on lines outside—far preferable to draping them around the inside of the cabin. On Saturday mornings, Mama rode along to town with Mrs. Thorne to buy what she needed to keep the Onishis in rice and other necessities.

At night, the cabin was stifling. They left the two windows wide open to let some breeze through, but the place quickly filled with mosquitoes. Between the high-pitched buzzing in her ears, the swatting sounds of her family, and the endless itchiness of the mosquito bites, Rose honestly thought it would be better to close the windows.

Until they did. They killed all the mosquitoes inside, and no more came in, but the cabin became unbearable. No one slept. Still, they had to rise before the rooster's crowing and be working at first light.

It was Mrs. Thorne who came to their rescue. She had not seen the Onishis most of that week, and when she did, she noticed all the red bumps on Tim's face and arms. "Frank, we must find screening for their windows before the mosquitoes carry this child off. How could we have overlooked such a basic thing?"

By the end of the day, screens had been tacked on over the cabin's two windows, held securely in place with narrow strips of wood. That night, the whole family slipped into blessed, deep slumber for the first time in weeks.

CHAPTER EIGHTEEN

Hong Kong - August 1942

Summer had come and with it, more heat than the Canadian soldiers had ever imagined.

"So much for our exotic vacation." Bert had not lost his ability to make quips. "At least we're not freezing."

The heat, however, had not stopped the problem of the painful feet, causing Rusty to think the young med student was right about it being caused by malnutrition. Their feet were no longer their biggest problem, though. With the filthy conditions, nobody in the camp was free of dysentery or diphtheria. Some appeared to have both. Could these skeletal figures, clutching their cramping stomachs, groaning in pain, covered in insect bites, bruises, and open wounds, survive to the end of the month? Some of the diphtheria patients had choked to death in their sleep, but still, the guards did nothing. Rusty listened to their wheezing in the night, making sleep impossible for everyone. But when the wheezing stopped, it was worse. The dead were buried in a common grave dug by whichever prisoners were still strong enough to wield a shovel.

Then came the morning Rusty himself couldn't get up.

"You okay, pal?" Bert reached out a hand to help Rusty.

"Just ducky." Rusty's voice came out as a whisper, his throat feeling as though it had closed up. When he reached out to grasp Bert's hand, he missed the mark. That's when he realized he couldn't see out of his left eye. He closed his right, and the room went black. Rusty's glasses had gone missing the day they were captured, but he'd gotten along all right without them until now.

"That's it." Bert grabbed Rusty's hand and pulled him to a seated position. "I'm taking you to the infirmary."

"What's the point?" Though the camp boasted its own infirmary complete with a doctor and at least one orderly, rarely did any of their patients live to tell about it. Its half dozen cots were always full.

But Bert insisted. He pulled Rusty to his feet and supported him around the waist—what was left of his waist—and together, they shuffled to the infirmary. To their surprise, the doctor took one look at Rusty and told him to line up at the front gate. A transport truck was due to arrive to take the sickest of the men to a hospital.

On this particular morning, at least one patient had dropped dead between the infirmary and the front gate. Four patients lay on stretchers on the ground, while a few more men lay or sat on the ground, too weak to stand. Behind them, still more stood in line.

"These fellows are in much worse shape than me." Rusty tried to turn Bert around. "Take me back to the barracks."

"Nothin' doing. I'll end up carryin' ya, and for a skinny runt, you sure are heavy."

Rusty was leaning hard on Bert, but he couldn't help it. He felt like a helpless baby, the pain in his throat overriding every other discomfort.

A military truck rolled to the gate, stirring up dust onto the already filthy men. Two Japanese soldiers with rifles jumped down from the back, threw open the canvas covering, released the tailgate, and began to load the stretchers. When they realized one of the stretcher occupants was already dead, they rolled him unceremoniously onto the ground and called for another to take his place. Once the weakest were loaded, those able to climb in under their own power quickly filled the back of the truck. Rusty wasn't going to make it.

"Full now," one of the guards announced, grabbing the tailgate to lift it back into place.

"Wait!" Bert shouted. "One more! One more!" With a mighty heave, Rusty would not have thought Bert capable of even under normal circumstances, he shoved Rusty onto the tailgate, then rolled him inside.

A stream of Japanese words came from one guard while the other knocked Bert to the ground with his rifle. But they left Rusty where he'd landed among the other sick men. The tailgate closed, and Rusty managed to pull himself into a seated position. Bert did a backward crab crawl for a few yards, then sat still.

"I'm all right." Bert waved to Rusty. "See you soon, buddy." He was still sitting there when the canvas flaps came down, engulfing the men in darkness. Though their guards both climbed into the cab, no one had enough energy to talk or to wonder aloud where they might be headed.

"Can you hear me?"

Rusty was hearing the voice of an angel. Had he died? The angel even spoke English! Beneath him, he felt soft bedding. The unfamiliar smell of something clean greeted his nose. The only clue that this might not be heaven—apart from the pain in his throat and feet—was the fact that he could not see a thing.

"Doctor, I think this one is conscious." The angelic voice held an urgency.

Rusty squeezed his eyes shut and opened them again. Nothing changed. Footsteps, then a male voice with a British accent. A hand rested lightly on his shoulder.

"Son, you're at the Bowen Road Military Hospital in Hong Kong. You've got diphtheria. The good news is, we're going to give you some medicine, and you'll be right as rain in a few weeks. All right? You're one of the lucky ones. We have only enough meds for the ones with a fighting chance. You understand me?"

Rusty tried to nod his head.

"Atta boy."

Why can't I see? Rusty's lips formed the words, but no sound came out. Then he heard the angel voice again.

"Don't try to talk. Can you see anything, soldier?"

Rusty could barely shake his head.

The male voice again. "That's probably from vitamin deficiency, son. We're going to fix that too. You just be patient. Now I want you to move your left toe."

Rusty focused everything he had, but he could not move any of his toes. He barely felt a needle being jammed into his thigh, then blissful unconsciousness overtook him again.

Over the course of the next three weeks, Rusty would awaken intermittently. Though he could feel himself becoming stronger, he still couldn't see. Gradually, he learned he was surrounded by other prisoners of war—including the medical team. His angel's name was Nurse Evelyn. From their discussions, he could tell others around him were dying and being carried out daily. Medicine and other necessities were in short supply, and the doctors needed to be resourceful. They also had to make difficult decisions about which patients would receive the limited medication and not waste it on those for whom it was too late.

Too ill at first to even grieve the loss of his sight, Rusty discovered that his hearing seemed keener. One conversation coming from some distance behind him left him with deep compassion for the doctors and nurses.

"I hate this." A feminine voice, but not Nurse Evelyn's. "I am becoming as cold-hearted as the brutes holding these poor fellows captive."

"You're not, Meg. You're doing the best you can, making impossible decisions." Rusty recognized Evelyn's voice.

"This is not what they trained us for—playing God."

"I know."

"And if they do recover, what kind of hell are we sending them back to?"

Rusty had wondered the same.

"It's hard. But we have to see it this way. Without our help, none of these fellows would make it. Not one. If we can help just one of these brave soldiers get home to his family, we can know we did our job."

Eventually, the pain in Rusty's feet subsided. His throat cleared and he was able to sit up. He began to take in small amounts of solid food. Better still, he could speak and ask questions. He voiced his biggest concern.

"Will my sight be restored?"

"I'm confident it will," the doctor told him. "I've seen this before. Be patient, soldier. Let your whole body heal."

But as the days and nights dragged on, Rusty fought despair. What good was it for his body to recover if he'd never see again? What would happen next? Just because he was in a hospital didn't change his prisoner of war status. Would he be returned to the camp if he was permanently blind? How could he possibly survive then?

Oh God, he prayed. *Do you even see me here, or are you blind too?*

Rusty longed for a familiar voice. He missed Bert and wondered how his friend was faring. Would they ever be reunited? He longed to feel Mum's soft hand on his forehead, to hear Dad's voice or his sisters teasing him. What would they think of their handsome, muscular brother if they could see his skeletal physique now?

I know you're there, God. Please be there.

Was he trying to convince himself? If he clung to the idea of God's presence—whether it was real or not—perhaps it would help him survive. And he must survive, if for no other reason than to spare his parents the loss of their only remaining son.

You're not alone.

The thought came to him as clearly as if he'd heard it spoken. With it, Scripture verses he'd memorized as a child began to drift in and out of his mind along with restorative sleep. *Be strong and of a good courage; be not afraid, neither be thou dismayed: for the Lord thy God is with thee whithersoever thou goest.*

One morning, when Rusty opened his eyes, Nurse Evelyn's voice was accompanied by a blurry white vision in one eye. By the next day, Rusty's other eye was picking up the movement of people around the room. His hope began to grow. To pass the time, he tried to engage patients around him in conversation. Most were too weak to respond. Others could at least whisper their names and where they came from. A fellow a few beds over said he was from Alberta.

"Got to see the Rockies last year before we shipped out," Rusty told him. "Never saw anything so pretty in my life."

"I know. Can't wait to get home." The soldier let out a sigh. "Got a girl waiting for me—even prettier."

"Then keep fighting, soldier. Get well and survive. You have much to live for."

The Albertan replied with a tremor in his voice. "Thanks, pal."

One of the blurry white figures moved toward him. "Good news, Russell." It was Nurse Evelyn. "Somebody knows you're here. You've got mail."

Rusty couldn't believe his ears. Mail had gotten through?

"Read it to me?"

"Be happy to." A chair scraped across the floor alongside his cot. "Return address says, 'Mrs. Frank Thorne, Spruceville, Manitoba.'"

"My mother." Rusty could hear the envelope being torn. "What's the date on it?"

"February fourteenth. Nearly … seven months ago."

February. Rusty had already been in prison for two months. Had his parents received word? Was he reported missing in action? Presumed dead?

Nurse Evelyn began to read. "*Dearest Rusty.*" She tried unsuccessfully to suppress a giggle. "Sorry."

"Don't be. I've been called Rusty as long as I can remember. Unless I'm in trouble, of course."

She laughed and kept reading.

"Today we received the letter you started on the train to Vancouver. The

116

mountains sound wonderful, and I'm so glad you got to see them. Maybe your dad and I will one day too. I do wish I knew where you've ended up, but I understand the need for secrecy and security. Things are fine here. We've heard talk about a program that will allow us to hire help for the summer and harvest work—families new to the area, willing to work. Your dad is keen to apply. It will be good to see at least one of the cottages occupied this summer and to have some good help. I know you'll be relieved to hear it as well. I'll write again when I know how that turns out.

Isabel Murphy had a healthy baby boy last week. Seems like yesterday you and she were competing in the Grade Eight spelling bee. Poor girl, her husband's been posted to Europe somewhere, and she has no idea when he will get to meet his son. She has moved in with her parents while she waits it out.

They've warned us not to share war news, so I'll trust you know more than we do. We're all doing our part on this end—there's talk of fuel rationing coming soon. I'm already sorting through seed envelopes saved from last year's garden and planning to increase the size of this year's. So thankful those drought years are behind us. Now if we can only bring this horrible war to a swift and peaceful end, my heart will be full. Looking forward to that day, and to seeing you again—hopefully soon. I'm saving sugar rations for another cake next time you're home. Until then, please remember all you've learned about God's love for you. I leave you with these words from Psalm 46: 'God is our refuge and strength, a very present help in trouble … He maketh wars to cease unto the end of the earth.' Love, Mother."

The nurse stopped reading, and Rusty swallowed past a lump in his throat. He could so easily picture Mum seated at her kitchen table, writing the letter, thumbing through her well-worn Bible for ways to encourage her son.

"Your mother has beautiful penmanship," the nurse said. "She sounds like a lovely person."

Rusty heard the rustle of paper again, then felt the envelope being tucked into his hand.

"Here. You hang onto this. Soon you'll be able to read it for yourself."

The chair scraped again, and the white figure moved away. Rusty lay with the letter clutched to his chest. If the military knew he was here, his parents must know by now that he'd been captured. That he was alive, at least. Had they received the silk or any of his subsequent letters?

Oh God, please comfort their hearts. And thank you for this program for farmworkers, whatever it is. By now, these workers would be well-established on the farm, and harvest would soon begin. Surprising, the measure of relief this brought him. He lay still, picturing his mother's garden laden with ripe, red tomatoes, corn, cucumbers, and bushels of greens. Eventually, he fell asleep, still hugging her words to his heart.

CHAPTER NINETEEN

The summer wore on, and Rose grew accustomed to the hard work. Though she hated the rough calluses on her hands, she appreciated the firm muscles in her arms and shoulders. While her back ached and sweat pooled inside her clothing, she and Tim looked forward to a cool dip every evening in the creek not far from the cabin. Dad and Mama often joined them, too, and even Ojiisan rolled up his pant legs and waded in on occasion. They splashed and laughed and washed away their cares along with the day's accumulation of field dirt.

On Sundays, they attended church with the Thornes. Spruceville Community Church was the proud owner of a pump organ. The woman who played it each week began pumping the pedals with her feet before the music began. From there, it appeared much like playing a piano, except with less finger movement, and she held down the chords longer. Every now and then, she'd push or pull out various stops.

"Looks like fun," Rose whispered to Tim, nodding in the direction of the organ.

Tim followed her gaze. "You should give it a try sometime."

"I don't want to get into trouble."

Linda and her family were there too. When they chatted after the service, it sounded as though her family's situation was much like the Onishis'.

"I heard we'll all be working together at harvest time, going from field to field." Linda swallowed. "I sure hope I can keep up."

Rose hoped Linda was right. It would be good to see more faces than her family's and the Thornes'.

The church people seemed to fall into two camps as far as the

Japanese were concerned. Some welcomed them and treated them like anyone else. Rose learned the Thornes had two married daughters, Shirley and Claire, who also attended church with their families. They both had children, but with all the church kids running around together, Rose couldn't keep straight which kids belonged to which family. Like their parents, the Thorne sisters seemed friendly.

A handful of people clearly thought the newcomers should not be there.

As Rose waited for her parents one Sunday after the service, she overheard one lady, Mrs. Pierce, advising the pastor as she shook his hand at the door.

"Don't you agree, the Japs should have their own place of worship, Pastor?" She held his right hand in both of her gloved hands, a large, white purse draped over one forearm. "Who knows what pagan ideas they might try to influence our children with?"

Mrs. Pierce looked older than Mrs. Thorne, so Rose sincerely doubted she had any children of an impressionable age to worry about.

The pastor's response made Rose glad. "I'm hoping their children will influence ours, Mrs. Pierce. They're the most respectful young people I know."

The woman didn't give up that easily. "Then perhaps an afternoon service just for them would solve the problem."

"I wasn't aware there was a problem." He looked around the room. "This building isn't exactly bursting at the seams. If that day ever comes, I would happily consider a second service to accommodate everyone. But each person would be free to choose which time of day they decide to come."

"But perhaps they would like something in their own language, with their own customs."

"Everyone will always be welcome here, as long as I am the pastor." He turned to shake the hand of the next person in line, and Rose tried to stifle a grin.

Mrs. Pierce muttered under her breath, "Perhaps it's time you weren't."

The following Saturday, Mrs. Thorne and Mama returned from town all smiles. Both held letters from their sons. They came out to the field where the others worked, waving their envelopes, eager to open them.

Mr. Thorne leaned on his hoe and wiped his brow. "Let's take a break."

While he and his wife sat on the grass a dozen feet away, Dad, Ojiisan, Tim, and Rose circled around Mama. She opened the letter from James and handed it to Rose to read aloud.

Dearest family,

I'm glad to hear you have found a farm family who is treating you kindly even if the work is hard. I sincerely hope they will allow Rose and Tim to attend school in September. I have good news and bad—depending on how you see it. I will not be joining you in Manitoba, after all. As I write this, I am in Ottawa! But by the time this letter reaches you, I will probably be somewhere else. When the military discovered my knowledge of the Japanese language, I was recruited to be a translator and interceptor of radio messages. I'm excited to be in the unique position of offering this service to my country and our allies. I know you will be disappointed that we won't be all together, but you can know I am safe and happy. I'm glad you insisted on Japanese school, Dad, and I'm grateful the language came easily to me. I don't know where I'll be going, but I will write again as soon as I have more information. Please don't be sad. This war can't last forever, and I'm glad to finally feel I have something significant to offer. Please write as soon as you can.

James

All five family members stood there, staring at the letter but not saying a word. Mr. Thorne would be disappointed too. He'd been hoping James might arrive by harvest time.

As Rose placed the letter back in the envelope, she became aware that Mrs. Thorne was crying. No one seemed to know what to do, so they all just stood there waiting—awkwardly trying to remain respectful. Mr. Thorne pocketed his son's letter and put an arm around his wife to comfort her. Had Russell Thorne been wounded?

Mrs. Thorne glanced their way, then turned and headed back to her house.

Mr. Thorne walked over to them. "Is your son all right?"

Dad explained the content of James' letter and then asked Mr. Thorne the same question.

"Russell is alive, but he's been taken prisoner. We should have received notice months ago that he was missing in action. I don't understand why we didn't." He shook his head. "Perhaps it's a blessing. We wouldn't have known if he was dead or alive. At least this way, we … he—"

The man pressed his lips together and gazed off into the distance, a furrow on his brow as deep as the ones in his fields. Finally, he took a deep breath and let out a sigh. Then he sniffed. "He and his buddy, also from here—Bertram Johnson—both captured. I need to visit the Johnsons, see if they've heard from Bert. And I need to go tell Russell's sisters." He cleared his throat. "Let's call it a day. Looks like rain might be comin', anyway." He turned and walked back to the farmyard without expressing any thoughts on the fact that James would not be coming for harvest.

When Mr. Thorne was out of earshot, Dad picked up his hoe. "Let's finish this row."

They all prepared for bed in silence that evening, torn between their happiness and pride in James' assignment and their sorrow that he wouldn't be joining them. They were also fearful for the Thorne family. Even with so little access to the news, they knew many soldiers did not survive POW camps. After they all settled into their beds, Rose thought she heard Mama let out a little sob. Then Dad spoke, just loud enough for all to hear.

"The Thornes have a son serving our country. Now, so do we. Our son is safer than their son. Let's be proud of James. Let's be thankful for this. Let's be good workers to show our support. Let's pray we will all be reunited soon."

Mama's sniffling diminished.

Just before Rose dozed off, her father whispered ever so softly, "*Shakata ga nai.*"

The following Sunday, Mr. Thorne and Mrs. Johnson both stood and requested prayer for their sons who'd been taken captive. Though Mr. Thorne merely said, "enemy forces," Mrs. Johnson specified, "by the Japanese." Immediately, Mrs. Pierce and a young lady next to her—her daughter, Rose assumed—turned and glared at the Onishi family. Rose quickly bent to tie her shoe. She had no desire to know who else might be staring at them. Would this be the end of their dubious welcome?

After a few more requests arose for the sick, for a good harvest, and for the return of Mr. Dickerson's prize goat which had wandered off, the pastor led the congregation in a heartfelt prayer. He prayed for Russell Thorne and Bert Johnson by name, asking God to protect them from harm, bolster their faith, and preserve their lives.

The goat was never mentioned.

CHAPTER TWENTY

After six weeks in the hospital, Rusty's eyesight was almost normal. He bragged to Nurse Evelyn that he'd guessed her hair color correctly—light brown and curly. He was eating two square meals a day and, while still too weak to move around, he could feel his strength growing each day. He wrote a letter home, assuring his family he felt fine even though his shaky handwriting would likely give him away. In his seventh week, he was able to take short walks down the hallway.

The Bowen Hospital had withstood heavy bombardment during the battle of Hong Kong. Rusty learned the original patients had been killed in their beds on that awful day, the staff beaten, taken hostage, and forced to care for wounded Japanese soldiers. Now the beds were occupied by prisoners of war, many of whom would never make it out alive. Those well enough to be discharged left with heavy hearts. Even Rusty's doctor, a prisoner himself, was apologetic.

"I'm sorry, Thorne. This will be your last injection," he said after eight weeks. "I hate what I'm sending you back to. But you are far from death now. Many others are not. We need your bed."

"Thanks, Doc. I know I'd be dead by now without you."

"You got here right on time." The older man shook his head sadly. "Others weren't as fortunate."

Nurse Evelyn handed Rusty a clean, folded blanket. "Goodbye, Rusty. Take this with you, and remember us."

Too overcome to speak, Rusty merely nodded and accepted the gift. He held it to his nose and breathed in the smell of it, knowing it would bring comfort if he could manage to hang onto it. He tried not to think about what he was returning to—starvation, filth, disease, lice, and brutality. He made up his mind to focus on seeing Bert and the other men again. Though still underweight, Rusty would now be the strong one. He could encourage the other men to the best of his ability and help keep them going. The snippets of war news he'd been able to glean did not bode well for Japan. He'd be able to give the men hope that surely, their captors would soon be defeated.

Rusty was surprised to discover he was being taken back to Sham Shui Po, which had now been combined with Northpoint prison. He braced himself. The beautiful place in which he'd spent his first weeks had become even more decrepit, the men more desperate. Would they be jealous of Rusty's relatively good health and the bit of meat on his bones? *Help me, God, to give them hope.*

Bert was the first to greet him. "Hey, Tubby."

If it hadn't been for knowing Bert's voice, Rusty wasn't sure he'd recognize his friend. Bert reminded him of a snakeskin he'd once found in his mother's garden, transparent and left behind to decompose. As though the slightest breeze would turn him to dust. Rusty tried to hide his shock as the two men embraced.

"I wouldn't wish you back here for anything ... but gosh, it's good to see you." Bert wiped a tear from his cheek.

The two friends spent the rest of that day filling each other in on the weeks they'd been apart. Bert couldn't get enough. He kept asking about the food, the nurses, the clean sheets. Rusty wasn't sure how helpful it was to keep describing it over and over, but when the other men gathered around, hungry for more, he told it again and again. Most important was his letter from home, which he read aloud.

"If the army could get Mum's letter to me, they know where we are, fellas. They've likely gotten word to your families. Your loved ones know you're alive."

Several men brushed tears from their cheeks.

"Best thing we can do for them is survive. If that means folding up your pride and putting it away until this ends, so be it. Do what you have to do. Your dignity will be waiting for you, safe and sound, when the war ends."

By the next day, the old familiar hunger had returned, and Rusty was once again counting flea bites, though they would soon be too numerous to track. As the weather turned cooler, some relief was to be found from the heat and bugs. But it was impossible to keep such thin bodies warm, especially at night. Even though the men continued to sleep huddled together on the floor, as many as ten of them died every day. It made no sense that some were taken to the hospital and others left to die. Morale had never been so low. Rusty himself despaired of making any difference at all. *Please*, he begged God. *Send an angel of mercy. Deliver us somehow!*

Then one day, his prayer was answered.

Hope arrived in the form of Red Cross packages. Although the guards kept most of them, each prisoner was given one parcel. Rusty carried his to the barracks and sat on a bunk, simply staring at it. Beneath the words *Canadian Red Cross Society*, he read, *Comité international de la Croix-Rouge*. Below that, *Geneve-Transit, Suisse*. The cardboard itself could be used for any number of things—to lie or sit on, to make a pair of primitive shoes, or even to write a letter home. The other men tore into theirs like boys on Christmas morning. "Thank you, Lord," Rusty breathed. Did the people who had assembled these parcels have any idea how they represented life itself? How they felt like love?

Then he opened his own and took each item out, one at a time. A one-ounce packet of salt and pepper lay on top, making Rusty laugh. Did it really matter to a starving man if he had such extras? Oddly, it made him feel human. Like he mattered to someone. He found a tin of sardines, another of corned beef, one of ABC salmon, and one of KAM. A six-ounce bag of coffee and an eight-ounce bag of sugar made him think of his parents doing without coffee and sugar back home. He pictured Dad valiantly trying to enjoy unsweetened Postum instead and Mum making her own tea from the chamomile she grew in her garden and dried each summer.

Boxes of raisins, prunes, and biscuits came next. Butter in a tin. A box of hard Maple Leaf cheese. Soap, blessed soap! Rusty raised it to his nose and breathed deeply. A large tin of KLIM powdered milk. The name the Borden company had chosen—*milk* spelled backward—was not exactly creative. But the product was more than welcome, and the tins themselves would later be flattened and crimped together to create tools such as miniature shovels. The biggest treat, an enormous Jersey Milk chocolate bar, rounded out his parcel. He promised himself he'd eat only one small square a day.

The parcels made a world of difference in the camp. The men knew someone was aware of their plight. Somebody cared. The food that filled their stomachs, if only for a short while, nourished their souls even more. Eyes that had grown dull now shone with life again. An air of hope permeated the bleak atmosphere. Even the guards were happier, producing a couple of can openers for the men to pass around. Rusty chose not to dwell on the parcels that had made their way to the guards' quarters.

Their children are probably needy and hungry, too, he told himself. *Be thankful for what you have. Besides, if it puts them in a better mood, it's better for everyone.*

Each day's bite of chocolate brought a different treasured memory to Rusty's heart and mind. Chocolate had been a rare treat growing up through the Depression, so the memories were specific and came keenly to the forefront. Eating his sisters' homemade brownies with the family while they all gathered around the radio listening to *Amos 'n' Andy*. Warm chocolate pudding at Grandma Thorne's house after school. A box of chocolates for the whole family to share on Christmas Day. The cake Mum used to make with leftover mashed potatoes and Hershey's cocoa. Steaming cups of hot chocolate around a bonfire on a chilly fall evening following a hayride with his church youth group. Going to the movies with Susie or with Bert and sharing a candy bar.

As tempting as it became to eat more than one day's allotment, Rusty found himself cherishing the memories more than the chocolate itself, making it easier to wait. He'd hold each day's memory close to his heart until it was time to see what the next day's bite would bring.

In some strange way he could not explain even to himself, Rusty sensed that these precious experiences from his past were more than mere memories. They held a key to his future as well.

By the time Rusty reached his last square of chocolate, he'd eaten all his other items. Even the soap had dwindled to a sliver. He held the chocolate for what felt like a sacred moment, wishing he could simply carry it around in a pocket, knowing how ridiculous and wasteful that would be. Sitting on a stump in the corner of the camp, a large roll of barbed wire nearby, he stared at the chocolate on the palm of his hand, contemplating how sweet it would taste and wondering which new, forgotten memory it might evoke.

When he raised his head, one of the same guards who had kicked Eli stared at him from a few feet away. In a blur, the guard's steel-toed boot shot out in the direction of Rusty's hand, hitting the protruding wrist bone so hard Rusty heard a definite crack. The chocolate went flying, landing in the dirt a few paces away.

The guard laughed uproariously. He took a moment to step on the chocolate, grinding it into the ground for good measure. Then he snickered as he walked away, convincing Rusty that he'd forever remember the sound of Satan's laughter. Hatred churned inside him like a pot of week-old coffee boiling over a campfire, dark and thick. With his right wrist throbbing, he waited until the guard disappeared around the corner. Then he inched his way to the chocolate, and with his left hand, peeled it from the ground.

His words to the men when he'd returned from the hospital with a full belly haunted him now. *Fold up your dignity and put it in a safe place until the war is over.* He began picking dirt and sand out of the chocolate. Then he slowly placed it on his tongue, where he let it melt and slide down his throat, taking bits of dirt with it. The remaining pebbles, he spit out. Then he closed his eyes and focused on the taste of the chocolate, waiting for the memory that would be sure to accompany it.

It came suddenly, like a snake from under a rock.

He is eight years old, standing in his parents' living room, a piece of stolen baking chocolate melting on his tongue. Guilt seeps into his heart even as the chocolate makes its way to his stomach. Ignoring the guilt, he licks his fingers before opening the big family Bible in search of his favorite picture—David nailing Goliath with one of his five smooth stones.

Instead, the book falls open to a picture of Jesus hanging on the cross, torn and bloody. The caption below reads, *"Father, forgive them, for they know not what they do."*

CHAPTER TWENTY-ONE

A s the orderly at the infirmary placed a primitive splint on Rusty's
wrist, he carried on a conversation with the armed guard standing
at the door. The mere sound of the Japanese language made Rusty want
to vomit as his insides churned with hatred.

His thoughts turned to Susie's current beau, the new doctor back
home in Spruceville. How many fractured wrists had that young
man treated in his sterile office, carefully applying snow-white strips
of gauze dipped in plaster of Paris? How many young ballplayers or
cowboys had he sent home with pain killers and warnings to be more
careful? Would they garner admiration from all their buddies, collect
signatures on their casts from all the girls? Rusty had never broken
anything before. He'd had no idea how much it hurt, and there would
be no medicine to ease the pain. The orderly and the guard laughed
together as Rusty walked away.

"I can't do it anymore, Bert," he told his friend back at the barracks.
"When we first came here, I thought it would be smart to learn a few
phrases in Japanese. I never did."

"Yeah. Still would be smart, I guess."

"Now it makes me sick just to hear it."

"I know." Bert stared off into the distance and sighed. "Remember
those missionaries who visited our church when we were kids?"

"We saw a few over the years."

"True. Well, one couple stands out to me. I can't even remember
where they served, but they told a story about speaking English and
having the natives hear them in their own tongue. That story always
fascinated me."

Rusty hummed a noncommittal response. He remembered the story well enough but wasn't sure he liked where Bert was going with it.

"They didn't even know the language! How does that happen?"

Rusty shrugged. He wished Bert would stop.

"Do you suppose if we started telling these fellas about Jesus, they'd hear it in Japanese?"

Rusty raised his sore hand to his chest, supporting it under the elbow with his left hand. "You gonna try it?"

"Maybe I should. I was never much for sharing it with English-speaking people, though, so I can't say as I've had much practice."

"And you might just get yourself beat." Rusty sucked in a sharp breath at another stab of pain in his wrist.

"Try to keep your chin up, pal. It will heal."

It was mealtime, and Bert rose to get in line for their twice-daily offering of watery rice. "I'll bring your chow back with me. I think I saw some carrots on the supply truck this morning—maybe there'll be some in the soup tonight."

Just as Bert reached the door, Rusty called out, causing his friend to turn. "Don't go converting any of those heathens, Bert. As far as I'm concerned, they can all rot in hell."

Bert locked eyes with him, and for a moment, Rusty thought he was going to say something. Instead, Bert simply sighed and headed toward the chow line.

A week later, Rusty's heart surged when mail call produced another letter from home. Clearly opened and censored, the letter was dated the previous May. He pulled it carefully from its envelope and unfolded it, noting some lines had been blacked out.

Dearest Rusty,

We were so thrilled to receive your letter and the parcel of beautiful silk fabric. Knowing you are all right gives us so much joy. I hope to make myself a dress with my piece—the turquoise one. Shirley took the red and

Claire the purple. They'll make dresses for themselves and their girls in time for Dominion Day. Thank you so much for your thoughtful gift.

Bert will be pleased to know his father got three wild turkeys from the flock that's been hanging around his place. He gave us one for Easter—all dressed and ready to go! We had the girls and their families over and made short work of that bird. As always, you were greatly missed. We still have a little turkey soup left—maybe one bowl each for your dad and me.

We are pleased and grateful that our help has arrived and are settled into the cottage. Naturally, we hoped for a few strong young men, but unfortunately, that was not an option.

Here, a couple of lines had been blacked out. Curious to know what his mother could possibly have written that wouldn't pass his own country's censorship, Rusty held the paper up to the light and turned it every which way. It didn't help. He kept reading.

They have no experience, so it is slow going, but they are hard workers and smart. We're confident they'll be up to speed by midsummer, when it really counts. Their daughter, Rose, is seventeen and their son Timothy, eleven. Very respectful young people. The whole family (except for the grandfather) comes to church with us, but I can't tell if they truly understand what it means to follow Jesus.

Speaking of which, I trust you are leaning hard on your faith wherever this war has taken you, my son. You know, Dad and I did our best to give you a good foundation, but it's up to you to keep growing in your faith by reading God's word and talking to him. On difficult days, tell him how you feel. He's big enough to handle it, and he already knows, anyway. You can't fool him. Stand up for truth and justice whenever possible—but if you're treated unfairly, remember that forgiveness is the mightiest power on earth.

We love you and pray for you daily.
Mother

Rusty replaced the letter in its envelope and jammed it inside his shirt. What did his mother know about it? What was the worst offense she'd ever needed to forgive? His father, for using the odd cuss word when a piece of equipment broke down? Rusty, for the time he sat on her sofa with a pocketful of overripe chokecherries that left a permanent stain? Justina Pierce, for her gossip and her rude comments at Jack's funeral?

Jack.

Jack had shattered his mother's heart over and over. When he talked back, when he skipped school, when he got caught smoking behind the barn and drinking behind the pool hall. When he stole tobacco from the general store. When he cracked Peggy Thompson's bedroom window throwing a stone in hopes that he could attract her attention and convince her to sneak out with him. His mother's heart must have broken over unanswered prayers, over all the misdeeds she knew must be happening. When Jack finally left home and didn't send word for months, Rusty had seen his mother on her knees at her bedside, weeping and beseeching God to save her son. Then, when the final word came—Jack's body found beaten in a back alley—Rusty was convinced it would be the end of his mother. Of both his parents, really.

But they'd surprised him. Oh, they'd grieved, all right. But as Rusty observed them over the course of the next months and years, his parents reminded him of King David. David pleaded so passionately with God to save his sick child that his servants feared what might happen should the child die. The child did die, but David rose and washed his face and looked to the future. Rusty's parents had clung still more tightly to their faith and to each other.

Rusty pulled out the letter and read it again. This time, it left him less angry. Mum did know what it was to forgive. She'd clearly forgiven God for not answering her prayers, and she continued to make petitions to him. She'd forgiven Jack. Probably even Mrs. Pierce. It was the Justina Pierces of the world, the bitter and vindictive ones, who had probably never learned to forgive. They carried their pain around with them like soldiers with gaping wounds, allowing those injuries to inflict more pain on others. Instead of healing, the wounds only festered and grew. Rusty had no idea who had hurt Mrs. Pierce or how, but he knew he did not want to be like her.

It seemed so obvious in others. But how did any of these examples relate to the cruelty Rusty now found himself subjected to, day in and day out? The injustice he witnessed all around him? Even if he could manage to forgive the Japanese for what they did to him personally, was it his place to extend forgiveness on behalf of others? Surely, to do so would seem like yet another cruel mockery, the invalidating of others' suffering. Forgiveness was not really his to grant. Was it?

I can't do it, God. I don't even want to. Make me willing to be willing.

He read his mother's letter once more, and by the time he reached the end, great tears fell down his face. He could almost hear her voice. *Forgiveness is the mightiest power on earth.*

Rusty clutched the letter to his heart and sobbed like a baby. *Help me, God. Help me.*

CHAPTER TWENTY-TWO

If Rose thought the weeding and thinning of the sugar beets was hard work, it was nothing compared to harvest. The one redeeming feature was the teamwork of the community and the air of excitement that went with it. All the farmers came together with their equipment—those with tractors as well as those with horse teams—and their workers. They'd converge on one field until done, then move on to the next. As grueling as the dusk-to-dawn hours were and as backbreaking the work, Rose couldn't help finding the whole process fascinating.

Mr. Thorne had explained how the sugar beets produced not only sugar but also industrial alcohol used in the manufacturing of munitions and synthetic rubbers. "You are all doing important work for the war effort," he announced as he organized everyone and assigned tasks.

First, the roots of the plants would be lifted by a plow pulled by tractor or horses. The rest was done by hand. One laborer would grab the beets by their leaves, then knock them together to shake free loose soil. Then he'd lay them in a row, root to one side, greens to the other. This was Rose's job. Even Tim got fast at it after some practice.

A second worker equipped with a beet hook followed behind and would lift the beet and swiftly chop the crown and stems from the root with a single action. Working this way, he would leave a row of beets that could be forked into the back of a truck box. Rose thought the beet hook looked like the grim reaper's sickle with its sharp hook on one end. She shuddered at how fast the more experienced workers used it.

When they broke for lunch, Rose sought out Linda, and they sat on the ground at the edge of a field eating sandwiches and apples they'd packed before sunup.

"How're you holding up, Linda?" Rose brushed her hands on her overalls in a futile attempt to clean them.

"Okay." Linda removed the brace from one leg and shook it. Small stones and clods of dirt fell from it, then she strapped it back on. She finished her food and lay back to rest.

Rose stayed seated, but she had no energy for idle conversation either. Even Tim was too tired to run around or play. He lay with his head in Mama's lap until a horn signaled it was time to return to work.

Spending their days half bent over, straddling the rows of beets, repeating the same motions over and over, gave Rose a lot of time to think. In her mind, she would often formulate letters to Freda or James with the intent of writing them later. By evening, she could barely find enough energy to wash and fall into bed.

Thankfully, all work stopped on Sunday. The Onishis still attended church with the Thornes. Rose was learning the hymns, her eyes following the notes as she sang. In the back of her mind, her fingers would fill in the extra piano notes to accompany the bland chords of the pump organ. Oh how she yearned to bring those notes to life!

On this particular Sunday, the pastor chose "Onward, Christian Soldiers" for an opening hymn, no doubt to bolster patriotism in these families who feared for the lives of loved ones overseas. When the hymn ended, Rose took her place on the hard, wooden pew and prepared to fight sleep through the sermon. Instead, the pastor made her sit up straighter when he brought a different meaning to the old song.

"We Christians need to unite as one and form a great army with the help of the Holy Spirit to fight against our *real* enemies, Satan and his demons." The man raised one finger heavenward. "The gates of hell cannot prevail against the church, the body of Christ. The battle is the Lord's. Satan has been defeated on the cross. Hallelujah! We are victorious by the blood of Jesus. We are not afraid."

If Satan was already defeated, why did Christians still need to fight him? And what did any of that have to do with her? It was all she and her family could manage to keep moving through the beet fields most days.

The service ended with all six verses of another rousing hymn about warfare, "Am I a Soldier of the Cross?" Again, Rose filled in the missing notes, the fingers of her right hand moving almost imperceptibly on the back of the pew in front of her. But when they reached verse three, Rose stopped singing and focused on the words.

Sure I must fight if I would reign;
Increase my courage, Lord.
I'll bear the toil, endure the pain,
Supported by Thy Word.

For some mysterious reason, those words sank into Rose's heart and kept repeating throughout the afternoon. Bearing the toil and enduring the pain fit with her parents' and her grandfather's philosophy, but the song offered much more. Support from the word of God. Courage. An opportunity to reign. What did it mean?

The whole family took Sunday afternoon naps to restore their energy for another grueling week ahead. In the evening, Rose sat at the little table in their cabin and penned a letter to Freda.

Sweet Friend,

Sorry I haven't written in so long. We are unbelievably busy, and I've never worked so hard in my life. I will never take another spoonful of sugar for granted as long as I live! You have no idea what goes into it. The Thornes and other farmers work just as hard, if not harder, so I can't say I hold any ill will against them. Plus, their son Russell (they call him "Rusty"—isn't that funny?) is in a prison camp somewhere.

We've received word from James. He won't be joining us after all, as he's been put to work as a translator. He's happy and that makes me glad, but I sure miss him, and we could use his help. Once harvest is done, Tim will be allowed to go to school. I don't know about me. The Thornes are not under any legal obligation to send me, and the one-room school down the road only goes to Grade Eight, anyway. I'll need to attend the high school in town if I'm ever going to finish Grade Twelve.

Enough about me. I want to hear everything that's going on. I was surprised you decided to work instead of starting college, but your job at the department store sounds kind of fun. I hope you'll soon work your way up the ranks and be a buyer for the ladies' fashion department or something! Do you see any of the old gang? Have you seen any movies lately? It would be swell to see a movie, but it seems those days are behind me. At least, until this stupid war ends and we can come home.

It means the world that you are keeping my concert dress safe, Freda. When I told Mama you had it, she let a tear slip down her cheek—something she almost never does, at least not in a way that she would let me see. So you know it means a lot to her too. Hopefully, I will get to wear that beautiful dress—somewhere—before I'm too old. No danger of getting too fat for it, that's for sure. What I wouldn't give to share a juicy burger and strawberry milkshake with you at Yoshitos' soda fountain again.

Sorry to complain. I know I should be more grateful. Another Japanese girl, Linda, lives on a farm down the road. Her legs are in braces from polio, but she works alongside us. I know my lot in life could be far worse, and I try to find something to be thankful for each day. Please fill me in on the latest movies and hit songs and singers and bands. I don't know anything. Dad gets Mr. Thorne's newspapers when he's done with them, but they're all about the war and politics. We don't even have a radio.

There I go, griping again. I'll stop now. Write soon. I miss you like crazy, but I guess that's obvious.

Love,

Rose

A supper and dance at the community hall celebrated the end of harvest, and amazingly, the Japanese families were included. Mama had been saving her sugar rations, and she and Rose spent the day making sweet *mochi* to take to the potluck. When the small, sweet balls were ready and carefully covered with a clean towel, preparations were made for everyone to take baths in the tin tub. When Rose's turn came, she scrubbed every inch of herself vigorously, paying special attention to her hands and nails. Sadly, only time away from the fields would truly rid her formerly delicate hands of the dirt stains and calluses. Rose took comfort in knowing she wouldn't be the only girl at the party with roughened hands.

The first thing Rose spotted when they walked into the hall was a piano. Old, worn, and pushed into one corner, it did not appear to be used much. Throughout the evening, her gaze kept returning to the lonely, forgotten instrument. Following the pastor's prayer of thanksgiving and blessing on the food, everyone ate more than their fill. Mr. Thorne, hair slicked back and dressed in his Sunday best suit with a brown tie, gave a speech to thank and congratulate the community for working together to harvest everyone's crops. "A special thank you to our new Japanese Canadian friends." He placed both hands on the lectern and glanced toward the Onishi family before taking in the rest of the room. "This work was new to you, and I can appreciate that. But you pulled your weight, and we couldn't have done it without you."

A round of applause went up, not necessarily the most enthusiastic, but clearly heartfelt from those who participated. Rose happened to glance at Mrs. Pierce as the clapping faded. She sneered at Mr. Thorne, her arms firmly folded across her chest. Next to her sat Spruceville's doctor and his new wife. While the doctor nodded and clapped politely, his wife glared at Rose with an expression easy to interpret—sheer contempt. Rose averted her eyes, determined to ignore the woman she'd heard referred to as Susie.

After the meal, the dancing began.

"With our usual band members all overseas," the emcee announced, "we've pulled together some old cronies to provide our music tonight. Come on up, fellas."

Four older gentlemen stepped to the platform and picked up instruments—an accordion, a guitar, a banjo, and a violin that reminded Rose yet again of Freda.

"Ladies and gentlemen, I give you the Plow Boys!"

Laughter and applause filled the room as the four men began to play rousing tunes like "Purtiest Gal in the Country" and "Joke on the Puppy." Couples quickly got up to dance. Little children began jigging in glee. None of it was Rose's first choice in music, but she couldn't stop tapping her toe and smiling at the happiness it generated. She was relieved no one asked her to dance.

When the band took a break, Rose's mother turned to her.

"Did you see piano?"

Rose nodded. Did her mother really think she might not have noticed it?

"You should play." Mama nodded encouragingly. "Surprise everyone."

Was Mama serious? Rose couldn't help letting a grin escape her lips at the thought. But she hadn't touched a piano for nearly nine months! And the room was full of people.

Mama smiled and kept nodding. "Go. Go!"

"I'll go with you, sis." Tim took Rose's hand and pulled her to her feet. Together, they slowly walked to the corner of the room where the piano stood. When they were about six steps away from it, Mrs. Pierce's daughter slipped onto the piano stool and began to pound out an error-ridden rendition of "Beer Barrel Polka" that would make the Andrews Sisters cringe. Rose stopped short. She pulled Tim back toward their parents and took a seat next to Ojiisan.

To Rose's surprise, Ojiisan spoke to her in English, something she had heard him do only a handful of times. "Good thing other girl get there before you, Rozu. Piano bad out of tune."

CHAPTER TWENTY-THREE

Rose shivered. The stove in the little cabin burned wood day and night, but still, the Onishi family huddled together inside its thin plywood walls. Mr. Thorne must have forgotten his plan to insulate it for winter. Dad said it was because the man was distracted by worry for his son. Rose had never experienced such cold, and from what church people told her, it was only the beginning. Some of them had organized a clothing drive, and the Japanese Canadians had been on the receiving end of warm coats and boots, homemade mittens, and scarves.

Tim had been attending the one-room school down the road since harvest ended, and he loved to go. The schoolhouse was warm, for one thing. He easily caught up to the others in Grade Four and excelled in his studies. The other students, for the most part, treated him the same as any other kid. He came home with stories about being chosen first for baseball teams at recess and about his teacher praising his spelling skills.

Rose had been set to start school as well, a prospect she welcomed with nervous excitement. Would the Manitoba curriculum include any music, and would her credits transfer to ensure she graduated in June? Then her mother developed pneumonia. Dad and Mr. Thorne decided Rose should stay home and help while Mama's recovery dragged on. During the worst nights, no one slept because of Mama's incessant coughing. Now her coughing had lessened, but the struggle had left Mama weak and thin.

Rose was too exhausted to feel sorry for herself. She spent her days managing tasks she had only assisted with before—cooking meals, cleaning the cabin, and washing the family's clothes. Everything took longer than it had back home, and Rose had to learn how to keep the woodstove stoked and how to heat water for every task—after pumping it at the well and carrying it back to the cabin. Mama wasn't always patient with the instructions she gave from her bunk, but the days she gave no instruction were far more concerning.

Rose feared *shikata ga nai* would become her own mantra. *It cannot be helped?* Of course, it could be helped! Surely, it could be helped. Couldn't it?

One Sunday after church, Mrs. Thorne gave Rose a used Bible. She'd never had one of her own, and she couldn't honestly say she enjoyed reading it or that she understood much of it. It sounded too much like the Shakespearean plays they'd been forced to study in school. Still, Rose enjoyed carrying the Bible with her to church and finding the passages the pastor preached from—it gave her something to focus on whenever Mrs. Pierce or her daughter glared.

During one of these Sunday sermons, Rose stumbled upon a Bible verse she decided to use as her own. It sounded so much better than "it cannot be helped." It came from the book of Isaiah.

But they that wait upon the Lord shall renew their strength; they shall mount up with wings as eagles; they shall run, and not be weary; and they shall walk, and not faint.

Rose didn't really know what it meant to "wait upon the Lord," but if she kept listening and reading, she might learn. The Bible—especially the book of Psalms—was rich with verses that encouraged her more than her parents' philosophy ever had.

The one positive side to Mama's illness was that Rose now accompanied Mrs. Thorne to town on Saturday mornings to do the family's shopping. Rose finally glimpsed the interior of the grocery store and post office. She visited the drugstore to pick up medicine for her mother and looked longingly at the soda fountain with its shiny, round stools topped in red vinyl. She caught a glimpse of style trends from the mannequins in the window of Helen's Dress Shop. Best of all, she got her own library card and began checking out her three-book limit at each opportunity.

As winter set in, however, these trips dwindled to once a month.

On the ride home one Saturday in early December, Rose cradled two books on her lap while she opened the third—Daphne Du Maurier's *Rebecca*.

"I've heard of it." Mrs. Thorne glanced over at Rose and smiled. "A bit creepy for my taste, I'm afraid."

Rose closed the cover. "You might be right." Next in the pile was *The Hobbit*, which she held up. "I hope to read this one with Tim."

"Can't say I've read it yet." Mrs. Thorne paused, then chewed on her bottom lip a moment before speaking again. "Rose ... you know the schoolteachers are encouraging all the young people to write letters to our boys overseas, especially the prisoners. They need encouragement. If you'd like to write to Rusty, I could enclose your letter with mine."

Rose jerked her head toward Mrs. Thorne. "What would I say? I don't know him."

"That doesn't matter, really. You could tell him about the books you're reading, your family, your work. Any news from home is a Godsend to the POWs. Only—there is one thing." Mrs. Thorne hesitated.

"Yes?" Rose waited while Mrs. Thorne focused on the road in front of her.

"The chance of letters actually reaching the prisoners is slim at best—especially if you mention the war or anything of a political nature."

"I really don't even know what's going on with the war." Rose watched the fence posts going past outside her side window. "It all seems so far away."

"I understand. But ... maybe ... it's best, if you do write, to only use your first name. Not your family name."

Suddenly, Rose understood all too well what Mrs. Thorne tried so carefully to say. Her family name was that of the enemy.

Though she promised to think about it, Rose couldn't imagine what she might say to Russell Thorne or any other soldier.

Christmas 1942 came and went like any other day for the Onishi family. They spent it stoking the stove, bundled in all their layers of clothing. One January morning before work began, Mr. Thorne knocked on the door of the cabin. Rose's father opened it and invited him in. The only thing Rose had to offer him was a cup of hot *genmaicha*—a beverage made with brown rice and green tea.

"That's kind of you, but I just finished breakfast." Mr. Thorne removed his hat and took a seat at the table, following Dad's lead. "How is Mrs. Onishi holding up?"

"Getting better." Dad stated it with confidence.

"Good, glad to hear it." Mr. Thorne cleared his throat. "Anna— that is, Mrs. Thorne—is concerned about the well-being of your family and asked me to visit."

Mrs. Thorne had come by the cabin earlier in the week—the first time since last summer—with some canned tomatoes and pickles.

Mr. Thorne continued. "I know this cabin is difficult to heat. We have two empty bedrooms in our house. One was our daughters' room, and one was our sons'—that is, Rusty and Jack shared it until Jack … um, left us." He cleared his throat again. "What I'm trying to say is, Mrs. Thorne and I think it would be a lot more practical for you all to come stay in those rooms for the winter. They're cold now, but if we open the doors, they'll warm up in no time."

Dad asked Ojiisan in Japanese if he understood what the man had said. Ojiisan responded with a nod and a stream of Japanese too fast for Rose to follow.

Mama was sitting up on her bunk. She, too, spoke to Dad in Japanese. This time, Rose could pick up enough to know her mother was not keen on the idea of moving into the Thornes' house. "This is Mrs. Thorne's idea?"

Mr. Thorne nodded. "Yes. I should have thought of it myself, really—I'm sorry I didn't. It's up to you, of course."

The eye contact between her parents spoke volumes. "We will need to discuss," Dad said.

"Certainly." Mr. Thorne stood and replaced his hat. Was he relieved her family had not jumped at the opportunity? "Take all the time you need. If you decide to move in with us and later change your minds, the cottage is still yours—no hard feelings."

Rose had never heard of such a thing. Besides Linda's family, a half dozen other Japanese families and several single Japanese men had arrived to live and work in the community surrounding Spruceville. None of them shared homes with their white bosses. How would that work? Would they gather around the same table, eat the same food? Would the Onishis be expected to do all the household chores while the Thornes put their feet up? What would happen when the Thornes' daughters came to visit? Rose wished her father would ask more questions, but it was not her place to speak.

While she waited, she imagined living in the house. *Oh, please, God, let Dad and Mama say yes.* Rose had never ventured past the porch of the Thornes' home, but the amenities she'd taken for granted while growing up—a warm room, indoor plumbing, solid walls, and electricity—had all become luxuries beyond her reach since leaving Vancouver. She'd gladly cook and clean their house if she knew she could crawl into a real bed each night and have a little more privacy.

"Walk Tim to school, Rozu." Dad brushed a hand across his forehead.

Rose opened her mouth to argue but then thought better of it. The adults probably wanted to discuss this new development among themselves. She bundled up in her too-large winter coat and trudged down the road alongside her little brother.

"I don't need you to walk me to school." Tim kicked at a stone. "They want to talk about moving into the house, don't they?"

"Yep." When would she ever have a say in anything?

"What do you think they'll decide?"

"If I know Mama, we'll stay put." Rose pushed her hands deep into her pockets and balled them up for warmth.

"That's what I was thinking too. What would you pick?"

"I'd move in, of course. You?"

"Of course. Who wouldn't?"

Rose shrugged. "Mothers who value their own territory over privacy and comfort."

CHAPTER TWENTY-FOUR

Nothing more was said until the family gathered around their little table for the evening meal. Rose had been trying to glean something from her mother's expression all day, to no avail. She decided not to ask. The more time it took for her parents to announce their decision, the longer she could keep hoping—and she needed something for which to hope.

Once the rice was dished up, Dad cleared his throat. "Mr. Thorne and I talked some more while we worked today, and we've reached an agreement."

Rose and Tim glanced at each other, then waited for their father to continue.

"Your mother would rather stay here, in the cabin."

Even though she expected it, Rose's heart sank. She studied her lap, trying to conceal her disappointment and wishing Mr. Thorne had made his offer in private, so she wouldn't have even known about the possibility.

"So I will stay here with her," Dad continued. "Tim, you will share one of the bedrooms with Ojiisan. Rose will take the other."

Had she heard right? Rose lifted her head to look at her father, who nodded slightly. Mama's face remained unchanged.

Tim spoke first. "Really? B-but … that means they'll need to heat the bedrooms *and* the cabin!"

Rose wanted to shush him in case the adults hadn't thought of that while knowing full well they would have.

"It's okay with the Thornes." Dad picked up his chopsticks. "They feel strongly that Ojiisan at least should stay with them. Ojiisan doesn't want to go alone. Mama doesn't want to go. We'll try it for a while. Now eat your food. You're moving in tonight."

Rose barely had time to think about it any further. She and Tim took only minutes to put their belongings together and help Ojiisan pack his. Mama remained at the cabin while Dad walked with them to the back door of the Thornes' house and knocked. Mrs. Thorne opened the door wide. A white apron with a ruffled bottom covered most of her dress, and a kind smile covered most of her face.

"Come in, come in. I'm so glad you decided to join us." Her hand fluttered to her chest in a nervous fashion. "I don't know why we didn't think of this sooner—it makes sense, don't you think?"

Rose took in the large farm kitchen. She'd made the wrong assumption about indoor plumbing. Mrs. Thorne's sink boasted a hand-cranked pump instead of hot and cold taps like she'd assumed. Still, it was a real sink with a real drain. The room also contained an electric stove and icebox, a big table with six chairs, and a hutch displaying pretty dishes. Faded yellow curtains graced the window over the sink. A set of round tins painted with red strawberries sat lined up on the countertop.

"My father still lived with us before he passed." Mr. Thorne flicked the light switch off and on. "We're lucky he was progressive enough to insist on running electricity out here before the Depression hit. People thought he was crazy. But soon after that, no one could afford it. And now, with the war on, they've put a hold on running lines out to any more rural communities. Dad was smart to get us in on it when he did." He tapped his foot on a large square in the floor with a handle on one side. "Here's the cellar door—we've got potatoes, onions, carrots, and apples down there. And all of Anna's canning, of course." Mr. Thorne demonstrated how to lift the lid, and Rose peered into the hole. A ladder led to a dirt floor. The light from the kitchen illuminated shelves filled with preserves.

Mrs. Thorne nodded. "We put milk down there, too, in winter."

"Let us show you the rest of the house." Mr. Thorne replaced the lid to the cellar and waved a hand toward another door next to the stairs.

"Bathroom's there. We hope to modernize the plumbing if this war ever ends." Rose peered in to see a chemical toilet, a washstand with a basin and pitcher, and a large, galvanized tub with a drain to outside. It all seemed luxurious compared with what she had grown used to.

"This way to the living room."

Tim, Rose, and Ojiisan set their belongings down and followed the Thornes through a doorway off the kitchen.

"We use this room a little more now that winter's here. In the summer, we only come in here to turn the radio on and off. Or to get to the front door." Mrs. Thorne chuckled.

Rose ventured into the room, and suddenly, her heart pounded, and her knees became wobbly. Was she seeing things? Against the south wall, covered in framed family photos, its wood shiny with polish, stood a beautiful upright piano.

"Do ya see it, Rose?" Tim nudged his sister with a sharp elbow.

But Rose could only respond with a slight nod as she stared. The piano was beautiful, even prettier than the one they'd left behind— though she felt disloyal to think it. Fresh longing swelled in her heart. If this had been here all along, how had she never heard it, not even the previous summer when the windows would have been open? How long since it had been played? Her hands began to ache with yearning.

Mr. Thorne seemed oblivious to the fact that all four members of the Onishi family were staring at the piano. He walked over to it and began pointing out the photos displayed on top. The first, in a large frame, was a head-and-shoulders shot of a young soldier. "This is Rusty." He paused a moment, as though he wanted to say more, then cleared his throat and moved on. "These are our girls and their families. I think you've met them all."

Rose recognized younger versions of Claire and Shirley in graduation caps, followed by wedding pictures and a group picture that included all the grandchildren. Last, Mr. Thorne picked up a picture of a teenage boy posing on the back of a horse.

"This is our son, Jack. We lost him in thirty-five. He'd be ... oh, let's see ... Anna?"

"He'd be twenty-seven now." Mrs. Thorne spoke in little more than a whisper.

Rose sucked in a small breath. She'd heard hints about the Thornes having another son but hadn't known he was dead.

Dad spoke up. "I'm sorry for your loss. That must have been very difficult."

"Thank you." Mrs. Thorne stepped over to the piano, took the photo from her husband's hand, and wiped the surface of the glass with her apron before replacing it. "We do miss him. Every day. But we are more blessed than many others. God has given us two wonderful sons-in-law and lovely grandchildren."

"Well, let's go on up." Mr. Thorne stepped toward a staircase leading from between the living room and kitchen. His wife followed.

Rose didn't want to leave the room and surprised even herself when she blurted out, "Who plays the piano?"

Mrs. Thorne stopped and turned. "Oh … I play a little, although I can't say it's been touched since … gosh, I don't know when."

Mr. Thorne filled in her blank. "Last fall when Rusty was home."

"Yes, you're probably right. He's the one who took the most interest. The girls can pick out a hymn with one finger if they have the music in front of them. Rusty can play all four notes."

Rose wanted to cry. It hadn't been touched? *All four notes?*

"Oh, he can do better than that." Mr. Thorne chuckled. "He even fills in some of the extra little notes that aren't in the book. Right?"

His wife nodded. "That's right. He's definitely the most musically inclined in the family—too bad he got my short, stubby fingers instead of his dad's long ones!" She laughed and carried on up the stairs.

Rose followed last in the line, taking one more glance over her shoulder at the piano, not daring to hope she might be allowed to touch it. But why not? Clearly, the Thornes did not value it that highly. *No, don't hope for it. Don't even think about it.* She focused on climbing the narrow staircase.

At the top of the stairs, four doors led off a central landing, all but one wide open.

"Here's our room." Mr. Thorne pointed at one door through which Rose saw a bed covered in a patchwork quilt. He waved a hand toward the closed door. "That one's a linen closet."

"Mr. Onishi, Tim … this will be your room." Mrs. Thorne entered a room containing twin beds, a dresser, and a nightstand. "This is Rusty's. I've put away his things."

Ojiisan and Tim followed. Rose stayed in the doorway, her father behind her. The walls were bare except for an embroidered sampler that read, *God keeps his promises.*

Tim stepped to the window and pressed his face against the glass. "I think I can see my school from here—when it's daylight."

"That's right, you will." Mrs. Thorne smiled at Tim and walked across the hall to the last room. She pulled a string, and the room lit up. "You can use this one, Rose. I've used it for a sewing room but can't say I've done much sewing lately."

Rose followed. The walls, one of which slanted toward the ceiling from about halfway up, were papered in pink roses. Covering the double bed was a homemade quilt in shades of pink and pale green, the same shade of green as the curtains on the gabled window. A white dresser stood against one wall, complete with a large mirror. On the dresser top sat a white doily and a fancy dresser set—brush, comb, and hand mirror. A small closet was tucked into one corner, and beside that, Mrs. Thorne's treadle sewing machine. Next to the bed, a white nightstand held an electric lamp with a pink shade.

"This is lovely." Rose wanted to pinch herself. Would all this space really be hers alone? What was the catch?

"I'm glad you like it. Our girls never appreciated that wallpaper much. It dates back to their grandparents' day. But I like it. And it certainly seems appropriate for a girl named *Rose*, don't you think?"

Rose nodded. She had never liked her name, but in this moment, she could hardly believe her good fortune. It may not be home, but it was more than she'd had for nearly a year. She stayed in the room, sitting on the bed, simply looking around after everyone went back downstairs. When Dad, Ojiisan, and Tim returned with all their belongings, Dad dropped Rose's bag in her room and turned toward her.

"Goodnight, Rozu."

"Dad, are you sure Mama won't change her mind? She'd be so much more comfortable here."

"I know she would, Rozu. But you know your mother. Don't worry about us. I'm glad you and Ojiisan can stay here. Enjoy it."

Rose gripped her father's elbow. "Dad … I don't know what I'm supposed to do, exactly. Should I come back to the cabin in the morning to help Mama?"

"Your first duty is to Mrs. Thorne. Just get up early, get yourself ready for the day, and report to her. She'll tell you what to do. She's a good woman, Rozu. You can see that, yes?"

"Yes."

"And make sure your brother's ready for school on time."

"I'll make sure he stops by the cabin to say goodbye before he leaves."

"Yes, good. You have a good sleep tonight. I'll see you tomorrow." He turned to leave.

"Dad?"

Her father turned around in the doorway.

"Did you see the piano?" Rose whispered.

Dad nodded. "I know what you're thinking, Rozu. You must wait to be invited."

"But why would they ever invite me to play it when they don't know—"

"Shh. All in good time, my daughter. All in good time. Be patient. Be useful. Helpful. I know you will do us proud."

CHAPTER TWENTY-FIVE

R ose awoke the next morning more rested than she had in months.
The room had seemed exceptionally quiet, even with the door
open to let the warm air circulate. She dressed quickly and ventured
downstairs, thinking she might be the first up. She was mistaken.
Halfway down, she could see Mrs. Thorne seated at the kitchen table
where a steaming cup of tea sat beside a fat, open Bible. The framed
photo of Russell, which Rose had seen on the piano, now sat on the
kitchen table. Mrs. Thorne was writing but raised her head when Rose
reached the bottom.

"Good morning, Rose! Sleep well?"

"Yes ma'am. Very well, thank you."

"Help yourself to a cup of tea from the pot—cups are on the shelf
there. I'm just writing to Rusty. I keep his picture in front of me when
I write. I suppose that's a little silly, but it helps."

Guilt flooded Rose's mind as she found a cup and poured herself
some tea. She remembered Mrs. Thorne's request from weeks earlier
but had entirely dismissed the idea of writing a letter to the woman's
son. Now she regretted it. It might be sheer selfishness, but she'd do
just about anything to be in Mrs. Thorne's good graces if it meant
playing that piano. She glanced toward the living room door, but the
layout of the house didn't allow her to see the piano without actually
entering that room.

"I think I'm ready to write a letter to Russell now, Mrs. Thorne."

"That's lovely, dear!" Mrs. Thorne pushed a chair away from the
table with one foot, indicating Rose should sit. "You can start right
now, if you like. We don't usually eat breakfast until eight this time of

year, and I do enjoy this quiet time of the morning. Don't you?"

Rose nodded to be polite. She'd never been allowed to sleep late, and she'd spent nearly twelve years rising early to practice piano before breakfast. Mrs. Thorne pushed a piece of pale pink stationery and a pencil toward her. "Would you rather use a fountain pen? I think I can find another."

"This is fine." Rose placed her teacup on the table, sat, and took the pencil. She stared at the blank page, chewing on her lip. "I'm not sure what to say."

"Oh, just introduce yourself a bit. I usually say a little prayer before I start." Mrs. Thorne took a sip of tea. "It's not possible for me to know what my son will most need when—or if—he reads my words. But God already knows, and he can guide me." She returned to her writing. Occasionally, she'd turn to the Bible, read something, then keep writing.

Rose studied the photograph of Russell Thorne. He had his mother's round face and fair hair, his father's eyes. The smile was all his own, though. The overall package was definitely attractive. But then, most fellows looked handsome in their uniforms, didn't they? She poised her pencil over the page. *Okay, God. If she's right, please give me some words for Rusty too. Something he can smile about.* She began to write.

Dear Russell,

My name is Rose, and I have been living and working on your family's farm since last May. Your mother suggested I write you, that it might be encouraging to you somehow. I don't really know what to say, but I will try. Your parents are gracious, kind people. I've met your sisters and their children too. They all miss you, of course. People at church speak highly of you.

It's been an education for my family and me to learn about sugar beet farming, although my grandfather (who is here with us) has always grown a small plot of vegetables. He helped your mother start a strawberry patch too. You can look forward to enjoying some berries when you return home. It's a lovely farm—I'm especially fond of the apple tree in the middle of the

*front yard. It was in bloom when we arrived, and we helped pick the apples
in September. When we first came, the big red barn with the milk cow and
the kittens seemed so like a childhood storybook I used to read repeatedly.
Can't remember the name of it now, but I loved that story.*

*My little brother Tim is eleven and attends your old school down the
road. He's especially taken with Lady, and she seems to like him as well, if
an eagerness to fetch sticks and incessant tailwagging whenever he's around
are any indication. Your mother says Lady is your dog, though. I'm sure
she'll forget all about Tim when you come back.*

*I am going on eighteen. I'm afraid I can't fill you in on the latest movies
and such. I haven't seen one in ages. Perhaps that doesn't interest you,
anyway. I like musicals best, but then—I am a pianist.*

Given that her piano career had been interrupted by the war and
she wasn't supposed to mention the war, she had little more to say.
Should she ask Russell questions about himself? Chances are, he'd not
be able to write back, anyway. Even if he could, he probably couldn't
give away much about where he was or what it was like. Best to keep
it generic.

*Who's your favorite singer or band? Obviously, I like Bing Crosby and
Frank Sinatra. The Ink Spots and Glenn Miller and Tommy Dorsey. And
you can't beat the Andrews Sisters for tight harmonies, can you? But honestly,
it's classical music that carries me away. Chopin and Bach, especially. I'm
not afraid of a little Gershwin, though. I guess I'm rambling. Your mother
tells me you play piano too. I hope I get to hear you play when you come
home, if we're still here. I guess your family won't need us anymore then,
though. That will be a great day for everyone, won't it?*

*Well, I don't know what else to say. I hope you are well and that my silly
letter brings a little joy to your day. I will write again when I can think of
more to tell you.*

Sincerely,
Rose

Just as Rose finished, the men clomped down the stairs. Mrs. Thorne began gathering the writing materials together. Rose read her letter over quickly and handed it to Mrs. Thorne.

"I hope this is all right."

"I'm sure it's fine." She took the letter from Rose, folded it, and put it with her own. "I'll send these off today. You can help me put Rusty's care package together if you like."

"Sure."

While Tim was at school, Rose and Mrs. Thorne baked a batch of oatmeal cookies and packaged them along with three pairs of wool socks Mrs. Thorne had knitted for Russell. She placed the letters on top, then they wrapped it all in brown paper.

"How do you know where to send this?" Rose held her finger on the string so Mrs. Thorne could tie a knot.

"The Red Cross sorts it out."

"Even for prisoners?"

Mrs. Thorne nodded. "They said on the news that Japan's emperor agreed to the Geneva Convention of 1929. It dictates that prisoners must be allowed to send and receive mail from family." Though she spoke with confidence, she must have recognized the glimmer of doubt on Rose's face. "I'm just going to pray this finds its way to our Rusty—on angel's wings, if necessary."

Late one night, Rose crawled out of bed to use the bathroom. As she passed the Thornes' bedroom, she thought she overheard them talking and stepped back. Both knelt by their bed. Mrs. Thorne was in tears. Mr. Thorne was praying, much too fervently to be aware of Rose's presence.

"Oh, God. Protect our boy, Rusty. Please, Lord. Bring him home. Preserve his life." A great sob exploded out of this usually calm man, causing Rose's own eyes to well with tears. He sucked in a gulp of air and continued. "Please, God. Bring him home."

She shouldn't be eavesdropping, but the captivating sight glued her to the spot. Her mind captured the scene as surely as any camera or sketch artist, and somehow, she knew it would affect her attitude in the future. When she finally crawled back into bed, she lay awake thinking about it for a long time. She would try to be more encouraging to the Thornes and put more effort into her letters to their son. Until now, she hadn't given much thought to what they were going through. She'd only been thinking of her own interrupted life and shattered dreams.

God, if you are there, help me make a difference. If I can encourage Rusty Thorne in some small way, show me how. Help me play a part in answering his father's prayers. In bringing him home.

When the next day's work was done, she sat down to write another letter to Rusty. The irony of him being held captive by the Japanese while she lived in the comfort of his parents' home was not lost on her. Of course, she couldn't say any of that.

A knock came on the front door. Mrs. Thorne went to the living room to answer it and welcome the visitor.

"Justina! What on earth brings you out here in the middle of January?"

Rose stiffened, her pencil poised above the paper. "Justina" was Mrs. Pierce, and Mrs. Thorne was inviting her inside.

"Have a seat on the couch where it's warm. I'll put the kettle on for tea."

"I'll have a seat, Anna, but I don't need tea. I won't be here long." The woman sounded intense.

"All right."

Rose could hear soft rustling as the two women sat.

"I'll get right to the point," Mrs. Pierce began. "I feel it's important for you to know, the most absurd rumors are going around town … that you're allowing your Japs to live inside your house with you. Well, I was just certain that couldn't be true, and I came out here so I can set the record straight myself."

Rose sat frozen, staring at the letter in front of her. Should she leave? Mrs. Thorne did not seem to be responding to Mrs. Pierce's query. When she finally did, her voice sounded cold and hard.

"Suppose there were some truth to this rumor, Justina. What

difference would it make?"

"What difference? Well … well, none to *me*, of course. I'm only concerned about *your* welfare, Anna. It's not true, is it?"

"Not that it's anyone's business, but the senior Mr. Onishi and his two grandchildren stay here in the house with us. We'd welcome the whole family if they so chose. It's much warmer in here, and we have the space."

Another silence before Mrs. Pierce spoke again. "I'm shocked, Anna. You of all people. With your own son—"

"With my own son, what?"

"Well, you know … being tortured by those heathens! They're the enemy. They're barbaric. How can you stand it? And besides, they'll rob you blind. Or worse, sneak into your bedroom and slit your throats while you sleep. I wouldn't even want them on my property, let alone in my—"

"What you do or don't do on your property is none of my concern, Justina. I'll thank you to leave now." Mrs. Thorne's voice sounded firm.

"Anna, listen to me. I'm only telling you this for your own good, your own safety. If you start treating those Japs like regular people, then the other farmers will follow suit, and pretty soon—"

"Pretty soon, what? Our fellow Canadians, who are no more at fault for this war than you are, will be treated like the humans they are? Like God's children? Is that what you're afraid of?"

Mrs. Pierce's voice became more subdued. "My only fear is for your safety, Anna."

"I highly doubt that. Goodbye, Justina."

With no further words exchanged, the front door opened and closed. Rose's heart pounded. With no time to slip outside or upstairs, she couldn't pretend she hadn't overheard. Mrs. Thorne let out a huge sigh. Mrs. Pierce's car started and rumbled down the driveway, Lady barking her disapproval all the way. Finally, Mrs. Thorne entered the kitchen.

"I'm sorry you had to hear that, Rose." She paused under the archway for the briefest moment, then walked swiftly to the sink where she'd left her apron.

Rose pressed her lips together, then took a deep breath. "Do you want us to move back into the cabin?"

"Absolutely not."

"We ... we sort of *are* the enemy, though. Right?"

Mrs. Thorne turned to face Rose. "Listen to me. We have *one* enemy, and that's the devil himself. He's my enemy *and* yours. And God's. He's the enemy of Japan and of every human who ever walked the face of this earth, whether they know it or not. He'd just as soon see every last one of us destroyed. Don't forget that. Now, I don't want to hear another word about it." She tied her apron around her waist. "Are you writing to Rusty?"

"Yes."

"Good. I'm off to town this afternoon. I can mail it with mine."

"Shall I come with you?" Rose didn't relish the idea of going out in the cold.

"I'd prefer you stay home and keep the fire going under the soup pot, Rose. And can you please give the living room a good dusting and polishing? Our ladies' prayer group is meeting here tomorrow." She began scrubbing on a heavy pot, then spoke softly. "With any luck, Justina Pierce will do her praying in the safety of her own home."

That afternoon, Rose found herself alone in the house for the first time. She dutifully fed the cookstove from the pile of split wood Ojiisan had stacked in one corner, trying to remember all she'd been taught about keeping it at an even temperature so the soup would simmer without boiling. She stood at the sink, pulling back a ruffled curtain to reveal the sunshine shimmering on glistening snow. She imagined this was her own home—safe and cozy, with no danger of being ordered to leave. The gong of the grandfather clock in the living room jolted her back to the moment, and she grabbed the furniture polish and rag Mrs. Thorne had left out for her.

She paused in the archway to the living room and surveyed its furnishings. She had avoided this room despite the way the piano called to her, knowing how hard it would be to see but not touch. Was it in tune? Did it have a rich sound? Working her way around the room, she left the piano for last. She dusted knick-knacks and polished small tables, wiped down the radio, and stacked books neatly. All the while, she thought about the piano.

When the only undusted item in the room was the piano, Rose cleared the photos from the top and stood on tiptoe to polish the surface. Then she thoroughly dusted each photo frame and returned it to its spot, taking extra time to study the picture of Rusty. He really was handsome. She tried to imagine his voice and mannerisms. Would he be like his dad? He resembled his mother more.

When all the photos were replaced, it was time to work her way down the intricate carvings on the front of the piano and across the keys. Her heart began to pound, the ache inside extending all the way to the tips of her fingers. Who would ever know if she played it? No one was home. The doors and windows were tightly closed against the winter weather—Mama would never hear from the cabin. The men wouldn't hear from the barn. She glanced around, then gently pressed middle C. A clear, clean note filled the room. Longing overcame her.

Rose lowered herself to the stool. Her finger went to F-sharp, then G-sharp. Her left hand hit a low C-sharp, and she began, from memory, Beethoven's "Moonlight Sonata." It had been a recital piece years ago when she was only thirteen. Now the piece came back as naturally as walking across the room, and she kept playing. With each bar, she became more lost in the music. She closed her eyes and let it carry her away. By the time she reached the first shift in the piece, she was no longer a displaced Japanese girl stuck on a prairie sugar beet farm. She was Rose Onishi, elegant and sought-after concert pianist, dressed in a gorgeous red ball gown and playing for an audience of thousands. The music continued to build, growing faster, louder. Rose bounced on the seat in spots, lowered her face toward the keyboard in others. Her fingers could still fly over the keys despite two years away from any piano.

Rose slowed down when she reached the closing notes of the full fifteen-minute piece, not wanting it to end. Instead of finishing the song abruptly as written, she held the final keys until long after the last vibration had dissipated. Only then did she realize her cheeks were soaked with tears.

CHAPTER TWENTY-SIX

April 1943

Spring arrived in Manitoba, and a sense of dread settled over Rose. On the one hand, the extended hours of sunshine, the emergence of flowers and leaves and green grass, and the call of songbirds lifted her heart. But on the other side was the knowledge that fieldwork would again begin in earnest. Even more, Rose no longer had any reason to stay in the Thornes' house. Ojiisan and Tim had moved back into the cabin as soon as the snow began to melt. Tim missed his mother. Ojiisan missed conversing in Japanese. Rose reluctantly planned to move out as well.

"Only if you wish to, Rose." Mrs. Thorne shook her head. "The room will sit empty if you go, and I can always use your assistance around here. You were a tremendous help when I was unwell, and we enjoy having you around." Mrs. Thorne had spent a few days in bed with the flu.

"Thank you." Rose answered softly, unsure what to do. "I think Mama would prefer I move back."

"Why don't you talk it over with your parents? I've already told your father you are welcome to stay here, but I don't want to come between you and them."

Rose's mother was hanging blankets on the clothesline when Rose went out to find her. Mama saw her coming and wasted no time.

"You moving back into cabin now?" She flapped a wet pillowcase in front of her with a sharp *snap* and hung it on the line with wooden pegs.

"I came to talk to you about it, Mama." Rose pulled more bedding

162

from her mother's basket and proceeded to hang it on the line. "Mrs. Thorne says I am welcome to stay at the house."

"That what you want?"

More than anything. Rose could not vocalize the thought lest it hurt her mother's feelings, as it surely would. "Well … I do like it there. I mean … a girl enjoys her privacy sometimes."

Mama nodded.

"It's not as though we don't see each other every day. Right?"

Mama bent over to grab the last item in her basket and hung it on the line wordlessly.

"But I don't want to make you unhappy, Mama. What do you want me to do?"

Mama took a deep breath and let out a long, slow sigh. She gripped her basket by one handle and let the other hang down near her ankle. Then she finally looked at her daughter's face. Gently, she reached up with her free hand and placed it on Rose's jaw. With her callused thumb, she slowly stroked Rose's chin and cheek.

"Rozu. There is no happy or unhappy. Nothing has gone the way we planned. This is not the life your father and I wanted for you. Or for us. Soon the work will become very hard again. You know that. The cabin is crowded. If staying in the house will give you a little joy, then okay. Stay in house."

Rose studied her mother's face and saw only sincere love. "Does Dad agree?"

Mama nodded. "We discuss. Last night. *Shakata ga nai.* It cannot be helped." She shuffled back to the cabin, where she hung the basket on the outside wall.

Rose followed in silence. She spent the rest of that day working alongside her mother, exchanging words only occasionally. After the laundry was all on the line, they carried the wash water to pour over tomato seedlings and pulled weeds from the extensive garden they shared with the Thornes. When Tim arrived home from school, he joined them, adding his welcome chatter to the quiet companionship. That evening, Rose helped her mother prepare supper and ate with the family in the cabin for the first time since Christmas. The family prepared for bed early, conserving as much energy as possible for the heavy workdays ahead.

"I guess I'll head back now," Rose announced to no one in particular.

Tim responded first. "'Night, Rose."

Mama and Ojiisan only nodded and climbed into their respective bunks. Rose's father opened the door and stepped outside with her. He took a seat on the wooden crate that served as a step and motioned for her to join him. The gray cat that hung around and kept the cabin free of rodents quickly found them. She rubbed herself against Rose's leg, and Rose reached down to pet her.

"Am I breaking Mama's heart, Dad?"

"No, Rozu. Your mother's heart has been broken many times, but not by you. Never by you. She wants only for you to be happy."

They sat together with no further words for a few minutes. Rose pulled the cat into her lap and was soon rewarded with a comforting purr.

"Dad? When the war is over, do you think we'll get to go home and pick up where we left off?"

It took her father so long to respond, Rose wondered if he had heard her.

"Ojiisan worries we will be sent back to Japan."

Rose scrunched her eyebrows. "*Back*? They can't send us back to a place we've never been. Can they?"

"I don't know what they can or cannot do."

"But I barely know Japanese! I don't even know which part of Japan Ojiisan came from. Or Mama." Rose suddenly wished she'd taken more interest, asked more questions.

"Your grandfather grew up in a small fishing village called NoTo. Mama's from a big city. Hiroshima. She still has relatives there."

"Is that where we would go, then? Hiroshima?" Rose had trouble wrapping her tongue around the long name.

Dad shrugged one shoulder and stared off into the pink and blue still lingering in the western sky.

Rose blinked back tears. "Canada is my home, Dad. Vancouver. I want to go home."

"Maybe we will go home, Rozu. I don't know. But we will not pick up where we left off. We will be changed. We will *all* be changed."

Over the course of the next several weeks, the farm work took over everything. Rose labored alongside her family and Mr. Thorne from sunup to sundown. At night, when she returned to the house, she barely had the energy to eat a few bites of food, wash, and fall into bed. The fingers that had softened over the winter grew callused again, black dirt working deep into every crevice. Though thoughts of the piano in the room below were always on her mind, the urge to play was overcome by the need to sleep. Letters to Freda and Rusty were reserved for Sunday afternoons, and Rose kept them short. She had not heard from Kenji and no longer wrote. Her friendship with him and their time at Tashme Camp seemed a lifetime ago.

CHAPTER TWENTY-SEVEN

Hong Kong, August 1943

Rusty and Bert had survived twenty months of captivity, against all odds. They'd seen others die beside them and in their arms. They'd watched men go mad with the horrors they'd been forced to endure. Now something was afoot. Rumor had it the Japanese Imperial Army was in trouble. The Battle of Midway had sunk what remained of their navy, and even their merchant ships now lay at the bottom of the sea. American submarines riddled the Pacific. Could this horrible war be drawing to a close?

On the evening of August 14, Rusty and any others able to walk were lined up along the side of the road. Two of the guards drew red chalk lines, one on their side of the road, one on the other. The men were ordered to walk across to the opposite line, with no understanding of what might happen to those who succeeded or to those who did not. Rusty decided to go for it. Whatever the future held for the successful men couldn't be any worse than what they'd already suffered.

He counted his steps. Twenty-three from one side to the other. He made it! Others collapsed. Rusty glanced around to see if Bert was one of the fallen, then he felt a hand on his shoulder.

"Congrats." Bert grinned. "We're fit as fiddles."

A guard's broken English came over the loudspeaker. "Congraturation. Prize one-way ticket to Japan. Go in morning."

The men returned to their barracks for the night, but Rusty couldn't sleep. Knowing it was his last night at Sham Shui Po lifted his spirits. If the Japanese were moving prisoners back to their own country, surely, there would be more food and other resources for them. But even as his heart absorbed this new hope, it broke for the men who hadn't made the draft. He spent the rest of the night going around to the beds of those who would be left behind, praying for them and encouraging them to keep their spirits up.

With the dawn, two hundred and seventy-six men shuffled out the south gate, which opened to reveal a massive ocean liner. As they neared the dock, Rusty could make out the boat's name in English letters—*Manryu Maru,* with the Japanese characters beneath. From a scrap of British newspaper that had somehow made it past the guards, Rusty had read of the Japanese raising and restoring Allied ships which the Allies themselves had scuttled rather than surrendering them to the enemy. Could this be one of those?

In a long line, the men proceeded across the gangplank. As he got closer, his hopes of a brighter future rapidly faded. From his previous times at sea, he'd become familiar enough with a ship's design to know they were not going to the interior cabins. They were being sent to the cargo hold.

Now Rusty understood why ships used to transport prisoners of war were called *hell ships.* If the Japanese believed the Allies wouldn't fire at them for fear of killing their own men, then the Japanese could use prisoners as shields. Rusty and the other men would be sitting ducks. And even if they did survive without being sunk, how many would die of starvation or disease or sheer panic before they ever disembarked? Rusty never thought in a million years he would wish to return to Sham Shui Po, but in that moment, he prayed for it.

Oh God, no. Please. Anything but this. Let something go wrong. Sink this ship right now! Take us back.

But from where he stood, he saw no option but to keep following. Down the steps they went, in single file, guards nudging them from both sides at each opening. "In," they grunted. The men walked past a mess hall and the engine room, then down another set of metal stairs. In front of the next doorway stood a mounted machine gun. A Japanese soldier sat on a stool behind it with his finger on the trigger, watching each prisoner disappear through the hatch into darkness. Rusty made eye contact for the briefest of seconds, but he knew the look. It said, *Go ahead. Give me a reason to shoot. Any reason.*

Behind him, Bert let out a moan.

"Stay calm," Rusty whispered.

"If they shoot at one, they'll get ten of us."

"Shh. They're bluffing. They wouldn't make that big a mess on their own ship." Rusty wished he could believe his own words. He'd seen enough to know the survivors would be forced to swab the deck and probably throw any wounded overboard.

Down into the cargo hull they went. When he reached the bottom, Rusty closed his eyes tightly, hoping they would adjust to the inky darkness. But when he opened them again, he couldn't see any more than he had with them closed. The space was already filled with prisoners, yet still, they kept coming. And coming. In a space that may have accommodated thirty men lying down, over a hundred fought for room to stand.

When all the men were packed in, their captors lowered two buckets into the hold—one filled with rice, the other empty. The hatch closed, and if Rusty had thought it was dark before, now he knew what utter blackness looked like. He put his hand in front of his face. It made no difference.

The engines began to roar and the *Manryu Maru* to move.

"Bert?"

"Over here, Rusty." The voice came from several feet away, but there would be no moving to get closer.

"Listen, men." Rusty hoped desperately his voice held some tone of confidence and authority. "I was blind for a couple of weeks. It's not the end of the world. We can do this if we help one another. We'll take shifts, take turns sitting and standing so we can get some sleep. Are you with me?"

The men counted off one to three, and every hour or so, the number ones would sit, then the twos, then the threes. The more claustrophobic among them would frequently scream or moan. The air was so short on oxygen, the smell so horrific, no one could take a full breath. Many passed out and were unable to take their turn standing.

After several hours—maybe days—the sea grew rough, and the boat pitched, adding a whole new level of hell as men grew increasingly seasick. The sitting-standing shifts were abandoned. When Rusty managed to sit, he drew his knees to his forehead and tuned out the sounds around him.

Oh God. I cannot do this. If I am going to survive, it will only be because you sustained me. Please, God. Don't let Mum and Dad lose another son.

At the thought of his parents, an old hymn came to mind, and Rusty focused everything on trying to recall the words.

Though the angry surges roll on my tempest-driven soul,
I am peaceful, for I know, wildly though the winds may blow,
I've an anchor safe and sure, that can evermore endure.
And it holds, my anchor holds:
Blow your wildest, then, O gale,
On my bark so small and frail;
By His grace, I shall not fail,
For my anchor holds, my anchor holds.

Rusty could almost see his parents standing in front of their church pew. His father would rumble through the bass line with enthusiasm, adding in the extra words, "my anchor holds, it firmly holds," while his mother sang the melody with her gentle vibrato. Neither of them had ever been at sea, but they'd certainly experienced the storms of life. They'd clung to their faith in God as an anchor. Could they even at this moment be drawing strength from this very hymn? Was it Sunday morning at home? Rusty had lost track of time, and his confused brain couldn't calculate the time difference, anyway.

Then he became aware of a different sort of prayer being prayed by a man nearby. "Send a torpedo. Please God, send a torpedo."

It was a death wish, and the man's pleas had to be stopped before despair spread like wildfire. Rusty felt around until he found the man's hand and held it firmly. "No, soldier. You're going to live. We're going to live. Listen to me."

The man kept up his mantra. "Send a torpedo."

Rusty didn't know what else to do or say. He leaned in and began repeating, "My anchor holds. My anchor holds." He hoped his voice would overpower the negative one. In time, the man grew silent. Rusty, completely exhausted, finally slept.

After three days, the men were allowed on deck for a few hours. The daylight was blinding, but Rusty took great gulps of fresh air and found a bucket of water from which he scooped a handful into his mouth before being kicked in the ribs by a guard. It was worth it. Never had a drink tasted better. He observed enough to learn they had docked at Formosa.

Returning to the cargo hull was worse for the men than the first time, for now they knew what they were returning to. An attack from a submarine could rip a hole right into their compartment, and they'd have no chance of survival. How many of them would go completely mad from the stress?

Rusty grew weaker and more discouraged. In his conscious moments, he tried to give a word of hope to those nearest him, but soon even that was too difficult. To maintain his sanity, he focused on whatever snippets of Bible verses and hymns would come to mind. Then his thoughts took a dark turn.

God does not see you—it is far too dark in here.

The voice was too strong to be any of the men.

And if he does see you, he certainly doesn't care.

Rusty was going mad. He must be. The voice seemed to be coming from the back of his head.

He must really hate you to allow this. Or maybe he's dead. He's dead and you're in hell.

Rusty wanted to yell for it to shut up, but he had no strength to yell. Instead, he summoned whatever strength he had left, gritted his teeth, and recited in a whisper some words memorized many years before. "For I am persuaded, that neither death, nor life, nor angels, nor principalities, nor powers, nor things present, nor things to come, nor height, nor depth, nor any other creature, shall be able to separate us from the love of God, which is in Christ Jesus our Lord."

He repeated the words. His voice grew a bit stronger. Then again. After the fourth time, he stopped to listen.

The other voice had been silenced.

The next time the hatch opened and the men were ordered up, Rusty could barely manage to unfold himself and move. As they made their way to the deck, men around him wept, and his own cheeks grew wet with tears. Those who weren't crying carried a haunted look, like walking dead. All were encrusted with their own filth.

He learned seven days had passed since Formosa. He learned they were in Osaka, Japan. And he learned they had graduated from mere prisoners of war to slaves.

CHAPTER TWENTY-EIGHT

Rusty and Bert eyeballed each other for the first time in two weeks. Almost as quickly as they could find each other on deck, they were marched across the plank to the dock, where Japanese soldiers waited.

"Stick together," Rusty managed to say to Bert.

The men hobbled to a train platform. The first hundred or so were loaded into cattle cars, far more than should reasonably fit. The doors were pulled shut. The train began to chug away while Rusty and Bert waited with another hundred or more men. What would happen to them?

Soon, a second train arrived. He and Bert managed to board the same car.

"Can't be any worse than the ship," Bert mumbled.

Couldn't it? No attempt had been made to clean away the animal filth, and black canvas tightly covered any openings. The train began to move in the opposite direction of the first train. They would not see those soldiers again.

Rusty's eyes adjusted. Yes. This was a slight improvement over the ship. At least, slivers of sunlight found their way through here and there. The men were free to speak.

"You're all knees and eyeballs, pal," Bert quipped.

"Thanks. I think we can officially say we've survived hell."

"Did you notice our beards and hair have stopped growing?" Bert rubbed a bony hand across his equally bony jaw.

"Thank God for small mercies." Rusty took a long, hard look at the emaciated man before him. While most of the other men's faces were either completely devoid of emotion or dark with hatred, Bert still had life in his eyes. "What kept you going in there?"

Bert's eyes began to well up, and he didn't answer at first. "You did."

Rusty thought he'd misheard. "Me? I didn't do anything."

"You did, though. I heard you singing."

Rusty stared at his friend. What was he talking about? He certainly hadn't had the strength to sing. Even if he'd tried, which he knew he hadn't, his voice would have been too weak for Bert to hear over the thrumming engines, the coughing and frequent groaning of men in deep distress.

"Bert. God must have sent you your own private angel or something. I didn't hear anything. And I'm tellin' ya, I didn't sing."

"It was no angel, Rusty. It was you. I know because you went off-key in all the same places you always go off-key."

Rusty stared. Had his friend become delirious like so many others? "What did I sing?"

Bert thought for a moment. "The one about the anchor in the storm. You know …" He hummed a bit, then remembered the words of the chorus. "'And it holds, my anchor holds … blow your wildest, then, oh gale …'"

The train finally stopped at Niigata POW camp on the northwest coast of Honshu Island. Rusty tried to remember the map he'd drawn for a Grade Four geography project on Japan. If he'd only known then what his future held, he'd have paid more attention.

The commander was Lt. Masato Yoshida, who, with his *Katana* sword in hand, informed the men they now worked for the Japanese Empire and would no longer be "free-loading guests," as they'd been previously. They would live out the rest of their days here, a fair and just consequence for being stupid enough to be captured. Any who refused to work would be immediately executed. Those too sick would have their food rations halved.

Rusty and Bert were assigned to the same hastily constructed barrack, a long wooden building with a dirt floor. Top bunks extended five feet above the bottom bunks, leaving little space between bed and ceiling. The men were divided into three labor groups. The first group would work in the steel foundry, toiling near hot furnaces for long hours. A second group was assigned to carry heavy loads of coal on their backs in the coal yard. Bert landed in this group. By the end of his first day, he was so covered in black coal dust, Rusty didn't recognize his friend.

Rusty was in the third group assigned to the dockyards. He would spend his future loading and unloading cargo—mostly coal and large bags of rice and beans. The biggest challenge was the cold. Rusty constantly shivered, his skin wet from ocean spray and riddled with goosebumps from the frigid wind.

"We're prairie boys," Bert teased. "You should be able to handle a little cold."

It was true. Rusty had experienced far colder temperatures back home in Manitoba. But he'd been carrying twice the body weight then, along with a warm coat. Now he worked in shirtsleeves and trousers that could hold three men his size.

This work assignment did, however, give the men a significant opportunity to provide food for themselves and their fellow prisoners. By tying their cuffs tightly around their ankles, they could allow rice and beans to spill from broken bags down their pant legs and carry it home to the barracks. They had to be careful not to be too greedy, lest their bulging pant legs give them away. In this way, Rusty's diet was supplemented to a survival level. While his muscles didn't exactly grow strong from the physical labor and his stomach constantly growled, he managed to keep going. He kept his head down and avoided the brutal taskmasters to the best of his ability.

One day, the prisoner in front of Rusty moved too slowly to suit the guard. He gave the man a blow to his shoulder with the butt end of his rifle, knocking him off balance. The prisoner slid across the narrow dock and plunged into the sea below. No attempt was made at recovery. If Rusty made any effort to save the man, or so much as said a word or even looked around, he would've been shot. And probably several others as well. Instead, he gritted his teeth and forced hard breaths out through his nostrils. *Do you see, God? Do you see?*

Rusty vented the emotions roiling inside after they carried their thin rice slop back to their barracks that night. "I hate them, Bert."

Face impassive, his friend paused with his bowl to his lips. "I know."

"How can I call myself a Christian and hate them? They're made in God's image too."

"I know."

"He told us to love our enemies."

Bert shoveled his last spoonful into his mouth, then licked the bowl. "I know."

"You're not helping." Rusty finished his own ration. "And don't say 'I know.'"

"I am, too, helping."

"Oh yeah? How are you helping?"

Bert turned his face toward the courtyard, where two Japanese guards openly shared a large Red Cross chocolate bar intended for the prisoners. He merely gazed at them a while. "I'm helping by listening, Russ. I hear you. God hears you too. He knows. He sees."

"But if he can allow you to hear me singing when I wasn't, why doesn't he just end this and free us? There's so much I don't understand."

Bert kept staring at the guards while they polished off the chocolate, licked their fingers, crumpled the wrapper, and threw it on the ground. Bert licked his lips and let out a long, slow sigh. "I know."

Miraculously, mail came through near Christmas. Rusty held a bundle of three letters from his mother and two from his sisters. He carried them back to the barracks like he might carry a precious newborn baby and laid them out on his bunk. He lined them up chronologically, determined to read them in order as they were written and to allow himself only one letter per day.

The first one from his mother included a letter from a girl named Rose.

"What's this?" Bert peered over his friend's shoulder.

"I don't really know. My parents hired a family to help with the beets. This girl is their daughter, I guess."

"Oh yeah? What'd she say?"

"Not a lot. Sounds like a sweet kid who just wants to write to a soldier. Go mind your own bee's wax."

What kind of strange arrangement had his parents worked out? It sounded as though the girl was sleeping in Shirley and Claire's old bedroom. He couldn't wait another day. Perhaps his sisters' letters would shed more light on the situation.

They did not. It was a treat to read of the antics of his nephews and nieces, though.

Over the coming days, he re-read all the letters, Rose's most of all, until he memorized them. Oddly enough, as he fell asleep each night, her words were the ones repeating in his brain and filling his heart with hope.

CHAPTER TWENTY-NINE

January 1944

Rose had tried to convince her parents to move into the Thornes' house for their second winter when Tim and Ojiisan did, but Mama kept stubbornly refusing.

"She's nice, Mama. She's not like Mrs. Kokura."

Her mother would not be moved. "At least we can be Japanese here."

Rose wondered what difference it would make to her mother's Japanese-ness if she slept in the house, but she gave up trying to argue. Mama only dug her heels in further when her daughter gave her all the reasons she should. At least, Mama's health had returned, and for that, Rose thanked God.

They'd survived another harvest. Tim was back in school. Everyone settled into the easier chores of wintertime.

Though Rose waited for another opportunity to play the piano, weeks went by, and she was never in the house alone. Guilt at disobeying her father's warning still burned in her heart, but it had been worth it. She'd do it again at the first chance.

Still, the desire to confess to somebody reared its head. She'd already told Freda in a letter, but it didn't seem like enough. Freda had no vested interest. No power to forgive. But if she told the Thornes she'd played their piano—the piano that had not been played since Rusty was home—not only might she never get another chance to play, but they would surely send her back to the cabin, and she'd lose the beautiful, private bedroom.

By March, the brutal cold of another Manitoba winter gradually gave way to a slushy, beige spring with the occasional snowfall and threats of late blizzards. Rose still longed for her west coast home, where tulips and daffodils would be in full bloom.

A letter from Freda confirmed it. Her friend hoped to secure a secretarial position within walking distance of her home. She wrote:

My bedroom window is wide open, and the fragrance of the plum tree blossoms is divine! I don't mind living with mom and dad for a year or two longer. That way, I can spend my earnings on gorgeous clothes instead of rent. I know it sounds superficial, but the war will end soon (please, God!), and I'll need to look good when all the men come home, right?

Speaking of fellas, are you still writing to Russell Thorne? Have you heard back?

Rose had been writing short letters to Rusty at least once a week, sometimes twice. What had at first felt extremely awkward as she tried to think of things to say had evolved into a pleasant pastime. When Mrs. Thorne added Rose's letters to her own, sealing the envelope without even glancing at Rose's pages, she felt confident her words were safe from prying eyes at home. Knowing there was little likelihood of the letters reaching Rusty made it easier to pour out her heart, much as she might with a diary—but with the added challenge of censoring her words so the real censors would not black them out. And if she came off like a foolish young girl, what difference did it make? Her letters gave the man something to read, hopefully, something positive.

Chances were, she'd never meet Rusty face-to-face, anyway. Odds were against his very survival, as cold-hearted as that sounded. But if he did make it home—Rose and her family would have returned to their own home before Rusty made it back to Canada. What did she have to lose?

Hello again, Rusty.

I hope it's okay that I call you that. Your parents and sisters always refer to you as Rusty, so it's hard for me to think of you as Russell. Today, I've decided to simply provide you with a list of things I love—not exhaustive by any stretch—and perhaps some of them will ring true for you as well.

#1. Music, obviously. I have a confession. My father told me not to go near your family's piano (other than to dust it when instructed to do so). But I have played it when no one was around. Only once, for about fifteen minutes. Of course, it seemed like only two minutes because I got lost in the music. I realize you can tattle on me to your parents in a letter, but I'm overwhelmed by the need to confess to somebody and will take that risk. Besides, somehow I have a feeling you won't tattle.

#2. May. I mean the month. June used to be my favorite, because that's when my birthday comes and school lets out and all. But since we moved to Manitoba and I'm no longer in school, May is my favorite. I love the promise of new beginnings everywhere—flowers and buds and baby animals and warm sunshine. Knowing there's a whole summer ahead to look forward to, even if it will be laden with hard work.

#3. Don't tell my mother, but your mom makes the BEST apple crisp! But then, you already know that. I don't know when I've tasted anything so utterly delightful! When it's still warm from the oven and topped with a little fresh, lightly whipped cream, oh my! You can put that in your mouth and forget all your troubles in an instant. Best of all, she is teaching me how to make it.

#4. Sundays. I am enjoying your church. The one we attended back home was formal and stuffy. Much larger. At yours, the people seem more real and down-to-earth (with a couple of exceptions!), and I enjoy your pastor's sermons. I hesitate to even call them "sermons." Some days they feel more like messages straight from God to me. You know what I mean? He really encouraged me with Scriptures from Joshua about how we don't have to be afraid because God is with us wherever we are, even when we didn't choose to be where we are. Maybe this passage will encourage you, too: "Be strong and of a good courage; be not afraid, neither be thou dismayed: for the Lord thy God is with thee whithersoever thou goest."

"Whithersoever" means the same as "wherever." But you probably know that already.

#5. Not that I'd ever admit this to him, but I enjoy my little brother's jokes and riddles. Yesterday he came home with this one: What five-letter word becomes shorter when you add two letters to it? I'm sure you know the answer ... "short." And then today, it was this one: Riddle: You draw a line. Without changing it, how do you make it a longer line? Solution: Draw a short line next to it, and now it's the longer line.

I'm out of space, so that's all for this letter. I hope you are well.

Yours truly,

Rose

P.S. The piece I played on your piano was Beethoven's "Moonlight Sonata," one of my favorites to play, not necessarily to listen to. Is that strange? Anyway, I could never choose a favorite. How about you?

Hello Rusty,

I had so much fun with the list of things I love, I decided to keep going. Can't remember what number I was on, so I'll just make an unnumbered list.

Sunshine. Especially the way it shimmers on the pond on a summer day. Or makes my little brother's hair shine.

Rain running down the outside of a windowpane when you're dry and warm inside.

The smell of clean sheets when you bring them in from the clothesline and make up the bed.

Ladybugs. (Although I don't think they are all ladies, or the species would have died out by now.)

The sound of children singing. The Sunday school kids gave a little concert last Sunday evening, so that's why it's fresh on my mind. My brother Tim sang in the choir too.

Fancy ball gowns. The kind I can only dream of wearing. Still, I know they are out there. I may as well throw in fancy shoes, too, while I'm at it. Like the pair Ginger Rogers danced in in Roxie Hart. *Did you see it?*

French braids in a little girl's hair.

The taste of a carrot pulled straight from the garden—I'd never eaten one so fresh before we came here.

The way piano keys beneath my fingers feel like an extension of myself—mind, body, and soul. Hard to explain, but so real.

I hope you don't find my little lists silly. Pastor says it's good to focus on the good in life, even in hard times. There's a Scripture about that, too, something about "whatsoever things are true or lovely ..." I don't know where that's found. Maybe you do. I hope and pray you can find some good around you, wherever this letter finds you. I confess I have overheard your parents praying for you, Rusty. They love you so dearly. I'm praying for you too. Your mother tells me God hears my prayers. I sure hope she's right. I'm certain he hears hers ... and yours too. He sees you, Rusty. He sees you.

Rose

CHAPTER THIRTY

June 1944

On June 7, Mrs. Thorne returned from a trip to town waving a newspaper and hollering as she ran out to the field. Rose looked up from her row of young beet plants as the others gathered around.

"The Allies have invaded France!" Breathless, Mrs. Thorne held the newspaper out to her husband, who took it in his dirty hands and shook the front page out to full size. Rose could see the big, bold headline: CANADIANS IN THICK OF IT AS ALLIES SMASH INLAND. She read smaller headings like "R.C.N. landed Canucks" and "The King calls for prayers."

Mr. Thorne began reading aloud. "Through a rolling ocean of clouds five thousand feet thick, Allied air forces threw eleven thousand aircraft of almost every type into the grand invasion of Europe today, bombing and strafing miles of Normandy's beaches and flying inland to break the enemy's communications."

He glanced up once, then continued. "Two things stood out in the air operations launched in support of the landings in northern France. The first was the mass of airplanes the Allies were able to put into the sky in weather described as 'just fair.' The other was the absence of German resistance."

Mr. Thorne kept reading through the article. By the time he reached the end, a huge smile lit up his face. "This is good news. This is really, really good."

"It won't be long now." Mrs. Thorne took the paper back. "This will all be over."

That evening, Rose read the paper for herself. Nowhere did it say how many lives had been lost, probably because no one yet knew. The paper was dated the previous day, June 6. The articles reiterated that the German defenses proved much less formidable than had been feared.

Rose didn't even know where Normandy was. Though it all seemed far away, the war had affected her life profoundly, and she wanted to remember this day. Surely, it would end soon. She could be reunited with Freda and her other friends back home. She could dare to dream again of completing her education and eventually approaching a concert stage, to the delight of an adoring audience. These years had been a setback, to be sure, but only a setback. She would use this experience to make her stronger. To deepen the passion. To increase the depth of emotion in her interpretation of music.

Her thoughts turned to Rusty Thorne. Would he have any idea there was good news on the horizon? Wanting to encourage him somehow, she wrote a few lines before retiring that night.

Dear Rusty,

It is June 7, 1944. I hope you remember where you were and what you were doing yesterday because my dad says it will go down in history as a significant date. I wish I could tell you all of it, but just let me say it is good news. Perhaps by the time this letter makes it overseas, you will be on your way home. Wouldn't that be wonderful? Spring fieldwork is well underway here. Maybe you'll be here to bring in the harvest, and I'll be back in school where I belong.

I wanted to share with you a portion of Scripture I came across recently. It has encouraged me because—from what your pastor says—sometimes "the enemy" means dark forces we cannot see with our eyes, but who are just as real and perhaps even more of a threat. Maybe it will bolster your spirits like it did mine.

"When thou goest out to battle against thine enemies, and seest horses, and chariots, and a people more than thou, be not afraid of them: for the Lord thy God is with thee ... let not your hearts faint, fear not, and do not tremble, neither be ye terrified because of them; For the Lord your God is

he that goeth with you, to fight for you against your enemies, to save you"
(from Deuteronomy 20).

None of us are in this alone. I'm learning that now, and I hope you are finding it to be true for yourself as well.

Sincerely,

Rose

August 1944

"It's some kind of miracle, Rusty." Bert entered the barracks, waving his letter from home under Rusty's face. Work was over for the day, and mail had come through for several of the prisoners—all of it torn open and much of it with missing pages or blacked-out lines, but precious mail, nonetheless. "There's some for you too."

Rusty tried to grab the bundle from his friend's hand, but Bert held it high. "What'll ya give me for it?"

"Hand it over." Rusty wasn't in the mood. He arranged the letters in order and opened the oldest. This one had clearly been part of a package, as his mother referred to enclosed socks and cookies. Rusty could only dream about how tasty those cookies might have been or how soothing Mum's home-knit socks would feel on his aching, blistered feet. Still, he determined to be grateful rather than dwell on who might be enjoying his gifts.

Thank you, God. The words from home are worth more than anything else.

Each letter from Mum included one from Rose. She was becoming more familiar with every letter. More willing to share her heart. In one, she confessed having played the piano when no one was home. Why on earth did Rose and her father think she wouldn't be allowed to play it? Surely, all she needed to do was ask. Mum and Dad would never be so unreasonable—would they? A burning desire to write back worked its way up from deep inside. Could he bribe a guard for some paper?

He forced himself to save the most recent letter for another day and fell asleep with Rose's words repeating in his mind. The girl sounded absolutely delightful with her lists of things she loved and her refreshing honesty. He pictured her nothing like his old flame, Susie. When he'd stood beside Susie, Rusty had always stretched, trying in vain to match her height. He imagined Rose much shorter. Where Susie had brown hair, Rose's was probably blonde. And with a name like Rose, he pictured fair skin with a pinkish complexion. He even went so far as to imagine her in a rose-colored dress with a flower in her hair.

Thoughts of Rose dominated everything as Rusty went through his monotonous, backbreaking work the next day. Forming replies in his mind provided something to occupy his thoughts besides the constant onslaught of abuse and deprivation.

"I know I'm being silly," he confided to Bert over that evening's rations. This night, they'd chosen to sit on the ground rather than inside the stuffy barracks. "It's just that we haven't seen any women in forever, you know? I keep thinking romantic thoughts about this girl, wondering what she looks like."

"Probably a lot like ol' Bossie." Bert drained his bowl and licked the bottom. "Why would a pretty girl want to write to the likes of you?"

Rusty envisioned his dad's best milk cow chewing her cud complacently. "Yeah. You're probably right. Still can't quit thinking about her, though."

"Nothin' wrong with that. You gonna write her back?"

The two of them wandered across the dusty grounds to their barrack building.

"Soon as I can get my hands on some paper."

"Tell her to write me a letter too."

"No dice. Get your own girl." Rusty climbed to his top bunk and pulled his bundle of letters out from under the blanket.

"She's hardly your girl."

"Maybe not yet. This war's gotta end some time."

"She'll take one look at your skinny carcass and run for the hills." With a victorious grin, Bert grabbed a bucket from the corner of the room and stepped out the door to fetch wash water.

"Jealousy does not become you!" Rusty called out, but his friend only chuckled as he walked away.

Rusty sat in the middle of his bunk and re-read every letter, in order. The ones from Rose, he read twice. He imagined her voice. When he finished, he reached for the one still-unread letter and pulled it out from its torn envelope. His mother's words helped confirm his vision of Rose.

If you've received our previous letters, you know that Rose is now staying in the house with us, along with her grandfather and little brother. She's become my right hand through a recent bout of flu, managing the cooking and cleaning like a pro. What a delightful girl! A little on the quiet side, but when she does speak, it means something. Not just a lot of silliness like other girls her age. Very respectful. And she seems keen to learn more about the Lord. I gave her a Bible and have seen her using it several times, even underlining significant verses.

His mother went on with the latest community and church news, updates on the farm work, and how the family had gathered for Easter dinner. Books she was reading and programs they enjoyed on the radio. Any references to news broadcasts or the war were glaringly absent. She closed with a prayer she prayed every morning and every night. *Lord, watch over Rusty. Give him strength to get through this day. Help him keep his eyes on you. Rescue him, Lord. Bring him home.*

Rusty wiped away a tear and turned his attention to the other sheet of paper—the letter from Rose.

Hello, Rusty.
Spring is here! I hope that wherever this finds you, you can see something colorful blooming and that it fills your heart with hope. Keep your chin up. Your mother showed me your high school yearbook. I hope you don't mind, but I read the things others said about you (like voting you "most congenial" and "most likely to succeed") and even the things written to you in notes in the margins. (To refresh your memory, someone named Lester wrote, "Thanks for all your help. I never would have made the team without

your encouragement." And a girl named Eileen said, "To Rusty, the kindest and sweetest boy in our class. Thanks for always sticking up for what's right.") From that, and from the comments and questions I often overhear at church, I can tell you are loved and respected. So even though we haven't met, I admire you, and I have every confidence you can and will survive your current situation and whatever ordeals are thrown at you. One day, you will look back on this horrible time, and you will see how God brought good from it. I read in Romans that "tribulation worketh patience; And patience, experience; and experience, hope." Does that mean we can't grow in patience and in hope without some sort of trouble? I think it might. My own troubles are insignificant compared to yours, but I think even I am experiencing this to be true.

Your sisters are a real gas. They came with their families for Easter dinner. Oh, how they carry on! There's never any shortage of laughter, except when someone mentions how much they miss you. They clearly love their brother dearly and pray for your return. From your photo on the piano, I can tell your little nephews resemble you. They've grown so much just since I came—I can only imagine the change you'll see when you get home. And you will get home, Rusty. I really and truly believe God will see you safely home.

All for this time,
Rose

Rusty lifted the letter to his nose and breathed in the scent of paper and ink. No hint of spring blossoms. No perfume. His imagination would have to supply those, and it did. Rose's words had lifted his spirit to a higher level than he'd experienced since leaving home. How was that possible, from a person he'd never met? He couldn't explain it. Perhaps that was it. Maybe the notion of a stranger who fully believed in him and in the hope of his safe return was the key. Except, she didn't feel like a stranger. In two short days, he'd become connected to this girl—like a lifeline. As though God truly did see him and was sending his promises through Rose. He couldn't wait to meet her, to hear her voice and see her smile.

His thoughts were interrupted by Bert's return with a pail of water.

But instead of taking the pail to the corner they used for washing, Bert set it down in the doorway and summoned Rusty over with a wave. "You said you couldn't remember the last time you saw a woman."

Rusty climbed down from the bunk and went to see what his friend was talking about. Darkness was falling. A jeep had pulled into the camp, and when it stopped in front of the commander's quarters, the driver got out and went around to the passenger side. Three teenage girls climbed out, dressed in bright, Japanese kimonos. Their flowery clothing reminded Rusty of Rose's wish that he'd see something colorful and draw hope from it. The driver escorted them inside.

Rusty's heart sank. "Is that what I think? Are they here for the officers and guards?"

Bert nodded. "Comfort women."

"They look like kids—fourteen, fifteen?" Rusty's stomach churned. Two of them giggled, hands raised to hide their mouths. "That's disgusting."

"They're not here by their own choice."

"How do you know? They're Japanese, aren't they?"

"More likely Korean or Chinese. *Ianfu*. Tricked into this by promises of work. I read something about this. You're right. It's just one more disturbing thing about this horrible war." Bert picked up his pail and moved to the corner of the room, where he stripped down to wash away the day's filth from the foundry.

Rusty made his way back to his bunk and tried not to think about the women or what was happening in the officers' quarters. He read Rose's letter again, hoping it would somehow cleanse his heart and mind. No matter what Bert said, those girls disgusted him as much as the men who used them.

"Maybe they deserve compassion, Lord," he whispered that night as he tried to sleep, clutching Rose's letter to his heart like a warm blanket. "But I can't help it. As long as I live, I don't think I'll be able to stand the sight of a Japanese man or woman without feeling revulsion. Surely, you can understand that."

CHAPTER THIRTY-ONE

Another Christmas came in Niigata. The men were made to work, the same as any other day. But the following day, Sunday, was a day off. They gathered in the barracks to sing Christmas carols, starting with "Jingle Bells" and moving into sacred carols like "Joy to the World." The captured soldiers became increasingly subdued as the singing changed to "O Come All Ye Faithful" and finally, as the sun set on another Japanese horizon, "Silent Night." Rusty knew every man in the room was longing for home and family.

By New Year's Eve, the men were in better spirits. A heavy snow had settled on the camp, making everything cleaner and brighter despite the cold and misery. To the Canadian boys, it was a taste of home. A good-natured but short-lived snowball fight ensued between Canadian and American soldiers, ending in the construction of a lopsided snowman.

"Let's call him 'Forty-five,'" suggested one of the fellows, holding up an empty hand in a mock toast. "May he welcome in a happier year, where this war finally ends and we all go home."

Rusty was inclined to agree. He chose not to participate in the outdoor festivities but spent his time writing as much as he could on the postcard he'd been issued—not knowing whether the card would ever reach home.

Dear Mum & Dad,
May this new year find you well. I have work to do now that makes the time pass faster. I'm glad you found help for harvest. Hoping by next harvest, it will be me. Give everyone my love. Tell Rose to keep writing.

That evening, the men shared cigarettes and food and stayed awake to usher in 1945. Less than two hours later, they were awakened by a loud crack. Rusty sat up on his bunk, nearly hitting his head on the roof. Had someone been shot in the middle of the night? Were they under attack?

The men rushed outside. Prisoners were streaming out of a neighboring barrack building. Its roof shifted sideways, the door twisting. Then, in one convulsive groan, the entire roof caved in. Rusty and the others ran to assist. As they began lifting the rubble to rescue the prisoners trapped inside, the shrill Tenko whistle blew, summoning them to roll call. Once again, they were forced to ignore their troubled comrades and line up to be counted if they wanted to survive.

By morning, they learned eight men had died in the collapse, and several more were wounded. The weight of the snow, which had brought such joy and freshness, had been too much for the flimsy roof. The men spent the next day clearing precipitation from the tops of other buildings lest another one crumple and the rest of that week cleaning up the remains of the fallen building. Its survivors had to find room in the other barracks, adding to the crowded conditions.

Just when he'd thought morale in the camp had finally taken an upward shift, it plunged. These new deaths and injuries almost seemed worse than the ones deliberately inflicted by their captors. The constant pain, hunger, filth, and threat of beatings had been more than anyone could bear. Now they couldn't even trust the roof above their heads.

The long workdays, the stiffness in his fingers, and the lack of writing material made it next to impossible for Rusty to compose letters. But when he managed to trade cigarettes for paper, he spent every spare moment for the next week working on one for his parents and one for Rose.

Dear Mum and Dad,
Thanks for your letters—a whole bundle of them came at once, and it was better than a six-course meal. The socks and cookies you mentioned never

made it, so maybe save yourself the trouble. I'm doing all right, working hard and doing my best to stay out of mischief. Thanks for encouraging Rose to write. I enjoyed her letters too. By the way, you need to let that girl play your piano!

Definitely hoping to see you before next harvest,
Rusty

How he longed to pour out everything happening around him, but Rusty had to spare his parents the horror of the full truth. If they could see a photo of him now, they'd be too distressed to carry on.

He set the letter aside and began the one that suddenly felt infinitely more important—the one he'd been forming in his mind ever since receiving the collection.

As Rusty prepared his letters for mailing, he prayed aloud. "God, it will take some kind of miracle for these to get through. But it's a miracle I ever received my letters from Rose, so I'm asking You to do it again. And I sure would love to hear from her again. Amen."

He slipped the letters to a prisoner named Fred who was wily enough to initiate bribery with the guards.

A week later, one of the prisoners went running past Rusty's barrack building shouting something about a bomber. The men rushed to the yard and faced the sky. A hulking green plane flew low enough overhead for its gray shadow to make its way across the camp.

"It's an American bomber!" one man shouted.

"It's a B-29!" another added.

The men trembled with elation and fear. If the B-29s had made their way here, the war must be coming to an end. The Japanese were surely facing defeat! But if those friendly planes dropped bombs, the prisoners were in as much danger as their enemies.

The men huddled in a crude bomb shelter night after night, the giant hole feeling more like a mass grave. With each explosion that sounded nearby, Rusty readied himself to meet God face-to-face. *If I'm not prepared to die, I have little reason to live.* But how sad it would be to lose his life now, so close to the end.

Once again, he turned his attention to the men and how he might help them. He sought out those who cried, who curled themselves into tight fetal positions, hands pressed over their ears, eyes tightly shut. *God, give me the words to say.*

To his surprise, often no words at all escaped his lips as he wrapped his skinny arms around one of his comrades and simply held him until he stopped shaking. Other times, he would repeat the same line over and over. "You are loved. You are God's precious child." It never failed to quiet a man, as Rusty rocked gently back and forth while speaking the words softly but firmly into his ear.

No one scoffed or belittled the men who so openly expressed fear. It was almost as though those who felt most deeply demonstrated emotions for them all. Even the attitudes of the guards softened. Did they know their days were numbered? Were they as fearful as their prisoners?

By day, the men's hopes lifted. The sightings of the B-29s told them they were not alone, not abandoned. Whether the Allies knew precisely where they were or not, at least something was happening. One man made the mistake of waving at a low-flying plane. The guards decided a lesson needed to be taught and gave the prisoner a brutal beating while the others stood in the parade square, forced to watch but helpless to assist. When the guards finally left, Rusty and Bert, along with two others, carried the man to his bunk. Several days passed before he was able to get up again. It was enough warning for the men to hold their smiles inside when they saw the bombers.

CHAPTER THIRTY-TWO

Rusty and the other prisoners were shocked one morning when they gathered for roll call. No smoke rose from the smokestacks at the steel foundry. Ever since their arrival at Niigata, the smoke had been incessant. If the fires ever went out, it would take days to relight them. Those charged with keeping the fires fueled had been warned of this often enough. But now, nothing was said. The stacks simply were not smoking, no matter how often Rusty double-checked to make sure his eyes weren't playing tricks.

After they were all counted, the men were dismissed with one simple phrase and no explanation—"No work today."

The same thing happened the next day, and the next. Almost gleeful at this unexpected holiday, the men discussed at length what it could mean. Surely, things were about to conclude. Would they survive whatever lay ahead? Would they soon be home, all this finally behind them? Or would the Japanese decide to kill them all before abandoning the prison?

Then one day, several U.S. Marine fighter planes flew over. These planes took off from and returned to aircraft carriers or islands, which meant they had to be based nearby. American troops were somewhere close. The men's spirits soared with every plane they heard.

No one blew the whistle for assembly in the parade square anymore. In fact, most of the Japanese guards had simply disappeared. Those who remained kept their distance. With free rein around the camp, the men found some paint and painted a white cross on the roof of the mess hall to indicate this was a POW camp. Would the fighter pilots see it in time? Would they believe it? Waffling between elation at their newfound freedom and fear as the planes banked overhead, raining bullets across the fence, the men watched and listened.

Then the foundry went up in flames. With explosion after explosion, the flames grew so high and so hot Rusty could feel the heat from camp. He couldn't take his eyes off the blaze, as though it could somehow heal his shattered heart and mind. Real hope of survival soared in his heart for the first time. God had not abandoned him! God would not let the Thorne family lose another son. For the next week, air raid sirens could be heard all around and became so prevalent that Rusty learned to sleep right through them.

"Rusty, get up!" Bert hollered early one morning as Rusty struggled to open his eyes. "Take cover!"

Rusty dragged himself from his bunk and followed the other men to their makeshift shelter. As he ran across the parade grounds, two B-29s flew toward them, dangerously low. What were they doing? Surely, they could see the white cross. Did they think it was merely a ploy by the enemy to keep them from dropping bombs?

The men hunkered down, waiting. With the foundry destroyed, they expected explosions from the harbor. Nothing happened. The planes carried on. The men waited in eerie silence for what felt like an eternity, although one brave man kept his wits about him enough to count. He declared that only three minutes had passed.

Rusty stuck his head out of the shelter and was greeted by a view more spectacular than the sunset over Hawaii or the Canadian Rockies. Dozens of huge barrels floated to the ground, each with its own parachute! He took a moment to absorb the glorious scene, then ducked back down to relay the happy news to the others.

"It's a supply drop," he shouted. He would not have been able to wipe the ear-to-ear smile from his face even if ten guards threatened him with their bayonets. No Japanese were around anymore. The men were free to dig into the supplies. Food, at last!

Several more heads popped up to verify Rusty's words. Then the commotion began, as men scrambled to be the first to reach the barrels.

"Wait!" Rusty shouted as the barrels swung unpredictably. "Wait for them all to land. Those are big barrels, forty-five gallons at least." And they were falling fast. "You'll get knocked right out if one hits you."

Most of the men listened, pulling back to safety. The barrels appeared larger as they neared the earth, the closest aiming just outside the camp gates.

Suddenly, two men pushed past Rusty and ran across the parade ground.

"Come back!" The men shouted from their hole in the ground as the skeletal figures dashed through the gates and stood holding out their arms as though they could catch the barrel. Rusty's heart lurched. Was one of them Bert? He looked around the bomb shelter for his friend.

"Bert? Bert!" The men's haunted faces all looked alike.

One of the men pointed toward the gates. "He's out *there*!"

Rusty crawled from the hole, trying to keep an eye on the falling barrels. "Bert!" he screamed.

With a thud, the first barrel hit the ground, and the two men made a dash for it. They weren't paying attention to the other cargo still falling. Rusty crouched, frozen in horror, as a second barrel clipped Bert's head, knocking him to the dirt. The army's logo on the side was obscured by blood before the barrel even hit the ground. Like massive silk angel wings, the parachute settled gracefully over both the barrel and Bert's body. Rusty knew beyond doubt that his best friend in all the world was dead.

Rusty had never felt so abandoned. How could Bert be dead when they'd come so far? When they had managed to stay together through everything? When they'd survived every horror the enemy had hurled at them? Only to die in this moment of victory and provision. It made no sense. Surely, God was nowhere near Japan.

Despite warnings to go slowly, the prisoners were too starved to take heed. Even the former med student didn't follow his own advice as the men tore open the supply barrels and began gorging themselves on canned meat and milk, cheese, chocolate, and crackers. All of them wept while they ate, and Rusty loathed himself for joining in. Like an animal, as though he had been reduced to a heartless beast by his enemies. But, like the others, he couldn't stop. When his stomach could hold no more, he collapsed near Bert's body. With one arm around his friend's remains, he wept harder than he ever had in his life.

"So close, Bert. So close." He kept repeating it through his tears.

Within hours, every one of the men was dreadfully ill. They didn't even mind. The food gave them enough strength to dig a grave for Bert. Rusty, who'd always been the one to share a word of hope from Scripture at these somber occasions, remained silent, completely numb. When the others picked up shovels to begin covering the grave, Rusty shooed them away.

"Let me do it. I need to do it. Alone."

One by one, the men left the graveside. Two stopped to briefly place a hand on Rusty's shoulder, but no one said a word. Rusty took one last look at his friend, then started closing the grave. He shoveled fast and furiously. Though he worked up a profuse sweat, he did not shed a tear or pause to wipe his brow.

When he'd created a high mound over Bert's body, Rusty patted it firmly in place with the back of the shovel. Then with one last angry heave, he thrust the tool into the dirt beside the grave, halfway up its handle. Without looking back, he stumbled to his bunk and collapsed.

In the following weeks, bombs continued to drop in the distance. Although it was frightening, each morning brought new hope. The men now ate their fill every day of powdered eggs and fried meat. They drank coffee and smoked cigarettes and began once again to speak of their sweethearts and families back home. They talked about what they would do when they got there. The optimism was contagious. Though free to leave the camp, they found nothing for them beyond the familiar fences. Any who ventured out returned quickly to the relatively safe boundaries.

Near the end of May, one man came back with an English newspaper. The headlines were victorious. The Nazis had surrendered, and the war in Europe was over! Surely, it was only a matter of time before Japan gave up as well. Could the men survive whatever might happen before rescue arrived?

Miraculously, a bundle containing mail was dropped in July. Although it was dated a whole year earlier, Rusty devoured Rose's words with a greater hunger than he'd had for the food rations.

Dear Rusty,

As requested, enclosed are two photos of me standing under the apple tree. They were taken on my 19th birthday, June 14th. I like the full-length one better. I was going to send you only that one, but your mother insisted you would want to see the close-up picture of my face. So you can blame her if you find it disappointing!

Rusty riffled through the pages and the envelope, but no photo could be found. "Filthy rotters stole it." He mumbled his frustration as he tried to shake the vision of other men passing around the pictures of Rose. He would simply have to continue imagining Rose's face until he got home.

Truth is, I didn't want to send it at all, but it's only fair. I get to see pictures of you any time I want, even if they aren't current. You certainly aren't hurting in the looks department. I don't think Susie's new beau is nearly as handsome, even if he is a doctor. I'm sure you'll have no trouble finding someone better and sweeter than her when you get home.

Your mom also took a picture of my whole family while she was at it. Tim is the only one smiling in it, but it's still nice to have. It sits on the dresser top until I can find a frame or maybe a little photo album of my own.

It's late and I'm exhausted, so I'll close off with these words I found in Habakkuk.

"Although the fig tree shall not blossom, neither shall fruit be in the

vines … the flock shall be cut off from the fold, and there shall be no herd in the stalls: Yet I will rejoice in the Lord, I will joy in the God of my salvation. The Lord God is my strength …"

This may seem like an odd passage to dwell on, but I chose it because I could relate, and I think you can too. The empty cattle stalls and sheep pens imply one of two things. Either there was anticipation of these cows and sheep that did not materialize, in which case there is great disappointment, or there used to be sheep and cows, but they are now gone, in which case there is great loss. Either way, the writer says he will still rejoice and be joyful. He recognizes God as his source of joy and strength, and God never changes. I hope this is true for you today, Rusty.

All for this time,

Rose

Rusty swallowed the lump in his throat. What did a young girl, safe at home in Canada, know about loss and disappointment? Rose had no idea. How could a God who allowed all this suffering, who allowed Bert to die in such a hideous manner, be Rusty's source of joy and strength? He found no joy in this. No strength.

Still, he kept reading the letter over. He couldn't deny Rose seemed to be able to draw more insight and depth from the Bible than any of the other girls he'd known. Frustration over the missing pictures and about his unrelenting attraction to a girl he'd never seen made him rumple up the letter with a huff.

Ten minutes later, he carefully smoothed it out and read it over again.

By late July, rumors began circulating about the Americans giving the Japanese an opportunity to surrender or face dire consequences. Rusty and the other men speculated about what it might mean. One fellow said atomic bombs were being tested in the deserts of Nevada. Some claimed those bombs were nowhere near ready, while others insisted one atomic bomb would destroy the entire planet.

And then it happened. From their camp in Niigata, no one could see the mushroom cloud that formed over Hiroshima on August 6 or the second one over Nagasaki three days later. But word filtered back to the men through civilians outside the fence. A sense of horror gripped Rusty. When would it end? Would the Americans just keep dropping more atom bombs until all of Japan—perhaps all of Asia—disappeared, and with it the Allied prisoners? Wasn't it enough that thousands of innocent civilians had died? How many children were lost or maimed for life?

Surely, the devil was in control.

Then the camp received surprise visitors, drawing a bunch of men to the main gate. Two American Marines stood there, clean and shaven, uniformed, and supplied with sidearms. The sight was so foreign, Rusty thought he was hallucinating. They seemed to be walking about freely and confidently. They carried an important message for the prisoners. General McArthur was in Yokohama! The war was over.

The Marines promised the prisoners they'd be rescued as soon as possible, hopefully within a week, and encouraged them to hang tough. While the others pressed in, asking for more details of what all had transpired and how this rescue mission would unfold, Rusty wandered away from the crowd. He walked directly to Bert's shallow grave, where the earth was only beginning to settle. He stood staring at it for a long time before he spoke.

"Oh, buddy. I don't want to leave you here. With all my heart, I want vengeance for this. But even if I could pull it off, I know you wouldn't approve. I sure hope you're happy now, because that thought is the only thing keeping me going. That, and Rose's letters. God willing, I'll be out of here in a matter of days and home in a few weeks. Even if it takes months ... we're free, Bert. Free! But I can't take you home, and it's killing me."

Rusty wiped the tears and sweat from his face with the back of one hand. "I know what you'd tell me. I need to forgive. Not in order to let those Japs off the hook, but to set myself free. I can almost hear you." He gazed off into the distant sky, where so recently bomber planes had delivered hope. "I just don't think I can yet, pal. I'm not ready. Maybe when I get out of here. Maybe when I'm safe at home. When I see the faces of my family and know this wasn't all for nothing. When I finally meet my Rose and hold her hand in mine."

He let out one long sigh. "Maybe I'll be able to do it then."

CHAPTER THIRTY-THREE

R ose looked up from her row of sugar beets to see her father and Mr. Thorne in a subdued discussion, heads bent over a newspaper. What had happened? If the war had ended, wouldn't they be jubilant? Why were they both so somber? She kept hoeing but kept one eye on her father until he walked over to where her mother worked a few rows away. He spoke to her briefly, then called Rose, Ojiisan, and Tim over.

"Mr. Thorne says we are done for today. Let's go back to the cabin. There is news."

As usual, Mama's stoic face gave nothing away. She followed Tim to the cabin, where they took time to use the tin washbasins before entering. Dad lay the newspaper across their little table so the light from the window could fall on it. The front-page headline made Rose gasp.

ATOMIC DESTRUCTION IN HIROSHIMA.

Dad began to read aloud. "Tokyo said today that the atomic bomb dropped by a B-29 Monday on Hiroshima literally seared to death 'practically all living things, human and animal,' and crushed big buildings and small houses alike in an unparalleled holocaust. Unofficial American sources estimated the enemy dead and wounded at one hundred thousand persons."

"Hiroshima. Isn't that where—?" Rose looked at her mother. Her face had gone completely white. Rose helped her settle into one of the chairs while Dad translated for Ojiisan.

Her father read a couple more paragraphs until Mama placed a hand on his arm. "No more."

Dad folded the paper, and the family sat in silence.

Finally, Tim raised a question. "Does this mean the war is over?"

Dad shook his head. "Only if Japan surrenders. I don't know if they ever will. It is more honorable to die."

"Mama?" Rose reached for her mother's hand. Mama allowed Rose to stroke the back of it gently, staring at their hands for several moments before she spoke.

"I have not heard from my sister since before the war. I do not know if anyone is still alive, even before this. Surely, now they are not. I only pray they did not suffer."

A knock at the door interrupted them, and Dad opened it to find Mr. Thorne, a folded piece of paper in his hand.

"Sorry, folks. With the news and all, I nearly forgot. A letter came for Rose. Tucked in with ours, from Rusty. It'll be several months old …" He held it out to Dad as his voice trailed off.

Dad took the page with a furrowed brow and a quiet "thank you." He waited while Mr. Thorne left, then closed the door and turned to Rose.

Rose accepted the letter, avoiding all four sets of eyes. Heart pounding, she stepped outside and settled on the swing in the Thornes' front yard before carefully unfolding the paper. She smoothed it out on her lap. Neat, masculine handwriting filled the page.

Dear Rose,

Thank you so much for writing to me. Your letters mean more than I can say. You sound like a wonderful girl, and I'm real glad Mother has you for help around the house and that your family is there for the farm work. The work is backbreaking, but it will make you stronger in every way. I know this from experience. If you haven't already, you'll soon get the swing of the harvesting knife and maybe even be able to enjoy the rhythm of the "chop-chop, slice, toss" repetition. (Well, maybe "enjoy" is an exaggeration. But there's a certain satisfaction in seeing the beets pile up, don't you agree?) With all those songs floating around in your head, I bet you can keep time to your favorite tunes as you work.

I love your lists—keep them coming! I love most of those same things, and it's great to be reminded they still exist out there, somewhere. Your encouragement about my coming home has given me a new lease on life, a new reason to keep going. Your faith that God's word is true even when we don't see it or feel it inspires me. Please write again, and send a photo of yourself! (If you don't have one, ask my mother to snap one with her Brownie.) Tell your little brother hello. He can write to me too. Tell him to give Lady a good rubdown for me. Now that she has Tim, maybe when I get home, she won't go completely nuts like she did last time. I'll curb my jealousy somehow.

Yours truly,
Rusty Thorne

Rose stared at the signature. He'd written back! She read it all again, then closed her eyes and held the letter against her heart as though she could somehow absorb his words into her very soul.

Lady trotted over and tried to sniff the paper. Could she pick up Rusty's scent? Rose held it out of reach lest the dog ruin it. Petting her with one hand, she read parts aloud to the dog.

"He thinks I'm a wonderful girl, Lady. My letters mean more than he can say."

The dog laid her head on Rose's lap, and for a brief moment, everything seemed right in Rose's world.

Three days later, the Americans dropped a second bomb on Japan, and by September 2, Emperor Hirohito had signed the official surrender documents. The war really was over.

"What will we do now?" Tim voiced the question on Rose's mind. "Can we go home?"

She shrugged.

Mr. Thorne had already asked Rose's parents to stay on through harvest. "We still need you desperately."

Dad, along with the other Japanese men on farms in the surrounding community, began meeting regularly to sort out their future. Sometimes they would travel to Winnipeg in twos or threes to solicit government assistance and information. Were they free to leave? Red tape seemed to be tying up everything. Rumor had it British Columbia did not want them back under any circumstances, but on what grounds could they keep them away? Others talked about going back to Japan, and Rose wondered whether there was even a Japan to return to.

Rose's heart soared at the idea of returning to Vancouver and finally pursuing her dream. But if she allowed herself to admit it, she longed more than anything to meet Russell Thorne face-to-face. In a letter to Freda, she wrote, *If nothing develops between us after we meet, then so be it. But if I don't at least meet him, I fear I will spend the rest of my life wondering what might have been.*

She supposed she was being terribly dramatic, but Freda loved that sort of thing.

In mid-September, two telegrams arrived on the same day. Rusty had been rescued from the POW camp and was preparing to board a ship that would take him from Japan to Vancouver. His parents were over the moon.

The second telegram came from Rose's brother. James had been released from his duties and was making his way to Manitoba to reunite with his family.

Mama's face broke into a smile. "James is coming here?" A load of grief suddenly lifted from her shoulders, making her look like a young woman again.

"Wonderful news!" Mr. Thorne clapped Dad on the back. "It could be winter before Rusty is discharged and able to come home. Your son can help us get the harvest in. I mean, if he wants a job. We need to celebrate!"

That night, Mrs. Thorne organized an impromptu party. Her daughters and their families arrived bearing food, and the Onishi family joined them in the house. The table was laden with treats, the air filled with joy, relief, and optimism. Rose was catching a glimpse of the Thorne family of days gone by, before the war and before the loss of their first son.

"I have a surprise," Mrs. Thorne announced. "We were so excited about the telegrams today, I didn't bother mentioning we received a letter from Rusty as well. I only read it an hour ago. It's old, of course. Most of what he says is no longer relevant. But I found one thing in his letter especially intriguing." She turned to Rose. "It seems a certain young lady has been holding out on us. Rose, why didn't you tell us you played the piano?"

Rose stared at Mrs. Thorne and swallowed. She looked at her parents.

Dad's face held a modest grin. "We thought maybe—" But her father couldn't finish his sentence. Mr. and Mrs. Thorne and their daughters all spoke at once.

"You play, Rose?"

"C'mon, Rose, let's hear you!"

"What would you like to play, dear?" Mrs. Thorne began pulling hymn books down from a shelf. "Oh, wait, I know! Something celebratory. Where's that sheet music? Maybe we could hear 'When Johnny Comes Marching Home.'"

Claire grabbed Rose by the wrist and pulled her to her feet. "C'mon, Rose. Give us a tune."

Rose's parents and Ojiisan nodded with approval.

"She plays real good," Tim chimed in. "Wait 'til you hear her. She's practically a professional."

Rose took a seat on the piano stool, her heart pounding. She turned to Mrs. Thorne. "What shall I play?"

"Whatever you like, Rose. I wish you'd told us long ago. We could have used some music around here."

The room grew quiet with anticipation. For the last several months, a hymn they often sang at church had particularly touched Rose. Only in her mind, the melody of "How Great Thou Art" blended perfectly with Beethoven's Fifth Symphony. Each time they sang it, the opening four notes reminded her of the start of the symphony. Bum-bum-bum-BUM. *Oh Lord, my God.* She'd already put the two together as a medley in her head, playing it over and over in her mind as she worked in the field or lay in her bed, mentally correcting her errors. Making improvements each time. She was sure she could play it now. Dare she try?

She placed her hands on the keys, closed her eyes, and waited a moment. Beethoven's familiar melody came like second nature, but when she transitioned to the hymn, greater concentration was required. Rose grew so absorbed in the piece she completely forgot about the people around her or where she was. The notes worked together exactly as she'd dreamed they would, as though the piano had only been waiting to do her bidding. Waiting for her to release years of soul-mending music held captive inside its framework. The piece built to a powerful finish, and when she'd played the final note, she lifted her hands high off the keyboard and held them there while the room and the people in it came back into focus.

The room was so quiet you could hear the clock ticking. Even the children were silent. Her parents sat beaming. Tears flowed freely down Mrs. Thorne's pretty face.

Claire and Shirley had tears as well. Their husbands and father appeared dumbfounded. Finally, it was Mr. Thorne who broke the silence.

"Rose. We had no idea. We had—" He slowly shook his head. "I don't even know what to say."

"That was absolutely beautiful." Claire smiled at Rose. "Mum? Wasn't it?"

Mrs. Thorne found a hanky and wiped the tears from her face. "Oh, Rose. Beyond beautiful. It was divine. I can't believe it. I feel so … so horrible that we didn't know. So sad and horrible."

"But why?" Rose studied Mrs. Thorne's face. "How could you have known?"

"Well, the secret stops here." Mr. Thorne stood. "This is a party, and now we have live music. Let's celebrate!"

Rose began taking requests, using sheet music when necessary and the hymnbook when someone wanted a favorite hymn that she didn't know. They spent the rest of the evening sometimes singing along, but mostly just enjoying Rose's talent.

After their daughters at last gathered their tired children and left for home, Rose's family returned to the cabin. As Rose helped Mrs. Thorne clean up the kitchen, guilt began to seep in until she couldn't hold it any longer. Better to blurt it out and get it over with.

"Mrs. Thorne, I have a confession to make. Tonight was not the first time I've played your piano."

"No?" Mrs. Thorne kept wiping the table.

Rose bit her lip before continuing. "I played it when no one was home."

"But Rose, you could have played it any time. Why ever did you not ask?"

"My father told me not to, that you might not want me to play it. So I didn't. Except … I did. Without permission. I'm sorry."

Mrs. Thorne stood up straight and studied Rose's face for a long time. "Then it was your father you disobeyed, not me. Perhaps it is he who needs to hear your confession. Perhaps not." She carried her dishcloth to the sink.

"What do you mean?"

"Your father meant well. But the piano was not his to deny. I would have gladly let you play it every day, had I known. I just never dreamed …" She paused to swallow. "And as a result, we were all robbed of something good."

"Should I tell him?" Rose dried the last glass and set it in the cupboard.

"If your conscience is telling you to, then I suppose you must. But sometimes it's better not to know. And as far as I am concerned, there's nothing to forgive, Rose. Nothing."

Rose thought about it as she dried the last plate.

Mrs. Thorne squeezed out her dishcloth and hung it up. "Rose, you are still new in your faith. Yet I see more spiritual maturity in you, more integrity, than in many people who have been Christians for forty years. I think this whole incident with the piano is like … like God's grace." She took a deep breath and let out a sigh. "His grace toward us is always available. Just waiting. But, so often, we let fear or guilt or lies keep us from going to him to receive it. We waste years in silence while the sounding board begs to share its riches. I feel as though it's me who owes you an apology."

"Why?" Rose hung her tea towel on the rack.

"For not asking you more questions. For making assumptions. I see now that … well, that it never occurred to me that a Japanese girl would have had such training, such ability. It was nothing but bigotry, plain and simple."

"Bigotry?" Rose had not thought of this woman in those terms. "But how could you have known?"

"Had I asked more about your life before you came here, if I'd taken an interest in what interested you, then I'd have known, wouldn't I?" Mrs. Thorne took both of Rose's hands in her own and studied them. "God did not create these hands for fieldwork, Rose. I am so sorry. Do you forgive me?"

Rose was speechless. She'd never heard an adult apologize to someone younger before. She'd been convinced she was the one who needed forgiveness, but now Mrs. Thorne was asking for hers? She stumbled over her response.

"Y-yes. Of course, but—harvest is almost ready to start. I have to help. We'll never get it all done without all hands on deck."

The two of them stood staring at each other. Mrs. Thorne pressed her lips together and then spoke. "No. I mean it. I'll convince Mr. Thorne somehow. And your parents, too, if necessary."

"But I'll need something to—"

Mrs. Thorne held up one finger. "For years, Miss Ingelson was the only person around here who taught piano. Now she's retired. She's too unwell to continue, and this community has been crying for a new teacher." She moved to the desk in the corner of the kitchen and pulled paper and a pencil out of a drawer. "Once word gets out, there will be no end of demand for you to give lessons. You can do it here."

CHAPTER THIRTY-FOUR

The next morning, Rose stood at the sink washing breakfast dishes when a car pulled into the yard. Claire climbed out and walked around the side of the house. Were those tear streaks on her face?

"Good morning, Rose." Claire stepped through and let the screen door slam shut behind her. "Are my parents inside?"

"Right here." Mrs. Thorne came down the stairs carrying an armload of sheets. "Your father's already out—" She took one look at her daughter's face, and the laundry fell to the floor. "What's happened?"

"Oh, Mum." Claire's tears started again.

"Is it Rusty? What's happened?"

"No. It's Bert. His parents got a telegram."

Mrs. Thorne's face went pale, and she sank into the nearest kitchen chair. Rose wasn't sure whether she should stay or leave. She grabbed a dish towel and slowly dried her hands, turning her back on the dishes. No one seemed to acknowledge her presence, so she stayed where she was.

"How? I thought it was over." Mrs. Thorne's eyebrows came together. "Was Rusty with him?"

"I have no idea, Mum. Bert's dad came over to the house this morning. He asked me to tell you and Dad. The telegram said only that Bert died in Japan, in the performance of his duties in service to his country, and that a letter would follow."

"I'll go find Mr. Thorne," Rose volunteered.

"Thanks, Rose." Claire took a seat across from her mother.

As Rose exited the house, she could hear Mrs. Thorne saying, "Oh, poor Gladys. Poor Henry. Oh, poor Rusty. How will he ever ..."

Rose found Mr. Thorne repairing a tire in his shop. "Mr. Thorne? Can you come to the house? Claire came with news."

Like his wife's, Mr. Thorne's face grew pale. "What is it? Is it Rusty?"

Rose didn't feel it was her news to share, but Mr. Thorne looked so stricken. "No, sir. It's his friend Bert Johnson. His parents received a telegram."

Mr. Thorne allowed a second for Rose's words to register, then headed for the house without saying anything. Rose followed and quietly began filling Mrs. Thorne's wringer washing machine with hot water from the reservoir at the back of the cookstove. Conversation continued around the kitchen table.

"Rusty must be devastated." Claire blew her nose into an embroidered hanky. "They've been together through thick and thin."

Rose knew this to be true. Rusty had mentioned Bert in his letters and how their friendship had sustained him.

"I think we should go see Henry and Gladys." Mr. Thorne looked down at the hat in his hands. "As soon as we can."

His wife nodded. "Yes. But not empty-handed. Let's take supper over." She rose from the table. "Rose? Once these sheets are in the water, can you please peel potatoes for potato salad? We won't worry about the rest of the laundry today. You can pour the dirty water over the garden when the sheets are done." Having something practical to focus on seemed to bring Mrs. Thorne back to life, and she started moving quickly around the kitchen. "Frank, bring me two fresh chickens as soon as you can get them killed and cleaned. I'll fry them up."

Claire rose to leave. "I'll stop by the Johnsons' on my way home and tell them you're coming with supper."

Rose spent the rest of that day helping with food preparations, hanging sheets on the clothesline, and making up the beds after they dried. Rusty Thorne was on her mind. He'd suffered so much, though he only hinted at the difficulties he'd faced. It had to have been much worse than he reported and probably far worse than she could imagine. How would he endure the loss of his best friend?

Rusty's parents had said they would continue to write to him until he was once again under their roof, in hopes that the military would see their letters delivered wherever he was. Rose decided she'd do the same, as soon as she finished her work and the Thornes had left on their errand of condolence. Before attempting a letter, she sat down at the piano. Mrs. Thorne's well-worn hymnbook was organized by themes, and Rose perused the index for songs of comfort. The first one she came upon was perfect. She played it through several times, allowing the beautiful melody and inspired words to fill her with hope about her own losses. She returned to the kitchen and began to write.

Dear Rusty,

Today we learned of Bert Johnson's passing, and I want you to know how terribly sorry I am. I know he was special to you, and I can't imagine how much you must miss him. I wish I could have met him. His parents have always greeted me with kindness and welcome. They seem like wonderful people, and I'm sure Bert was too.

I came across a hymn you are probably well familiar with, though it was new to me. The last verse seems especially meaningful right now, and I hope it will bring you comfort. I pray the melody sticks in your head, wherever you are, and drives the truth of the healing lyrics deep into your hurting heart.

"Does Jesus care when I've said good-by to the dearest on earth to me?

And my sad heart aches till it nearly breaks, is it ought to Him? Does He see?

Oh yes, He cares; I know He cares, His heart is touched with my grief;

When the days are weary, the long nights dreary, I know my Savior cares."

Even with this sad news, we all feel so grateful to hear of your release and that you will soon be home. I don't know whether I will still be here when you arrive, but I do wish you all the best and would be happy to continue writing in any case—if you like. I also wanted to thank you for telling your mother I play the piano. We had quite the party here the night we received word of your rescue (before we learned about Bert), and I have been welcomed to play the piano as much as I want. After my work is done, of course. Your mom is determined to line up some piano students for me to teach!

Your dad says you will not likely be here in time for this harvest (we begin next week). However, my brother James will soon be joining us. He's strong and will be able to work twice as fast as I can once he gets the hang of it.

Again, all my condolences on the loss of your dear friend. War is so senseless.

Rose

Sunday's church service was a messy blend of celebration over the end of the war and sorrow for the Johnson family. Rose learned a little more about the awful way Bert had died. It seemed impossible. Since they had no body to bury, the family requested that his memorial service wait until Rusty and a half-dozen other Spruceville boys came home.

"It's going to be difficult enough for them all." Mr. Johnson spoke to the congregation from his seat on a pew. "It would be even harder if they couldn't share this with us." He glanced around at his family. "And it will be a comfort to us to have them present."

Rose admired the man's courage and transparency. No wonder Bert had been such a man of integrity and a faithful friend to Rusty.

After the pastor closed the emotional service with prayer, he asked, as always, if anyone had any news or announcements pertinent to the congregation before they went their separate ways. Mrs. Thorne stood.

"I know some of you have been searching for a new piano teacher for your children since Miss Ingelson retired, and I'm pleased to let you all know that we have a very accomplished pianist, with teaching experience, in our midst."

Rose sucked in a quick breath. Mrs. Thorne placed a hand on her shoulder.

"Rose here will be offering lessons at our home. I know we're not in town, but it's not that far by bike, and it will be worth it. Now, Rose—you don't know this, but I've spoken with your parents. Any money you earn will be set aside so you can continue your education in piano performance as soon as you're able."

The pastor nodded. "Thank you, Mrs. Thorne … and Rose. Anyone else?"

Rose glanced around the room. People smiled and nodded. Her parents were practically beaming. Mrs. Pierce, however, stared back with her usual crossed arms and disapproving expression.

"If not, then you're dismissed." The pastor stepped down and hurried to be the first one to the door so he could greet his parishioners individually.

Rose remained seated with Mrs. Thorne. Within minutes, they were approached by two mothers and one teenage girl, all inquiring about piano lessons. Times and costs were agreed upon, and Rose stood to leave. By the time she joined her family at Mr. Thorne's truck, two more parents had stopped her to discuss lessons for their children. Rose climbed into the back of the truck and sat beside Tim. Ojiisan took his place in the middle of the front seat and waited. When Mr. and Mrs. Thorne approached, Mr. Thorne whispered something to his wife.

Mrs. Thorne's reply, however, was fully audible. "What does she mean by 'conducting business at church'?" She let out a snort. "I don't give a fat fig what Justina Pierce thinks." She swung the door open and climbed in. Rose couldn't tell whether Mrs. Thorne said more about the issue or not. It didn't matter. Her mind already raced with possibilities for the students she was taking on.

Rose spent most of the afternoon thinking about how she would test each student to determine their skill level. She jotted down some of the best teaching techniques her own teachers had used and imagined herself helping each child grow to love the piano as much as she did. Most of all, she relished the new freedom to play it herself. That evening, she played for a solid three hours.

The following morning, as soon as Mr. Thorne had left the house, Mrs. Thorne placed a hand on Rose's elbow. "Rose, dear, we need to talk."

They sat together at the kitchen table, Rose's heart pounding. Had they changed their minds? Mrs. Thorne sounded serious and sad.

"I'm so sorry to say this, Rose, but I spoke too soon. I overstepped. Mr. Thorne is happy to have you playing the piano and giving lessons— but not until harvest is over. He says we really still need everyone helping, or we'll never get the crop in. I'm sorry." She took both of Rose's hands in hers. "It kills me to see these hands doing that work, it truly does. He just doesn't understand."

"It's all right." Rose swallowed her disappointment. "Really. I mean, I expected to work the harvest before this, anyway, and it wouldn't feel right to know that my family—everyone—is out there working when I don't have to. And I've done this often enough to know how it goes, how much help it takes. You don't need to feel bad. We can start the lessons afterwards. I'm sure my students will understand."

Mrs. Thorne studied her a long time. Finally, she smiled. "This would almost be easier if you got mad."

Rose smiled back. "I do get mad sometimes. But not at you. Sometimes, it's the government. Sometimes, it's my own parents, a little, though I know none of this is their fault either. It's just the whole war. It's unfair to everyone."

Mrs. Thorne nodded. "That it is." She patted Rose's hand. "Your mature attitude gives me hope for the future of this country, Rose. God has promised to redeem and restore all that is wrong in our world, and he will for you too. Somehow, someday. I hope you can believe that."

Rose nodded. "I want to."

"And I hope this will be the absolute last sugar beet harvest you will ever have to work as long as you live."

On Tuesday, James was due to arrive in Winnipeg. Restrictions had not yet been lifted on how far the Japanese could travel from their host farms, so Mr. Thorne agreed to drive the whole family to Union Station in Winnipeg. Rose had not been there since they arrived three-and-a-half years earlier. Except for the different season, it looked the same as she remembered. But she had changed immensely.

Mr. Thorne waited in his truck while the Onishi family waited on the platform. When the train pulled in, Rose could feel her heart pounding. She had not seen her brother for nearly four years. Would they even recognize him?

She didn't have to wonder long. James was the first passenger to step off the train. Tim spotted him immediately and started jumping up and down, calling his name until James saw them and came over. He carried a duffel bag in each hand and was dressed in simple civilian clothes—brown pants, a plain, blue shirt, and a gray fedora. Though he looked older and huskier, his perpetually serious expression had not changed.

While other passengers ran into the loving embrace of relatives and friends on the platform, James' family greeted him with smiles and handshakes. Rose wished she could give him a big hug, or at least hop around him like Tim did. But that would be considered unacceptable to her parents and to Ojiisan. James would probably feel embarrassed too. She settled for a handshake and warmed inside when her brother placed his other hand on her shoulder.

"Hey, there, little sis." He squeezed gently before pulling his hand away and picking up the bags he'd set down. "You're all grown up!"

Tim led the way back to Mr. Thorne's truck amid rapid-fire conversation in both English and Japanese. Mr. Thorne waved and climbed out of his truck. He reached out to shake James' hand. "Frank Thorne. Pleased to meet you, James. Welcome!" He took one of James' bags and slung it into the back of the truck. "You'll need to ride in back, I'm afraid."

"Not a problem. It will give me a chance to catch up with these squirts." James tousled Tim's hair and wrapped one arm around Rose, making her blush. Dad climbed into the back with them, while Mama and Ojiisan took their spots in front with Mr. Thorne. The ride home seemed to go by in record time. Questions volleyed back and forth in a volume akin to yelling so as to be heard above the wind, the roar of the truck's engine, and the crunch of wheels on gravel.

Rose peered through the window into the front seat. Even from behind, she observed a lightness to her mother's posture and countenance. Knowing Mama, her heart was filled with joy to have all her children around her at long last—regardless of where they were or how unknown their future. For now, they were together. Nights were growing colder, but they had a roof over their heads, and they had work. The 1945 sugar beet harvest would begin the following day.

CHAPTER THIRTY-FIVE

March 1946

Spring had arrived by the time Rusty was finally discharged from the army. He didn't mind the delay. The thought of returning home made his insides quiver and his chest tighten. He didn't want to face Bert's parents. Surely, they would take one look at him and wonder why God had spared Rusty and taken Bert. It should have been the other way around. For the hundredth time, he wished he'd joined his friend on the field that day the barrels dropped. If he could go back, he'd run deliberately into one of them.

He'd spent the months going through the motions, doing whatever he was assigned to do, feeling nothing. The other men had been surprised the first time he joined them for celebratory drinks when they disembarked in Vancouver.

"Didn't take you for a drinker, Preach," one fellow teased. "Glad to see you stoop to our level for once."

"Aw, leave'm alone," someone else said. "He's earned it."

Rusty didn't respond but threw back enough drinks to numb his feelings. The next day, regret and a headache plagued him. But when the next opportunity arose, he repeated his actions, if only to escape his tortured thoughts. While his body was returning to health with plenty of food, medical attention, and fresh air, the memories of the past four years invaded his mind, and night terrors continued to shorten his sleep. Many nights, he awoke to find himself sitting up in bed, his sheets tangled and damp. He'd been wrestling Japanese soldiers in his dreams, trying to keep himself between them and Bert. Failing every time.

So when word came that they were finally boarding a train for Winnipeg, Rusty didn't even try to notify his parents. He wasn't ready for anyone to meet him at Union Station. He'd get to Winnipeg, collect his discharge papers, and take his time going home. It was too early for spring planting, anyway. They wouldn't need him yet. And Rose was probably long gone. A letter had reached him in late February, and Rusty pulled it out to re-read on the train.

Happy New Year, Rusty! Can you believe it's 1946? We had a quiet Christmas. The extreme cold kept everyone home. They even canceled the Sunday school concert, which was unfortunate. I'm sure there were lots of disappointed little kids, and maybe some relieved ones too.

My brother James arrived in time for harvest. As I predicted, he learned quickly, and I know your dad was relieved when the beets were finally trucked to the train and he could turn the cows out onto the field to forage for the tops. Your father got James and Dad involved in the curling club, and James has made new friends already. He's more outgoing than I am.

We had a huge potluck feast at church to celebrate the war's end. Of course, a parade is being planned for when you and the other fellows finally get home. There's been much discussion about whether it's better to celebrate first and then hold a memorial service for Bert, or would the other way around be best. Do you have any thoughts on that?

Now that you're back in Canada, do you have lots of free time? James and I saw The Harvey Girls—*have you seen it?*

I was also inspired by the newsreel before the movie started. It wasn't really news anymore, but it's been so popular they keep playing it. It shows Princess Elizabeth working as a mechanic for the British military, in coveralls and all! Her parents were visiting her. I loved it. Good for her, I say! My brother wasn't convinced. "Just a publicity stunt," he claims. James can be a bit cynical. I think the princess is perfectly lovely and really brave. Good qualities for a future queen, if she outlives her father. It's hard to imagine singing "God Save the Queen" instead of king, though.

I'm rambling. I'll close for now. Haven't heard from you in a while ... guess you're busy. Again, I'm glad you're back in Canada at least and hope you'll soon be discharged. I doubt I'll be here for your homecoming either way. My father is inquiring about work in Winnipeg, and if he finds a job, we'll all go with him. Your parents made it clear we are welcome to stay and keep working here. In fact, your mom insisted that last year's harvest was my last time for fieldwork, that she will keep me busy indoors, between piano lessons. I do like the sound of that!

In any case, I am extremely proud and grateful to be a Canadian—in spite of everything.

Sincerely,

Rose

Rusty folded Rose's letter and put it back in his duffel bag. The girl he had so longed to meet, whose letters had convinced him he was falling in love sight unseen, now seemed far too good for him. If she thought her brother was cynical, what would she think of Russell Thorne, the drunk? The depressed? The lazy? The silent? The filled-with-bitterness?

What did she mean by *in spite of everything*? Sure, her piano dreams had been put on hold for a while, but so what? Surely, she could pick up where she left off. She'd never left her country, never been separated from her loved ones. What did a girl like her understand about being a prisoner? About having every moment of your life dictated by others?

They would probably make a horrible match.

So why couldn't he stop thinking about her?

The fellows were circulating an *Archie* comic book, and when it came to Rusty, he perused the cover and passed it along. He preferred staring out the train windows. The mountains that once held him in awe and made his heart soar with praise and worship to their creator may as well have been a crumbled heap of rubble. As the Rockies gradually settled into foothills and then rolling prairie, his heart grew even heavier. He leaned his head against the window, but sleep eluded him as his thoughts raced on.

Perhaps it would be best if Rose were gone when he got home. Though part of him still desperately wanted to meet her—if for no other reason, to satisfy his curiosity and see if she looked anything like he imagined—another part worried his mere countenance might frighten her off. His reflection in the mirror revealed only an empty shell. Though his body was returning to its former weight, he still appeared undernourished. Worse than that was the hollowness to his eyes that he feared would never change. How could it? There was no way to unsee the things he'd seen or to gain back all he'd lost.

CHAPTER THIRTY-SIX

Two other soldiers from Spruceville, both of whom Rusty had known casually before the war, were with the group that got off in Winnipeg. Bill was older than Rusty and had spent most of his time in France. Eddie was younger. A draftee who'd never left Canada, he'd spent the war chauffeuring officers around on Vancouver Island.

Eddie's family waited on the platform to meet him at the station. Their happy smiles and jubilant squeals almost made Rusty wish he'd contacted his parents to let them know he was coming. A tap on his shoulder made him turn away from the emotional reunion.

It was Bill. "Anybody here for you, Thorne?"

Rusty shook his head.

"Not feeling ready to go home yet?"

Bill's brown eyes held his, filled with silent understanding. Together, they watched Eddie's family leave. Then Bill bent his head toward Rusty again.

"We could hang around in the city a couple of days, give ourselves some time."

Rusty nodded. "We could. But as soon as Eddie gets back to Spruceville, word will be out. My parents will wonder what became of me."

Bill sighed. "Yeah. Mine too."

The pair of them walked slowly to the bus station, half hoping they'd miss the next bus to Spruceville. Though they said little, a sense of comradeship quieted Rusty's heart.

As they stood in line for tickets, Bill turned toward Rusty. "I heard Bert Johnson didn't make it."

The offhand statement hit Rusty like a punch to his midsection. He should respond somehow, but he could barely breathe. The image of that supply barrel falling from the sky, knocking Bert to the ground, and the parachute settling over his body was back in an instant. He gave his head a shake to erase the picture.

Bill was waiting for a response.

"No. He didn't." Barely a whisper, it was all Rusty could manage.

Bill said no more. They bought their tickets and boarded the bus, prepared for at least a ninety-minute ride with the frequent stops along the way.

Once they were rolling, Bill attempted conversation again. "Got a girl waitin' for ya?"

Rusty's mind flew to Rose, but he didn't think she'd even be around. And even if she was, could he really call her his girl? Would she want anything to do with him once she realized he was nothing like the man she'd thought? He boiled his answer down to two words. "Not anymore."

"Wait a minute. Weren't you and that Pierce girl an item? Sally? Sandy?"

"Susie. That ended long ago. She took up with the new doctor in town. They're likely married by now, with half a dozen kids. How about you?"

Bill smiled. "Nope. I'm unattached, but if my mother has her way, I'll be engaged to Helen Murphy by summer."

Rusty chuckled but the conversation ended. His heart grew heavier as the bus rumbled closer to home. By the time they reached Spruceville, darkness had fallen. They stepped off the bus and found a pay phone outside the little cafe that doubled as a bus station. Rusty waited while Bill called his parents. Ecstatic shrieks carried through the receiver.

Bill hung up. "It's all yours. Unless … you want to catch a ride with us. We go right past your place."

Rusty considered it. Something about walking up the lane toward home, being greeted by Lady and her wagging tail before any humans knew he was coming appealed to him. "Sure, if your parents don't mind."

"Of course, they won't. It'll take them at least forty minutes to get here, though. Dad was out milking. Want to go grab a drink? I don't know about you, but I could use a little extra fortification before I see my family again."

Rusty agreed, and they walked across the road to the town's lone watering hole. Rusty had stepped inside the Spruceville Hotel only one time, when he was around fifteen. The combination hotel and pub was run by the parents of a former classmate, Ralph Foster, and Ralph's family had living quarters in the back. Rusty had once gone home with Ralph after school to work on a history assignment. Out of curiosity, Rusty had poked his head inside the pub on their way through the lobby. He'd been left with the impression of dim lighting, cigarette smoke, a sour odor, and sad music. The Depression had been in full force, and Rusty had wondered how anybody could afford booze or cigarettes. It held little appeal for him back then.

Though the establishment had been taken over by new proprietors, it was just as Rusty remembered. The music had been upgraded to a wooden jukebox, however, and Bill plugged it with a nickel. Seconds later, Doris Day and Les Brown crooned "Sentimental Journey." Bill ordered shots of whiskey for them both. The place was about half full, and Rusty kept his face forward at the bar, hoping no one would recognize him—especially anyone who'd known Bert. He threw back the whiskey and ordered another while the words of the tune teased him.

"Stupid song," Rusty muttered as he took another drink.

More than anything, he wished he and Bert had never volunteered to serve their country. What good had it done? Even if they had eventually been drafted, they would have stayed in Canada and avoided imprisonment. It would have made no difference to the outcome of the war, except that Bert would still be alive.

But, of course, it wasn't patriotic to say such things.

A loud voice behind him jolted him back to reality. "Russell Thorne, is that you? Well, as I live and breathe! Look, fellas, it's the Thorne boy. Home from the war."

An old neighbor, Clem McCarthy, approached. Clem thumped

Rusty on the back as though they'd been close friends. "Welcome home, son! Your parents must be so proud! Spent your time in the Pacific, did I get that right? Sorry about the Johnson boy. That's a crying shame. Let me buy you a drink."

Two more free beers came Rusty's way, courtesy of hometown well-wishers. He didn't even like beer, but he downed them regardless, welcoming the numbness that replaced his despair.

From the window, Bill spotted his parents across the street. "C'mon, Rusty. Grab your gear."

Rusty complied, wavering slightly but now fortified to greet his family and even Rose if she was still around.

Bill held the door open for him. As he walked through, three young men in civilian clothes approached. Rusty didn't recognize any of them, but the face of one caused his heart to race. Suddenly, faster than Rusty could think, his arm seemed to take on a mind of its own. His fist contacted the man's face. The man fell backward, landing on the concrete outside the hotel. His buddies helped him up, and Rusty prepared to deliver a second blow. But somebody was holding his arms.

"Thorne! What are you doing, buddy?" Bill and Clem pulled him back. "C'mon, let's get you out of here."

The man Rusty had hit swiped at his bloody nose and shuffled back a step or two. His two companions glared at Rusty. "The war is over, pal," one of them said, rolling his shoulders back. "Maybe you didn't hear."

Bill and Clem steered Rusty across the street, keeping a firm grip on his arms. "Who was that, Thorne? Why'd you haul off and hit him?"

Rusty didn't trust himself to speak. He stared at his fist, clenched and unclenched it, hardly believing what he'd done. He had no idea who he'd just hit.

But Clem knew. "I met that young fella at the curling rink a few weeks ago. He's working on one of the beet farms around here. Nice guy. Name is James Onishi."

CHAPTER THIRTY-SEVEN

The next thing Rusty knew, he was waking up in his own bedroom in his parents' home. How had he gotten here? His head pounded and his eyes burned. Try as he might, he couldn't recall anything past having a drink in town with Bill. Bill's parents must have brought him home. *Oh no.* Mum and Dad must have seen him drunk.

A glimmer of light entered through the half-open door, revealing the outline of his uniform on the chair and his boots, socks, and duffel bag on the floor. Under the covers, he wore only his undershirt and undershorts. As he lifted a hand to his forehead, trying to remember, the silhouette of his mother formed in the doorway. She peered in, her pink chenille bathrobe a comforting sight. Was she real? It wouldn't be the first time he'd had this dream.

"Mum?" His voice was a pathetic croak.

"I thought I heard you moan." She stepped into the room and approached his bed.

"What time is it?"

"Almost five. How are you feeling?" His mother sat on the edge of the bed and placed the back of her hand on his cheek. "Got a headache?"

Snippets of the previous evening came back. Insisting to Bill that he be dropped off at the road. Climbing out of a vehicle at the end of his driveway and throwing up. Stumbling toward the farmyard and being greeted by Lady, who was exuberant at first and then subdued when she sensed his condition. For the life of him, he couldn't remember seeing his parents or coming to bed.

"Mum, I'm so sorry. This is not how I imagined it. Not how I planned it." A tear began to run down one cheek.

His mother sat on the neatly made bed that had been Jack's. "It's not exactly what I envisioned, either, son. But you're here. That's what counts now. You're alive, and you're right here, under our roof. I've prayed for this day since you left." She stood. "I'll bring you some aspirin and a big glass of water. I want you to drink it all and go back to sleep for a few hours. Okay?"

When she returned, Rusty did as he was told. The familiar taste of the farm's well water went down like a balm for his spirit. *I'll wake up refreshed, back to my old self, and never take another drink. It's the least I can do. Maybe Mum and Dad will forget the homecoming like a bad dream.*

"I'm going to open your window a bit. The fresh air will do you good." Mum pushed up the frame and braced it open with the stick that sat on the sill for that purpose. "Now go back to sleep."

"Mum?" There was one thing Rusty just had to know. "Is Rose still here?"

His mother smiled. "She's asleep in the next room, Rusty. You'll meet her soon enough."

Sometime later, Rusty awoke sitting straight up once again, drenched in sweat and heart pounding. He'd been fighting the Japanese, arms flailing against the tangled bedding. Even though he was awake, he was certain he could still hear them talking. Panting, he looked around. He was in his own room back home. He took a deep breath and let it out slowly. He flipped his pillow to the cool side and lay back down. Then he heard it again. Male voices, speaking Japanese! But he was awake. Wasn't he?

He lay still, listening. The welcome sound of birds chirping in the treetops allowed him to relax. Then the voices started again—and they sounded as though they were right outside his bedroom window.

"I've got be dreaming." The sound of his own voice convinced him he wasn't.

He threw off the covers and stumbled to the window. In the dim light of early morning, two men stood in front of the barn. One looked old and stooped over. Both gestured with their hands when they spoke. He couldn't make out their faces, but whatever language they spoke sounded exactly like the hateful one he'd heard for far too long. He thought he recognized the word for shovel—*shaberu*. Either the war was back on and the Thorne farm had been invaded, or Rusty was hallucinating.

It had to be the latter. What was in those drinks last night? Perhaps he really was still asleep. He closed the window, but instead of climbing back into his bed, he crumpled to his knees beside it.

"Oh God. If you're still there and you hear me, you've got to help me. I'm in worse shape than I thought. These visions are so real. If they show up in my room, I'm done for. I need to quit drinking. But I'm going to need your help with that too."

He crawled between the sheets and let his extreme fatigue carry him into slumber. Just as he was dozing off, he recalled hitting a Japanese face as he left the pub the night before. That was impossible. There weren't any Japanese people within sixty miles, maybe more. But he'd hit *someone*, of that he was certain. Was it some local, perhaps even an old friend? Was his mind so far gone it was altering the facial features of innocent bystanders to look like the enemy?

The third time Rusty awoke, it was gradually and to the sound of beautiful music. In his half dream, he followed a forest trail overgrown with weeds. With a sickle in hand, Rusty cleared the path as he went along, propelled by a sense of urgency at something left undone. The strains of classical piano urged him forward as he tried to reach the source of the music.

When he opened his eyes, the sun was high in the sky. The cause of the music became obvious. It was his mother's piano. And the fingers producing the incredible melody had to belong to Rose. He closed his eyes and soaked in the wondrous sound, letting it soothe his aching heart and mind. He was really and truly home! He'd made it. He was safe. No one could hurt him. There would be plenty to eat. Even now, he thought he smelled bacon and toast. His mouth watered. The hallucinations from the earlier morning hours lost their grip.

Soon he would meet Rose!

Wow, Mum wasn't kidding. She is *good!* Rusty had never heard such a skilled piano player. If he didn't know better, he would think he heard two pianos being played at once, both by talented pianists. Rose's dream of becoming a concert pianist was not simply pie in the sky. She belonged on a stage. Surely, now that the war was over, she could continue her pursuit and fulfill the dream. The world needed to hear her.

He swung his legs over the edge of the bed, reached for his trousers, and pulled them on. While he would probably still appear thin to his family, the new uniform he'd been issued upon his rescue had since been replaced with a larger size, and he'd grown into it. Checking the small mirror on his bedroom wall, he ran a hand through his hair. A glance out the window revealed only a handful of chickens scratching around the barnyard. No hallucinations, Japanese or otherwise.

Rusty tiptoed down the stairs slowly, not wanting to distract Rose from her playing for even a moment. He didn't know the name of the piece she played or its composer, but it seemed to be building to a big finish. His heart pounded. He was finally going to see this girl whose letters had so captivated his attention and whose words had sustained him through his darkest days. When he reached the bottom, he turned to his right and leaned against the doorframe between kitchen and living room.

At the piano with her back to Rusty, appearing completely absorbed in the song, sat Rose. Even though she was seated, he could tell she was smaller than he'd imagined. More surprising was her hair. It wasn't blonde or curly as he'd expected, but black and straight. It hung past her shoulders and shone in the early spring sunshine streaming through the window, reminding Rusty of Veronica Lodge, Archie Andrews' comic book girlfriend. He relaxed against the doorframe, arms crossed and one foot over the other as the young woman's delicate-looking arms managed to draw enormous volume out of the old piano. Two tiny hands with incredible span clearly held more strength in them than they ought. Rose's frame moved with the rhythm of the music, her head leaning in toward the instrument and back again, as though she and the piano were one. The entire scene was so lovely, Rusty thought his heart might burst right then and there. He closed his eyes and allowed the music to flood over him.

The kitchen door opened and closed, and he turned to see his mother coming in with a basket of eggs. He raised a finger to his lips and nodded toward the piano. His mother smiled, set the basket on the table, and joined him in the doorway. Rusty placed an arm around her shoulder, and she wrapped both of hers around his midsection.

Rose played through the climactic finale of the piece and brought the song to its close. Her hands stayed poised over the keyboard for a second, then reached for a pencil and notebook that lay off to the side. She jerked upright when Mum began to clap.

"Bravo, Rose! Beautiful as always. Simply beautiful!"

Rose's hand flew to her chest, and she turned around with a quiet gasp.

"I've got someone for you to meet." Mum kept talking, but Rusty couldn't understand any of the words. He stood frozen in place, his mother's voice an infuriating buzz in his ears.

The girl at the piano was looking him straight in the eyes, but it was not Rose.

The girl at the piano was Japanese.

CHAPTER THIRTY-EIGHT

Rose nearly jumped off the piano stool at the sound of Mrs. Thorne's voice. She'd thought she was alone in the house and had warmed up with Beethoven's "Two Rondos," which she knew from memory. When she turned, the image of Rusty Thorne that had seared itself into her brain from gazing at his photographs suddenly came to life. He stood next to his mother in an undershirt, army pants, and bare feet. Though he was thinner than she'd imagined, she would know him anywhere.

More importantly, his face registered an expression she could only interpret as absolute horror.

"Look who got home late last night." Mrs. Thorne's smile was victorious. "I'd like you to meet my son, Rusty."

Rose felt her mouth gaping open. She quickly pulled it shut and swallowed.

"Rusty, this is Rose Onishi. Not that the two of you need much of an introduction, but just to make it official—"

Mrs. Thorne's sentence was cut short by her son's words. "She's Japanese."

He continued to stare at Rose, and she could do little more than stare back.

"Well, of course. You knew that." Mrs. Thorne hung onto Rusty's arm.

Rusty's posture stiffened. He finally tore his gaze from her and glared at his mother, his head shaking and his jaw slack.

"Rusty, I told you. I'm sure I told you! Rose's family is part of the relocation ... from Vancouver ... after Pearl Harbor? They came here to work on the farms ..." Each sentence grew fainter, the last trailing up like a question. "I'm certain I told you."

Rusty scowled at Rose and said nothing to relieve the tension.

She stood and held out her right hand. "Pleased to finally meet you, Rusty." Though she tried to speak with confidence, a tremor weakened her statement.

Rusty did not respond. His accusing gaze swung back to his mother. "How could you do this to me?"

Mrs. Thorne blinked rapidly. "How could I do what? Rusty, I told you—"

"You told me nothing! You deliberately deceived me."

"I didn't! I did not deceive you, Russell. I never dreamed—"

"Was Dad in on this too? Where is he? Those were Japs out by the barn this morning, weren't they? They're here!"

Rose wanted to run, but with the two of them standing in the doorway, the room's only exit was the front door. She stood frozen in place as Rusty and his mother faced each other.

"Rusty, we assumed you knew. You have to believe me!"

He poked a finger toward his mother's chin. "I cannot believe you lied to me." Then he turned and clomped up the stairs.

Mrs. Thorne followed him. "Rusty, we did *not* lie to you. *Ever.* I'm sorry! Maybe that letter never made it through, I don't know. We had to be so careful not to say anything political, maybe we—"

A door slammed upstairs.

Rose grabbed her chance to flee through the kitchen, hot tears stinging her eyes. She was expecting a piano student in fifteen minutes. She'd go see her mother at the cabin and allow things to cool down in the house.

But Mrs. Thorne must have heard the back door close and ran after her. "Rose, wait!" She called from the step. "Come back. He'll settle down. He's just ... surprised, is all. This won't make any difference once he's over the shock."

Rose stopped, but she didn't want to turn around lest Mrs. Thorne see the tears welling. She blinked them back. "I think it's best if I wait out here for a bit, Mrs. Thorne. I'll come back when Marla Jean arrives for her lesson."

Rose arrived at the cabin and explained to her mother what had happened. Mama listened, nodding as though she'd expected this all along. "You move back to cabin now. Your father will find other work soon. Then we all leave. Stay together."

Rose stared back. They were leaving? "But planting starts in a few days!"

"They can hire others now." Mama kept stitching. "And they have their son home."

"But Mama, there isn't room for all of us in the cabin with James here. And the piano's in the house!"

Her mother sighed. "Rozu. Your brother came home with a black eye last night."

"What? James got in a fight?"

"Not much of a fight. He got hit just for being Japanese."

"By who?" Rose couldn't believe it. With only a few exceptions, the people of Spruceville had been so welcoming.

"A soldier. We don't know who." Mama abruptly stopped talking when Tim came inside.

"Hi, Rose. Did you hear? James has a shiner." Tim handed a basket of eggs to his mother and turned to leave again. "You should see the other guy." Laughing at his own joke, he let the screen door slam behind him. Then he hollered over his shoulder, "Marla Jean's here for her lesson!"

Indeed, her student pedaled her bicycle down the lane. Rose would have to wait to find out more about James' fight. She stepped out into the yard, but her feet faltered when Mrs. Thorne came out of the house and strode out to meet Marla Jean. She conversed with the girl a moment, then Marla Jean turned around and left, peering back over her shoulder at Rose as she pedaled away. What was going on?

With her shoulders slumped, Mrs. Thorne approached. "I'm so sorry, Rose. I had no idea Rusty would be like this. I suppose I should have realized, given his circumstances, but I—I didn't think. For today,

I think it's best if you avoid the house. His father will talk with him when he gets in from the field. I'm sure everything will be all right. He simply needs a little time."

Rose should have known things were too good to last. She spent the day working with her mother, but her mind remained on Rusty. The expression of horror on his face when he first laid eyes on her kept playing over in her head—much like the time she and Freda saw *Bride of Frankenstein*. She hadn't been able to get the images out of her head for days.

How on earth had she been so naive as to entertain notions of romance? Even friendship with Rusty seemed out of the question now. How could she face any of the Thorne family again?

After supper, she started a letter to Freda to tell her all about it.

I'm mortified, Freda. I wish Mrs. Thorne had never encouraged me to write to Rusty in the first place. What was she thinking? But in a way, it's my own fault. I shouldn't even be here anymore. I am twenty years old! I should be making my own way in the world by now, figuring out how to get back into school and once again pursue my dreams instead of letting everyone else dictate what I do. But the money I've managed to save from teaching piano isn't nearly enough. I feel so stuck. I'd begun to believe God was going to work all this out for my good, but now I'm not so sure.

She abandoned the half-finished letter, not sure if she'd ever have the heart to send it. Freda's last letter had revealed she was moving on with her life, had met a wonderful fellow and would probably be engaged by Christmas. It would take at least that long for the ban against Japanese Canadians in Vancouver to be lifted, enabling them to return. If Freda was a newlywed, she'd not have much space for Rose in her life, let alone her home.

Meanwhile, where was Rose to sleep? James had taken over her former bunk in her parents' cabin. The other cabin was occupied by four single men Mr. Thorne had hired for the season, all of them itinerant laborers who had worked last year's harvest.

Mama was already on top of things. She seemed almost pleased with this turn of events, humming as she and Rose placed clean sheets on the bunk beds. Tim and James would share one, freeing a top bunk for Rose. "It's good for us to be all together again."

Rose couldn't find an opportunity to ask James about his black eye. He and Dad spent a large chunk of the day in town, trying to formulate plans for their next step. Since his arrival, James had gotten involved in the community, worked hard, and made friends. But that was before the soldiers came home—the ones who'd fought the Japanese or been imprisoned by them. If the Onishis were no longer welcome in Spruceville, where could they go? Reports were coming back about other internees finding jobs in Winnipeg, only to be unable to secure housing. Those who managed to rent apartments did so by saying they were Chinese. One rumor said the government was trying to send all of them back to Japan.

She prayed from her bunk. *Oh God, if you're listening, please let everything blow over. I love my piano students—I don't want to let them down. I love my room in the house. If you're going to take it all away, please help me stop loving it all so much. Most of all, help me to stop loving Rusty Thorne.*

CHAPTER THIRTY-NINE

R usty sat at the kitchen table, drinking a tall glass of milk and trying to talk some sense into his parents. Darkness was falling on his first full day at home, and this was not at all how any of them had pictured it. After storming away from his mother and Rose, he'd tried in vain to sleep some more. Then he'd ventured out to the front porch where he couldn't see the workers' cabins, the barn, or the beet fields. He'd sat on the step, petting Lady for most of the day. Dad had joined him briefly, bringing him a sandwich and asking him if he wanted to talk. He hadn't.

His sisters and their families had come for supper, and he'd managed to put on a happy face. The matter of the Japanese was avoided. Now everyone had returned home, and Rusty didn't want to face another sleepless night, knowing the enemy was outside his window.

"I don't understand how you and Mum could have agreed to this, Dad."

His father wrapped both hands around a coffee cup. "First of all, these folks are as Canadian as we are, son."

"Rose doesn't even speak Japanese," Mum chimed in.

Rusty held up a hand to stop her. "We'll get to her later. I still don't understand what they're even doing here."

"Rusty, we'd have lost everything by now if it weren't for the Onishi family and the other Japanese. Plain and simple. You know how hard the work is, how difficult it's always been to find dependable help for the summer and harvest. With all the labor force gone—overseas, or otherwise working for the war effort—we'd have been sunk. Just as surely as if we were hit by a German U-boat."

His mother continued. "Meanwhile, B.C. was booting the Japanese out of the province, fearful they'd help Japan attack us, somehow. They were rounded up and placed in camps. Rose had to give up her education, her piano studies—"

"They were prisoners, too, Rusty." Dad drew a callused hand across his whiskered chin. "Not like you, I know, but—"

"No, Dad. You *don't* know. You weren't there. You didn't see what I saw. I couldn't tell you about it in my letters, how awful it was, how brutal. But—" His voice broke. "They were monsters. And then ... and then Bert ..."

The room grew silent except for the ticking of his mother's kitchen clock and the distant croaking of bullfrogs through the open window.

His mother placed a hand on his arm. "Rusty, we're so sorry about Bert. So sad for his family and for you."

Rusty cleared his throat and gave his head a shake. He wasn't ready to talk about Bert or think about visiting the Johnson family yet. "All right, so ... what happened? The government came up with a brilliant plan to put the Japanese to work in Manitoba to replace the farmworkers?"

"That's about the size of it, yes." Dad nodded. "Some of the farmers were skeptical, at first. But it was a way to keep the industry going."

"We finally had a huge demand for the beets," Mum added. "Sugar couldn't be imported from anywhere anymore."

Dad rose to refill his coffee cup from the pot on the stove. "It seemed like a good plan. I still think it was. For us, at least. None of this has been fair to them."

"Fine. They saved the farm. That still doesn't explain how you could have encouraged Ro—" He couldn't even say her name. "Why on earth did you persuade her to *write to me?*"

His mother wrung her hands. "All the young people were encouraged to write letters, Rusty. Rose hasn't been able to attend school with the others. She's made few friends, and she's had no social life. I thought it would be good for her. And for you. Tim wrote letters of his own, to complete strangers—"

"And why was there not one word, in her letters or yours, to indicate she was a Jap?"

Dad returned to the table. "Rusty. We love you. We know you've been through hell over there. But this is not who we raised you to be. Rose and her family are not the enemy."

"You keep saying you know, Dad. But you don't." He was raising his voice, but he had to get through to them somehow. "If the truth about what went on behind all that barbed wire ever comes out, then maybe you'll get it."

But his mother wouldn't let it rest. "Rusty, please believe me when I tell you I was certain you knew. That you were fine with it. That you might have heard what was going on back here at home and put two and two together." She paused to press her lips together, then took a deep breath. "I'm sorry—I shouldn't have assumed. We never knew how much of our letters would be censored or if you'd receive them at all. What about the photos we sent?"

Rusty shook his head. "I never got any photos. If I had, that would have been it for me right then and there, I can tell you that."

"Oh, Rusty! How can you say such a thing?" Mum gripped his arm, but he rose from the table.

"I'll work hard for you, Dad. I will. But not with those people." He headed for the stairs. "I'll visit Bert's parents tomorrow, and then I'll help you get this year's crop planted. Just get rid of those Japs."

"Rusty—" Mum began, but Dad hushed her softly.

His father's voice trailed after Rusty as he climbed the stairs to his room. "Give him time, Anna. He'll come 'round. He just got home. Give him time."

Rusty hardened his heart. It would take more than time for his parents to see the light. But he had no words to describe what the Japanese had done to him and the other men. His parents hadn't seen the skeletal men walking around, barely able to stand some days. They hadn't witnessed the beatings, the deaths. They hadn't helped dig graves or suffered the pain of electric feet or gone blind or lived in their own filth for weeks on end. Nothing would make them understand.

Rusty made sure his window was tightly closed that night, but his sleep was interrupted many times. At least once, he found himself sitting straight up, drenched in sweat and trembling like the leaves on the aspen tree beside his old one-room schoolhouse. At some point, he must have disturbed his parents, for he awoke again to the outline of his mother, kneeling by his bed and mouthing silent entreaties.

Her prayers must have been effective, for the next thing he realized, it was daylight. He got up, determined to get his visit with Bert's family over with. Downstairs, his father poured fresh milk through the cream separator while his mother scrambled eggs at the stove.

"Sorry, Dad. You should have woke me for milking."

"Figured you needed your sleep."

Rusty took a plate of eggs from his mother and sat at the table. "I gotta start earning my keep around here."

"Then I'll wake you tomorrow." Dad smiled and joined him at the table. "Let's say grace."

Rusty stared at his plate and listened to his father pray.

"Lord, our hearts are filled with gratitude to you for bringing our boy home. I ask you to comfort all those for whom that isn't the case. Thank you for these provisions from your hand. Please bless them and guide us through this day. Amen."

Mum murmured an *amen* of her own, and Rusty lit into the food.

"Best eggs I ever had, Mum."

His mother pressed her lips together to stifle a smile. Hopefully, the arguments of last night would not surface again.

"I'm visiting the Johnsons today. Suppose I'll need to pump up my bike tires."

His parents exchanged a glance Rusty couldn't interpret. "Take my truck." Dad focused on spreading butter on his toast. "Keys are in it."

"They'll be so glad to see you." His mother wouldn't look him in the eye either.

When he walked from the house to his father's truck, he glanced toward the cabins. There sat his bicycle, leaning against the side of the nearest cabin. Immediately, Rusty's fists clenched and his jaw clamped shut. A Japanese boy came out of the cabin, jumped on the bicycle, and headed down the lane with a book bag slung around his shoulder and neck. What Rusty might have done next had he not been interrupted by a wet tongue on the back of his hand, he didn't know. Lady stood waiting for attention, tail wagging.

"Hey, girl." He gave the dog a brisk rubdown, then continued to the truck and yanked open the door. "C'mon, hop in. You can be my courage." The bicycle was nearly forgotten as he steered the truck in the opposite direction. What in the world would he say to Bert's mother and father?

Within fifteen minutes, he sat on the Johnsons' front porch, waiting with a cup of coffee. Mrs. Johnson had welcomed Rusty with a long, tight embrace before she even said a word. When she did speak, it was only to whisper, "Thank you for coming," and to explain that she needed to find Bert's father.

Lady greeted their dog, Shep. The two were siblings from the same litter, and now, even in their advanced age, their kinship allowed them to flop comfortably on the porch and fall asleep side by side. Rusty soaked in the coolness of the morning, the bright Manitoba sunshine, the blue of the sky, and the notion that he was truly free. Free to come and go as he wished, to eat when hungry, to sleep in a clean bed when tired. Being here, at Bert's house, drove home the fact that his friend had not lived to see this. How could he possibly tell Bert's parents what had happened? Did they know the hideous truth?

"Rusty." Bert's father had entered the house by the back door and was still drying his hands as he stepped out onto the porch.

Rusty rose, and the two men wrapped their arms around each other. Neither said another word, nor did Rusty feel the need. He'd spent many hours in this home, eating meals at their kitchen table, climbing trees, building forts, learning basic mechanics from Mr. Johnson alongside his son, teasing Bert's sisters. Mrs. Johnson took a seat on one of the rockers, wiping her eyes. Rusty and Mr. Johnson sat across from her.

"We don't need all the details, Rusty." Mr. Johnson pulled a handkerchief from the pocket of his overalls and blew his nose. "I know this is difficult for you. Just tell us what you want to tell. We're so glad you're home."

It was exactly what Rusty needed to hear. Guilt over his surviving when Bert didn't had been almost too much to bear. That the Johnsons were glad he returned, even without Bert, meant more than he could say.

"We all knew Bert was made of good stuff," he began. "The war proved it. I never would have made it without him. The times when I wanted to give in to despair, he was always there. He knew what to say. And not only for me. He encouraged everyone. He did you proud."

They passed a tear-filled but pleasant hour, recalling happy memories of Bert. When Rusty suggested it was time he was on his way, Mr. Johnson rose. "C'mon around back with me, Rusty. We got somethin' for ya." He wrapped an arm around Rusty's shoulder, and the two dogs lumbered after them.

Mr. Johnson led him into his machine shed. There, shiny as new, stood Bert's 1930 Ford with the V-8 engine. "Polished it up as soon as I heard you was comin' home. It's yours now, Rusty."

Rusty squinted at Bert's father, his jaw slack. Slowly, he shook his head. "I can't—"

"You're gonna need a way to get around." Mr. Johnson pulled a key out of his pocket and studied it a moment. "B'sides, I can't drive that dadgum thing. Too unstable with the souped-up engine. I never know if I'm gonna make the turn or veer off into the ditch."

"It can be a handful, all right."

Mr. Johnson held the key out toward Rusty. "Just take the key for now and come back for it when you can."

"You sure about this, Pops?" Bert's familiar nickname for his father slipped out automatically.

The man's eyes began to glisten, and he cleared his throat. "He'd want you to have it. I know he would. Yes, I'm sure. We're sure. It's only right that you take it." He waved the key again. "You probably worked on it as much as Bert."

Rusty shoved the key into his pocket and stared at the Ford.

"I'll leave you alone for a bit." Mr. Johnson shuffled out of the shed.

Rusty couldn't bring himself to get inside the car. Not yet. He walked around it. Bert had picked up Rusty for school nearly every day, and the pair of them had cruised down the main street of Spruceville as though they owned the town. They'd gone on double dates, picked up hitchhikers, and ventured into the city half a dozen times. Last time he remembered sitting in this car was when he was home on furlough, before Hong Kong. A lifetime ago. He'd driven so Bert could take a nap on the passenger seat. Rusty could almost see him there now, his long legs splayed out at awkward angles as he slouched to rest his head against the doorframe.

He peered through the window. From the rearview mirror dangled the same two items that had hung there since graduation day—the tassel from Bert's mortarboard and a little wooden cross.

Rusty folded both arms on the roof of the car, lay his forehead against them, and wept.

CHAPTER FORTY

Dad, Ojiisan, and James were heading out for a day of planting, to be followed by Rose and Mama as soon as they finished packing lunches, when a knock on the cabin door surprised them. When Dad opened it, Mr. and Mrs. Thorne stood there. Mr. Thorne gave a greeting, and then Mrs. Thorne asked for Rose.

Rose stepped outside while Mr. Thorne stepped inside. Was the whole family being dismissed?

"Rose." Mrs. Thorne twisted the hem of her apron with both hands. "I'm so sorry to have to say this, but we … we need to move you back into the cabin. I thought it would be only for a night or two, but … I didn't understand how difficult this would be for Rusty. He's left for a couple of hours, so now is a good time for us to move your things. I'll help you."

Rose looked back over her shoulder, but her father had closed the door. She followed Mrs. Thorne to the house, enduring her apologies the whole way.

"No need to be sorry." Rose's lifetime of hearing *shakata ga nai* served her well now, though she'd grown to loathe the words. She knew how to deliver the correct response. "It is your home, and it was Rusty's long before it was ever mine."

"He'll come around. I know he will." Rusty's mother must have repeated the line three times before they finished gathering Rose's meager belongings and changing the sheets on the bed. But even if it were true, if Rusty were to "come around" and accept Rose and her family as hired help, it would never erase the memory of the horrified look on his face when he first saw hers. The best-case scenario would be Rusty's tolerance, perhaps civility. Never friendship, no matter how warm and personal his letters to her had been. She gathered them now from the desk drawer and placed them in her satchel. She could add them to the woodstove the next time she saw a fire going in it.

"Can you manage everything?" Mrs. Thorne stood with the bundled-up bedsheets in her arms.

"Of course." Rose left the room without a backward glance and headed down the stairs, her satchel in one hand and a small box in her other arm, laden mostly with books. A sense of banishment filled her heart with shame, far more than it had when their family left B.C.

Mrs. Thorne followed. "I'm going to miss you, Rose. I will especially miss hearing you play our piano. It's just not possible right now. I hope you can understand."

At the bottom of the stairs, Rose paused to peek into the living room where the piano displayed stacks of recently used sheet music.

"What about my students?" she ventured.

Mrs. Thorne sighed. "Don't worry. I'll ... talk to them all. You won't have to. I'll think of something. Maybe ..."

But her voice trailed off. They both knew there was not another piano within a reasonable distance.

"It's only for a little while, I'm sure of it," Mrs. Thorne repeated.

"My father hopes to move us elsewhere." Rose shifted the load in her arms. "Mama insists that, until we can return to Vancouver, we should stay where we are and not disrupt things twice. And that we need to stay together, wherever we go."

"I know, Rose. And Mr. Thorne has been trying to help. But right now, he's asking your father to stay another season. We need you."

"But—what about Rusty?" Rose shook her head. The whole situation seemed ridiculous and impossible. Were they expected to stay hidden from Rusty's sight while still working the farm?

"Rusty will just need to keep his distance, and ... we hope your family can give him the space he needs. For a while. I know it's a lot to ask. He'll come around."

Rose swallowed hard. Nothing about this had been fair—why

should it be now? She turned and walked back to the cabin alone.

She found it empty, everyone having left for the field. Rose grabbed her hat and headed out to join them. She spent the rest of the day becoming reacquainted with the feel of black Manitoba soil working its way deep into her hands. At lunch, the family gathered at the end of the field farthest from the yard where the five bento boxes she and Mama had filled with rice and pickled vegetables waited in the shade of an elm tree. Sitting on the grass, she and James carried on their own quiet conversation.

"I saw the young Mr. Thorne this morning," James murmured. "Driving away in his father's truck. I was leaving the barn after milking."

"Did he see you?" Would Rusty's reaction to her brother be the same as it had been to her?

"I don't think so. He watched Tim leaving for school, though. And I'm pretty sure I now know who hit me the other night."

Rose swiveled her head toward James, taking in the bruised skin which had faded to shades of green and yellow. Did he mean what she thought he meant?

"Rusty?"

James nodded. "Don't tell his parents. Or ours."

"Why not?"

"No point making things worse." James took another mouthful of rice.

"But James, that was just wrong! You didn't do anything. He shouldn't have—"

"Shh. I mean it, Rose. I guess I shouldn't have told you."

"Why are you so calm about this?"

James sighed. "Because I get it. And because I don't think it will happen again."

Rose stared at her brother. Whatever his experiences had been as a translator for the Allies, they had changed him. Though she couldn't understand how he could so easily let this go, she admired him for it.

James scraped up the last remnants of his lunch. "You're his friend, right?"

"I thought I was." Rose stared off across the field toward the house. "When he didn't know I was Japanese, I was. Now, I don't know what I am."

"He's had a shock. It's understandable. If you care about him, best thing you can do—we can all do—is keep our distance and help get this crop in the ground and out again. Show him we're not the enemy. Show him we're the opposite."

Dad had agreed to stay on through harvest. Mr. Thorne had promised a small raise in pay, one that would allow the family—if they saved and pooled their earnings—to travel back to B.C. in November after harvest ended. Finally, there was a concrete plan.

Rose missed the piano and her students like crazy. She missed the pretty bedroom and the warm chats with Mrs. Thorne. She desperately missed her privacy. But, like she wrote to Freda, she was claiming a Bible verse the minister had used in a recent sermon: "I can do all things through Christ which strengtheneth me." It seemed like a more affirming and solid philosophy than her parents' ideal of "It cannot be helped."

Somehow, Rusty Thorne kept his distance while he worked with his father and some local hired men in other fields. A memorial service had been held at the church for Rusty's friend Bert, but the Onishi family did not attend.

They no longer sat in the Thorne family's church pew but at the back of the sanctuary with the other Japanese families still remaining in the community. They arrived separately moments before the service began and were the first to leave. Between coming and going, Rose would try hard to focus on the pastor's words but often found herself staring at the back of Rusty's head. How could this be the same man who had responded with such warmth to her letters? Who even seemed to admire her from a distance?

He needed prayer, his mother said. So she prayed. And she noticed. If anything, the man was becoming more handsome as he grew healthier and filled out his clothes. His mother's meals, fresh air, and farm work were clearly doing him good—physically, at least. Only when it was time to open a hymnbook was Rose able to forget Russell Thorne was in the room. While she sang the words, her fingers floated over an imaginary keyboard in her mind, adding flourishes and trills to every bar of music.

When Mrs. Thorne offered Mama a 1946 wall calendar for the cabin, Rose began crossing off the days, counting how many remained until the end of October when harvest would end. Surely by then, the path would be clear for them to return home. She needed something to look forward to. She wrote the university to ask how to reapply for the program she'd once been guaranteed—with no idea how she'd pay for it. She penned letters to Freda, planning a reunion no later than Christmas. She would not allow herself to consider whether her optimism for the future might be misplaced.

CHAPTER FORTY-ONE

As Rusty stood next to his parents in church, his father's rich baritone warmed him. The congregation belted out "Oh to Be Like Thee," but he could not bring himself to sing along. What did any of these people really know about anything? About the *if onlys* that haunted him?

If only Bert had survived, Rusty would have someone to talk to who completely understood. If only the last few rows of the sanctuary weren't filled with the enemy, it would be easy to focus on God. To forget. If only he could go about his daily work without wondering which of them was spying on him or might appear from around the corner any second. If only he could sleep through the night without waking in a cold sweat, convinced the enemy held him by the throat.

Maybe then he could sing along.

He closed his eyes and listened. They sang about being like Jesus, forfeiting earth's treasures in order to wear the perfect likeness of Christ. *Full of compassion ... loving ... forgiving ... tender ... kind. Holy, harmless, patient, brave. Meekly enduring cruel reproaches, willing to suffer, others to save.*

Rusty could hardly stand it. Before the war, he'd wanted all those things too. He'd begged God to make him more like Christ. To be able to forgive anyone for anything. To do good in the world, to make his life, his words and actions count for something. To make his parents proud. To be a good Christian son and an excellent soldier.

But that was then. Now, he only wanted to survive. Sure, his body had survived the war. But his soul felt injured beyond repair. Dead. And no hymn writer, no matter what they may have endured, could resurrect a dead spirit. And as for God? Somewhere along the line, God had stopped paying attention to Russell Thorne.

As the hymn ended with the final words, *Stamp Thine own image deep on my heart,* Rusty sighed with relief. Next was the Lord's Prayer, and he raised his voice along with the others. Surely, he could do this much, fake it if necessary. And he did fine until the end.

Forgive us our trespasses … as we forgive those who trespass against us.

He couldn't do it. It was one thing to ask God's forgiveness for his own sins, petty misdemeanors by comparison. He could even forgive his parents for hiring the Onishis and for deceiving him. They didn't know any better. But if God wanted him to forgive the Japanese who had treated him and the others so brutally, then God was asking too much. It would be a slap in Bert's face and in the face of every other man who had died at those barbarians' hands if Rusty forgave them.

I'm not asking you to forgive what was done to others. Only to you.

Rusty knew that familiar voice, but he'd grown adept at ignoring it. He shook it away as the congregation took their seats and the pastor began his sermon.

It was on forgiveness.

Of course. How typical. What could that pastor possibly know about forgiving? He'd sailed to Canada from Russia or somewhere before World War I and had been here ever since, safe and healthy and fed.

Rusty counted the hymn books in the back of the pew. Then he counted the letters in the book's title. He counted his shoelace holes.

"For if ye forgive men their trespasses, your heavenly Father will also forgive you: But if ye forgive not men their trespasses, neither will your Father forgive your trespasses."

The preacher's words, which Rusty knew to be the words of Jesus, pierced their way through his attempts at distraction. Next Sunday, he would stay home.

Could he remember how to count to ten in French? *Un, deux, trois, quatre, cinq, six, sept, huit, neuf, dix.* Six sounded like *cease* and ten like *dease.* What came next?

The pastor's voice broke through again. "Forgiveness is not something you do for the person who wronged you."

How on earth did you say *eleven* in French? *Concentrate, Thorne. You know this.*

"What others did to you is between them and God. Forgiveness is something you do for yourself."

Onze, that was it! Right, onze. What came next? What did he mean, *something you do for yourself?*

"It's setting yourself free. Not allowing that person to hold you prisoner any longer."

Prisoner. Rusty's hands began to tremble. He balled them into fists, then opened them wide and closed them again to make the quivering stop. What did the preacher know about being a prisoner?

"God has given you the power to open that door, to walk through to freedom by setting the other person free of your anger, hatred, and vengeance. He's also given you the power to hang onto it, to let it eat you alive. The choice is yours. Do you want to be free? Or do you want to stay in a place of imprisonment?"

Rusty wanted to run out of the church, but he was wedged between his parents on one side and his sister and her brood on the other. Plus, leaving now would mean walking past all those faces at the back of the room. Surely, the preacher was about to wrap up his sermon. *You can do this, Thorne.* Douze. *That's how you say twelve in French. Sounds like* booze. *Which actually sounds pretty good about now. A good stiff drink.*

Finally, the pastor closed in prayer. The congregation stood to sing one last song. Rusty grabbed the hymnbook and turned to the right page—a hymn called "Deeper and Deeper." This time, he'd sing along with the crowd.

And he did. Until they reached the third verse.

Into the cross of Jesus, deeper and deeper I go, Following through the garden, facing the dreaded foe. Drinking the cup of sorrow, sobbing with broken heart, "O Saviour, help! Dear Saviour, help! Grace for my weakness impart."

Rusty stopped singing. He brushed away a tear that had somehow escaped. *No! I will not do this. Not now. Whatever's going on, I'll make it stop. Maybe I do need help. But not today.*

He was never so glad to see a church service end. He continued facing forward for several minutes while the room cleared. *Give them time to get out of sight, Thorne. Out of sight, out of mind.*

The next Sunday, Rusty found an excuse to stay home from church. Once everyone had cleared out, he grabbed a tin bucket from the kitchen and looped his belt through its handle. The saskatoons should be nearly ripe. If he could pick a pail full, maybe his mother would forgive his missing church. He stepped out the back door and called Lady, who was happy to scamper alongside. It would be his first trip into the woods along the creek since he got home. The shortest path to the best berries would take him past the workers' cabins, but since everyone was gone to church, it shouldn't matter. Besides, he'd walk fast.

At the first cabin, the one the Onishi family used, he increased his pace—then nearly jumped out of his skin when a voice came from inside. Rusty stopped short. Was his imagination playing tricks? Lady trotted back and cocked her head to the side in a puzzled doggy expression. Rusty took a few steps closer to the cabin and stood where he had a clear view through the window. An old man sat on his knees in front of a small statue of Buddha. Rusty had seen a few like it, but larger, in Hong Kong. A candle burned in front of this one. The man held a little book open in his hands, and a small, rope-like object dangled from one wrist. He seemed to be chanting the same phrase over and over.

"I forgot about the old man." Rusty breathed a sigh of relief as he scratched Lady between the ears. "Should've known this one wouldn't be in church with the others. The old heathen."

Rusty knew Rose's grandfather was part of the Onishi family but had not seen him up close before. He'd also figured out the man he punched in town was Rose's older brother, James, and that James had served the military somehow during the war. Though he regretted hitting him, he wasn't going to say anything to anyone. James had probably never figured out it was him. Best to leave it alone.

He continued walking, scouting out berries and trying to forget the grandfather's presence. How could Mum and Dad tolerate pagan worship on their own property? They probably didn't even know the half of what went on since these people came. Maybe Rusty could enlighten them. The geezer was probably trying to rain down the wrath of his god on those who had defeated Japan. *Well, good luck with that, old man.*

But by the time he returned to the house via a different route with a full pail of berries, his entire family had gathered for a chicken dinner that extended late into the afternoon, forcing him to put the encounter with the elderly Buddhist from his mind. Rusty spent the afternoon chasing and wrestling with his nieces and nephews under the oak trees in the yard.

And he spent the rest of the summer avoiding the Japanese workers while toiling harder for his father than he ever had before the war. The work had always been exhausting, but now the freedom to do useful labor that would provide for all of them energized Rusty. Working hard and staying busy kept his mind off the pain. Some weeks, he went to church with his family, and other times he stayed home. In addition to the fieldwork, he did the milking, chopped wood for his mother's cookstove, and helped her in the garden. If he ever found a spare minute, he tinkered on Bert's car. He still couldn't think of it as his.

He attended a couple of community events but returned home with an emptiness in his gut that made him want to avoid the public. These events always included girls happy to dance with him, but Japanese people frequently attended too. Not the Onishi family, of course. They had agreed to keep their distance.

One night, he drove home from a gathering while patting himself on the back. *You're getting better, Rusty. You can tolerate those people and not smash their faces in.* As long as no one asked him to work side by side with them or talk to them, he'd be fine. And surely, no one would ask that of him. Not even God.

He went to bed so exhausted every evening that the dreams and night terrors diminished. But one night, he woke desperate for a drink of water. With a huff, he threw back the covers and crept into the hallway, tiptoeing so as not to disturb his parents. But apparently, something had already disturbed them. Though their room was still swathed in darkness, their door had been left ajar, and Rusty heard their voices, including his own name. He paused before he reached the door, lowering himself silently to the floor.

"Lord, we know you love him even more than we do," his father prayed. "Please, meet him where he's at. You know what it's going to take to break through this wall he's put up."

Then Mum chimed in. "Help him to see these people the way you see them, God. As your children, just like you see us. Give him your heart, Lord. Help our Rusty. He's suffered so much. He needs you so much. Fill him with yourself and your love, I pray."

"Soften his heart so he can forgive the wrongs done to him."

"Show us how to help him."

Rusty swallowed hard. He sat there, motionless, until his parents' voices stopped and he heard the even sound of their breathing. He crept back to bed, somehow no longer needing a drink.

With mid-August came a minor lull in the workload as the sugar beet plants had overtaken the weeds and needed only time to grow larger. Rusty cut hay and helped his father bale it for the milk cows come winter and picked endless cucumbers for his mother to pickle.

"Let me help you with that, Mum," he offered one day. "What do you want me to do? Scrub the cukes? Wash jars? Pack the jars? Put them in the canner?"

His mother smiled. "You know what would really make me happy?"

Rusty glanced around the cluttered kitchen. "Pick some dill?"

Mum pointed to a basket where freshly picked sprigs of dill sat waiting and ready. "Got plenty. I'm fine here, really. But I've noticed you still haven't unpacked."

She was right. Rusty had been home for months, but his army

duffel bag still sat on the floor of his room. He wasn't sure why. It wasn't like him to be sloppy.

He sighed. "Guess I'm not a messy teenager anymore. I'll go do it now."

"Thank you." Mum returned to washing her canning jars, humming as she worked.

Rusty climbed the stairs. He took a moment to stare at the duffel, still sitting where it had been dropped his first night home. He didn't even know who had carried it up. Dad, probably. It would be good to get it out of sight, to put those memories elsewhere. He reached in and pulled out various items of clothing, toiletries, and the new Bible he'd claimed from one of the supply barrels that had landed in the camp shortly before his release. The Bible reminded him of Bert and the awful way he died. He quickly placed it in a dresser under some socks and closed the drawer.

The last item in the bag was a bundle of letters—every word from home he'd managed to hang onto. He untied the string. He'd placed Rose's letters on top. Something churned in his gut as he studied his name written in her delicate handwriting. He could picture those dainty hands he'd seen covering the keyboard with such skill that day, holding a pen and carefully writing words just for him.

I should burn them.

He set them aside and leafed through the others instead. His parents' and sisters' letters reminded him of their prayers, and he quickly restacked them. He retied the string and added the bundle to his sock drawer. Then he shoved the empty duffel bag to the back of the closet. Now, what to do with Rose's letters?

The screen door downstairs slammed. Was someone coming or going? He looked out the window. His mother was heading for the outhouse.

Perfect. The stove was probably good and hot. He could toss in the letters, and they'd be transformed to ash by the time Mum returned. He dashed down the stairs, grabbed the lid lifter, and prepared to throw the letters into the fire. To his surprise, the stove was cold. Mum must have decided to wait until all her jars were filled and ready to go. *Phooey*. By the time he got a good blaze going, she'd be back and asking questions. He grabbed a couple of matches from the tin match holder hanging beside the stove and headed outdoors. Lady was immediately at his side.

"Hey, girl. Wanna help me burn something?"

The dog's tail wagged automatically as she trotted happily beside Rusty. He'd head down to the old swimming hole where he and Bert used to skinny dip and build bonfires to dry off beside. He hadn't been there since he got home, but surely, the stones they'd placed in a circle would still be there, no matter how overgrown they might be with weeds.

Ten minutes of walking, and he'd found the spot. Clearly, someone had been using the fire pit recently, probably teenagers. Rusty lay the letters in the center of the circle and lit his first match on one of the rocks.

Don't be dumb, pal.

Rusty could have sworn he heard Bert's voice. He turned all the way around, even though he knew the voice was in his own mind. He closed his eyes, hoping to hear it again—if for no other reason than to feel close to his friend. The heat of the match singed his fingers, and he dropped it into the sand, where it quickly fizzled out. No problem. He had another.

But he could easily imagine what Bert might say. *Don't be dumb, pal. At least, read 'em first. Then if you still want to burn them, go ahead.*

Rusty sat on the sand with a sigh. Maybe he should read the letters once more. Maybe there'd been some clues he had missed about Rose's heritage because he wasn't looking for them. Maybe he owed her—and his parents—that much. He grabbed the first one. Lady completed her rounds of exploration and plopped down, pressing herself against him. There she stayed, like a warm comforter, while he re-read every single word Rose had written.

CHAPTER FORTY-TWO

"It's so unfair," Tim complained to Rose and James as the three of them picked potato bugs off the plants in their family's garden plot. "Just because *he's* home, *we* have to stay out of sight."

"I know." Rose had watched through the windows of their hot, stuffy cabin while the Thorne family played on the lush lawn on Sunday afternoons. She'd seen Rusty giving his nieces and nephews under-ducks on the old swing and heard them laughing and pleading with him to "go higher, Unca Russy!" She'd even heard piano music drifting through the window screens, performed by someone who knew how to play "all four notes at once" from the hymnbook. Meanwhile, she and her family remained stuck inside their little cabin, trying to read or nap. They ventured out to the swimming hole only when the coast was clear.

"I'm tired of it, too, Tim. But it won't be much longer. As soon as harvest is over, we'll be gone and free to go out whenever we want."

"She's right," James added. "Try to be patient. I wouldn't trade places with Rusty Thorne for anything, not if I had to go through what he did."

How did James know what Rusty had gone through? And did she really want to know? Perhaps it was best not to ask.

"It's still unfair." Tim's usual optimistic nature had soured since he'd turned fourteen. Rose hoped the old Tim would return soon.

"Nobody said it was fair." James dropped a handful of beetle larvae into the jar of gasoline they all shared. "It's war."

James had returned to them so different. He'd left for the road camps angry and bitter yet returned more compassionate. When she'd asked him about it, he only shrugged. "Some things are too hard to explain," he'd said. "I thought I'd seen the worst in humanity when they forced us to leave home. But others suffered far worse. The best thing we can do now is be patient with one another, to refuse to be defined by our injuries."

Rose prayed for God's help to take those words to heart and make them her own, to be patient and understanding. To live the rest of her life with optimism and hope.

"Are we going home to Vancouver after harvest?" Tim voiced the same question Rose had been wondering about. Her father had made no promises.

James sighed. "I don't know."

The year before, *Time* magazine had run a headline: WHO WANTS JAPS? NO TAKERS. The mayors and premiers of all the western provinces and even Prime Minister King sent the same message, most of them hoping for re-election. The Japanese were to go "home" to Japan. The Canadian government was paying its citizens to leave, and some had agreed. While the war had still raged, her parents had received their letter offering the option of leaving voluntarily and having their expenses paid—or risking being kicked out later with no assurance of compensation. Dad had shaken his head, folded the letter, and put it away with other official papers. "We are Canadians," was all he said on the matter.

And they were not completely without supporters. In January, thousands had gathered in Toronto to protest the bill that would send them all to Japan. The loudest voice, according to the newspaper Dad brought home, belonged to a Jewish rabbi, of all things. By then, the world was learning that millions of Jews had been murdered and mistreated in Nazi concentration camps. Abraham Feinberg told the crowd, "The ghost of Hitler still walks in Canada. The thing for which Hitler stood has been inscribed on the order-in-council which punishes little children for crimes they couldn't commit."

Now the war was over, the soldiers were home, and still, British Columbia was bolting and locking its doors. The Onishis' abandoned possessions had all been sold, presumably to cover the cost of their relocation. From memory, they'd compiled a list of items worth nearly seven hundred dollars—funds they hoped would get them home. Dad's shoulders slumped when a letter from the Custodian of the Japanese Evacuation included a check for only twenty-six dollars. He cashed it and gave Mama the money for groceries.

Rose had received no reply to her letter to the university.

"I think Dad's working out a deal with Mr. Thorne," James continued. "I don't know the details yet, but it would mean Dad owning his own beet field and a place to live. Don't tell him I said anything, though."

Rose stood upright and stared at her brother. "You mean we might stay? Here? But how—?"

"Shh." James broke off a leaf laden with insect eggs and dropped it into the jar. "Nothing is definite. Our best plan of action is to keep working hard and make this as uncomplicated for Mama and Dad as we can."

Rose returned to work, but not without a grimace. Life was anything but uncomplicated.

When the job was done, she volunteered to carry the jar of gas and dead bugs to the fire pit, where it could be left and used to fuel the next campfire. Halfway there, she jumped when Lady trotted toward her along the winding trail. The dog would not venture off the yard alone. Who was with her? Rose stopped, but not in time. Rusty was coming around the next bend. She whirled and headed back, quickening her pace.

"Rose, wait."

Did she actually hear it, or was it her imagination? She slowed down.

"Rose?"

It was him, all right. She stopped but still didn't turn around. Then Lady's nose nuzzled her hand, and she dropped her gaze. She stroked the dog's ears, then slowly turned toward Rusty. He'd stopped about eight feet behind her. She looked at his feet first, then up to his hand. It held a bundle of letters, and she immediately recognized them. She raised her eyes to his face.

Rusty waved the letters slightly. "I guess I never—I never thanked you for these."

Rose nodded. "It's okay. You're welcome." She turned to go.

"Rose, wait."

She stopped again.

"I don't hate you. I … want you to know, I don't hate you."

This time, Rose turned all the way around and met his eyes. She paused, taking a deep breath. "I don't hate you either." Even as she said it, it seemed like the biggest understatement of her life. At best, she should feel ambivalence toward this man who'd appeared so disgusted the first time he'd seen her face. But looking into his deep blue eyes now stirred a deeper longing.

They held the gaze for several seconds, then Rose moved toward the house. But again, Rusty called out.

"Where were you headed?"

Rose stared at the jar in her hand. "Oh. Right."

Never feeling more awkward, she turned and continued on her original path. Rusty stepped aside to let her pass. She almost cringed. What would he smell as she walked by? The gasoline? Her own perspiration from working in the heat? The lingering scent of Mama's *tsukemono*? Chastising herself for such pointless and superficial thoughts, she kept walking past Rusty.

She let out a huge breath when he called, "C'mon, girl," and the underbrush crunched as he and Lady started moving toward the yard again.

She'd relive this strange encounter every night for weeks as she fell asleep.

Harvest time arrived, and with it, the crazy-early mornings and intolerably long days. At least, the heat of summer was behind them, but as the days cooled, fewer hours of sunlight meant plunging temperatures. Although they worked up a sweat in the warm afternoons, Rose and the other workers bundled up for the early morning hours. Even then, her hands often grew numb with cold. She'd "graduated" to handling the sugar beet knife two seasons earlier. But even with practice, it remained tricky to maneuver the sharp, heavy tool—especially if Rose allowed herself to focus on anything other than her work.

And allow it, she did. Although weeks had passed since his proclamation that he didn't hate her, she was still thinking about Rusty Thorne one morning when she'd only been at work half an hour. Did he think about her? Would they ever move toward friendship? Why couldn't she free herself of her ridiculous notions of romance?

She grasped a sugar beet in her stiff fingers, brought the knife down, and froze. The sharp blade had fallen two inches too far to the left—across the pointer finger of Rose's left hand—slicing all the way through both the finger and the sugar beet in one swift swing and sending her finger sailing into the black dirt.

CHAPTER FORTY-THREE

Grateful to be working another harvest alongside his father, Rusty didn't mind participating in every aspect of it, from pulling the beets to chopping the tops off and laying them in rows, to forking them into the backs of the trucks or driving the truck to the train yard, where they'd shovel them up into the train car. It was great to feel strong again and to know he could drink all the water he needed, that there would be a hot breakfast every morning, thick sandwiches for lunch, and his mother's delicious, home-cooked meals at supper. He went to bed too exhausted to dream and rarely awoke with night terrors. When he did, his mother was often at his side. She'd encouraged him to say the name of Jesus aloud whether she was there or not.

"Other people are never our real enemies, Rusty. The actual enemy is invisible to our human eyes but very real. He seeks to kill, steal, and destroy. He is the enemy of all people because we are made in the image of God, whom he hates." Then she would read Scriptures to him about how we "wrestle not against flesh and blood."

Rusty had heard all these things since childhood, but they'd never hit home as they did now. And calling on Jesus did, indeed, seem to quench his fears.

Try as he might, though, thoughts of Rose Onishi were never far away. The day he'd re-read her letters and decided not to burn them had sparked a shift for him. Rose's words had reminded him it was the girl's heart he'd found so attractive and that her heart had not changed. The only difference had been Rusty's arrival, and with it, the revelation of Rose's heritage—about which she could do nothing. This is what he told himself, and it made complete sense—as long as he wasn't looking at her.

Then he'd encounter one of her family members in passing, and that same old churning in his gut would start all over. When his dad asked him about it, suggesting it might be time to end all the cautionary distance, Rusty shook his head. "I'm working on it, Dad, but this is best for now. Please."

He knew his father was trying to understand. At the same time, Dad didn't want to lose the best help he'd ever had. "We're asking a lot of them," Dad said. Rusty didn't disagree.

The whole situation was again on his mind as he climbed into the truck, ready to haul another load of beets to the train. Just as he was about to start the engine, he heard a ruckus off toward the east field. Dad sprinted toward him.

"Rusty! Wait!" Dad ran to the truck and opened the door, huffing and puffing. "There's been an accident! Rose needs to get to the hospital. Now!"

Rusty stared at his father, trying to comprehend what he was saying. *An accident? Rose?* But Dad was tugging on his arm, pulling him out of the truck.

"Take Bert's hot rod. It's the fastest thing we've got."

Suddenly, it seemed the entire farmyard was full of people, yelling and coming from all directions. Mum materialized out of nowhere, carrying her laundry basket and shouting that she had ice. The Onishi family ran toward her. James carried his sister in his arms. Someone's jacket was wrapped around Rose's left hand. She appeared as limp as the sick and dying prisoners Rusty had himself carried to the infirmary for attention that never came.

"I'm going with you!" Mum shouted. "Rose's mother too."

"Get the car," Dad hollered at Rusty.

Rusty managed to pull the key from his pocket but held it out to his father. "Here, Dad. You go."

"No, Rusty. You have to. I can't drive that thing! Come on, son. Soldier up."

Rusty didn't have time to contemplate his father's plea because suddenly, George Onishi stood before him. The man looked Rusty right in the eye and uttered one word. "Please."

His mother grabbed his arm, and together they ran to the hot rod. Mum climbed into the front seat while she kept shouting instructions. Rusty was barely aware of James laying an unconscious Rose across the back seat, her head resting in her mother's lap.

"Go, go, go," Mum yelled. Then she turned around to Mrs. Onishi. "Is there a lot of blood?"

"No."

"Where are we going?" Rusty started the engine and took off toward town. Spruceville had a small clinic with one doctor—Susie's new husband. But Rusty had no idea how extensive Rose's injury might be.

"They're not going to be able to help her here, Rusty. We'd only lose time. Head for Winnipeg." His mother handed a bottle of water to Mrs. Onishi. "If she revives, offer her this."

In exchange, Rose's mother handed Mum a bundled sheet. The woman's voice quivered. "Take this, please."

Mum carefully took it from Mrs. Onishi and laid it gingerly on the ice.

Rusty frowned. "What's that?"

His mother didn't respond at first. Finally, she swallowed hard and answered. "It's Rose's finger."

Rusty sat with both women in a waiting room at Winnipeg's General Hospital, studying the tiled floor. Rose had revived enough to stand when they arrived at the emergency entrance but quickly collapsed against her mother again. Rusty had caught her up and held her as James had done. It took only a moment for the hospital staff to wheel out a stretcher. Rusty laid Rose on it.

They had placed the bundled finger on Rose's abdomen as they carted her away.

Now there was nothing to do but wait and pray, which both mothers were doing plenty of. Rusty sent up a few prayers of his own, but he doubted they sounded much like those of the two women.

Oh God. This can't be happening. Rose wouldn't have even been in that field if it weren't for me. She'd be safe in the house, giving piano lessons. Where she belongs. He leaned forward, elbows on his knees, hands covering his face. *How could I have done this to her? How could I be so selfish? Oh God, oh God, oh God.*

The image of her seated at the piano was all he could envision now. Those moments before he'd seen her face. The surprise at the shiny, black hair. The tiny hands dancing up and down the keyboard. Owning it. Her small body swaying to the music. The incredible skill that impressed him and moved his heart before he'd even come downstairs.

Oh God, you've got to save her finger. You've got to! I cannot be responsible for this. Please, God. I'll move out if I have to, I'll leave the farm. I'll do anything. Please save Rose's finger. Save her dreams. Please.

Between prayers, the words of Rose's letters rolled through his mind. Like old friends who knew and understood him, her words were always encouraging and affirming. They always brought joy to his heart. How could he have treated her so hatefully?

Mrs. Onishi walked to the desk to ask a nurse if there was any update on Rose. When she returned, Rusty and his mother looked up expectantly.

"She says if it's taking a long time, that's a good sign. It means they're trying to save her finger."

But she had no sooner taken her seat than a doctor in surgical garb came walking toward them. "Mrs. Onishi?"

Rose's mother merely nodded.

"How is she?" Mum moved to the edge of her seat.

"She's stable, but I'm terribly sorry to tell you we simply cannot save the finger. There's far too much dirt ground into the tissue. The blood vessels are filled with dirt. Trying to attach it would put Rose at great risk of infection. We don't want to chance losing her whole hand, or more. We've stitched it up at the first knuckle." He indicated on his own hand where the stitches were. "Is she right-handed?"

Rose's mother nodded.

"Well, that's something, then." He sighed and made a note on his clipboard. "And she's got youth on her side. She'll recover quickly and learn to adapt. I can put you in touch with other patients who've suffered the same injury."

Rusty's mother swallowed hard. She glanced at Mrs. Onishi, then turned back to the doctor. "She is a pianist."

The doctor's face went pale. "I'm so sorry." It was barely a whisper.

"Would it have made a difference?" Rusty challenged him. "If you had known?"

He studied Rusty for the first time, as though trying to comprehend his relationship to the patient. Then he slowly shook his head. "No. It wouldn't have. But knowing does make it much sadder. Again—I'm so sorry."

Rusty tuned out as the doctor continued to discuss things like antibiotics and length of stay with Rose's mother. What would happen next? Could Rose keep playing piano? He remembered reading about a soldier who'd been a piano player and lost his right hand in the Great War. The story went that the man had been near suicidal until someone introduced him to a couple of pieces of classical music written for the left hand only. The man had tried them reluctantly at first. Eventually, he'd come to understand that although he would never again be a concert performer, the gift of music did not die with his hand. It was in his heart and mind. He could still produce beautiful music and teach other gifted people how to as well.

Surely, Rose would be able to do the same, and more.

But would she ever be able to forgive Rusty for what he had done?

CHAPTER FORTY-FOUR

Muffled voices pulled Rose out of a wonderful, dreamless sleep. They called her name, asking if she could open her eyes and cough for them. But she didn't want to do either. Her eyelids felt as heavy as milk pails filled to the brim. Her left hand was on fire. She tried to jerk it away, to pull it out of the flames, but it wouldn't budge.

"Can you hear me, Miss Onishi?"

Go away. Let me sleep. Rose didn't have the strength to make her lips move.

"I'm Dr. Collings. Can you open your eyes for me?"

Her eyelids fluttered open and clamped shut again. In that brief blur, she glimpsed two figures leaning over her, both dressed in white. One man, one woman.

"Rose?" It was the woman's voice this time. "You've had an accident, but your surgery is over, and you're going to be all right. We need you to try and wake up. Give us a cough if you can."

Then Rose remembered the sugar beet in her left hand, the knife in her right. She'd performed the action so many times before. Why now? Why this time did the knife come down across her hand? She saw the finger landing in the dirt, inches away from the beet top. Had she screamed? She couldn't remember. She had to get back to the field! She had to rescue her finger. She opened her eyes fully then. The pain in her hand was searing, but she tried to sit up.

"Lie back, lie back." The nurse held both hands against Rose's shoulders, preventing her from moving. "It's too soon to sit up. Can you relax?"

My finger! Rose wanted to shout, but it came out garbled. "Mmffh!"

"Can you cough for us?" someone asked again.

Rose gave a few weak huffs.

"Atta girl, very good. Try again."

Rose wanted to scream. Her finger was lying in the sugar beet field, and they were asking her to cough! It made no sense. She coughed for them, anyway, hoping they'd leave her alone so she could go back to sleep. But it was becoming easier to hold her eyes open. The room was coming into focus. Bright lights made her squint. A pale blue blanket covered her lower body. An unfamiliar smell assaulted her. Iodine? Bleach?

"Call me immediately if she shows any signs of shock." The doctor capped his pen, placed it in his pocket, and left the room.

"My ... hand ..." Rose managed to squeeze the words out, but they sounded weak even to her. She lifted her head, trying to glimpse her hand. All she saw was a bundle of white bandages.

"I know, Rose. Your hand has been injured, but we've stitched you up, and you're going to be okay. I know it hurts. I've given you something for the pain." The nurse sounded so kind. She reminded Rose of Mrs. Thorne. "You can rest now. I'll be nearby, and your family is waiting to see you as soon as you're fully awake."

Rose let her eyes drop shut and sighed with relief. She'd be okay. The nurse had said so.

The next time she opened her eyes, Rose's mother was leaning over her.

"Mama?" Her voice was still croaky.

"Hi, Rozu. Yes, it's Mama. I'm here."

Were those tears on Mama's cheeks?

"My finger ..."

"Here, Rozu." Mama reached for a glass of water and held the straw to Rose's lips. "Can you take a sip?"

Rose put her mouth around the straw and drew in several swallows. The water felt good going down, but she needed answers more than anything. When Mama put the glass back, Rose tried to sit up. Her mother helped her, adjusting the pillow so she could lean against it. The room spun for a moment, but when it stopped, Rose counted three other beds. Two were occupied by other patients. One was neatly made.

Though her entire finger still burned with pain, the odd shape of the bandaging told her it was gone. She peered into her mother's grief-stricken face.

"I'm so sorry, Rozu. We tried to save it. Tim found it in the dirt, and we rinsed it and brought it with us, but … they couldn't. Too much dirt. Too much time." Mama sucked in a gulp of air, and a shudder went through her body. "Too risky. I'm so sorry."

Rose shifted her gaze from Mama's face back to her hand. It had to be a bad dream. That's all it was, a dream. She'd wake up and find herself in her own bunk in the cabin, ready to head to the fields for another day. Another day of her last beet harvest ever.

"Do you understand what I'm saying, Rozu?"

If only Mama would stop talking, the horrible dream could end. She clamped her eyes tightly shut and waited.

Daylight was fading, creating a soft glow across the room the next time Rose awoke. This time, Dad and James were in the room, seated on chairs near her bed. "How did you get here?" she murmured.

"In Mr. Thorne's truck." James stood and stepped closer. "I drove. Tim's here too. He's with Mama."

"How're you feeling, Rozu?" Dad tenderly laid a hand on her cheek, bringing tears to her eyes. So it wasn't a dream. She studied her hand again, this time raising it a few inches off the surface of the bed.

"It's completely gone, isn't it? They couldn't save it?"

Dad and James both shook their heads slowly, their faces sad.

"But you're going to be okay, Rose. Once it heals, once you've had time to practice … you'll get used to it. You'll see. In time, you won't miss it."

Rose could tell her brother didn't fully believe his own words, but he was trying. For that, she loved him.

"You'll still be able to play the piano, Rozu."

"Dad's right, Rose. You will. With your skill, why ... give yourself some time, and no one will even know the difference."

Rose sighed. She appreciated what they were trying to do, but she needed time for the reality of her loss to sink in. "Maybe save those ideas for later, James. I can't even think about that. Not yet."

"Of course. I'm sorry."

Dad suddenly let out a single cough and quickly left the room. James watched him go, then turned back to Rose. "He blames himself."

"That's ridiculous. I was the one with the knife in my hand."

James sighed. "I'm so sorry this happened to you, Rose. I'd gladly switch places with you. Any of us would—Dad, Mama, Ojiisan. Even Tim."

Rose nodded. "I'm sure that's true."

"We love you, Rose."

A tear slipped down her brother's face. These displays of emotion were so unusual for her family, it was nearly too much to bear. Why had no one uttered the old motto yet? Maybe Rose should do it.

"*Shakata ga nai.*"

The painkillers Rose received allowed her a reasonable sleep the first night. But when she awoke in the pre-dawn hours, the realization of what had happened jolted her like a set of giant cymbals in the middle of a pianissimo lullaby. Her hand throbbed. To take her mind off the pain, she closed her eyes and imagined playing through scales on a beautiful grand piano, working her way through them one by one. But every time she needed the pointer finger of her left hand, the pain pierced her concentration. She tried to think of how she could play anything without that finger. It was not going to work. It wasn't possible. Her dream was over. Just when she'd begun to hope again, it was over. And she'd done it to herself.

A stirring to her right caused Rose to open her eyes. Someone still sat beside her—a man. He appeared to be asleep, leaning with his arms crossed on the edge of her bed, his face resting on them.

"James?"

He jerked awake then, too, and raised his head. She must be dreaming now, for sure. She was staring into the teary, tortured face of Rusty Thorne.

CHAPTER FORTY-FIVE

Rusty's mother had returned home with Rose's dad and brothers. Rusty asked to stay with Mrs. Onishi, who curled up and fell asleep across three chairs in the waiting room. A kind nurse brought them each a blanket. When he was sure no one was watching, Rusty had sneaked into Rose's room. With the first sight of her lying there, her left hand wrapped in a big white bandage, Rusty was undone. James had told him Rose understood her finger was gone and could not be repaired. For the longest time, he'd simply stood there, staring. Though it was only his memory, he could almost hear her beautiful piano music.

Eventually, he'd taken a seat beside her and, in the dim light, begged God for mercy. It was his selfishness that had landed Rose in this place. His hatefulness and prejudice. Rose had nothing to do with the evil that had been done to him in Hong Kong and in Japan or in that horrible hell ship between the two. Nothing. Yet he'd held it against her as though she were one of them when she'd only wanted to be his friend. To encourage him and speak life into his unspeakable nightmare.

He recalled his weeks in the Hong Kong hospital, how the experience of blindness had made him appreciate his sight. Now he could see that he'd been spiritually blind as well. The old Rusty had gone off to war determined to be the good son, the faithful Christian, the confident soldier. The new Rusty understood that living the Christian life was not possible, not in one's own strength. Pride had been his undoing.

Oh God. Forgive me. Rose does not deserve this. Please, Father. Forgive me. Help me forgive them—all of them. Help me.

Time seemed to stand still, and Rusty sensed something sacred all around him. His tears finally subsided, and he sat with his forehead propped on his arms on the edge of Rose's hospital bed. He stayed that way until Rose began to stir.

When he lifted his head and peered into her face, still more tears sprang to his eyes. Though he wanted to speak, no words would come. She looked so fragile. Small clumps of field dirt still clung to her hair, now matted and dull. Her skin was, for the first time, paler than his. Slowly, she opened her eyes and focused on his face. His heart just might stop.

"Rusty?" Her voice came out barely above a whisper.

"Shh," he whispered back. "They don't know I'm in here."

He studied her eyes. They were not and never had been the round, blue eyes he'd once imagined. But they were every bit as beautiful. Maybe even more because they were truly hers. This was the same girl who'd made him laugh with her silly jokes, with stories of his dog and her little brother. The girl who had gifted him with words of hope and life. She stared back at him with sadness and something else. Fear? Was she afraid of him? She certainly had reason to be.

"I did this to you." The words tumbled from his mouth.

Rose scrunched her brow. "No, Rusty." She shook her head slowly.

"I did, though. If I hadn't been so—so hateful, so stubborn, you wouldn't have been in that field at all. Can't you see that? You'd be giving lessons at our piano, you'd be—"

"Stop it."

"I'm sorry, Rose. I'm so very sorry. I need your forgiveness." Rusty let the tears flow down his face unchecked.

Rose held his gaze a long time, but he couldn't read her expression. She let out a long sigh before she spoke. "I suppose I could blame you, Russell Thorne. Would that make you happy?"

Rusty leaned back in the chair. He wanted Rose's forgiveness, or maybe her anger. But this, he had no idea what to do with.

"I could blame my father for bringing us to Manitoba. Or *your* father for putting me to work in the field. Would that make *them* happy?"

"Rose, what are you—"

"I could blame the Canadian government for moving us out here, or the B.C. government for booting us out. I could blame Japan for dropping that bomb. I could blame the Nazis for starting the whole stupid war."

Rusty swallowed. Where was she going with this line of thinking?

"I could blame myself for being so careless with that sharp knife. Or the cold weather. Or the God who controls it. For the rest of my life, I could blame and blame and blame. Don't you see?"

Her gaze was so intent, Rusty could hardly breathe. He *did* see. "None of it would restore your finger."

"It would not. But it would eat away at everything that's left of me."

His mouth dropped open. It hadn't even been twenty-four hours since the accident. How had Rose drawn these conclusions so quickly?

Rose wasn't done. "I forgive you, Rusty. And I want to be your friend. But you also need to apologize to James."

Rusty squinted. "James? For what?"

"The night at the pub? When you first got back to Spruceville?"

The image of his fist meeting James Onishi's face suddenly grew crystal clear. So it *had* actually happened.

Rose wore a funny grin. "You know, that was his first and last visit to that establishment. He didn't even make it inside. I kinda wish I'd seen it."

Rusty winced. "I'm so sorry, Rose. I had no idea—"

"Don't tell *me*." She closed her eyes.

Rusty kept gazing at her face in wonder. How had he missed seeing her? Really, truly *seeing* her?

He jumped to his feet when a nurse entered the room.

"Sir, what are you doing in here? You'll have to leave." She pointed a finger toward the door.

"Can't he please stay?" Rose pushed herself partway up. "It helps to have someone here."

Did she mean it? Whatever painkillers they'd given Rose were probably altering her thinking. Surely, he'd feel the full effects of her wrath once the drugs wore off.

"I'm sorry, but you'll have to come back during visiting hours."

Rusty started to leave the room, but Rose tried one more tactic. "He's a veteran!"

The briefest hint of a grin appeared on the nurse's face, and she gave Rusty a respectful nod. "I thank you for your service." Then she turned back to Rose. "Sorry. No exceptions."

As he reached the door, Rose called out. "Rusty?"

He faced her again.

"See you later?" Rose's eyebrows were raised in petition.

She really wants to see me again! Rusty's throat felt as though something had lodged itself there, and he could only nod in agreement. He returned to the waiting room where Rose's mother still slept.

Rusty spent as much time in Rose's room as he was allowed the following day, but he couldn't abandon his father in the middle of harvest. As he returned to the fields, his heart ached to spend every minute at Rose's side. He doubled his efforts, working alongside Rose's family during the day and driving the truck to the train station late into the night. A cloud seemed to hang over the entire farm. Everyone knew of Rose's amazing ability and her ambitions. Now her dreams were shattered, and it was all Rusty's fault. Surely, they blamed him. No one spoke of Rose, at least not to him.

Before dropping exhausted into bed at night, he would read her letters yet again, sometimes falling asleep with them scattered around his bed. Always, his prayers remained the same. *Oh God. How could I have been so blind? I love this girl. I know she'll never be able to love me back, but help me make it up to her somehow!*

One morning as they were finishing breakfast, he made an announcement to his parents. "When Rose is released, I want her to move back into her room upstairs. I'll move out if she wants. I'll make a bed in the barn loft or something. I want her to be comfortable and to know she's welcome here."

His parents stared at him, motionless. They glanced at each other before Dad cleared his throat to speak. "I'm sure that can be arranged if that's what Rose wants."

"Thank you, Rusty." His mother's response was little more than a whisper, but her smile lit up her face as she began clearing away dishes.

"While we're at it"—Dad pushed his chair back from the table— "I've got an idea regarding the Onishis I want to run past you. Walk with me to the barn?"

"Sure." Rusty left the table and grabbed his cap from the hook by the back door. "Thanks for breakfast, Mum." He followed his father outside and took a deep breath. "Actually, Dad, there's, uh ... there's something I want to talk to you about too.

"Is it about the Onishi family?"

Rusty stifled a grin. "Well ... one particular member of the Onishi family."

CHAPTER FORTY-SIX

Rose remained in the hospital for a week, taking both pain medication and penicillin to fight off any infection. She followed the doctor's instruction to keep her left hand elevated to prevent swelling. Nurses changed her dressings daily, checking for signs of infection or bleeding.

"Your hands and fingers contain many sensitive nerve endings," the doctor explained. "Even after it's all healed, you will feel sensitive to cold and pain for a year or more. You might even feel as though your finger is still there."

"Yes, I do!"

"That's called phantom pain, and it's very common. It only means those nerve endings are still sending messages to your brain. Hopefully, in time, that will diminish."

The nurses instructed Rose on how to care for her hand once the stitches came out and she was home. A therapist showed her some exercises she could do to keep her hand as strong as possible and explained how the loss of a finger is a blow to the whole hand, arm, and nervous system. She was told the loss of a thumb would have been far worse. One nurse admonished her to be glad it wasn't her dominant hand. She was warned about possible side effects from the drugs. She was given sympathy, guidance, and encouragement.

No one was able to tell her how to keep playing the piano.

Mama and Mrs. Thorne came to bring her home. Mrs. Thorne must have read the disappointment on her face when she said, "Rusty's dad needs him in the field today," as though she owed Rose an explanation. Rose stepped outside the hospital walls and smiled at the crisp autumn day while she took a deep breath of fresh air.

It wasn't until the ride home that reality began to settle in. Staring at her bandaged hand, Rose's numbed emotions turned to anger as she tried to grasp the fact that her finger was gone for good, her career as a concert pianist shattered in a million pieces. For what?

She faced the window, hot tears stinging her eyes at the sight of other laborers in the beet and potato fields. Trucks loaded with vegetables lumbered down the road, reminding her life went on. The all-important harvest took precedence over everything. No one cared about one little pianist whose life had ended—or may as well have ended. As long as the world could have its sugar. As long as the farmers could trade their produce for cold, hard cash. As long as the seed producers and equipment manufacturers and railroads and refineries and warehouses and grocery stores could continue to turn a profit, the world could go on.

There would always be other piano players.

By the time they pulled into the Thornes' lane, Rose only wanted her bed. Having been surrounded by people every moment since the accident, she ached for privacy. Hopefully, her mother would return to the field so Rose could be alone in the cabin to cry her eyes out. Then she'd escape into an exhausted sleep until the terrible moment, seconds after waking, when the realization of what had occurred hit her like another blow to her hand. She wanted to throw something, hit something, kick something. Scream. But she had to sit there on the front seat of the truck, her mother perched stoically in the middle and Mrs. Thorne at the wheel.

To Rose's surprise, Mrs. Thorne stopped the truck in front of the big house instead of driving nearer to the Onishis' cabin. She turned to face Rose.

"We have a little surprise for you, Rose." Her smile seemed nervous. "You can have your room back. If you like. It's all ready."

Her mother nodded. "It would be best, Rozu. You will get more rest."

Rose swallowed hard. She glanced up at the window of "her" room. A bouquet of fall flowers rested on the sill. Obviously, from Mrs.

Thorne's perennial garden, they showed off brilliant shades of gold, orange, and purple. She closed her eyes. How could she step foot back in that house, walk past the piano she could no longer play, sleep across the hall from Rusty, whom she still loved despite his rejection? Sure, he'd been all apologetic at the hospital. But that was guilt talking. By now, it would have worn off. At best, Rusty would feel only indifference toward her. He'd clearly not been eager to be involved with her trip home.

"No, thank you." The words were out before she could think, and they sounded colder than she intended.

"Rozu!" Mama's tone told Rose she was being rude and ungrateful. Next, Mama would probably try to dump *shakata ga nai* on her.

"It's all right, Rose," Mrs. Thorne hastened to say. "If you're not ready or prefer to be with your family, I understand. But—"

Rose opened the door and climbed out of the truck. When she stood upright, the farmyard spun for a moment. After the dizziness passed, she headed as swiftly as she could toward the cabin, ignoring both women as the truck doors slammed behind her.

"Rozu!"

"Rose, wait!" Mrs. Thorne's pleading voice close behind her stopped Rose. "I want you to know your room will be ready and waiting for you whenever—*if* ever—you want it. We really hope you'll consider it."

Mama caught up to Rose, and the expression on her face revealed her mortification. Rose managed to pause and murmur a "thank you" to Mrs. Thorne. Then, as an extra measure, she added, "And thank you for bringing me home." Hopefully, that would be enough to appease Mama. It was all she could manage.

Just then, the Thornes' back door opened. His arms laden with bedding, Rusty stepped out and let the screen door slam behind him. He spotted the truck before turning his eyes toward the three women standing like statues in the yard. "Oh. You're back. Didn't hear you pull up." He cleared his throat. "Welcome home, Rose."

Rose stared back. "I thought you were in the field."

"I am. I mean—I *was*. I'm just, uh ... it's lunch break, so ..." Rusty walked toward them.

Rose focused on the blankets in his arms. "What are you doing?"

Rusty glanced at his mother, then lifted his chin toward the barn. "I'm just, uh, fixing up some space for myself in the loft."

Rose followed his gaze. "Why?"

"I thought you'd feel more at home in the house if I wasn't there."

Rusty was willing to move out for her? He really must be feeling guilt-ridden. She imagined him trying to sleep in the barn year-round. "It's going to get awfully cold soon, at night."

"I've endured far worse. I'll be fine."

"There's no need. I won't be in the house." Rose turned and continued in the direction she'd begun. She knew she was behaving rudely, but she didn't care. Rusty Thorne and his mother could think whatever they wanted. Mama could go ahead and feel embarrassed. Rose needed to cry, and she didn't want anyone else witnessing it. Besides, if she didn't lie down soon, she'd drop.

The cabin felt warm even though the fire in the stove appeared to have gone out hours before. Rose didn't have the strength to climb to her top bunk, so she lay on Ojiisan's lower bunk instead. She was staring at the bottom of the upper bunk, begging sleep to come, when Mama walked in. *Here it comes.* She rolled over to face the wall.

Instead, Mama scurried around the cabin for a few minutes, then left again. When Rose sat up, a cup of water, a sandwich, and her medication sat on the shelf between the bunks. Mama had no doubt returned to work. Life went on.

When Rose got up to use the outhouse, she saw a package sitting on the kitchen table, wrapped in brown paper and string. It was addressed to her, and she recognized Freda's handwriting immediately. She tore into it, then caught her breath. Beneath a folded letter lay the black satin concert dress Freda had rescued from the Onishis' apartment all those years ago.

"Oh God." Rose's plea escaped her lips in a whisper. "Why now?" She lifted the dress by its shoulders and held it up for her first close-up view of her mother's loving gift. How she had longed for such a dress!

That seemed like a lifetime ago. She gently gathered the shimmering fabric and held it close to her heart, burying her face in the coolness of it. "Why, oh why, now?"

She opened Freda's letter.

Hey Rosie,

I'll have to make this letter short so I can get to the post office before they close. I wanted to let you know we are moving. I'll write you all the details soon, but Mom is making me clean out closets and drawers and get rid of things. I decided it was time to send you the dress. Please don't view this as me losing hope of your coming home. On the contrary, I see it as my hope that you will need this dress for a concert or recital soon, now that the war is behind us. Don't give up on your dream, Rosie. I haven't. If you can't get here, then I would really like to come there. Someday. Take care, my friend. Write soon. Please have someone take your picture in the dress and send it to me. I so wish I could see it on you in person! Your music box, however, I am keeping—and I want you to keep my necklace too.

Love,

Freda

Rose let the letter fall to the floor. She buried her face in the beautiful dress and sobbed, not caring whether her tears ruined it forever.

CHAPTER FORTY-SEVEN

Late that evening, Rose's family came in weary from another full day of harvest. Each of them greeted her in their own way. Tim was eager to see Rose's hand and tell her he was the one who'd found her finger in the dirt. "I'm sorry they couldn't save it." His earnest face made Rose want to cry all over again.

"Thanks, Tim. Me too. But it would never be the same again, even if they could have put it back on. I might have had even worse problems."

"Yeah. That's what James said too." He turned and joined Mama at the stove.

Ojiisan patted her on the shoulder, sadness in his eyes.

Dad sat beside her on the bunk. "Good to have you home, Rozu. Does it hurt bad?"

"Not so much anymore."

Dad nodded. "Good. That's good." He cleared his throat and turned his gaze toward the window, even though it was too dark to see anything outside. "I would give you my finger if I could." He looked at his hands, folded in his lap. "I would give you my whole hand."

"I know, Dad."

Slowly, he rose and moved to the table where Mama poured tea.

Finally, it was James' turn. In his hand, he carried a jar stuffed with purple and white wild asters. He held them out toward Rose, and she accepted his gift, holding it on her lap while she examined the delicate petals and yellow centers. These would be the last wildflowers of the season, and her brother's efforts to give her a gift of beauty warmed her heart. She patted the bunk beside her, inviting James to sit. Instead, he kept standing.

"Feeling up for a walk?"

At the table, Mama, Dad, Ojiisan, and Tim gathered around tea. While Tim blatantly stared straight at her, the adults were clearly trying to be more subtle. Their faces focused on their teacups while their body language told her they were listening, following Rose with their peripheral vision. As though her brains and intuition had hit the dirt along with her finger.

"Sure." She set the flowers on the windowsill and grabbed a jacket off its wall hook. "It would be good to get some fresh air."

Outside, she let James lead the way. They walked quietly down the lane to the road that ran along the edge of the field where Rose's accident had occurred. Only dirt clods remained.

James broke the silence. "Two more days and we should be done."

"Good. What happens then?" Rose lifted her face toward the broad prairie sky, where a billion stars twinkled.

"I guess that's going to depend a lot on you."

"Me? Why me?"

"Well ... a lot happened while you were gone. We had a visit from the Thornes. Mr. Thorne and Rusty, to be exact." James shoved his hands in his pockets as he walked along.

"Oh? Is the deal still on? For Dad to buy one of the fields?"

"Well, that's just it. Dad went to Mr. Thorne and told him maybe the idea wasn't a good one after all, in light of your accident. That it might be better for us to leave. No painful reminders for you or for them. No hard feelings, and so on." James kicked at a stone.

"*Shakata ga nai?*"

"Something like that, yeah. I told Dad he should at least discuss it with you first, but ..."

"I don't see why. Nobody has consulted me on anything. Why should they start now?"

James sighed. "Anyway, Mr. Thorne came to say he really hoped Dad would continue with the plan. Said he admired what hard workers we all are, and he thought he and Dad could make good business partners. He even sweetened the pot."

"How?"

"Well, you know the house Rusty's sister lives in—Shirley, is it?"

Rose nodded. Shirley lived down the road a mile, and Claire lived in town.

"Turns out her husband is building them a new house. It's nearly finished. The old one they've been living in belonged to Mrs. Thorne's parents. It needs work, but Mama and Dad could have it free of charge … to fix up or live in until they can rebuild. And the yard site it's on is right next to the field they were discussing."

"Okay." Rose had seen the new house going up. Naturally, Mr. Thorne's offer would sound inviting to her parents, especially since no other doors had opened. "I still don't see what any of that has to do with me."

"I'm getting to that. After Mr. Thorne finished his piece, we found out why Rusty had come with him." James let out a low chuckle. "He asked Dad's permission to court you."

Rose stopped. "What? Did you say *court me?*"

James' eyes twinkled, convincing Rose that he was trying to suppress a laugh. Why would he toy with her at a time like this? Maybe he didn't understand how Rusty's interest would fill her heart with hope. She'd play along.

"Have you ever heard of anything so old-fashioned in your life? *Court* me?" Even as she made light of it, her heart pounded. Did Rusty truly want her after all?

"Well … yes, actually. I have. You never met our Grandma Onishi, but I remember her a bit. She sailed from Japan as a 'picture bride' for Ojiisan. They'd never met face-to-face until she got off the ship, sent by her parents in response to Ojiisan's request by mail. All they had were a few letters and pictures sent back and forth. Now *that's* old-fashioned."

Rose had heard this story so many times that when she and Freda were little, they'd played "Picture Bride" for fun. "Well, since you put it that way, at least I'm not going to be anyone's picture bride."

"Of course not. I think Rusty's parents suggested asking Dad. He wanted to honor our family's tradition and really didn't know what might be required. Nor did his parents."

"Do *we*? Do we even know what our tradition is? I'm sick and tired of being Japanese, James. Look where it's got me." A larger stone appeared in Rose's path, and she kicked it hard into the ditch.

"Rusty told Dad and Mama he'd grown to care deeply for you through your letters but didn't truly realize it until he saw you in the hospital. He said he had a chance to tell you his feelings then, and he wanted permission to pursue your relationship further."

Rose stopped again and turned to stare at her brother. It was impossible to read his expression in the darkness, but surely, he wouldn't joke about something like this. Would he? "You better not be pulling my leg, James."

James held up both palms. "I'm not, I swear." He turned around and they headed back.

Rose shook her head. "I don't remember what all Rusty and I talked about at the hospital. I must have been too looped on painkillers."

James chuckled again. "Rusty claims he was even more impressed with you after that, with your ability to process what had happened and not lay blame. He said you helped him see how important it was for him to forgive those who wronged him too. Or to at least start that journey."

"Did he ever figure out it was you he slugged the night he got home?"

"Yes. And he apologized for that too."

Rose was still shaking her head. "Golly."

"I know. I like him, in spite of everything. I don't know why, but I can't help it. I think he's a good guy who's been through some hellish experiences. But he clearly cares about you. He just wanted to make sure he followed proper protocol and was respectful."

Rose could certainly empathize with not being able to dislike Rusty Thorne, even if she didn't fully understand why she cared so much for him. She wished she'd been a fly on the wall of the cabin while that conversation took place. "What did Dad say?"

James shrugged. "What else could he say? He said it was up to you, Rose."

CHAPTER FORTY-EIGHT

A restless night provided Rose with the perfect excuse to stay home from church the next morning. She wasn't ready to face Rusty, for one thing. As for facing God, well … she could have that show-down right here.

But her family proved anything but understanding. Even Ojiisan had decided to attend church with the family this day. "You come," he said, with no further explanation.

"You have to, Rose." Tim pulled on her good hand. "You won't regret it."

"I'm too tired." She lay back on her bed.

"No, you're not. You're too mad. At least, be honest about it." James' assessment made her want to spit.

She glared at him. "Well, if I wasn't before, I am now. Wouldn't *you* be?"

"Probably. Please, Rose. Just come today. It's important. After that, if you never want to go back, that's your business."

Her parents waited, already dressed in their Sunday best. Mama held a covered rice dish.

Rose frowned. "Is there a potluck today?"

Mama nodded.

"But the harvest feast is soon … next week? Two more weeks, maybe? Why would they have a potluck now?" Wouldn't everyone be happy to go straight home from church and rest on their one day off?

Dad stood at the door, hat in hand. "Please come, Rozu."

Rose recalled her father's declaration of the previous evening, how he would give her his whole hand. She knew it was true. Though her parents had never said *I love you* or expressed affection with hugs, she knew she was loved. There was no need to make this more difficult for them than it already was. They were not to blame. She dressed as quickly as she could, fumbling with the buttons on her dress and cussing under her breath at the missing finger.

A lot had indeed happened while Rose was away, and not only at the Thorne farm. Inside the sanctuary, Japanese families sprinkled the pews instead of filling the back rows. Mrs. Thorne stood, waving for Rose and her family to join them. As Rose followed her parents, both Japanese and white friends greeted her with smiling faces, pats on the shoulder, and soft *welcome home*s. Rose returned their smiles, stifling her amazement. Thank goodness, the seat that opened for her fell between her brothers. Rusty sat at the other end of the pew, out of her line of vision.

When they stood to sing, Rose couldn't keep herself from her old habit of mentally playing the piano. But each time she needed her left forefinger, she fell behind while trying to sort out how to adapt. By the end of the third hymn, she'd decided her middle finger and thumb could share double-duty and that certain keys would be easier to play in than others.

If she remained content with playing hymns, she'd be fine.

After the singing, the pastor gripped both sides of the pulpit and made an announcement.

"We want to welcome Rose Onishi back with us today." As he leaned on the podium, beaming at her, and people smiled and nodded in her direction, her cheeks flamed. "Rose, we are all sorry about your loss. We've been praying for your swift healing and for your encouragement. After the service today, we'll be having a potluck lunch in your honor, and we have a little surprise for you, so I certainly hope everyone plans to stick around."

Rose didn't catch a word of the sermon after that. What kind of surprise could this small congregation possibly have in mind? Would she be expected to speak? She glanced at James, but he only imitated Mama's stoic, know-nothing face as he focused on the pastor's message.

As the final chords of the doxology faded, Rose followed the others toward the church basement. Delicious aromas made their way upstairs. From the landing halfway down the stairwell, she could see tables and chairs had been set up. Her tummy rumbled—from nerves or hunger, she wasn't sure which.

"What's this all about, James? The harvest feast is coming up. This seems—"

"—excessive?" James finished the sentence for her. "I agree. Way too much fuss for one little finger." He grinned at Rose. "Looks like I'm not the only one." He lifted his chin toward the main doors at the top of the stairs, and Rose followed his gaze.

Mrs. Pierce stood buttoning her coat with a frown. "Our girl was hospitalized for a full ten days when she had her appendix out." Though she appeared to be speaking to her husband, her voice drifted down the stairwell full of people. "We nearly lost her. Nobody made a fuss like this when *she* came home." She pulled on her gloves. "It's completely ridiculous. Treating a little Jap like some kind of celebrity." With that, she swung the door open and made a dramatic exit, her husband following meekly behind with a red face.

Rose wanted to hide. But to her surprise, it seemed few people had heard Mrs. Pierce, or if they had, they chose to ignore her. They continued down the stairs. The pastor whistled through his fingers to get everyone's attention. When the room grew quiet, he said grace, concluding his prayer with, "We thank you, God, for Rose's safe return to our fold. Amen." He opened his eyes and smiled. "Dig in!"

The room returned to noise and activity. Mrs. Thorne led Rose to a specific seat while one of her piano students presented a plate filled with more food than Rose could eat. It really did look good, and Rose ate along with the others as a spirit of joy filled the room. Despite herself, her anger was lifting. She'd never seen such a mingling of the Japanese with the community at large. Could this really be a result of her accident?

When everyone had eaten their fill, the pastor stood again. "Well, as I've said, we have a special something for you today, Rose. But first, I'd like to thank Rusty Thorne for not only suggesting but also organizing all this. Would you like to say a few words, Rusty?"

Her hands trembled as Rusty rose and took his place next to the pastor. This was all his doing? He'd become a bit of a hero in this church since arriving home. What on earth would he say? She clasped her hands together tightly in her lap, still terribly mindful of the missing digit.

Rusty cleared his throat, and it was enough to silence even the children. "Most of you have known Rose Onishi far longer than I have. What you may not know is that she wrote to me when I was overseas. Her kindness and encouragement often kept me going through dark days. I can't even describe how much I cherished those letters. Meanwhile, back here in Spruceville, Rose and her family kept my parents going through their own dark days when they didn't know whether I was dead or alive." Rusty's voice began to tremble a bit, and he paused before continuing. "I can't explain how much it means to me, and I want to take this opportunity to publicly thank them—for all of that."

Rose glanced at her parents as she swallowed back her own emotion. Dad acknowledged Rusty's words with a polite nod while Mama dared to allow an almost imperceptible smile to appear.

"However, it wasn't until I had the opportunity to talk with Rose in the hospital that God showed me, through her, how beautiful a human heart can be when we learn to forgive. The community I came home to looks very different than the one I left. It came as a shock, at first. But I now know it's a better community than the one I left." At this, Rusty waved a hand around the room. "Diversity has made us stronger, and I hope it never returns to the old way again. Rose reminded me we are all God's children, and he wants us to forgive one another, love each other, work together to bring his kingdom to earth. To be part of the answer when we pray, 'Thy Kingdom come. Thy will be done on earth.' It takes all of us. It takes holding onto love and giving God our hurts. Getting that backward, holding onto my hurt and resentment, wanting vengeance, only harms me. I see that now. And I have you to thank, Rose."

Rusty focused on her for the first time. "Thank you for setting an example, for me and for this whole community. I hope it will truly start to feel like yours really soon." He turned toward the pastor, who shook his hand before Rusty took his seat.

"Thanks, Rusty. Well said. I couldn't agree more. In a couple of weeks, we'll be celebrating another harvest—one that would not have been possible without the help of everyone here." He focused on Rose. "We're all so sorry about what happened to you, Rose. You, of all people, with your skill. But we're confident this isn't the end of your piano playing. In fact,"—he held up a sheet of paper—"on this sheet is a list of names of former and new piano students who wish to start lessons as soon as possible. The Thornes have already promised their piano for your use if you want it."

Even from a distance, Rose could tell the paper held enough names to fill her schedule. With her good hand, she covered her mouth. Was this really happening?

"And secondly, we're taking up a collection to be presented to you after harvest is complete. It's to help you finish your education. We're doing it at that time for two reasons. Folks will have more money, and it will give us time to spread the word. A lot of people will want to participate and to dig deep." He smiled at Rose, then turned to everyone else. "So tell everyone!"

Rose's bandaged hand went to her chest as she looked around the room. Dad and Mama were both beaming at her, her brothers laughing at her shock. People applauded and smiled. Last, she made eye contact with Rusty. His eyes glistened with tears, and she thought her heart might burst at his warm smile.

For the next forty minutes, well-wishers expressed both their sadness for Rose's loss and their encouragement for her future. Students eager to resume or begin lessons came to say hello. Finally, when only a few people remained, Rusty took the seat next to Rose.

"Getting tired?"

Rose searched his face, still worried this might be merely his attempt at appeasing his conscience. But only kindness was reflected in his eyes.

"A little. Thank you, Rusty. You didn't have to do all this."

His blue eyes were almost piercing in the afternoon sunshine streaming in through the basement window. "I wanted to. And I meant everything I said, Rose. I've been reading up on some of the things that went on here in Canada while I was away. It was wrong. What was done to you and your family and so many others was just wrong."

Rose shook her head slightly. "It was nothing compared to what you went through."

"It's not about comparing. But the things you said really made sense. I don't want to become a bitter old man. If I do, the enemy wins. It was all for nothing."

"Well, the things I said might make sense," Rose admitted. "And I probably even meant them at the time." She focused on her hands in her lap. "I've been pretty angry since I got home. I don't think I fully comprehended everything when I delivered all that wisdom."

"It's still true, though." Rusty reached out and took her uninjured hand in both of his. "And you have every right to feel everything you need to feel. Including anger."

Rose sighed. His hands, callused and rough, held hers tenderly, and she wished he would never let go. "As long as I don't feel angry forever?" She gazed up at him with a smile.

"Well. I know a bunch of piano students who will want the Miss Onishi they've come to know and love. Not an angry one."

She smiled wider.

Mrs. Thorne was heading their way when Rusty leaned a little closer. "Can we continue this conversation with a walk this evening?"

Rose nodded, and Rusty pulled his hands away. Was it her imagination, or did he seem reluctant to do so?

CHAPTER FORTY-NINE

R usty could hardly believe the changes in his own heart. He felt like the luckiest man alive, walking down the gravel road next to Rose, his hand in hers. Though nothing was the same as he'd imagined it while still in that hellhole of a prison camp, his heart soared at his new reality. The sun that had ravaged his skin in Hong Kong now cast glorious hues across an achingly beautiful western sky. Overhead, a late flock of Canada geese honked their freedom as they stretched their necks southward, their V-shape affirming the victory God's healing hand had wrought.

Thank you, Lord, for showing me Rose's heart first. Otherwise, I'd have written her off without giving her a chance. Thank you for finally opening my eyes. Make me deserving of her. Since the accident, this had become his daily prayer.

"I have so many questions for you, Rose. I want to know all about you, all about your life back in Vancouver. About how you ended up here, and everything in between."

Rose smiled. "I have something to ask you too." The twinkle in her eye almost took his breath away.

"Oh yeah?"

"Yes. Did you really go to my father with a question?"

Rusty turned his attention to the horizon, which would soon hide the sinking autumn sun. "I … may have. Why? What did you hear?"

Rose laughed, a melody as lovely as anything from the piano. "James told me you asked Dad for permission to court me."

Rusty rubbed the back of his neck and let out a fake laugh. "Well, I can see where your brother's loyalties lie. Can't say I blame him on that score, though."

"So … it's true, then? He wasn't just giving me a hard time?"

Rusty stopped and turned toward her. He wanted to take her left hand, too, but was still cautious of her injury. To his surprise, she placed it on top of his right hand as she waited for his answer. "It's true. I suppose it was a dumb question. My parents suggested it … that it might be considered proper protocol."

Rose grinned. "I thought it was sweet."

"Well, that's a relief. Your dad said it was up to you."

She nodded, then pulled one hand away, and they continued walking. "My parents used to assume I would only date a Japanese man. They weren't too pleased when I went out with a white fellow back home, but I think they came to realize it was inevitable. Our school was mixed, our church was mixed. I had a lot of white friends."

"Is your friend Freda Japanese?" Rusty tried to remember what Rose had written about Freda.

"No. She's still in Vancouver, hoping for my return." Rose fingered the treble clef around her neck. "It doesn't look as though that's going to happen, not unless I eventually make my way back on my own. That would break Mama's heart. I think she and Dad are pretty sold on the plan to partner with your father. At least, Dad is."

"My parents knew I had feelings for you before I did, Rose. Mum's intuitive, I guess. They love you a lot, but Mum warned me some. She told me marriage is challenging enough without adding in the element of different cultures."

Rose's face had turned red. Rusty tried to backtrack. "Oh—I'm sorry. I don't mean—that is, I'm not—I'm not trying to rush you into anything. I just …"

To his relief, she began to laugh. "It's okay."

They'd reached the one-room grade school Rusty had attended and from which Tim had graduated the previous spring. Rose took a seat on one of the swings, and he gave her a gentle push.

"I want to get to know you better, Rose. I want to get to know you really well, and really quickly."

She laughed harder. "I would like that too."

"So ... is that a yes, then? We're an item?"

Rose put her feet down to slow the swing. "I guess we're an item."

Rusty caught the swing by the seat, pulling Rose toward himself and holding her there. "We're going to be met with opposition, you know. Maybe not from our parents, but from the community at large. Sure, they were great today. But today wasn't about us being a couple."

Rose nodded. "I know."

"And because of that, even though I don't want to rush you, I need you to know ... I don't see much point in our courting, or dating, or whatever we decide to call it ... unless marriage is a real possibility. I want you to know that up front."

With their faces mere inches apart, Rusty longed to wrap his arms around her, but if he let go of the swing, she'd sail away from him. To his surprise, Rose released the rope with her uninjured hand and raised it to his cheek.

"Rusty Thorne." She searched his eyes while she gently touched his jawline. "I know it makes no sense. But I felt a connection with you from the moment your mother pointed at your photo on the piano and said, 'this is our son, Russell.' While we were writing back and forth, it was easy for me to imagine us being together." She slid her hand down his neck and rested it on his shoulder. "You and your parents have taught me so much—about God, about myself. About human nature. By the time I read your first letter, I knew I loved you. And ever since ... well, I think I've been trying to convince myself how foolish that was. Especially after our first face-to-face meeting."

"I'm so sorry, Rose. Bert told me I'd be crazy if I let you get away." Rusty tightened his grip, pulling her closer. "I can't believe I almost did. I'm so, so sorry."

"I am too. I'm sorry for everything you went through. I'm sorry you never got my picture. I'm sorry the whole situation was never painted clearly for you." Rose slipped both hands around Rusty's neck.

He wrapped his arms around her waist and lowered her from the swing to her feet without taking his eyes off her face. "I want to kiss you so much."

"Then what are you waiting for?"

The words were barely a whisper, and Rusty leaned into the invitation gladly. Their lips met in the softest, sweetest kiss he'd ever known.

By the end of October, Rose and her family were settled into the house down the road. Rusty spent as much time with her as he could. She would arrive on his old bicycle in the afternoon, then spend an hour or two at the piano, working on her own skills until her students began arriving for lessons after school. Depending when the last lesson ended, she sometimes spent more time practicing. To Rusty and his parents, her playing sounded as skilled as ever, but her frustrated growls made it clear that she did not agree. When she was done for the day, Rusty would walk alongside as she pedaled home. If the weather was bad, he'd drive her in Bert's hot rod. They'd converse the whole way, then talk some more on the front porch or in the living room. It was always hard to leave, and Rusty found himself loving Rose more with each visit.

Then the snow began to fly.

"I've been thinking," Rusty's mother announced one evening at supper." The notes of "Hot Cross Buns" came from the piano in the other room, along with Rose's patient voice as she instructed her young student. "It's getting far too cold for Rose to be walking or biking over here every day. I think we should move the piano to their place."

Dad looked up from his baked potato, his eyes round.

"What?" Mum jabbed her fork into a carrot. "You don't agree?"

Dad swallowed. "I'm just surprised, is all. That was your mother's piano."

"And that was my mother's house." Mum pointed a thumb in the direction of the Onishis' home. "So it can go where it always used to sit when I was a kid. It'll feel right at home. It will be much more convenient for Rose and closer for her students who come from town."

"Are you saying you want to give it to her, or would this be a loan, or …" Dad let his question trail off.

Mum shrugged. "Why do we have to define it?"

Rusty didn't want to get in the middle of it. Could Rose hear any of the conversation from the other room, or was she too focused on her work?

Dad scratched his bristly chin. "Well, I think it's a fine idea, but only if everybody understands what the deal is from the start. I mean, if things change …" He glanced at Rusty, then busied himself with his meal.

"He means if Rose and I break up." Rusty whispered the painful words.

His mother held his gaze for what felt like an exceptionally long time. "That's not going to happen. I think we all know it."

Dad studied him too. "Is your mother right, son?"

Rusty grinned. "I sure hope so. I can't imagine ever ending things with Rose."

"So what are you waiting for?" It was Dad's turn to grin. "Marry the girl!"

Was his father serious? He looked back and forth between his parents. "You mean it?"

"She's practically part of the family already. Make your mother happy."

Mum's face was beaming. "Then we can call the piano our engagement present!"

Rose had used part of the money she received from the congregation to pay for the correspondence courses she needed to complete high school. She planned to finish them by spring and had talked about the possibility of enrolling in Teacher's College next fall.

"Is that what you really want?" Rusty asked that evening as they walked hand in hand.

Rose shrugged. "I got a taste of teaching school at Tashme. I liked it all right. I can do it."

"But it's not your first love."

They continued strolling in silence until Rusty began to think Rose hadn't heard him. Finally, she spoke. "My dream of being a concert pianist is over, Rusty. I'll never know what I might have been spared."

"What do you mean?"

"I mean ... if I didn't have what it took to make it, even *with* my finger, then I've been spared a lot of heartache and humility."

"Wow, that's quite a way to look at it, but ... you would have made it, Rose. Are you sure it's not still possible?"

Rose let out a low *hmph*. "That's sweet of you to say. But no. I figure I've been spared either way. I had this glorified picture of what that life would be like, but in reality, I think I'd have hated traveling all the time, staying in strange places, being away from my family. Maybe never having a family of my own."

"You almost sound convincing."

"I'm serious. If I get a teaching job, who knows? I may or may not be able to teach music at school, but I can always teach piano on my own."

"Even if you marry a sugar beet farmer?" Rusty teased.

"If I marry a sugar beet farmer, I will be a sugar beet farmer too." Rose smiled up at him. "I'll just pay someone else to swing the harvesting knife. And I will *always* make time for piano, no matter what."

"In that case, sweetheart, I'll throw your own words back at you."

Rose raised her eyebrows. "What words?"

"What are you waiting for?" He lowered himself to one knee, holding Rose's fully healed left hand in his own. "Will you marry me, Rose?"

The smile he'd come to love more than any other in the world lit her face as she nodded. "I would like to marry you very much."

"Even if it means being called Rose Thorne for the rest of your life?"

Her smile didn't dim. "You think I haven't already thought of that a thousand times?" She pulled him to his feet and wrapped her arms around his neck. "Yes. Even then."

EPILOGUE

September 22, 1988

If my big sister Rose ever regretted marrying Rusty Thorne, she certainly never showed it over the next forty years. Following their wedding in 1947, a few people were scandalized. But by the time their boys came along, everyone seemed to have settled down and accepted it. Rose taught school for a few years and gave piano lessons for decades, teaching and influencing pretty much every kid in the community— white, Japanese, whatever. The church bought a piano so they could enjoy having her play on Sundays, and the old folks' home brought her in as regular entertainment. She even gave a few little concerts for various benefits. She's a bit of a celebrity around here.

We buried Ojiisan in the church cemetery in 1962, and Dad alongside him twenty years later.

With few memories of our life before Manitoba, I had no desire to go back west. I took over our parents' farm like Rusty did his. Mr. and Mrs. Thorne still live in the old house with them. James became a lawyer. We might have succeeded in completely burying the events of World War II were it not for the curiosity of Rose and Rusty's boys. Once Jack and Bert opened that can of worms, there was no stopping them.

They'd grown up knowing they were half Japanese, but they never thought about how we all ended up here in Manitoba until they reached their twenties. Out of respect for our parents, we never talked about the internments and relocation or about our beginnings in B.C. Nobody did. It was like a code of honor among the Japanese Canadians. *Shakata ga nai.* It cannot be helped. So reluctant were the

Issei and Nisei to discuss their shame that it took the next generation to start asking questions. It certainly wasn't in their history books at school. First, Bert and Jack began grilling Rusty about his years in Japan. Rusty preferred not to talk about that either. "It's forgiven," he'd say. "No need to dredge it up."

But the boys persisted. They involved their cousins and other youngsters in the Japanese community. I wasn't shocked when Rose got involved in the long, drawn-out fight for restitution, but I sure was impressed when Rusty did too. My brother-in-law was a man of integrity, but he'd had a lot to forgive. Why should he seek justice for what happened to *us*?

Though Manitoba's Japanese Canadian Citizens' Association had formed in 1946, it wasn't until the eighties that momentum for the Redress Campaign began. Rose and Rusty got so involved, it seemed they were running to meetings every week. They participated in council sessions to decide on the position to be taken during negotiations with the government. A committee was formed to raise funds and to educate Canadians.

In 1986, the committee walked away from what the government called its "final offer," which involved some money for the community as a whole but nothing for individuals. Nothing to compensate for all the property and income lost. So the group decided to make it a human rights issue, contacting famous Canadians for support. Over forty-five hundred people, representing unions, churches, and municipal governments, supported them. A rally was held on Parliament Hill last spring. We saw some of that on television. The collective voices of the coalition sent a message that Canadians would not be satisfied until a redress agreement was reached.

In August, they held a meeting to determine individual compensation. It certainly didn't hurt that U.S. President Reagan announced his government was awarding a twenty-thousand-dollar compensation package to each formerly interned Japanese American.

In the end, we all agreed that Rose, Rusty, and James would travel to Ottawa for the September announcement.

"Tim," Rusty said to me. "You should go in my place. You're Japanese."

But he'd been far more involved than I had. They'd all been. They deserved the honor. Rose was nervous to fly, but she agreed to it when her old friend Freda called to say, "Rosie, you *have* to go!"

The rest of us gathered at my place to watch on TV. My wife, Katie, went overboard preparing Japanese dishes. Our daughters came early to decorate the house with Canadian and Japanese flags. Mama, at eighty-eight, lives with Katie and me. She sat in her favorite easy chair, holding her framed photo of Dad. James' wife, Connie, joined us. It was standing room only after Jack and Bert arrived with their families.

All eyes were riveted to the TV as Prime Minister Brian Mulroney rose to speak in the House of Commons. "Mr. Speaker, nearly half a century ago, in the crisis of wartime, the government of Canada wrongfully incarcerated, seized the property of, and disenfranchised thousands of citizens of Japanese ancestry. We cannot change the past. But we must, as a nation, have the courage to face up to these historical facts."

He talked about there being a world of difference between regret and a formal apology.

"It is fitting that representatives of the National Association of Japanese Canadians are present in the visitor's gallery on this solemn occasion because today I have the honor to announce, on behalf of the government of Canada, that a comprehensive redress settlement has been reached with the National Association of Japanese Canadians on behalf of their community."

As the TV camera panned the balcony, we strained our eyes to spot Rose, James, and Rusty. We never did see the men, but we saw Rose. She was wearing the black satin dress Mama made for her years ago. Katy helped her alter it a bit for this occasion, although my sister has managed to maintain her girlish shape more than most women, I think. The dress was a surprise for Mama. She recognized it immediately and bounced gently in her recliner, pointing at the TV with one hand and covering her mouth with the other.

The prime minister continued. "… no amount of money can right the wrong, undo the harm, and heal the wounds. But it is symbolic of our determination to address this issue, not only in the moral sense but also in a tangible way.

"Most of us in our own lives have had occasion to regret certain things we have done. Error is an ingredient of humanity. So, too, is apology and forgiveness. We all have learned from personal experience that, as inadequate as apologies are, they are the only way that we can cleanse the past, so that we may, as best we can, in good conscience, face the future. And so, Mr. Speaker, I know that I speak for members on all sides of the house today in offering to Japanese Canadians the formal and sincere apology from this parliament for those past injustices against them and against their families and against their heritage. And our solemn commitment and undertaking to Canadians of every origin that such violations will never again be countenanced or repeated."

Both houses—the House of Commons and ours—burst into loud applause. There wasn't a dry eye in my living room. Even stoical old Mama couldn't stop smiling and cheering. Her face was wet with tears as she hugged Dad's picture close. The cameras panned the gallery again where the occupants stood to applaud.

In addition to the apology, the government offered $21,000 to each individual directly affected by the internment, the creation of a community fund, pardons for those who had been wrongfully imprisoned during the war, and Canadian citizenship for Japanese Canadians and their descendants who had been wrongfully deported to Japan at the war's end.

Weeks ago, we discussed what we might do with the money if it came. Mama plans to split hers three ways for us kids. Katy and I want to help our grandkids with college when they're older. If I know James, his will go to some worthwhile cause.

Rose hopes to take Rusty and their boys to Japan and then Hong Kong. She wants to see if we have any relatives left in Hiroshima and bring something home to Mama. Rusty wants to see what's left, if anything, of the camps where he was imprisoned. Perhaps he needs closure. A talk he delivered to our church congregation about it had most of us in tears.

"If not for my experiences there, I might have lived my whole life believing I could be a good person in my own strength, that I was a genuine follower of Jesus. By the grace of God, the wrongs done to me revealed who I was, and by the grace of God, I have forgiven those wrongs. But I want to go back to remember and to pay respects to Bert. I want to thank God for sparing my life, for bringing me home to Rose, and for granting me the power to forgive and heal. For making me so much more than a psychiatric casualty of the war and preventing me from becoming like those who abused me so unspeakably."

I pray the trip will be all that and more for them.

For me, it feels like a release of long-held shame. No one is pretending money can erase wrongs. But it's an acknowledgment of injustice. Of remorse. Of affirmation that, though treated like criminals, no Japanese Canadian was ever convicted of war crimes.

We were good Canadians all along.

AUTHOR'S NOTES

For years, I tried to let the idea of this book go. A story about a Japanese Canadian girl relocated from Vancouver to a Manitoba sugar beet farm during World War II was obviously not my story to write. When I realized this fictional girl would start writing letters to the farmer's son, imprisoned in a Japanese POW camp—I knew for sure the story was far too big a project for me.

But God wouldn't let me take the easy way out. You can read the full story on my blog, here: https://terrietodd.blogspot.com/2019/08/from-as-if-to-what-if.html

I owe my inspiration for this story to my friend Terry Tully and his mother, Osono. Although Terry's dad did not go to war like Rusty Thorne, he was the farmer's son who married the Japanese girl interned on his family's sugar beet farm here in Manitoba. I deeply appreciate the creators and all the participants of the CBC documentary *Facing Injustice*, including Terry and Osono.

I couldn't have begun this tale if not for the many writers who have courageously written their own and others' true stories from those years. You could say I collected the experiences of many real-life individuals and piled nearly all of them onto my characters. If the harshest ordeals faced by Rusty and his fellow prisoners seem too horrible to be true, I assure you that I held back in many instances for the sake of my readers' sensitivities. The real-life stories reveal the depths of depravity to which humans can sink when they don't acknowledge their creator, who made every human in his own image. They also affirm the value of recording those stories accurately and not trying to change history.

For the story of Rose, I leaned heavily on the books *Obasan* by Joy

Kogawa, *The Enemy that Never Was* by Ken Adachi, *Torn Apart: The Internment of Mary Kobayashi* by Susan Aihoshi, *Years of Sorrow, Years of Shame*, by Barry Broadfoot, *Too Young to Fight: Memories from our Youth During World War II*, compiled by Priscilla Galloway, and *The Translation of Love* by Lynne Kutsukake.

I couldn't have created Rusty's story without first reading the biography of American World War II hero Louis Zamperini, *Unbroken: A World War II Story of Survival, Resilience, and Redemption* by Laura Hillenbrand, which was also made into a movie. A subsequent movie, *Unbroken: Path to Redemption*, tells the rest of Zamperini's story of forgiveness and grace following his return to America. Victor Stanley Ebbage's book *The Hard Way: Surviving Shamshuipo POW Camp 1941-45* was also enormously informative.

Forgiveness: A Gift from My Grandparents by Mark Sakamoto was tremendously valuable in developing both Rose's and Rusty's journeys. For insights into sugar beet farming, I found *Sugar Farmers of Manitoba* by Heather Robertson immensely helpful.

If you enjoyed this book, I hope you will read my other novels as well: *The Silver Suitcase, Maggie's War,* and *Bleak Landing.* All are set in Manitoba during the war years. In 2020, I also published an anniversary collection of my favorite pieces from the faith and humor column I write for my local newspaper. You can find links to *Out of My Mind: A Decade of Faith and Humour* and to all my books on my blog at www.terrietodd.blogspot.com. Please watch for my next novel, *The Last Piece,* releasing November 2021.

I'd be thrilled to hear from you at terriejtodd@gmail.com. And remember, the best thing you can do for any author is to leave a review of their books on Amazon, Goodreads, or wherever you can!

Finally, my most earnest prayer is that the freedom found only in Jesus Christ will fill your heart and that you'll fully grasp God's truth that forgiveness is the mightiest power on earth.

Terrie Todd

GLOSSARY OF JAPANESE WORDS AND PHRASES

Bento: a home-packed Japanese lunch box.

Bushido: samurai moral values, most commonly stressing some combination of sincerity, frugality, loyalty, martial arts mastery, and honor until death.

Genmaicha: a Japanese tea consisting of green tea mixed with roasted popped brown rice.

Ianfu: "Comfort women," the women forced as sex slaves for the Imperial Japanese Army during World War II.

Issei: A Japanese immigrant to North America.

Katana: a Japanese sword characterized by a curved, single-edged blade with a circular or squared guard and long grip to accommodate two hands.

Kodomo no tame gaman shi masho: "For the sake of the children, let us endure."

Misoshiru: Japanese soup made from *miso* paste (fermented soybeans) and *dashi* (fish stock)

Mochi: a Japanese rice cake made with glutinous rice flour.

Nemaki: Sleep wear, kimono.

Nisei: A person born in the U.S. or Canada whose parents were immigrants from Japan.

Ojiisan: Grandpa. (Not to be confused with *Ojisan*, which means *uncle*.)

Onigiri: steamed rice formed into balls and usually wrapped with *nori* (dried seaweed).

Picture bride: the practice in the early twentieth century of immigrant workers (chiefly Japanese, Okinawan, and Korean) in Hawaii and the

West Coast of the United States and Canada selecting brides from their native countries via a matchmaker, who paired bride and groom using only photographs and family recommendations of the possible candidates.

Shikata ga nai: "It cannot be helped," or "Nothing can be done about it."

Tsukemono: literally, "pickled things."

Bibliography of Hymns Used

(Public Domain)

Chisholm, Thomas O. 1866-1960, "O To Be Like Thee"

Graeff, Frank E.1860-1919, and Hall, J. Lincoln, 1866-1930, "Does Jesus Care?"

Habershon, Ada Ruth, 1861-1918 and Stebbins, George C., 1846-1945, "A Sunset Nearer"

Martin, W. C. (William Clark), 1864-1914, "My Anchor Holds"

Smith, Oswald J., 1889-1986, "Deeper and Deeper"

Watts, Isaac, 1674-1748 and Arne, Thomas A. 1710-1778, "Am I A Soldier of the Cross?"

Watts, "I Sing the Mighty Power of God"